winner: John Whiting Award; nominated: Olivier Award for Best Comedy), *Babies* (Royal Court Theatre; winner: *Evening Standard* Award for Most Promising Playwright; winner: George Devine Award) and *Rupert Street Lonely Hearts Club* (English Touring Theatre, Donmar Warehouse, Criterion Theatre; winner: *Manchester Evening News* Award for Best New Play; winner: *City Life Magazine* Award for Best New Play). Other plays include *Corrie!* (Lowry Theatre and national tour; winner: *Manchester Evening News* Award for Best Special Entertainment), *Canary* (Liverpool Playhouse, Hampstead Theatre and English Touring Theatre), *Hushabye Mountain* (English Touring Theatre, Hampstead Theatre), *Guiding Star* (Everyman Theatre, Royal National Theatre), *Boom Bang a Bang* (Bush Theatre), *Mohair* (Royal Court Theatre Upstairs) and *Wildfire* (Royal Court Theatre Upstairs). Jonathan also co-wrote the musical *Closer to Heaven* with the Pet Shop Boys.

For television Jonathan has created and written three series of the BAFTA-nominated *Gimme Gimme Gimme* for the BBC, two series of *Beautiful People* (winner: Best Comedy, Banff TV Festival), the double-BAFTA-nominated *Best Friends, Von Trapped!* and *Birthday Girl*. He has also written for *Rev* (winner: BAFTA for Best Sitcom), *Shameless, The Catherine Tate Show, At Home with the Braithwaites*, *Lilies* and *Murder Most Horrid*. To date he has written over one hundred episodes of *Coronation Street*.

Jonathan's film work includes *Beautiful Thing* for Film4 (Outstanding Film, GLAAD Awards, New York; Best Film, London Lesbian and Gay Film Festival; Best Screenplay, Fort Lauderdale Film Festival; Grand Prix, Paris Film Festival; Jury Award, São Paolo International Film Festival).

But perhaps most telling of all, he also won the Spacehopper Championships at Butlins Pwhelli in 1976.

His novels are *All She Wants*, *The Confusion of Karen Carpenter*, *The Girl Who Just Appeared*, *The Secrets We Keep*, *The History of Us* and *The Years She Stole*.

THE
YEARS
SHE
STOLE

Jonathan Harvey

PAN BOOKS

First published 2018 by Pan Books
an imprint of Pan Macmillan
20 New Wharf Road, London N1 9RR
Associated companies throughout the world
www.panmacmillan.com

ISBN 978-1-4472-9822-9

1 3 5 7 9 8 6 4 2

A CIP catalogue record for this book is available from the British Library.

Typeset by Palimpsest Book Production Ltd, Falkirk, Stirlingshire
Printed and bound by CPI Group (UK) Ltd, Croydon, CR0 4YY

For my husband, Paul Hunt,
and my Best Woman, Julie Graham.

ACKNOWLEDGEMENTS

Continued thanks to Wayne Brookes, Jeremy Trevathan and all the team at Pan Macmillan for publishing this book. Also to my agent Gordon Wise for his continuing sage advice, and to Michael McCoy for handling all my other writing work.

Thank you to Angela Sinden for sharing her insights on how it feels to be pregnant, and to Philippa Perry for sharing her insights into how someone might become a private investigator. Especially big thanks to my parents Maureen and Brian for taking me on so many holidays to Butlins as a child that I didn't need to do any research for that section of the book. Thanks to Didi Schmiterlow for allowing me to name a dreadful PA after her; she, of course, is anything but.

Debbie and Andrew Rush bid a considerable amount of money for Moodswings Network to have a character in the book named after Debbie's wonderful mum Margaret Mary Lavery. Moodswings is a Manchester-based charity that gives information, advice and ongoing support to people with mood disorders and other forms of emotional distress. So thank you Debbie and Andrew.

To Linda Wilson, I finally got you in there.

And to Paul Hunt, we finally got there.

PROLOGUE

SHIRLEY

Birmingham, 1981

The cracks. If I don't step on the cracks in this pavement then all will be well, all will go according to plan. If I don't step on the cracks then the gods will smile down on me, I will be the lucky one, I will succeed in my mission. But it's hard to monitor the progress of my feet when I'm ducking beneath the branches of a weeping willow. I spit the leaves from my mouth and wrestle the fronds that stick to my coat, hoping against hope that the soles of my shoes haven't made contact with the cracks underfoot.

Free of the tree, I look up to the sky. All I can see is bunting. There really is no escaping it today. Every street in this neighbourhood is criss-crossed with red, white and blue triangles flapping in a breeze I cannot feel. I wonder if the residents have kept these decorations locked away since the Silver Jubilee. Four years seems a long time to keep something in a drawer on the off chance, yet so few of them look brand new.

Did people really do that four years ago?

'Oh don't put them in the bin, Marjorie. We might have a royal wedding in a few years. Stick them in the bottom of the sideboard instead. I feel another street party coming on.'

'Whatever you say Gilbert.'

I very much doubt it.

Some mums and dads are in the middle of this street, starting to arrange trestle tables. I see a little girl, red faced, crying in a deck chair. She is wearing a bowler hat covered in tin foil. Sellotaped onto the tin foil is a cut-out of the happy couple, Charles and Diana. But that little girl is looking anything other than happy. I know how she feels.

The next time I look down – I will spend a lot of time looking down today, avoiding eye contact, it's the only way – I see a bandy legged crow strutting towards me. He seems as unimpressed by the day's events as the little girl. I shoo him away with a jab of my right foot.

I know that time is running out. I hasten. If I don't do this quickly, soon the streets will be full and I will be noticed. I cannot afford to be noticed, not after all my intensive planning. Today is the climax of everything I have been working towards for so long and I must not screw it up. I have practiced for this day so many times, now I need to come good.

I have had umpteen elocution lessons. I now sound so different you'd never guess it was me. All trace of my accent has disappeared. Well, when I want it to. And today it is imperative.

My father's car is a Jaguar. And he drives it rarther farst.

The man in the moon came down too soon.

Yes. You would hardly know it was me.

And today I don't want anyone to know it's me. If anyone stops me, or asks me the time, I have to sound convincingly un-me. I'm even thinking in received pronunciation. That's what the elocution teacher told me this new accent is. Received pronunciation. RP for short. It suits me, too. It lends me the air of a lady. And till today is over, I need anyone who sees me to see someone other than me.

You know, this old lady's coat I'm wearing suits me. The pinched waist accentuates my bust and the A-line drop is very forgiving on my thighs. Burgundy is not a colour I'd usually choose but then I wouldn't normally be wearing a chestnut wig either. It looks good on me, whoever 'me' is today. Again, the neutral lipstick isn't normally my kind of thing. But then there's nothing normal about what I'm about to do. In fact, this is a very abnormal thing.

I chose this city because it is nowhere near my home town and I have no links to it, but I've grown to like it over the last few weeks. I wasn't sure how to proceed when I first arrived, but then I saw her. And somehow I knew she was my destiny.

I'm no midwife, but as soon as I saw her I knew she was days from dropping. She was waddling along outside Birmingham New Street station. When she got on a bus, I got on too. When she got off, I followed suit. She lived in a nice area. Semi-detached houses, wide roads, weeping willows, the works. The sort of place where mothers leave their babies outside the front door in prams all the time. It could be any area in Britain. She lived in a nice house on the corner of two roads. Across the road from the house was a bus stop. It turns out nobody seems to mind if you sit at a bus stop all day, watching. Everybody just thinks you're waiting for a bus. And from said bus stop you have a wonderful view of the back garden.

Four days ago she returned from the hospital with her husband – he must be her husband, the area is too well-to-do for illegitimacy, plus they're both wearing wedding rings – and a plump baby in a carrycot.

3

Three days ago she started leaving the baby out in the back garden in a pram in the sunshine for twenty minutes at about ten o'clock. The baby seems as good as gold. Not a peep out of her.

I am of course hoping this is a regular thing.

I am of course hoping she is out there today.

What sort of parent leaves their child unattended outside their house? It's like an invitation to abduct. She may as well stick a big sign in the pram. An arrow pointing downwards.

PLEASE. TAKE MY BABY.

Honestly, the everyday habits of the suburban mother never cease to amaze me.

And today is a most excellent day. No-one will give two hoots about me, all eyes will be on their television screens. Today is not royal, it is regal!

I turn from this street to the next, the bunting is sparse now. I wonder if her road is republican – no trestle tables here.

I reach the bus stop and look across the street.

My heart sinks. There is no pram there. I feel a panic rise in me as I lower myself onto the pebble-dashed seating. I have to try and be calm so I can think rationally.

If it isn't going to happen today, it will happen one day.

I just really want it to happen today.

I look again at the house. Quite a new build. Mid-seventies maybe. Windows not too big, this is good. And the road we're on is on a slope. It was meant to be the perfect site. A hop over the wall, or a push through the back gate that leads to the back path to the garage. Either would do. Lots of greenery to hide behind. A welcoming house. Nothing foreboding here. A perfectly pleasant house. An inviting house.

A woman ambles up and sits next to me. Shit. This is not part of the plan.

4

She's about my age. She has been crying. Why is everyone so sad today? It's meant to be a day of national celebration, for God's sake. I look away. I don't want her to remember me tomorrow. 'Oh yes, there was a woman in a burgundy mac at the bus stop.' I just want to blend into the background. And actually it's good that she's in some sort of distress. Maybe someone she loves has just died. Perfect. She'll be in no mood to remember me if that's the case. Yes, crying at the bus stop, today, right at this moment. This can only be a good thing. In fact, it can be a most excellent thing.

Eventually a bus comes and she gets on and it drives off. And as it sails out of view I see something magnificent. The pram is now in the back garden.

Deep breaths. Deep breaths.

I stand. I cross the road. And I head to the back gate. I open it as quietly as I can. I can hear pop music floating out from the open back door. I will have to be quick. As I approach the pram I hear raised voices. Heart in my mouth, I quicken my pace.

RACHEL

Marrakech, 2017

Chapter One

'Rachel? It's Pam. I think you should come home. Your mum . . .' I hear a catch in her voice. 'Your mum's not got long.'

I don't know what to say. And, coward that I am, I say nothing. Just then my phone vibrates and I don't know what's going on. Is Pam sending weird messages down the line?

'Pam?'

'Yes?'

I then realize I have another call coming through so I look at my handset. I have had a mobile phone for about a zillion years; you'd think I'd be able to handle 'call waiting' by now. I hit a button, any button, and soon I hear my PA's voice.

'Hi Rach, it's me.'

'Oh, hi Didi. Actually, now's not a good time.'

'What time is it?'

Er, My Mum's Dying Time?

'I'll call you back in a wee while.'

I never say 'wee while'. And for some reason I even said it with the whiff of a Scottish accent. I'm in shock. McShock, even.

I don't know where this Scottish thing is coming from.

I realize that by cutting Didi off I have now cut Pam off as well.

9

Instead of trying to find her number I find myself pacing the room, glad of the air con. I feel the leather flooring beneath my bare feet and each step feels like a step on ice.

My mobile rings once more and in a daze I answer. It's her again.

'Pam, sorry about that.'

'There's something weird going on with your phone,' she says. 'It's not going ring ring, it's just going beep. Like a long beep.'

'I'm abroad, Pam. I'm working.'

'Oh, right. Where are you?'

'Morocco.'

'Oh, right.'

'Marrakech.'

'How soon can you get back?'

'I'll look into flights and let you know. I better get onto it now.'

Again I hang up without so much as a goodbye.

I lie on my bed for five minutes, staring at the ceiling. I am catatonic. The stillness is reassuring; it brings me comfort. It also brings me out in a bit of a sweat.

I stay there another five. And another five.

It's as if I am paralysed with shock. My head is blank with white noise. This will not do. I have to get. My. Shit. Together.

As the sweat is still trickling down my neck I grab a towel and dry it, while I open my laptop and start looking into plane times. Then I remember that I have a PA who is paid to do exactly this job for me.

I phone her.

'Oh, is it a better time now?' she asks, with a slight hint of sarcasm to her tone.

'Didi, I need you to do something for me,' I say with brisk

efficiency. 'I need to come home. I need you to get me a flight to London as soon as possible.'

'But you've got three dinners to go to tonight.'

'My mother's dying, Didi. I need you to prioritize this and do it now.'

'I'm so sorry, Rachel.'

'Me too. Call me back.'

She calls back ten minutes later.

'D'you want the good news or the bad news?'

'The good news.'

'That guy I met last week? He wants a second date.'

'What's the bad news?'

'There are no more flights to London tonight.'

'You're joking.'

'No.'

SHIT.

'Okay. Get me onto the first one in the morning. I'll let Pam know.'

'Great. Who's Pam?'

'My mum's next-door neighbour.'

'Actually. Ben was wondering whether this was actually necessary.'

Ben is my boss. Ben makes Madonna look easy-going.

'Whether what's necessary?'

'You going home.'

'To see my dying mum?'

'That's right. In fact, he said, "Over my dead body."'

'Tell him to go fuck himself.'

'Do you really mean that, Rachel?'

'Yes, I do. And forget booking the flight. I'll do it myself.'

'Oh, I don't mind doing that –' and then she lowers her voice

– 'I just can't do it on your company credit card. I think he's still a bit het up about the JuJu Quick hoo-ha.'

I really can't be bothered to argue. I hang up.

Let me explain. JuJu Quick is an international pop star. With huge ideas above her station. I work for Ben's company Venus Travel and we organize all her travel around the world. Recently we had a massive problem on our hands when the address of the five-bedroom town house I had found for her to stay in while she was recording a new album in Toronto was leaked to the press and she threw a hissy fit. We very nearly lost her as a client. In fact, Ben was so desperate to win her back he promised her a week in Marrakech, so I have come to the hotel we have planned for her to check everything is in place for her arrival. I also have to go everywhere on her itinerary and make sure it's up to her sort of standard. Basically I have to go to every shop she's likely to go in and eat in every restaurant we have booked for her. Tonight I was meant to be doing three in one go.

My phone rings again.

'Any joy?' Pam asks, all niceties dispensed with.

'No,' I reply, trying my best to sound both disappointed and frustrated. 'I've been on the phone to the airline. I can't get a plane till tomorrow. I promise you, Pam, I'll be home as soon as I can. I really must go, Pam. This'll be costing you a fortune.'

'Well . . .'

But before she can say any more I hang up and head to the bar.

If you think travelling on your own as a woman is bad, try travelling on your own as a pregnant woman. In the hotel I get pitying, sanctimonious looks. Outside in the souk, the stall-holders assume I have mislaid my husband or that 'he come along later'. But in the hotel there's no escape, you can't pretend.

They know I'm on my own and the absence of any man is the elephant in the room. Or the elephant in the riad.

In Marrakech hotels aren't really called hotels; on the whole they're called riads. A riad, as far as I'm aware, is a traditional Moroccan house with a garden or courtyard at the centre of it and the building constructed round it in a sort of square shape, with rooms off the central space.

The riad I am staying in is very fancy. It has to be; JuJu Quick only does fancy. Fancy schmancy, my mum would say. And this place is the epitome of that. Hence the leather floor in my room. And hence the feeling that I'm in some old episode of *Ab Fab* where they come to this hot country to pick up knick-knacks and rugs. Knick-knacks and rugs are what the souk is famous for. Honestly, you could get lost in that city-wide maze of a market for weeks. It's got to the point where I daren't go out there, I'm so sick of getting lost and asking for help to get me back here.

I go up to sit on the roof of the riad looking out over the sun-bleached city, the canvas coverings of the outdoor market stalls, the tiled roofs of the souk, the clock tower overlooking the main square, in the distance the Atlas Mountains. Although it's blisteringly hot here and I am grateful for the shade of an olive-green canopy, over there the mountains are dusted with snow. I take a deep breath, slowly exhale, and think of the words that Pam has said on the phone.

My mum has not got long left.

I order a non-alcoholic mint julep and try to put those words to the back of my mind. Like it's normal to feel so little when you hear your mum is about to die. Like it's normal to think, well, if I just stay here long enough I might not make it in time and will be saved the deathbed farewell. If only I wasn't pregnant. If only I could drink a proper drink, a proper mint julep, and ease the journey to blocking it all out. I'd even drink gin tonight, and I hate gin. There's something about the taste, makes me feel anxious and sicky. And I love a good drink!

But I can't. I'm just not capable. After everything my mum has done to me I still love her. So I take out my phone and try looking for flights online.

I'll be honest. When we had to do our damage limitation exercise with JuJu, it was my idea to send her to Marrakech, and why? Because although I have done a whole heap of foreign travel through work, it's one place I've always wanted to visit but as yet have not had an excuse to. When I suggested it, Ben thought it was a glorious idea.

I was first drawn to Marrakech because of my slight obsession with Doris Day. Although not close to my mother now, growing up we did share a love of old movies. They were some of the few times I remember her being happy, curtains drawn on a Saturday afternoon, cigarette on the go, television on in the corner of the room with some Technicolor dance routine or Doris Day emoting over a picket fence.

The Man Who Knew Too Much has long been one of my favourite Doris Day films and, even as a child, when I first saw the shot of that bus squeezing under the arch as it entered the riotous town square on its arrival in Marrakech, I knew I would have to visit it one day. I just never thought it would take me till I was thirty-six. Thirty-six and up the duff. In retrospect, not the best place to come when heat is an issue for you. The staff at the riad have been very kind and furnished me with my own fan, with which I waft myself now. They've also given me my own parasol for when I venture outside. All very good but I can see it in their eyes every time they look at me. *Weird Englishwoman about to drop, coming here in the heat, silly moo.*

'You model yourself too much on Doris Day,' Jamie used to say. 'Sometimes I feel like I'm with her and not with you.'

Which was, frankly, ridiculous. And now, looking back, was just a good excuse for him to draw away from me.

Yes, I might do my hair like Doris did in some of her movies. I've always liked to bleach it and keep it cropped short. Even now I'm pregnant I haven't slacked with the bleaching brush. I'd always believed that hair dyeing wasn't allowed if you were 'with child', a bit like soft cheese and cartwheels, but even the bores on mums-to-be chat rooms seem to think that these days it's okay to try to keep up with the latest follicle fashions, no matter which trimester you find yourself in. But to say I model myself on the star is taking it a bit far. That gives the impression that I wander through life expecting everything to be apple-pie perfect, that I enter kitchens in a soft-focus glow and a Fifties buttercup-yellow frock with a chuckle in my voice.

Oh no. I am definitely far too bitter for that! But that didn't stop Jamie making a typically hurtful jibe. Now I look back, he was often belittling me.

I remember once saying to him, 'Don't belittle me.'

To which he replied, 'Bit hard with those hips.'

The irony is that in some of Doris's most successful films she was paired up with the delectable Rock Hudson and we were meant to believe that they were a crazy, heterosexual, will-they-won't-they couple, whereas history informs us that Señor Hudson was of course gay, and sadly went on to die from an AIDS-related illness. One of the first high-profile stars to do so. And like life imitating art, so the same happened with Jamie. Oh, he didn't die of AIDS. He just came out to me. Shortly after the twelve-week scan. Great timing.

I'll never forget it. He started crying as the nurse showed us the shady image of the outline of our baby. As the sound of the heartbeat filled the room. I thought the moment had moved him to tears. But then afterwards he'd blurted out – and I always thought people never really blurted anything out . . . it seems so childish – he blurted out, 'I can't do this any more. I'm gay.'

'You're what?'

'I'm gay.'

It was like someone had driven over me with a steamroller.

Actually, that happened to me once. When I was little.

Well, it did and it didn't.

I loved drawing as a child and could spend every waking hour from dawn till dusk doodling away on scraps of paper. One day Mum bought a long roll of white wallpaper for me to draw on. When her back was turned I lay down on the wallpaper and drew round myself with a marker pen. I then went out of the back door and ran round to the front door and rang the bell. When Mum opened the front door I held the wallpaper up in front of me and said, 'Mrs Taylor! Your daughter has been run over by a steamroller!'

I honestly thought she'd buy it. I honestly thought she'd scream and faint or gnash her teeth or beat herself around the head with her rolling pin.

Oh no. Instead I heard, 'Get in, Rachel. I didn't even know you were out.'

Yep. She moaned. And I felt so stupid.

And back there, in the hospital, that's how it felt. Not only had I been steamrollered but I'd also been humiliated. Again, I felt stupid.

And to make matters worse, as I processed the information Jamie had just given me, all I could think to say was . . .

'You're gay?'

He nodded. And I added, 'Just like Rock Hudson.'

At that he had turned on his heel and walked out.

Relations had obviously cooled for a while. With me not answering, never mind returning his calls, his texts, his Facebook messages.

There was no way I could have a termination now I'd seen an actual photograph of its outline. There was no way I could get rid when it had stopped being a cluster of cells and become an actual person. Oh, don't get me wrong, I'm not some happy-clappy pro-lifer, far from it. I just could not go through with getting rid of a baby I'd ALREADY NAMED.

God, what a bastard.

That's what I renamed him in my phone.

Oh, look. It's BASTARD calling. Get lost, BASTARD.

And, okay. It was very childish of me, when Jamie changed his profile picture on Facebook to a screenshot of the scan, to write underneath it *Who says it's yours, prat?*

Though I was quite proud that the comment got seventeen likes and several of his friends commenting 'LOL', etc.

But over time relations between us had become more civil.

Civil actually to the point where he has recently started to get on my nerves with his new-found over-attentiveness. When I said I was jetting off to Marrakech he went into meltdown.

Are you sure you should? It's a long way from home if anything goes wrong? You might get raped.

WHAT?

Are you sure it's a good idea going somewhere so hot? What if you get the squits? You don't even like aubergine that much.

WHAT?

Well, it's just I've heard a lot of Moroccan cooking involves aubergine.

RIGHT.

And then when he heard I was going on my own it got even worse.

What if you pass out on the plane? What if you die in your hotel room and no-one finds you for days?

ENOUGH ALREADY, ROCK!

If only he'd been so attentive when we were together.

Instinctively I grab my phone and send him a text.

My mum's dying.

I wait. The only good thing about having a gay ex-boyfriend who's fathering your child is that you call all the shots. He has to be nice to me at the moment as he feels so guilty about what has happened. I know he will reply soonish. And indeed he does.

Shit. I'm so sorry Rach. What you gonna do?

Getting first plane back. Laters.

Laters xxxx

I order another non-alcoholic mint julep as I have found a flight in the morning that has space on it. But before it arrives I'm already regretting it as I hear a familiar voice calling, 'Rachel!' and without even turning to see who it is I know it's the other Single Woman on Holiday on Her Own. Brigit from America. 'RACHEL!' she calls again, and I turn and smile, seeing her sidle up to me.

The problem with Brigit has been that she's never really understood I'm here to work and not to have a scream.

The other thing with Brigit is she doesn't understand my current need for personal space. I'm six months gone. When I first got pregnant I was convinced I'd be constantly feeling claustrophobic or agoraphobic. And for a while I did feel both.

I hated the idea of being squeezed in tight anywhere – tube journeys were a nightmare. But then open spaces freaked me a bit too. I felt too vulnerable, like a gust of wind could lift me off the planet and jettison me into space.

But then this was soon overtaken by an almost constant feeling of joy. Of excitement. I wanted to stop people in the street and tell them, 'I'm brewing a baby in here, babes!'

I didn't. I'm not daft. But I did feel like it. I walked around like I was surfing on a wave of euphoria.

I remember telling Jamie, not long after we'd split up, just how euphoric I felt.

He thought about it a while. Then said, 'That was a Eurovision winner a few years back.'

'What was?'

'"Euphoria". By Loreen. Swedish. Wadda song!'

Cue an eye roll from me.

And then that high was overtaken by a feeling of over-protectiveness. Nobody was going to hurt my bump. Again, tube journeys were a nightmare, but fortunately I live very centrally in London so I just took short cab rides or walked.

And Brigit is useless at not accidentally jabbing me in the stomach, or banging into me. She is useless with personal space. As she heads towards me I instinctively flinch.

'Oh gee, have I had a shoporama today!' she calls. 'I totally nailed the souk, Rachel. Totally bartered my ass off. I am EXHAUSTED. I'll have what you're having. Two of them, Pedro!'

Pedro. She always calls Mohammed 'Pedro', for some reason. Possibly a racist one.

'I got this heavenly little table, they're wrapping it and bringing it round for me later. God knows how I'll get it on the plane, maybe as hand luggage, I just don't know. But I had to have it.

You know when you just know? Oh, and look at this dress I got for twenty bucks. They saw me coming.'

She fishes a floral thing out of a brown paper bag.

'Massive rip in it, God knows what I was thinking but I was in the ZONE. Know what I mean, Rachel? And I had to have it. What've you been up to?'

Oh, finally. She's interested in me.

'Actually I can't stay here.'

'Sun too hot? Let's take these inside. My veranda is TO DIE FOR. Come on, let's walk and talk.'

'No, I have to go home.'

'Oh.' She sounds most put out.

'My mum's dying.'

'Oh.' And that oh was much more dramatic. I almost ask her to say it again. Once more with feeling, Brigit. OH!

Well, there's no arguing with it really, is there? Your mum's your mum's your mum. I ignore the mint julep as it arrives and practically run back to my room.

I can do this. I can get back to Blighty.

The one thing that makes me realize I should be heading back to England is the idea of getting there too late. I imagine myself arriving and the funeral already underway. In my absence Pam has had to organize it and I arrive halfway through and nobody knows who I am. The house has been sold and the proceeds given to the local cats' home.

Actually, this wouldn't surprise me. But even if this is what Mum is doing I know I owe it to her to at least pull my weight. Get back there and supervise everything so that I know her wishes are carried out, even if I do walk away with nothing. I am her daughter, she gave me life, that is my responsibility now.

And of course if I get back sooner rather than later I will get a chance to say goodbye.

I suddenly feel very guilty. Even if I have never been that close to her, she brought me into the world; is it not now my job to see her out of it? But what am I doing instead? Baking in the sweltering heat on the roof of a house in Marrakech. Good work, Agent Taylor.

But I have an excuse. The wifi in this very expensive place keeps freezing. I have now been trying to choose my seat for twenty minutes. That can't be right, surely.

Every step I take in this building, every corner I turn, each staircase I hurry down, it's like running through an advert for interior design. The green-and-white tiled floors, the bougain-villea in huge tan pots, the multi-coloured rugs, all look like they're camera-ready for a magazine shoot. Shame then there's a squat, fat woman running through each potential photo look-ing alarmed.

Back in my room I fire the iPad up and look for flights to London on there. I must be starting to panic because I keep spelling Marrakech wrong, and then London wrong, and the page keeps freezing as I'm clearly doing something else wrong. As the panic increases I hurl the iPad onto the bed and scarper down to reception, where the nice black woman from London is sitting feeding a tortoise.

You have to be really careful in this riad. On the ground floor they have tortoises everywhere.

Yes. Real live ones.

I'm really glad I'm not drinking; I dread to think how many I'd have killed if I was meandering tipsily back to my room one night!

I tell the nice woman what's going on and she tells me to leave it with her. An hour later she comes to my room looking disheartened and confirms that the next flight I can get out of here is tomorrow morning. I'm here for the night.

'I'm so sorry,' she says. 'But I have managed to get you on the ten a.m. flight tomorrow.'

I tell her it's okay, order room service, and once I've nibbled my way through a few chicken skewers decide I might take one last trip to the Jemaa el-Fnaa.

I should be going to three restaurants. They're all expecting me and have tasting menus for me to try so I can tell Ben I've tried everything on the menu and what I recommend. But I just can't face it. I need to be amongst people. Not doing something akin to a five-star Bushtucker Trial.

I've never been anywhere like the night market in Marrakech. The hustle and bustle in the town square in the daytime is one thing, but as the old pop song goes, 'in the evening, the real me comes alive', and it certainly does here. One of the things I love about this city is that it feels like nothing you could find in England. There's no Starbucks or KFC to make you feel you're in yet another identikit place. Marrakech is the real deal, no imitations here, thank you. I've never known an atmosphere like it. I've never are seen crowds like it. Now normally I'm not a big one for crowds, but the energy of this place and the excitement of the people here are infectious; all bets are off. You want a snake charmer? They've got one. Actually they've got several. You want your photo taken with a monkey? Roll up, roll up! Actually, I wouldn't bother rolling up; the monkeys (wearing nappies) don't look like the best-treated animals on the planet. In fact I seem to recall that one of the on-location tales about *The Man Who Knew Too Much* was that Doris's love for animals and her fight for their rights began in this very square. She refused to continue filming until she saw that the horses queuing up to do horse-and-trap rides were fed properly. Looking around tonight I wouldn't bet much money on any animal-rights advancements since then.

Aside from the market stalls, small circles of people gather round various entertainers. It might be a musician playing the accordion, it might be a woman painting hands with henna, though my particular favourites are the men who sit gabbling away as onlookers stare wide-eyed. I asked a guide on my first day here what was going on with these particular groups, and I was told that these were Storytellers. They told exciting stories and people flocked round to be entertained. I loved it. It was like this was the origin of radio and television. It seemed so raw and immediate, and it does again tonight. I can't understand what the stories are that they're telling, but again, like the other night, the people listening are enraptured. And it strikes me as apt, because this square is full of story for me. For this is the square where Doris Day and James Stewart walked as Broadway star Jo and her doctor husband Ben and had their son Hank abducted from them. I remember the shock I felt when I first saw the film as a kid. The idea of that horribly weird British couple kidnapping the little boy and keeping him hostage in that eerie church in Brixton. It made me feel sick to the core. Even I, with my odd upbringing in a dark country cottage with only my depressed mother for company, knew that was preferable to being held hostage by the baddies in the film. Though of course at such a tender age I believed every second, every shot of the film. It was real and they were really horrible. Now, of course, I appreciate how well cast the movie was. Hitchcock baddies were always so good. Their faces always looked so troubling, or distinctive, that you remembered who they were any time they popped up on screen.

I look around. Above the sea of sparkling lights are the roof terraces of various hotels and restaurants where tourists sit and eat and watch the cacophonous spectacle below. I could willingly sit on one of those terraces and watch the movement below as if gripped by the best TV series in the world.

But I'm only doing a whistle-stop visit tonight and so I push on and savour the sights and smells of the food cooking on the stalls, the spices for sale, the nuts. I pause awhile next to a snake charmer. Back home I am petrified of snakes. But here it just seems so natural, so much a part of the fabric of everyday life, that there doesn't seem anything to be scared of.

Behind the snake charmer a woman is reading fortunes. She sits on the floor under a huge embroidered umbrella, turning over cards from a pack and placing them on a low plastic table for a woman in front of her. She is talking animatedly. But then catches my eye and freezes. She stops talking. Her change in demeanour is so obvious that her customer can tell there's something up and she looks round to see what her fortune teller is looking at. I smile awkwardly, wondering if I've broken some social rule here. Maybe there is a reverence attached to fortune telling that I am unfamiliar with and I shouldn't be eavesdropping. Maybe this is like me shoving my head in a confessional box back home, earwigging on someone's sins. I mouth the word 'Sorry' – for what it's worth – and move on, looking away. I walk towards the horses, the big line of horses and traps waiting to take tourists on trips around the town. I breathe through my mouth, keeping my nose blocked as the smell here is far from fragrant. I try to put the look from the fortune teller to the back of my mind. Her stare was so unsettling. But then I feel someone tugging at my top and I look round, worried someone is pickpocketing me.

It's the fortune teller.

I stop in my tracks. Now I have turned round it's like she's unsure what to say.

'English?' she says, her accent thick.

24

I nod.

She looks as if she's trying to work out the right words.

'Be careful,' she says. 'You are about to go on a difficult journey. Be careful.'

And then she turns and heads back to her stall.

I quickly start to walk as fast as I can back in the direction of my riad.

A difficult journey? She has to be a charlatan, surely. Someone hanging out there to put the fear of God into people, encouraging them to sit for a reading to prove things couldn't possibly be that bad. Well, she won't get the better of me.

Before I leave the square I twist my neck and look back. She hasn't moved. She is standing there watching me, a tiny figure in the fading crowd.

I hurry on.

Chapter Two

I squeeze myself into the taxi while I'm still shouting at Ben.
'No, Ben. I'm not shirking my responsibilities. I have returned
home because my mother is DYING.'

The cab driver peers at me over half-moon spectacles. I
swear I've not seen half-moon spectacles this side of a period
drama.

'Where to, love?'

'Beaulieu village, please. Sparks Lane.'

He starts the car up and asks the inevitable question. 'On
your holidays?'

'No, I'm from here.'

This is what happens when you come from a beautiful part
of the country; everyone assumes you're not from there but on
holiday there. Actually, one of the downsides of coming from
somewhere so picturesque is that you're then spoilt when it
comes to holidays. There doesn't seem much point in heading
anywhere pretty; you've had pretty on your doorstep all your
life. It makes you set the bar higher, or go somewhere urban
that can't compete.

It's then that I hear Ben's voice and realize I'm still on the
phone.

'I'm just really worried about JuJu Quick.'

'Yeah well, I'm really worried about my mum.'

'When will you be filing your report on Marrakech?' And then he quickly adds, 'Your unfinished report. Your incomplete report. Oh, this just gets better.'

'I don't know, Ben. I tell you what, though. If she does die tonight I'll lean on the coffin and get typing. How's that?'

'There's no need to be like that, Rachel.'

'Is there not? Apologies. I tell you what. If you're so worried about Marrakech, why don't you send JuJu to that place you know in Ibiza?'

'That's not funny.'

I think it is, actually. Last year I found out Ben had gone to Ibiza with other man behind his then-boyfriend's back. I was sworn to secrecy about it and it's a timely reminder to him to not mess me about too much because I have that threat hanging over him. Not that I'd ever really ring his ex-boyfriend up and tell him. But he doesn't know that.

I hear him say quietly, 'Take as long as you want off. I can go to Marrakech tonight.'

'Finally,' I say. I meant to say thank you but . . . oh well. I hang up.

God, this taxi's uncomfortable. And the seat belt digs into my swollen belly. If there's one type of person I now have empathy for it's obese people.

All my life I have completely taken for granted the ability to run up a flight of stairs, run for a bus, and that while you do these simple activities you won't get completely out of breath.

There have been times I have lain in bed at night and realized I've not cleaned my teeth. But the effort that would be involved in getting out of bed and heading to the bathroom. It's too much. So I don't do it. I just lie there, hoping to sleep.

And don't get me started on sleep patterns.

Okay, well, do.

All my life I've loved lying in bed, face-down in the shape of a starfish. It's my best position for getting to sleep. Well, just try doing that with six months of gestation in your belly. Although I'm not supposed to, I can only sleep on my back or, at a push, on my side. And if sleep comes it's a blessing. The baby presses down on my bladder so I'm constantly in need of the loo. Oh, and never mind how windy I've become.

Let me think of nicer things.

Let me concentrate on something else.

I know. The view!

The view from the taxi really is beautiful. It's probably part of the reason I work at the exclusive end of the travel industry, for a company that isn't even listed in the phone book. If there still is such a thing as the phone book. I want to help other people see places as beautiful as this.

Pretentious? Moi?

I'm sure I'll get over it.

Autumn is well and truly over and winter is on its way. The trees in the forest are so naked I almost blush. And I really notice a chill in the air. Dorothy, you're not in Marrakech any more!

I see the taxi driver giving me a long hard look in his rear-view mirror, working out why, if I'm from round here, he doesn't recognize me. He catches me catching him.

'Never seen you before,' he covers.

'I'm elusive,' I say, as if reading his mind. But he looks confused.

'You what?'

'I said I'm elusive.' And then I smile.

'Oh, right,' he says. 'I'm Tony.'

I decide it's probably best for me to keep my trap shut the rest of the way.

I know every inch of this journey, every second of the time it takes. Nothing I see from the cab window is new. This is an old part of the country, steeped in its own traditions. Change rarely happens here, and certainly not on the route from the railway station to my mother's house. I mean, don't get me wrong, there's not much to see, just acre upon acre, mile upon mile of scrubland and the odd clump of trees. In the distance the hills on the Isle of Wight. The occasional pony munching on grass. Even more occasionally a deer will dart out in front of the car, making the driver slow down, then bounce away to the trees on the other side of the road.

Fortunately the tourist season is over now, so the road is clear. In the summer this would be crammed with traffic, all driving at a snail's pace, slowing down to show the kids a donkey, a horse, a tree. I know all these roads from riding them on my bike as a kid. It would be me, a rucksack of sandwiches and a bottle of pop, my bike, and that was it. I was a solitary child, not helped by my mother packing me off to a grammar school miles away. When I came home I didn't mix with the other kids in the village. They either went to boarding schools or went to the local state school and therefore thought I was snobby because of my 'nice' accent, even though they had no idea that home life was very down at heel. Mum was a dinner lady at a local senior school and also did dressmaking to make extra cash. She was a good seamstress and could copy any frock, more or less, if you showed her a picture of it. This made her a popular choice for some local brides, though she didn't always like the resulting attention her dresses brought. 'Don't put it in the paper you got your dress from me,' she'd insist, if she knew a bride was having her picture in the local paper, though I never knew why.

It was only after I left the area for good and moved to London that I started to meet like-minded people. I had grown up believing that no-one else in the whole of the New Forest was like me and that I needed to get to the big bad city to find my soul mates, and then on one trip back I discovered a quirky cafe had been opened on the high street by a woman who'd moved from London, Cliona. It was best-buddy love at first sight. And then love at first bite when I tried her Rocky Road Pie. For me she was a sharp blast of fabulosity in a landscape of dreariness. She dyed her hair pillar-box red and wore it in a victory roll. She wore fishnet stockings and frocks that wouldn't look out of place on Jessica Rabbit. Her heels were higher than the World Trade Center. And she had the filthiest laugh I'd ever heard. Irish by birth, she had lived for years in London before moving here with her trendy hubby Joth, another hipster type who seemed to dress like something out of Dexys Midnight Runners in their dungaree period, and would often be found in the local pub, strumming on a banjo for no apparent reason. And then a series of weird things happened. Someone stole Joth's banjo and it was found burning on top of Cliona's car. Then someone painted the word DIE on the window of the cafe. It was so hard to get off that in the end Cliona had to get a new window put in. And then someone cut the brakes on Cliona's car. Fortunately she realized as soon as she got in the car and so avoided doing some big dramatic *Help I can't stop my car and I'm approaching an insanely busy junction and the lights are red* type of scenario. Nobody knew who might have had it in for Cliona, till one day a woman walked into the cafe with a pair of espadrilles and asked Cliona if Joth worked there. Cliona answered that he did. The woman then asked if she could pass on the espadrilles to him as he had left them at her B&B when he was staying with his girlfriend last night. Now as far as Cliona was concerned, Joth had gone to visit family in Newquay. Cliona covered, though, and acted dumb, asking questions about Joth's lovely girlfriend, and the woman from the B&B was remarkably loose lipped.

The B&B was only a few miles down the road. As Cliona eloquently put it later, 'Talk about shitting on your own doorstep.'

By the time Joth arrived back later on his espadrilles, along with the rest of his belongings, were neatly packed in suitcases for him. And standing outside the cafe on the pavement.

Of course he did that male thing of bleating on about how he'd never wanted to hurt her and how he'd been manipulated into a relationship by this psycho woman. Cliona didn't want to hear. But she did hear enough to report the new girlfriend to the police for cutting her brakes and defacing her property. She was now in prison for attempted murder, and Joth was single once more.

I'd only got to know Cliona properly because I'd been in the cafe when the B&B woman arrived with the Dexys Midnight Runners shoes. After she'd left Cliona had been so upset she'd poured a pot of tea directly into my lap instead of into the cup and when she'd taken me into her kitchen to wipe me down she'd burst out crying and told me her whole sorry tale.

And then when I'd found out what I'd found out about Jamie I'd gone to the cafe on my next visit home and cried on her shoulder. Our shoulders wet with each other's secrets and sadness, we were now firm buddies, and what was nice about our relationship was that it didn't matter how long we spent apart; once we were back in each other's orbit we could pick up exactly where we had left off last time.

Soon we're in the village, the mill pond still as a mottled mirror and on the other side of it Palace House, the stately home, looking twice as big as usual since it's reflected in the pond. We cross over it via the stone bridge and to my right I see a family picnicking on the banks of the pond, a donkey standing behind them, clearly wanting to be fed. They used to have rock, pop and jazz concerts at the Palace when I was growing up and, because I couldn't afford the tickets, I would come to this bridge with my own picnic and sit and listen to the music floating across the water for free. We head up the high street. More donkeys, one eating something from the bin outside the village shop. The village shop that hasn't really changed since I was a child – no barcode scanning here, they're still on stickers and free paper bags. We pass the ice cream shop, the chocolatiers, the photography studio that still seems to be showing wedding photos from the eighties as their latest fare, the hairdresser's and the teddy bear shop. What a high street! We pass the village school and the phone box, always so handy as the phone signal round here is pretty much non-existent. And every paving stone holds a story of my past. Falling over on a wonky kerbstone and grazing my knee, sheltering in the phone box because it was raining and I couldn't find Mum. We head on past the garden centre that was boring as hell for a little girl but which I now find strangely enticing and gorgeous – but then it has had a makeover and does evening meals and cutesy breakfasts and you can buy all sorts there, not just boring old plants. In fact it's the sort of place I could imagine working, were I to move back here.

'Just at the top on the left, please. By the gate, thanks,' I say to the driver.

These cabs don't get any cheaper, I think to myself as I hand over a crisp twenty-pound note. It doesn't pay to not have your own transport in the countryside. You can't just nip on a bus here. I see him looking at me again as he takes the note off me, still wondering why, if I am so local, he hasn't seen me before.

Well, sadly that's what happens when you're the daughter of a recluse and your mother doesn't let you have any friends round for their tea, or to play, or for a sleepover. I'm making the whole experience sound so gruesome. It wasn't really, it was all I knew. It's just I know different now.

I look up the street. There's a light on in the cafe window at the corner that bends to the main road leading to Lymington. Dare I just nip in and see Cliona? Tell her I'm back? I can't. I've come back to see my dying mum. I can't go to the cafe, surely. It wouldn't be right.

I could pop in for five minutes. See an old friend. No harm in that, is there?

I look at the gate that leads to the path that leads to Mum's house and Pam's house. The hinges are red with rust and the paint is falling away like it has alopecia. I drag my pull-along suitcase to the top of the high street and the quirkily named Hipster Teapot. But before I can even get there I hear someone calling.

'Rachel? Rachel? Where you going?'

I turn and see Pam.

'Oh, hi Pam. Yeah, I'm just coming.'

And I trudge back towards the gate.

Pam is dressed in Crocs, woolly socks, some kind of skirt that looks like the sort of thing a dog would lie on in the back of a Land Rover, and probably is, and a badly stained hoody that, when she turns round to lead the way, gives the impression that she studied at Yale. Where she got it from I have no idea, nor do I have the inclination to try to find out. She's about Mum's age, sixty-ish, but always looks older as her attitude to grooming is very much from the foreign-war correspondent's school. I.e., you don't bother because a bomb could go off any second.

She is clutching a box of ice lollies. 'It's all she wants to eat,' she explains, and I assume she can only be talking about my mum.

'How is she?'

'Dying,' she says abruptly. But then that's always been Pam all over. She doesn't call a spade a spade. She calls it a bloody shovel.

'Well. I'm back now,' I say, and it sounds pathetic. I can almost hear her thinking AND WHAT? But it feels hard to say anything at the moment and it not sound crass. She doesn't reply so I try to explain.

'So you're not having to deal with everything on your own.'

'Oh, I don't care about that. She's been good to me in the past, bless her. I'll be all right.'

And I think it's probably best to continue to the house without saying any more.

The only car that comes down this dirt track these days must be Pam's. Even the postman parks on the high street and walks the rest of the way. As a result it's all overgrown and weeds cover the odd pothole so you've no idea you're going to trip into it until you're actually doing it.

And then we come to a break in the road. The track leads left and right. If you turn right you go to Pam's cottage. Left and you go to ours. I follow her down the left track and there it is. My childhood home, the place that more often than not felt like a prison. And now it looks so inoffensive and, of course, loaded with sadness.

Seeing my mum so tiny and frail isn't a shock. She's tinier and frailer than the last time I saw her but Pam has kindly, or unkindly, depending on how you view it, been sending me regular photographs of her, tracking her progress, usually accompanied with texts reading *Doesn't she look awful, Rach?*

Really thin now. Cancer porn, I decided it was, like she was getting off on it. I'm sure she'd say she was preparing me so that seeing her wouldn't be a shock, but there also seemed to be something of the illicit excitement about the texts. Still, at least she was too old and fuddy duddy to be on social media and broadcasting the spectacle to all and sundry.

Mum is in residence in the living room. Fast asleep on the sofa bed.

'Jane? Rachel's here.'

Mum doesn't stir.

'She's not . . .'

'What?'

'Well . . .'

'Dead?!'

'It's just . . .'

'No, you daft brush. She's sleeping.'

But then Pam leaned over as if checking for signs of life, suddenly alarmed. And then nodded her head as she heard something that put her mind at rest.

'Put the fear of God in me then, you did.'

'Sorry, I couldn't hear anything. And she looks so still.'

'SSH!'

'What?'

'She can bloody hear you.'

And then she turns to Mum again and practically shouts at her, 'JANE. RACHEL'S HERE. SHE'S COME ALL THE WAY FROM MONGOLIA.'

'Morocco.'

'Morocco. Isn't that nice?'

And then she looks at me.

'Is it full of Muslims?'

'It's a Muslim country, yes.'

'Then you're lucky you didn't get raped. I'll put the kettle on.'

She heads into the kitchen. I'm too shocked to respond. But then she calls through.

'Mind you! You are pregnant!'

'Yes, I'm fully aware of that, thank you Pam.'

I let it lie for a minute but then can't help myself. I call out, 'Actually, it's not that rapey a country, Pam!' and then add as an afterthought, just to hammer it home, 'Morocco!'

Suddenly she is in the doorway, an ice lolly still with the wrapper on in her hand. 'It is,' she says firmly. 'I've looked into it.'

And then she returns to the kitchen.

Already Pam is making my blood boil.

She always does this. Makes some outrageous claim and then argues that it has to be true as 'she's looked into it'. Like the time she insisted that the actress Michelle Collins was from the New Forest. I had Googled her instantly to read, just as I'd thought, that she hailed from the London Borough of Hackney, but no. Pam insisted that she was New Forest born and bred and that her father Colin Collins had run the Fleur De Lys pub in Pilley. When I suggested that maybe, if this story had come from Colin, he might have been lying, she shut me down with, 'Nobody's lying, it's true. I've looked into it.'

I follow her into the kitchen to find her sucking hard on the ice lolly. She looks embarrassed to be caught.

'I'd opened it for your mum,' she says between sucky slurps. 'Seemed a shame to waste it.'

I shake my head like it doesn't matter.

'Why not take your things to your room?' she says, like this is her B&B and I am her guest, as if I've never been here before. But I can't be bothered to argue with her, and do what she says.

The cottage has been stuck in the sixties, style-wise, since the seventies, when Mum redecorated and made everything look ten years out of date. Bar the odd bit of carpet replacement since, very little has changed. Outside it might look like something from the cover of a box of candied fruits, but inside you feel like you're stuck in an episode of *Heartbeat*.

My bedroom is something of an exception. My bedroom is stuck in the eighties. A pink wrought-iron single bed and a black, white and red striped carpet. It's like a headache come to life, but when I was younger I thought it was so sophisticated. My teenage posters still adorn the walls; I've never been that bothered about taking them down. I honestly thought I was going to marry H from Steps back then, judging by the number of posters I have up of him and the group. Little did I know he'd turn out to be gay too. God, I can't half pick 'em! I dump my case on the bed, unzip it and quickly rip out a cardy from inside. Sometimes I forget how cold this house can get. Mother has never been a big fan of central heating.

I go into her bedroom and open her left-hand wardrobe, where I know the boiler lives. Of course the heating is off. I flick it across to ON and the house feels like it rattles into action. It does actually vibrate as pipes that haven't seen any action in months suddenly flood with hot water, excited to finally be put to some use.

When I return downstairs Pam is reading something on her phone. She is sitting at the kitchen table and speaks without looking at me.

'Have you put the heating on?'

'Yes. I was cold.'

'Put a pully on.'

'I've put a cardy on.'

Pam looks up and inspects me, then looks away.

'The heat doesn't agree with her.'

'I won't have her freeze to death.'

'She loathes the expense.'

'With respect, Pam, she's not the one who's going to have to pay the bill. I am.'

'We'll have no talk like that, thank you.'

I sigh and open the fridge door. There's not much in there. A few tomatoes. Half a pint of milk. Some tinned meat that's been upturned on a plate.

'If you're hungry there's some spam there. Got it in for you. Make a lovely sandwich with those tomatoes.'

I can think of nothing less appetizing but as she's clearly 'gone to a lot of trouble' – or at least her tone of voice tells me she has – I pull the plate of spam out and grab the bread from the bread bin.

'Any news on whatsisname?' she asks. And I know she means Jamie.

I haven't told Mum or her what really went on between us. I just told them he'd left me for someone else, which was bad enough, but I was worried back then that if I told them the truth they'd think less of me. Probably daft, but there is an element of humiliation to discovering your man is gay. I worried that people would see me as a bad judge of character, gullible, easily hoodwinked. Or some humongous fag hag who was obsessed with the queens. I was neither, or at least I didn't think I was. And I wanted to keep it that way.

'Is he still with that tart?'

'I don't know, Pam. And I don't care.'

'Well you should do, he's the father of your child.'

'I'm going to be fine, Pam. Please. Don't worry about me.'

'Oh, don't you worry. I've got bigger fish to fry, love. Like her in there. Dying.'

As I have my back to her, slicing the spam for the sandwich, I allow myself a little eye roll.

'Does she sleep a lot, then?' I ask, trying to change the subject.

'She hasn't really been awake since Thursday.'

Right. Well, I didn't know that.

'Floats in and out. You know. Probably the morphine.'

I concentrate on making the sandwich.

'Look,' says Pam. And there's a sudden honesty in her voice I don't recognize. 'I know you and your mum have never been the closest mother and daughter on the planet but . . .'

I turn and look at her.

'But it wasn't her fault that she didn't bond with you. She had . . . she had problems.'

I can't quite believe I am hearing this. Frankness like this is a stranger to these four walls. I look at her, alarmed.

'Just . . . I think it's really good that you're here now. I . . . I think it's really decent of you, all things considered.'

And I'm not sure quite what to say to that. So I just say a quiet, 'Thank you,' and return to sandwich making.

I can't be a normal person, can I? A normal person would now say, 'What do you mean? It wasn't her fault that she didn't bond with me? What are you insinuating? What happened back then?'

But instead I make a sandwich in silence.

I then take the sandwich into the living room and eat it, again in silence, staring at my mum. She sleeps on. And though I fear at first that I might become upset, I don't. The over-riding feeling I have is one of numbness. See? I am not a normal person.

Sometimes I think I want that on my tombstone. *I was not a normal person.* Or . . . *Eeh she weren't normal.*

I wonder what will be on Mother's. *Didn't have much to say, really.* That would be a good one. Or. *Silence then, silence now.*

Forever silence. There is, of course, something so apt about the silence in the room, not even the ticking of a clock, as this for me was always a house of silence. But the silences of my childhood were heavy silences, loaded ones, passive-aggressive ones. Cunning silences that actually spoke volumes, that told me for some reason this woman resented my mere presence. I put it down to me reminding her of my father. She never told me this was what was going on, but it was an easy enough assumption to make. I often thought she was dishonest. And so when she told me, and reiterated the fact, that she hadn't known my father long and that she had tried to keep in touch with him but he had proved elusive (ah, that's where I get it from!) I didn't really believe her.

Of course, me being me, I never told her this, I never challenged her about it. I just went with the flow. And fortunately, after a fashion, I didn't have to keep up the facade for long, as it was always soon time to be heading back to the railway station and the lucky escape of school.

She told me once that he was a travelling salesman who had been drinking one night in the Turfcutters Arms when she'd done a brief stint behind the bar. He was staying at the pub and one thing had led to another. She only recalled that his name was Ambrose and, she revealed one night after a bit too much gin, he had the biggest willy she'd ever seen. Just what you always wanted to know about your father.

The memory had always repulsed me, rather, but tonight it makes me smile. I pine for the ticking of a clock. I want to lean over the bed and put the television on. Any sort of noise, any sound will be welcome tonight. Anything to stop the loudness of my brain.

I have too many questions for her but I fear it's too late. This is it. This is the end.

'She's not doing the death rattle,' Pam says suddenly. I didn't even know she was still here. I look up and over to her. She's in the kitchen doorway again. 'Few more days in her, I reckon.'

Is this it? Is this how life ends? You lie on your couch with the television off and your daughter eats a spam sandwich and your friend stands in the doorway and we all just wait? There should be wailing, gnashing of teeth, histrionics, deathbed confessions, promises. Instead. A spam sandwich with a side order of ennui.

'I might nip out for a couple of hours,' I say to Pam.

She shrugs. 'Well, I'm not going anywhere.'

I head to my room to change. As I do I call Cliona.

'Rachel! I had no idea you were back! To what do we owe the pleasure?'

'Oh, just a dying mum, you know.'

'Oh God, I'm sorry. Anything I can do, sweetheart?'

'Well. Yes. I was just wondering if the ten o'clock club was on tonight?'

'You fucking betcha. I'll book us a cab.'

Margaret Mary Lavery lives in a big house at the top of a small hill on the other side of the Beaulieu River. In her youth she was a stunner. She still turns heads now at seventy-three. In her youth she was a glamorous actress on the telly. But those days are long gone and now she lives life to the full with a steady flow of cheap white wine and menthol cigarettes, the mainstay of her diet, topped up with the occasional chicken salad or boiled egg. Since her husband died she has been lonely, and every night at ten o'clock she hosts the ten o'clock club for any one of her friends who wishes to turn up and get drunk. Sometimes she celebrates alone. Sometimes with Cliona. Sometimes a few other people. But tonight it's just the three of us.

I first met Margaret at the village fete. I found her rowing with the woman on the 'guess the weight of the cake' stall. She was full of expletives and passion, disagreeing with what she was hearing about the cake's weight. I was instantly drawn to her, and a little bit obsessed. I'd then followed her round the fete, in the vain hope that we might fall into conversation. Eventually we did in the queue for the ladies' loos. And when I dropped the C-word in front of her it had the desired effect. She grabbed my arm and told me we'd be friends for life.

The moon is high in the sky. The ultimate streetlamp that lights all around. The water in Margaret's pool lies still, the moon reflected perfectly, unmoving in it. And sweeping down her lawn to the jetty the river lies still too, a glass shelf, the moon sailing on it.

'Full moon,' Margaret says with excitement, as she pops the cork on the champagne. The rivers of bubbles into our eager glasses are anything but still. Once they are full, a toast is raised.

'To Rachel's mum.'

'TO RACHEL'S MUM!'

'Even if she is a bit of a cold-hearted cow,' Margaret adds, and there isn't a trace of bitchiness in her tone, just sympathy. She's always felt sorry for me; it's just the way it is. I want so much for her to be proud of me, or happy for me, but the sympathy card always wins. She has so much joy and love in her heart, and offers it generously, that she can never understand people who aren't like-minded.

'And to trusty Pam,' says Cliona.

'Oh God, yeah. Trunchball,' adds Margaret, though she doesn't really know what this means. I think it is from a long-forgotten memory of Miss Trunchbull from the Roald Dahl book that she must have read to her nieces and nephews, but it has latterly been conflated with 'Wrecking Ball'. Either way it feels apt. Pam can be a bit of a quiet monster who destroys everything in her wake.

'And anyway,' Margaret continues, 'families are created not given. And here is our little ensemble. To real family!'

And again we toast. 'To the ten o'clock club!'

Margaret then regales us with tales of her new cleaner, a Filipino woman who goes by the name of Baby and travels everywhere on a 'ghastly' moped at fifty miles an hour, honking at everything to get out of her way.

'Are you sure you're not making her up?' Cliona gasps, between giggles.

'No! I mean yes! Well, she's real anyway. As is that God-awful scooter.'

'But there aren't any Filipinos in the New Forest.'

'Well, there are now. And I'll tell you something else.'

'What?'

'They're facking good cleaners. Whenever she does my parquet I swear, it's like a bally ice rink in there. Lucky I haven't broken a hip. I could lie there for days in a puddle of my own incontinence. But hey. I'll have gone down in a clean house. To cleaners!'

And this time we toast cleaners. Suddenly Margaret looks disorientated.

'Music. Shit. I haven't put any on.'

We know it's dangerous for Margaret to play her music late at night. She doesn't give two hoots about the neighbours. 'Why should I? The nearest one's half a bally mile away!' But because she lives at the top of a hill, and the hill leads down to the river, any music she plays seem to hurtle down the water like a bouncing bomb, ricocheting into the houses lining the river. And in a posh enclave like this, people have no idea that neighbours can be anything other than silent. I sometimes wonder how they'd cope living in Brixton like I used to, the smell of 'de 'erb' permeating from next door's yard, the low-level drum and bass accompanying everything I did. I got used to it after a while, but some of my neighbours here might never sleep again, were they confronted with it. Margaret disappears into the houses to meek bleats of 'No, Margaret!' and 'Not too loud, Margaret!' from me and Cliona. But true to form the next thing we hear is a VERY LOUD Frank Sinatra belting it out. It seems like the water in the pool and the river itself start to tremble like there's a tsunami heading for the south coast; somewhere in the trees a flock of once-sleeping birds takes flight.

'They don't make them like this any more, darlings,' Margaret says, eyes shut tight, leaning against the doorframe as if the beauty of his voice is too much to take, savouring every bar.

'Well, they do,' Cliona says, 'it's just you're not familiar with them.'

'Oh fuck off, you boring little popstrel,' Margaret spits, heading back to join us. God knows why Cliona bothers to argue with her; it is a pointless battle she always undertakes. Margaret will soon annihilate her. No-one knows music like Margaret knows music. At least, that's what Margaret thinks. 'Amy Winehouse, I grant you. But where is she?'

Cliona goes to say 'dead' but Margaret pounces on her before she can open her mouth.

'EXACTLY. And Adele, at a push. But what about Looby Lu?'

'Who?'

'Makes dresses.'

'Sorry?'

'Married to oojameflip.'

'Who's oojameflip?'

'Got the kids. Never smiles.'

'Victoria Beckham?'

'Don't you DARE sit there and tell me she can sing.'

'Well, she can, actually. I think you'll find she's earned a considerably larger sum of money precisely from singing than anyone round this table.'

Margaret looks like she's smelt blood and she's going for it.

'I'm not talking about earning money. I'm talking about singing. Do an impression of Victoria Beckham singing. SEE, YOU CAN'T. BECAUSE NO-ONE KNOWS WHAT SHE SOUNDS LIKE.'

'With respect, Margaret. Victoria hasn't been a professional singer for quite some time. Your argument is rather outmoded.'

'Good. I like outmoded. Outmoded suits me. And careful what you say. You're sitting on an outmoded chair on an outmoded terrace by an outmoded pool by an outmoded house. This place is the epitome of outmoded, so ya boo sucks to you, you little trend-setter.'

It's got ugly. Cliona shouldn't have challenged Margaret's world view. I try to rescue the conversation.

'I suppose I better start thinking of music for Mum's funeral.'

'Oh, don't ask this one,' Margaret says, jabbing her finger in Cliona's arm. 'It'll be all Spice Girls and skinnymalinx.'

'I've always thought Audrey Hepburn for a funeral. "Moon River". You can't beat that as the coffin rolls away.'

Margaret shuts one eye and uses the other to eye Cliona suspiciously. 'Now that, my dear, might be the best idea you've had all night.'

And it seems relations are back on track.

We stay chatting till midnight, when Margaret announces that she is sleepy, and disappears inside. When we hear the door being bolted we realize she's not coming out again and we'll have to find our way home. I've only had one drink as I am with child, but Cliona is tipsy and leans into me as we walk all the way home. It's a cool evening, the sky is clear, and the night feels eerily full of promise. Even though I have come home to witness my mother dying, I feel the buzz of potential in the air.

Cliona and I say goodbye on the high street and I watch as she staggers back to the cafe.

When I get to Mum's cottage I'm as quiet as I can be as I let myself in.

I stand in the hallway and realize I can hear people talking in the living room. Soon I realize the voices are Pam's and Mum's. Oh good! Mum is awake!

I am about to open the door and burst in full of the joys when I hear Mum's voice, weak but stern, saying, 'No. Rachel must never know.'

I stop in my tracks. What on earth are they talking about?

'So you're not going to tell her?' Pam asks.

'No.' Mum replies. 'I'll take that secret to my grave.'

Chapter Three

I push the door open. Although it's late every light in the room is burning bright. Overhead, uplights, a bedside light. It's an unforgiving arena to walk into. There's a connection between Mum and Pam that's as close as if I'd walked in on an illicit couple canoodling. And they break apart quickly, as if caught out. Mum recovers equally quickly and, eyes lighting up, croaks out a speedy, 'Rachel! Pam said you were here! Oh, come and let me look at you!'

I move and sit on the bed alongside her, taking her hand, pretending I've not heard what I heard through the door. After a few stilted sentences Pam is keen for us to call it a night.

'Your mum's tired.'

'Plenty of time for sleeping when I'm gone,' she replies, and that's most unlike her. Unlike her to disagree with anyone quite so blatantly. And unlike her to joke about something so serious.

This isn't the mum I'm used to. And this is a side of her I suddenly like.

'I won't tire her out too much, Pam. Promise.'

Pam looks to Mum. A hesitant, unsure look. Mum glances away and smiles at me and squeezes my hand.

'I want to hear all your news.'

Pam beats a polite retreat and says she'll see us in the morning.

'Pam says you've been away. Africa?'

'Morocco.'

'Gosh. Was it interesting?'

'Yes.'

'*The Man Who Knew Too Much*.'

'Exactly. I saw the market square and I went for dinner at the hotel that they filmed a bit of it in. It's a beautiful place.'

'I'm sure. And how's baby doing?'

'Mother and baby are doing just fine.'

'Do you know if it's a boy or a girl yet?'

'I don't. I want it to be a surprise.'

'If it's a girl, call it Jane.'

'Right.'

I wasn't sure what I thought of that, actually.

'Don't worry, dear. That was a joke.'

A joke? My mother never made jokes. And when was the last time she called me dear? Actually, has she ever called me dear? This is like having a whole new mum.

'Can I do anything for you?' I ask, expecting her to maybe ask for a glass of water. Or an ice lolly. But her response wrongfoots me.

'Did you come by car?'

'No, I don't have one. There's not much need in London.'

'Can you borrow one?'

'I don't know. Possibly.'

'Or hire one.'

'I'll try. Why?'

'I'd like to go to the seaside.'

'Okay.'

'Before I die. I'd like to dip my feet in the sea.'

'Of course. We'll do it tomorrow.'

'Wonderful. And for now . . .'

'Yes?'

'I'd love an ice lolly.'

'I'll get you one.'

Later, as I lie in my single bed, I think that this is not the woman I've known. I savour each sentence she's said to me, the warmth and love that accentuated every sound. The light in her eyes, reflected from the many bulbs in the room, but nevertheless it made her look so content. Does this mean the cancer has spread to her brain? Does this mean that actually, in the morning, she will have forgotten all about her request and will therefore have scant desire to visit the seaside? Is it even worth me looking into hiring a car to take her there or anywhere? Mind you, a little run-around while I'm down here will save me a fortune on taxi fares. I'll look into it first thing. Maybe tomorrow she will remember her wish to get a little sand between her toes, but maybe she will also revert to being the same distant mother I've always known. Maybe she was giddy from being embarrassed to have almost been caught discussing her secret, the secret she has to keep from me, and she prescribed herself some enforced out-of-character jollity to cover the salacious thrill of the near miss. Maybe now she is sleeping she is back to normal. Maybe the relief of having got away with it will make her sink back to being herself again. Either way, I know if we do visit a beach tomorrow then I will be asking her what secret she is keeping from me. I'll have few other chances to, and at the end of the day I have to ask myself – what have I got to lose?

Pam is really hacked off that I'm taking Mum out.

'She's not well enough,' she says, crossing her arms as I help myself to some past-their-best Corn Flakes.

'It's what she wants,' I counter.

'It's abuse.'

'As if.'

'You'll kill her.'

'I'll try my very best not to.'

'You're not taking my car.'

'I don't need to. I'm borrowing Cliona's.'

'Who's Cliona?'

'The woman from the cafe.'

'I'm sorry?'

'The Hipster Teapot.'

'Oh, that God-awful place. Marjorie Lyons took her grandson in there and d'you know what they did?'

'Haven't a clue.'

'Served home-made lemonade in a jam jar.'

'Gosh, I've never heard of that before. Ever.' She doesn't clock my heavily sarcastic tone.

'Well, it's true. She took a photograph on her phone to prove it.'

'Wow.' I should really snap out of this sarcasm.

'And now you go in there and tell all and sundry what's going on with your mum, presumably?'

'Not all and sundry. I know the woman who owns it. She's my friend.'

She doesn't reply to that.

'I didn't just do some mad dash up the high street screaming, "Need to take my dying mum to the beach, can someone lend me their four-by-four?" I'm not Challenge Anneka.'

'It's a four-by-four?' She's sounding impressed now.

'Yes. What difference does that make?'

'None. I still don't approve.'

'Are you going to barricade the door so we can't get out?'

'How do you propose to get her out, incidentally?'

'I will be borrowing a wheelchair from that wheelchair place in Lymington.'

'Oh, you've got all bases covered.' Now it's her turn to sound sarcastic. I almost spit out my Corn Flakes. I don't. But I almost do.

'Well, what you rather I did, Pam? Hmm? Give her a fireman's lift?'

'There's no need to be sarcastic.'

'I'm not being sarcastic.'

She pulls a face that tells me she begs to differ.

'Would you like to come with us?' I say, meaning, *Is that your problem?*

Please say no. Please say no.

'I want no part of this. I can't believe you're doing it. It's nasty, that beach.'

'I haven't said where I'm taking her yet.'

'The currents. It's a dangerous place.'

'I'm not going to make her swim, Pam.'

'Good, coz she can't.'

'I know.'

'Neither can I.'

'I know.'

'If I was to jump in that sea that'd be it. I'd be a goner. Same with the river out the back. I have to keep my wits about me.'

She's making this about her.

'I mean,' she continues, 'people don't have an appreciation of how downright dangerous nature can be.'

'Yes. I know what you mean.'

'Look at Noah's Ark.'

'Well, exactly,' I find myself saying, even though I have scant idea what she is talking about. I see she then starts to hate herself for having forgotten that she was meant to be having a go at me.

'I still disapprove, basically,' she says.

'Look on it as a morning off,' I proffer.

She shrieks with derision and heads out of the kitchen into the garden. Heading home, presumably.

Fancy not being able to swim. Fancy getting through your whole childhood without a successful trip to the swimming baths. What was it in my mum and Pam's upbringings that meant their parents didn't insist they learned to swim?

I instinctively reach for my stomach and imagine my unborn child with armbands on. Diving into a pool. An Olympic swimming champion. Just like . . . like . . .

Okay, so I can't think of the names of any famous swimmers.

Except maybe her, the one who was in the films. Esther someone?

I can't think of anything.

Oh, well. I'd better get on and do this.

I can't quite believe Cliona has let me borrow her ginormous car. It's a Range Rover Sport. It feels so high up. It IS so high up, I feel like I'm driving a tank. I'm seeing the forest from a whole new vantage point. If they had a regular bus service round here then this is what it'd feel like to be on the upper deck.

Talking of bloody buses, I have to swerve awkwardly when the local tourist double-decker comes zooming towards me and runs me off the road. I stupidly think everyone will understand I have some very precious cargo in the passenger seat. So I stupidly expected the tourist bus to pull over to let us go past. No such luck, of course.

Fortunately the lanes leading down to the beach are only surrounded by grass, so it's not like I've crashed into any buildings or anything. I pull back onto the lane and put my foot down. I do a side eye thing to Mum, worried this might have tipped her over the edge, or worse, off her seat, but I am relieved to see that she is asleep.

At least I hope she is asleep.

All the way to the beach I pray in my head. Please keep her alive. Don't make her be dead. Please let her be alive.

Not because I particularly want her not to die. She has suffered so much, she can go when she wants. But more for the selfish reason that I want her to see the sea. I want to have made a wish of hers come true. Also, I've gone to a bit of trouble hiring the wheelchair. Sixty quid for a month. I doubt she'll last that long and I have visions of wheeling myself round in it, making her funeral arrangements. I see people feeling sorry for me. *Oh, her poor disabled daughter, wheeling round planning everything, bless her.* Or, *Isn't she speedy in it? And her, a cripple.*

But then I banish this thought from my head as it is cruel and unnecessary and right now I think that if I entertain any negative thoughts, if I think bad things, then the bad thing will happen to my mum. And by that of course I mean the BIG bad thing. As enough bad things have already fallen in her lap.

And then I wonder again if the cancer is affecting her brain. Has it spread there? I didn't even ask Pam about how advanced it all is. I know it's nearly the end, but I don't actually know where it's travelled. I see her body as a network of roads and motorways, canals and rivers. I picture the bastard cells moving round the roadways; some travel fast, some slow. Has it gone as far as her brain? And if so, maybe that is what affected her personality change last night.

I know there is nothing of her now. I know, despite wrapping her in two fleeces, a dressing gown and an overcoat, that she was remarkably light to carry to the car. In fact I'm starting to think that the wheelchair was a bit over-the-top. Maybe the fireman's lift isn't completely out of the question. And now I have images of me walking through Lymington market with Mum in a papoose round my neck.

I have to stop thinking like this or bad things will happen.

The wheelchair is a good thing. They are not confining, they are liberating. This wheelchair will afford Mum some dignity as we move from the car to the beach.

The good thing about the New Forest is that you are never more than five minutes away from a beach. Well, that's certainly how it feels living in Beaulieu.

I swing a slow right down Thorns Lane, a thin finger that points to the sea, and eventually I slow down and pull over by what looks like a field that just drops into the ocean. I get the wheelchair out of the back of the car and push it to the passenger door. Mum is still asleep. I open her door and lean across her to undo her seatbelt. Still, she doesn't stir.

Please. Don't let her have died as I swerved to avoid the tourist bus earlier. I don't want to associate her passing with that ridiculous open-top green thing with the big orange sun on the side. The tourist bus that drives round all the time, breaking the speed limit, without a single passenger on board. I want her death to be beautiful. If she is going to go today, at least let her die on the beach, smiling.

'Mum?' I say, quite forcefully.

And, thank God for that, she wakes with a start.

'Where are we?'

'The beach. We've just got to get you down that footpath. Should be all right in this.'

I indicate the chair.

'Can you put your arms round my neck? I'm going to lift you out.'

She slowly moves her arms round my neck.

'You shouldn't be doing this,' she reprimands.

'Well I am, so less of the back chat, Mother.'

'In your condition,' she adds.

'Well, you're hardly Ten Ton Tessie, Mum.'

And before you know it she is in the chair.

'Hang on, I've brought a picnic.'

I grab my rucksack from the boot and hoick it onto my shoulders.

Time to brave the footpath.

As I push Mum along I feel the wheels glide over wet muddy leaves, stones and the odd twig, and I wonder if this is what it will be like pushing my baby round when she comes. Is this what it will feel like tucking her into a buggy and trundling her along the muddy pathways of the countryside? Will we have a better relationship than I've had with the woman in this chair? Well, I definitely hope so, or else there's little point me going through with the whole performance. And some days that's what it feels like. A performance. Because it's an effort, a drag. There's no-one to share it with, so some days it feels like a pointless performance. But then I have to remind myself that in a few months' time I will no longer be on my own. Ever. Well, not for a good few years anyway. And I shan't be packing this little one off to boarding school. Eventually we make it to the beach.

A horse is standing in the sea. The water tickles its ankles as it stands there looking out towards the Isle of Wight, unseen today in the dampness, and I have no idea how it got here. I ignore it and fall to my knees alongside the chair.

'Good?' I ask. And Mum nods. She stares at the horse.

'He doesn't look very happy, does he?' she comments, and I shake my head.

'No. I don't suppose he does. Mind you. Which of us is ever happy?'

And I see a wry smile on Mum's face.

'You've all your wits about you, haven't you?'

She nods slowly. She does everything slowly. She is literally winding down. She speaks slowly. She breathes slowly. That smile, yes, she even smiles slowly.

I take the rucksack off my back and unload its contents onto the shale. This isn't the nicest beach in the world, but hey, it's a beach. It's all rocks that I have no chance of wheeling the chair across. Every now and again there's a low wall of little knobs of wood, the occasional tree, and then the sea. And that's it. I'm glad I wrapped Mum up well.

'Still want to get your feet wet?' I ask, as I pop the cork of the miniature bottle of champagne.

I look at her as I pour it into two beakers. She is shaking her head slowly.

'No. Now I'm here. This is enough.'

I hand her a beaker. Then clink it with mine.

'Cheers!' I say enthusiastically.

'Cheers back atcha,' she says wistfully.

We sit in silence for a bit, staring out at the sea. The horse doesn't move once. The sea is brown today. With the yellowing spume it looks like shandy. After a while I work up the courage to ask her what I've been dying to ask her since last night.

'Mum?'

'Aha?'

'You know last night?'

'I think so. Memory not what it was.'

'When I came in I heard you saying to Pam. Well. Well, Pam was asking you if you were going to tell me something. And you said . . . you didn't know I was outside. I swear I wasn't eavesdropping, I just happened to hear it.'

She isn't looking at me. She keeps staring at the sea.

'And you said. You said . . . you'd take that secret to the grave.'

And still she doesn't turn to look at me.

'Can I ask . . . what is it you were talking about?'

'If I tell you . . . then it won't be a secret.' And now she does turn to look at me, and I see she is smiling.

'What?' I am more insistent, and return her smile.

'Is nothing sacred?' she says, shakes her head and looks away. 'You'll kick yourself when you find out.'

'Is it my dad? Were you talking about my dad? And who he was. And stuff like that?'

'Oh, Rachel.'

'What?'

I can hear in her voice she feels sorry for me.

'Mum, what?'

'You're going to feel so silly,' she says.

'Why? What is it?'

'Pam was asking about my special recipe for pumpkin pie.'

I display a wry smile but inside I'm screaming. Ever so gently. A muffled scream. The sort you do in the middle of the night, just as you're waking up from a bad dream. You think you're screaming the house down. In reality you're emitting no sound. I know she is lying. But you can't argue with a dying woman. So the lie goes unchallenged.

'I knew it'd be something like that!' I chuckle, and she wrinkles up her nose, amused.

The horse steps to the shale from the water and goes about nibbling at the leaves on a nearby tree. Next time I look at Mum she has fallen asleep. She looks cold. I worry this might finish her off and remember there's a blanket in the car so I make the decision to run back for it. I'm only gone for less than a minute but on my return Mum is awake, her eyes wide, almost with fear.

'Sorry. I went to get you this.'

I wrap the blanket round her, knowing that Cliona wouldn't mind.

'I was all on my own.'

'Yes, I know. I'm sorry.'

'Good practise.'

'Don't say that. No need to be on your own now. I'm back. And I'm not going anywhere.'

'I don't want to be on my own.' And as she says that her hand reaches out from under the blanket and clasps mine and it kind of breaks my heart because she needs me. It kind of breaks my heart because finally I feel like the parent and she is the child.

'You're not, Mum. You're not,' I say, and I cuddle into her and stroke the short downy grey hair on her head. Pam's cut it all short for her so she looks like a reject from Greenham Common. It suits her. She looks gamine, elfin. Not just like a woman with short hair dying of cancer.

I misjudged her head. Most of your heat loss comes via your head and I didn't think to bring a hat or put something on her head to keep her warm.

'Are you cold?'

'No, I'm okay.'

'Are you sure?'

'Stop fussing.'

'Drink your champagne.'

'I'll be tipsy.'

'Well, it's not like you're driving.'

'This might be my last drink.'

'I doubt it. I have a feeling this could be the start of a rocky road to alcoholism.'

'It might kill me.'

'Shit. STOP NOW.'

And the pair of us laugh. A lot. Eventually we settle and she takes another swig of her champagne.

'So,' I say. 'We've done the beach. Is there anything else you want to do before . . .' Why did I say 'before'?

'. . . Before too long?'

'No. My bucket list is very short.'

'This is a bucket list?'

'Well. A very small bucket. A thumble.'

'Thumble?'

'I mean thimble.'

'I like thumble. It's like a thimble, but has a bucket-esque quality to it.'

'Are you going to be okay, Rachel?'

'I'm going to be fine, Mum.'

'Oh, good. Because that was next on my list.'

'Two done in one day. We're just living life in the fast lane.'

'Dying in the fast lane.'

And that does make me smile.

'Oh hello, black humour,' I say, 'pull up a chair. I've been expecting you.'

'I'm a bit cold.'

'Then let's get you home.'

The good thing about the Range Rover Sport, I discover on the way back, is that at the push of a button you can warm your seat up, so Mum gets so toasty in the car that she actually asks me to drive her round for a bit so she can see the scenery.

'Aren't we lucky? Living in one of the most beautiful places in the world?' she says quietly.

'Yes. We really are spoiled.'

'I don't like it particularly. I've never liked it really. But there's no denying it's pretty.'

I look at her, alarmed. It's the first time she's ever told me she doesn't like the area.

'I thought you liked it here.'

'It was a good place to hide away, I guess.'

'Who were you hiding from?'

She shakes her head, pulling a face as if she doesn't know, or doesn't want to say, or even that it's not important. But then she says, 'Me, probably. I don't know.'

Maybe the cancer is affecting her brain, and this is how it's showing itself.

But then I realize she is just being honest. In cancer veritas. I don't know why I should be so surprised when she spent most of my childhood in a catatonic state. I can only imagine she was depressed for most of her adult life. She rarely seemed happy, so why should it be such a biggie that she didn't like where she lived?

'Have I asked you about Marrakech?'

'Er, no, not really.'

'Memory like a sieve.'

'That's okay. I'm really forgetful.'

'Was it lovely?'

'Yes, it was stunning. I loved it.'

'Not too hot?'

'Really hot. But really beautiful. They had tortoises in my hotel.'

'What?'

'They had tortoises in my hotel.'

'Yes, I thought you said that. Where were they?'

'Just . . . roaming about on the ground floor.'

'Roaming?'

'Yes. Not very fast. But yes.'

'How odd.'

'Very.'

'I like these seats.'

'I know, they're great, aren't they?'

'Whose car is it again?'

'Cliona's.'

'Oh, yes.'

'From the cafe.'

'Yes. Jam jars.'

'Yes. Jam jars. Pam was saying.'

'Pam says a lot.'

And we share a chuckle.

When eventually I pull up outside the cottage Pam runs out with a tea towel in her hand, purple of face.

'I was worried sick! Where the hell did you take her? Bournemouth?'

'No, just Sowley,' I say as I'm getting out of the car.

Pam is at the passenger door now and I realize it's pointless to try to stop her from carrying Mum inside herself.

'Hello, love. Where's she been dragging you, then? Blimey, it's hot in there, isn't it? Like a flaming sauna.'

'She likes it,' I say.

'She'll get a shock once she's in her cold place again. Come on, Trouble. Let's get you indoors.'

And I watch her carry Mum inside.

Later, Mum is sleeping. I've been to Tesco and am trying to make a fish pie. I have no idea why I think a fish pie is such a good idea – it's not like she's going to eat it, but I guess it's as good as any other sturdy dish that can tide us over and can always be reheated. I am assuming Pam is taking her meals over here now. She certainly never seems that keen to leave. She hovers as I prepare the fish.

'What fish did you get?'

'Well, I just got pre-prepared chunks.'

'Pre-prepared?'

'Pre-prepared chunks, yes.'

'Bet that was pricey.'

'What d'you want me to do, Pam? Jump in the river and stab what I can see with a protractor?'

'A what?'

'A protractor. Oh, it doesn't matter.'

'Money to burn,' she mutters to herself.

I know what will shut her up. I know what will change the direction of our evening.

'What secret will Mum be taking to the grave?'

'Beg pardon?'

'I said – what secret will Mum be taking to the grave?'

I turn to look at her. She does a very good impression of someone who hasn't the foggiest idea what I might be talking about.

'I heard you. Last night. Before I came in.'

I don't take my eyes off her and I see her neck redden with nerves. I know she's not going to tell me.

'It's just talk, init?'

'She said, "Rachel must never know".'

'I honestly can't remember.'

'You can. You're lying to me.'

'I'm not, Rachel.'

'And earlier. When I first arrived. You said . . . you said it wasn't Mum's fault we'd never been that close but . . . she had had problems.'

'Did I?'

She gives the impression that it wasn't that important. Can't be, if she can barely remember it. Eventually I return to cooking.

'Did she have a breakdown?' I ask quietly.

She doesn't reply.

Eventually she comes closer to me and takes my hand and removes the knife from it. I look at her.

'I don't know what you'd call it. And I don't know what brought it on. But yes. She couldn't do anything for herself. I did it all. She saw a few doctors and they all dosed her up on pills.'

'It's nothing to be ashamed of.'

'Not now. Very different then. She asked me not to tell you. She wanted to . . .'

And I finish her sentence off for her. 'Take that secret to the grave.'

That night I have such vivid dreams. Mum and I are driving around 1950s London in an open-top car. For some reason she has morphed into Doris Day but as this is a dream it's absolutely fine. We're having a gay old time, as gals did in those days, off on a bout of shopping. Hat boxes surround us and Mother can't stop laughing. We really are having super fun.

I wake. And realize there's someone in my bedroom. Disorientated, I think it's Mum.

'Mum?'

But the voice I hear tells me it's Pam.

'Rachel?'

'Mm?'

I sit up and put the bedside light on. Pam looks pale as a sheet.

'She's gone.'

Chapter Four

Pam isn't speaking to me.

I don't really care.

I said what I said in the heat of the moment but also because it's quite possibly what I believe 99.9 per cent of the time, and if she doesn't like it she knows what she can do. Which is what she has done. Which is to a) lump it, and to b) bugger off.

So. Peace and quiet for me now.

When I got in from Tesco last night the rather hideous orange-patterned cushion that sits on the armchair next to the sofa bed was positioned so that the patterned bit was facing out, facing the room. When I saw that Mum was dead I also saw that the cushion had been moved so that the patterned bit was facing inwards, towards the chair, and that the plain orange bit was now facing out.

All I said was, 'Is this what you used?'

And she hit the roof.

It must have been the most unusual sight. Two grown women having a scabrous row across a bed in which a woman lay dead, and hissing at each other like snakes, keeping everything screamed in whispers till eventually I burst out with, 'I don't know what we're keeping so quiet for, it's not like we're going to fucking wake her!'

To which Pam protested, 'You will rue the day you insinuated I killed your mother.'

Well, what am I supposed to think? The two of them have, or had, this unspoken language between them. No-one could get close to my mother like Pam could. And then I go sniffing around asking the pair of them if there's anything they want to tell me and . . . okay, so Pam tells me some sort of story about Mum having a breakdown . . . but the next thing I know is . . . Mum has died? Suddenly? And Pam just happened to be sitting next to her, unable to sleep, at two in the morning? Something doesn't add up. And I've told her so in no uncertain terms.

She came round this morning and seemed most put out that I hadn't dropped my assertion that this is what'd happened. Even me saying, 'Don't worry, I've not told the doctor,' didn't seem to make it any better.

I know. I just know. Pam killed my mum.

And do you want to know what else?

I don't care.

Pam says I'm in shock and that's what's making me make these bizarre claims. But that is not the case. I'd say the shock was more to do with the fact that I am surprised I am so grateful she did it. Our worries are all over. For now.

But Pam just won't back down. So I told her she was no longer needed and that I can sort a funeral and . . . oh, who cares what I said? What's done is done. Now I really do have to get on and sort the service, and this house, out.

The house is now so empty and eerie. And suddenly I feel as if I'm staying in a museum. Come. Look. This is what life looked like last century. Pull up a chair and spend hours transfixed by the psychedelic wallpaper and matching curtains. Maybe I should offer it up to TV companies who want to film something set authentically in the past. Maybe I could charge money for photoshoots. Maybe I could give guided tours.

Mother is now 'resting' at an undertakers' in Lymington. I went with this particular company because the woman I spoke to on the phone informed me they had 'unrivalled views of the river', which of course is completely useless for the deceased, as I pointed out, and then she pointed out that it was very nice for the relatives. 'And we all love water,' she added. Well yes, perhaps. Maybe not if you couldn't swim, or had an aversion to washing. Or if you'd survived the *Titanic*. But there was something so oddly reassuring about the idea of selling a place for the dead on the views from the window that I couldn't help but agree to go with them.

It's a competitive world down here, funerals. So many people come to the area to retire that there are in fact four different undertakers in Lymington. Yes, I officially grew up in the place where people come to die.

It's Tuesday. The vicar is going to drop by before lunchtime, apparently. I have no idea how long it will take to get a slot for a funeral. I'm not even sure if I want a church funeral. She never went to church in her life. But I didn't know who else to call and the woman from the funeral parlour said this vicar was lovely, and had given me his mobile phone number on a Post-it as if she really was really tight with the in-crowd, so what could I do?

The doctor came out. I didn't know doctors still came out. But I suppose I couldn't really drag a corpse into the health centre and say, 'Any chance of a death certificate, love?'

Cause of death. Lung cancer.

Oh well.

When she arrived, the funeral woman asked if I was feeling upset. I said I felt remarkably chipper. She nodded like this happened all the time and told me, 'You're on autopilot.' And I'd nodded back. Then she'd added quickly, 'That's not me saying you are an actual pilot who flies planes and stuff; it's more a saying. Vis-à-vis the numbness one feels after a death and stuff.'

I was really glad I'd gone with this undertaker. You really can't beat someone who manages to get 'vis-à-vis' and 'and stuff' in the same sentence.

She looked at my stomach and gave a tight smile.

'Is your husband going to be joining you soon, Rachel?'

'No.'

'Oh.'

'There isn't a husband.'

'Oh.'

'Yes.'

'My sister's a lesbian.'

'Sorry?'

'My sister. Jeanette. Her partner Tina's a scream.'

'I'm not gay.'

'Oh. So . . .'

'Yeah.'

'Sorry.'

'No, it's fine. I'm just single.'

'Single gonna mingle.' And then she emitted a filthy laugh. Which I thought was very unbecoming for an undertaker. And then she added, 'I usually wear my hair in a bun on the big day. Just so you know. Bit more respectful.'

'Fine by me.'

'It's just . . . sometimes people do like to know these things.'

'Great. No, well . . . I . . . look forward to perusing your bun.'

'Thank you, Rachel.'

And then she asked me to leave the room while 'we make Mummy comfortable'.

Five minutes later the house was empty.

Am I on autopilot? Or am I just not going to feel too sad because things were rarely good between me and this woman I called my mother?

And yet. And yet.

And yet yesterday I got a glimpse of how it might have been. Maybe that's why I feel such anger, currently, towards Pam. Not so much that she did what she did, just the timing of it. Could I not have had a wee bit longer with this changed person? Clearly not.

If anything, that is what I mourn right now. The lost chances. The lack of closeness. This woman who gave me life but then pushed me away at every opportunity finally welcomed me in right at the very end. She didn't ask Pam to take her to see the sea; she chose me.

But I have to be honest with myself. Had she survived a week longer, a few days longer even, nothing much would have changed. We wouldn't have spent days and nights joking and bonding, she hadn't the energy for that. But she might have been more honest about the supposed recipe for the pumpkin pie.

I never really liked her pumpkin pie. That's how I knew she was lying. She knew I wouldn't have thought that'd be any great shakes. Yet she still came out with it.

Oh well. Pam has furnished me with an explanation. I will just have to accept that and move forwards.

I have so many decisions to make. Do I stay in London? Do I leave my job? Do I move down here, lock, stock and barrel? What do I do?

But I suppose one thing life has taught me: at times of trouble, at times of stress, don't rush into making any big decisions.

Those decisions can wait.

For now I just have to get on with the business of burying my mother. And maybe, perhaps, trying to make amends with Pam. Well, we'll see about that one.

But for now, I guess it's as good a time as any to put the oven on and heat up the fish pie.

I wasn't expecting the vicar to be handsome. Forgive me for making sweeping statements but I'm not sure any supermodels have ever come from this neck of the woods. As Cliona once put it, 'Round here it looks like there's a lot of family and not much tree.' But when Father O'Neill ('Please, call me Tom,' he says in a soft northern accent) arrives he is disconcertingly easy on the eye.

'I bet your church is busy,' I say without thinking, as I show him in.

'Sorry?'

And then I feel caught out. I've said too much. So of course I cover.

'Well. With this area being a bit more traditional than most. I bet they're flocking to church.'

'We're hanging on in there, put it that way.'

'Oh good.'

'Are you a churchgoer yourself?'

'No. Complete atheist in fact.'

'Ah.'

'But. You know. Tradition and all that.'

'And was your mum religious at all? I . . . didn't see her as a member of our congregation.'

'No, she was an atheist too.'

'Maybe you can tell me a bit about her,' he says, as he takes a seat on the sofa. The sofa bed on which she died.

After a while it becomes clear that I've not given him too much information.

'Sorry. I bet people usually know way more than this.'

'Well, if she led a quiet life . . .'

'Unusually so, really. Actually, we didn't get on.'

'That's okay. I'm not here to judge.'

'It's a bit pathetic really, isn't it?'

'Not at all. There's no rule book for how we should get on with our parents.'

'I thought there was. The Bible.'

'You've done nothing wrong, Rachel.'

He really is incredibly handsome. If my life were a Hollywood romcom I'd be bedazzled by him and he by me. And he'd put down the cup of coffee I'd have made for him by now, when in reality I put the kettle on as the doorbell rang and haven't returned to it since, and he'd say, 'I've always wanted to fall in love with a pregnant woman.' And we'd waltz off into the sunset, doing a joint funeral/wedding in which he not only buried my mother but also took my hand, and anything else he fancied for that matter, in marriage.

But I'm not. I'm me and I'm here and I've got a feeling Father O'Neill's gay. Call me paranoid, call me whatever, but he's just a little bit too groomed. His nails are perfectly cut. I've never really trusted a man whose nails were better manicured than mine. And his shoes are shiny. And he looks like he's had his teeth whitened. Jeez, how much are they putting in that collection plate of his? And he looks like he's no stranger to the tanning towel. He's like a *TOWIE* vicar. And he's Church of England. I didn't know C of E vicars could call themselves 'Father'. It's all very 'come to daddy', and it unnerves me somewhat.

And then he goes and spoils the Hollywood romcom illusion

by asking if he can use the bathroom. So I point him up the stairs, hoping to hell it's not too untidy. And when he doesn't return for a few minutes I get a bit mortified on his behalf that he's clearly not just having a wee up there and is, no doubt, doing a number two. And for some reason I am torn between finding this completely hilarious and completely outrageous. Hasn't he got his own toilet he can do that sort of thing in? How would he like it if I popped round to the vicarage and had a cup of tea and then suddenly adjourned to his smallest room and stayed there for the rest of the day?

Still, I suppose the lesson I should take from this moment in my life is a new motto. Even pretty people poop.

I might cross-stitch it into a cushion and give it to him as a present. I wonder if I could do that in time for the funeral?

I wonder if I could learn to cross-stitch, full stop.

Okay, so that's a bad idea. Having a vicar upstairs using your toilet for such a long time clearly makes me nervous.

To distract myself I have a quick look at the notes he's jotted down on a pad on the table next to the couch. He's written:

Jane Taylor
Aged 62
Born Sheffield
Parents Edward and Connie. Only child.
Quiet childhood. Always loved countryside. Moved to
   NF in 70s.
Gave birth to Rachel after brief rltnship 81
Liked a quiet life.
Dinner lady
Loved television.
Hetty Wainthropp Investigates.

Would like the Hetty Wainthropp Investigates theme
  music during service. CHECK CD.
Neighbour Pam cared for her
Pam like sister to her in absence of fam
Loved animals

I hear the toilet flush. I move to the kitchen to busy myself
with some pot washing. Then I hear the water going. He must be
washing his hands. He'll be down soon enough. Then I hear the
air freshener being shot around the bathroom. He'll be down
now. And then, oh for pity's sake, what are you DOING up there,
man? Then I hear the window being opened.

Finally the bathroom door is unlocked and I hear him
hurrying down.

'Right, where were we?' he says jovially.

Taking the biggest shit in Christendom! I want to say, but
instead I hear myself saying, 'More tea, vicar?'

'I've not had any.'

'Sorry. Some tea, vicar?'

'Maybe not. I'm . . . terribly sorry but . . . I've not been very
well. In your bathroom.'

'Which end?' I say, before I realize it's a pretty impolite
question.

'Oh!' he almost shrieks, 'I was just shick.'

He says SHICK. SHICK!

'I mean sick,' he says meekly. And we share a smile. Knowing that both of us have now had to have the image of him
pooing in my bathroom.

I like the word shick. I think it would be a good medical
term to cover the times one is so poorly it is coming out of both
ends. He explains he thinks he has food poisoning from a

dodgy prawn, and very nearly cancelled coming here but felt he had to. Great. Now I feel guilty.

To try to change the subject I pour him a glass of water and ask him how he got into vicaring.

Yep. I actually use the word 'vicaring'. Though it doesn't seem to bother him.

'Well, it's an interesting question,' he ruminates.

It's really not, I want to say, I was just burbling to move us away from the talk of toilets and the like. But, sure. You're a vicar. You would find it interesting. I'll just have to stand here smiling and pretending to find you fascinating. Which admittedly isn't too hard as you're devilishly easy on the eye, so I'll just admire your nostrils, or your teeth, or your fulsome lips as you talk at me. I might even take in one or two words of what you're saying.

'My route to "vicaring", as you call it –' and he gives a wink as if to say he approves of my sense of humour – 'was certainly circuitous to say the least.'

My hopes for him as a PNB (Potential New Boyfriend) are dashed. The syntax involved in the phrase 'circuitous to say the least' reminds me too much of Julie Andrews as Mary Poppins saying she's 'practically perfect in every way'. Any desire I've had is extinguished like a cigarette in a puddle.

'I started out in the legal profession. Not very exciting . . .'

Oh God, I'm here for the long haul. This could take forever. Why doesn't he tell me what kind of nappies he used to wear while he's at it?

'Solicitor's clerk. Lots of hanging around at magistrate's courts, knocking about with the reporters and whatnot. Then a friend and I set up our own private investigation service.'

Now that IS interesting.

'Really?'

'Yes.' He seems offended I think he's capable of lying.

'So they . . . actually exist?'

'They do.'

'You were a private investigator?'

'I was.'

'Miss Marple in a dog collar.'

'Oh, I wasn't the least bit religious back then. In fact it was one of my clients that led me to Jesus.'

And then he starts telling me about a man who thought his wife was playing away and how he and his friend had followed her and found out that she *was* playing away, with the local priest! All very scandalous, but he was very taken with his first experience of setting foot inside a church.

'And it kind of snowballed. Or skyrocketed. From there.'

'And did your friend become a vicar as well?'

'Which friend?'

'The one you set up the agency with?'

He laughs and shakes his head. 'No, she's still tracing missing persons to let them know they've been left fifty quid in Great-Uncle Harry's will.'

And then it's as if he sees my eyes glazing over, because he adds, 'Don't knock it. It's a living.'

I have another almighty row with Pam on the Wednesday. She takes offence at me changing the locks on the back door, thinking I have done this on purpose to keep her out, but the truth of the matter is I go to the shops and lose my key and, bar breaking a window, I can't get in. I call out an emergency locksmith – I have to go to the phone box on the high street to do it as my mobile won't give me any bloody reception – and he advises that the lock is so decrepit, which is true, he's not trying to rip me off, that I should have a new one fitted. Which I do.

An hour later Pam comes round with a trifle to make amends and when she can't get her key in the spanking new lock, decides to have the mother of all kick-offs.

So we're still not speaking.

'After everything I've done for that woman!' she screams through the door. 'After everything I've done!'

No amount of me explaining what has actually happened will placate her, so in the end I tell her to fuck off and she does.

Cliona has called a few times but I don't want to speak to her. Same too with Margaret. I'm just not in the mood today. In fact, I think ignoring my phone is best, full stop. I just don't want to talk to anybody now. Maybe I will tomorrow.

I head upstairs and go into her bedroom. She can't have been in here for a while but it's tidy and the bed is made, and suddenly I have a pang of guilt about Pam. A Pamg of guilt, maybe. Clearly she has kept this room 'nice'. I sit at Mum's dressing table and look out of the latticed window behind the mirror at the overgrown shrubbery of greenness, and then above at the pale blue sky. The dressing table and mirror themselves are MFI – standard 1970s fare. The table has a pink pleated skirt running round it on a track. I used to think it was covering hidden secrets when I was a little girl. But a quick look under the skirt showed me it was only hiding a load of dust on its legs and the skirting board beyond.

On the table is a tray with a brush and hand mirror set, inlaid with mother of pearl. The brush looks like the sort of thing you'd groom an Afghan hound with and I can't imagine or remember my mother ever using it. There is a layer of dust on the mirror that looks like a fine trace of powder, as if the table had been recently used. I want to write something in it with my finger, but I can't think what.

I could write 'BYE' rather dramatically.

Or 'Jane' . . . and some kisses.

I could draw a big willy, like I'm a kid in primary school.

A happy face.

A sad face.

Or I could do as I choose to do and just leave the dust lying there untouched, unmoved.

A bit like I am. Unmoved. Where are the tears? Where is the damning realization that suddenly, now she is gone, I loved her so much I could cry. And do.

But instead I sit there as if I am an actress on a theatre set, waiting for the play to start, waiting to pretend that she meant more to me than she did.

Suddenly someone is knocking at the front door.

Maybe it's Pam come to make amends.

I hurry down but when I open the door I see Cliona. She's clutching a bottle of champagne.

'Thought we could celebrate her life?'

'Bit selfish. I can only have one.'

Margaret steps into view. She is brandishing a bottle of grape juice. 'Which is why we also brought this. Get some glasses, love. I'm parched.'

Oh well. Looks like I have company.

Because the pair of them are so nosy, we are soon back up in Mum's room and pulling it apart. Cliona has recently started selling some vintage (second-hand) clothes as a sideline at the cafe and is wondering if any of Mum's stuff will do. I am more than happy for her to take whatever she wants, but twenty minutes of pulling things out of the overstuffed fitted wardrobes and it is quite clear that a woman who admired Hetty Wainthropp is not going to have any amazing gowns hidden away for a rainy day. The clothes are all depressingly mumsy-ish. Very twin-set and pearls with the omission, sadly, of the pearls.

It all started off so well. It felt like high jinks at a boarding school once the teachers had buggered off to the pub or something, pulling frocks out of cupboards to try them on and play dress-up. And then realizing that none of them was particularly nice, and the allure of the game was lost. It was tarnished. And the atmosphere deflated.

Margaret is having a root around in a chest of drawers, one of which appears to be full of knick-knacks and bracelets and plastic necklaces.

'Hardly Aladdin's cave, dear,' she says forlornly, then shoves the drawer shut again.

'I told you,' I say, 'there's nothing of interest here. Hers was a grey world. A beige world.'

'Greige,' suggests Cliona, and we all have a chuckle at that.

'When Mummy died,' Margaret says wistfully, lolling back on the bed alongside me, 'we found a little box of letters we knew nothing about. Love letters. She'd been having the most wonderful affair with a married man.'

We offer up murmurs of intrigue and excitement. A bit like the Pink Ladies singing 'tell me more' in 'Summer Nights'.

'All those years I felt sorry for her, leading such a solitary existence since Daddy passed away. And all the time she was rogering a bookkeeper called Barry, three streets away. Dirty bitch.'

And then she smiles.

'Dirty, wonderful bitch.'

'I suppose we all have secrets,' Cliona adds, holding a swing coat up against her and glancing in the mirror to see what it looks like. Before returning it swiftly to the wardrobe it came from.

'I don't think I have,' I suggest. 'I'm pretty much an open book, I think. Does that make me boring?'

'A little, darling,' Margaret says, wrinkling her nose. 'You better do something about that.'

And then she slides off the bed and opens another drawer.

Maybe it's not so bad after all. Maybe it's a good idea to have company at the moment rather than hiding away. Maybe human beings are meant to be social animals rather than isolated Idas.

It's nice to feel something, when previously today I've felt like I was feeling nothing.

Cliona pulls out a mini fur coat from the wardrobe.

'Now THIS is more like it.'

And suddenly I can see her in it.

I'm running down the stairs and she is in hot pursuit, wearing that awful coat. We are rowing about something.

What are we rowing about?

That's it. I'm off school for the summer holidays and I want to go to Southampton for a day out with my friend Claire, who lives in Holbury. Claire's mum is going to drive us to Hythe to catch the ferry over to Southampton and I'm really excited, only Mum is adamant I can't go.

'You don't know who's out there!' she's screaming.

'I'm going and that's that!'

I stormed out of the house and slammed the door so hard it felt like the world fell off its hinges, never mind just the front door.

She was meant to be going to a function that day, up at the golf club with some other dressmakers. One of the larger lady members who availed herself of their services, as 'You just couldn't find anything on the high street for the big boned', had offered to spoil all of them by treating them to afternoon tea there. Mum had bought a hat from that fancy place on

Lymington High Street and then dug out the mink. I didn't give her a second thought once I'd left the house.

When I got back I found her lying on her bed, staring into space. She still had the hat and the mink on.

At first I thought she was drunk. Sometimes she got drunk. Not often, but sometimes. But then I realized she was just catatonic. And that she hadn't even left the house. All dressed up for a high tea she never went to.

'Why didn't you go?' I asked her.

'Fuck off, Rachel,' she said with no feeling. Monotone.

So fuck off I did.

The memory of it stings me. Maybe the hat is in the wardrobe too. The memory of the unpredictability of my mum stings anew. Again and again. This is why I felt so little sadness today. Because sometimes she just wasn't very nice to me. Yes, she was lovely recently. And the other day. But I've had a lifetime of her lying on that bed, all dressed up and swearing at me because I'd done something she'd perceived as some kind of slight.

I will never tell my child to fuck off.

I will never buy a hat from that fancy place in Lymington.

And I will never wear mink, that's for sure.

Margaret is groping through the bottom drawer of my mother's chest. She is pulling a face and I see it's because she is trying to yank something out that appears to be stuck in there.

'You all right, Margaret?'

She nods and eventually pulls out a fading yellow piece of knitwear. The softest yellow. A fairy yellow. Like it's a mirage, a colour from the past. As though, if you took it in your hands, it would fade away like the memories with it. And I recognize it instantly.

'That was mine,' I say. And she passes it to me.

It's weird. I don't remember seeing any photos of myself in it as a baby. Not that mother had that many photographs of me as a baby, it has to be said. But there is something chemical that instantly connects me to this piece of wool. I unfold it into my lap and lift it to smell it. It feels so familiar.

'It's mine,' I say again.

I turn it to see the back. It's not a blanket; it's a tiny little baby coat. My coat.

But something on the back of it surprises me.

The others can see from my face.

'What's the matter, Rach?'

I turn the coat up to show them.

A name is knitted into the back of the jacket in pale grey wool.

A name that is not mine.

Diana.

'I thought you said it was yours?'

I nod.

'So who's Diana?'

'I don't know.'

SHIRLEY

1978

Chapter Five

'I wish we were at the Butlin's in Minehead, Shirl,' our Josie said, carefully attaching the false eyelash above her right eye.

'Why, what's wrong with this one?' I said, helping myself to a cheeky sip of her Bacardi while she wasn't looking.

'They've got a monorail there. Can you imagine that?'

'Wow, that's sounds so good.'

'I know. A monorail.'

I thought for a while, then worked up the courage to ask: 'Josie?'

'Aha?'

'What's a monorail?'

'Oh, it's like a railway in the sky. Goes round on one rail.'

'From cloud to cloud?'

'No, you daft apeth. God, you've got your head in the clouds, you. No, it goes from place to place. At Butlin's, like. So. Like tonight. We might leave the chalet and head to the Gaiety Theatre on the monorail.'

'Really?'

I couldn't for the life of me picture it.

'Oh yes, Shirl. These days, monorails and whatnot. It's the only way to travel.'

Our Josie was what they called a beauty. All the blokes

fancied her round our way. Some nasty people said she'd had half of them but I knew that wasn't true. She was just a popular lass. That's all. She had green eyes, like a cat, all almond-shaped and shiny. And a blonder head of hair you couldn't imagine. She flicked it up at the sides like a proper pop star who had someone else doing their hair – oh, she was proper gorge was our Josie.

Like folk always said, 'She's the pretty one. You got the brains, Shirley.'

But who wants to have brains when you can have flicky-up hair like our Josie?

And on top of that she had a cracking bust. I'd read about her bust at a bus stop once. It was the one near Mumps Bridge. Some blighter had written: *Josie Burke. Best tits in Oldham. Fact.*

She pretended to be all embarrassed about it. But I thought it was proper lovely, that.

Best tits in Oldham.

I remember telling me mam about it. Ooh she went right peculiar, she did.

'Shirley Burke, wash your mouth out this instant. You don't say tits, you say bosoms. Honestly. Folk'll think you were dragged up, and we all know you weren't. Not by a long slice of the sausage.'

Whatever that meant.

Some folk said Mother had ideas above her station.

Which was funny, coz she actually worked at Oldham station. In the cafe there. Buns and a cuppa. You couldn't beat it really.

Any road, here I was. Butlin's Pwllheli. The best Butlin's in the land, according to some. And our Josie was going in for the Holiday Princess Pageant, tonight at the Gaiety Theatre. I couldn't wait. She'd bought this smashing catsuit off Rochdale

Market, that Mam said looked obscene but Josie and I both knew was gonna right wow the judges, especially when she teamed them with those new cork platforms she'd borrowed off her mate Sunita.

Sunita was one of them Pakistani types. Loads of folk called her names. We never; we thought she was really pretty and cool. And her mam worked in a shoe shop so she had all the latest footwear. And coz we never called her names, she'd lent the cork platforms to our Josie for the whole holiday. And we were gonna be there a fortnight, so it was dead dead generous when you thought about it.

'How are you feeling, Josie?' I asked, offering her her own Bacardi glass now she'd got all her false eyelashes on.

'Me ring's playing me right up. Always does when I'm nervous. Anxiety goes to me shitter.'

'I hope you're not gonna use language like that on stage tonight, lady.'

'Piss off will I! I'll be all ladylike and kittenish. Saying I want to help blind folk across t'road and promote world peace.'

'Aye, you're a good liar!' And we did, we fell about laughing.

See, that's the thing with our Josie. She has to work hard at being sophisticated. All the other girls in these beauty contest things, it seemed to come natural to them. But with our Josie it was a bit of an act. Before she went on stage I had to remind her not to belch or do her dirty laugh, or wink at the fellas in the audience and mime having a pint with them later. Like the time she came second in Miss Runcorn Shopping City, last year, 1977. I reckon she'd've walked that if she hadn't answered as she did in the interview round, when the host – a handsome bloke from the local radio station – had asked her, 'And what are your plans for the summer? What do you intend to be doing?'

And she'd squeezed his bum, let out a throaty chuckle, and gone, 'You, chuck, you!'

Half the audience had gasped, the other half had roared. But that was our Josie all over. Once she opened that foghorn gob of hers, opinion was always divided.

I'd've been so much better than her at playing the game. But then, as the lads in my class always said, I did have a face like a bag of spanners.

Sixteen, I was. Sixteen. Near old enough to be an old maid. Sixteen and never been kissed. You can't blame fellas. Every other girl in my class was prettier or dirtier. Even Mongy Mary had snogged Fat Larry up the back of the chemistry block. And she had one foot bigger than the other. Maybe I was just destined to a life on the shelf. A bit like our Aunty Glad. She'd never married and she was ancient. So likelihood was she'd never had a snog neither. But it didn't seem to bother her. She'd just lived as the maiden aunt alongside my granny all these years, putting her first and looking after her like the ladies in waiting did for the Queen. I thought I'd be happy doing that for our Josie for the rest of my life. I just wasn't sure she would be!

'Right. Check all me outfits, come on!' Josie hobbled from the bathroom into the bedroom of the chalet where I'd laid out her other costumes on the bed. There was the swimming costume. She lifted it up, all cornflower blue and gorgeous, and sniffed the crotch.

'That's better.'

'Yeah, I swabbed at it with TCP. Staining's gone now.'

'Nice one Shirl, you're a star.'

'Oh, I don't know about that.'

'And this is my disco look?'

Our Josie was a right good disco dancer. That's what she was going to do in the talent section. She always wowed the crowd with the routine she'd copied from watching an episode of *Blue Peter* where Peggy Spencer was teaching Lesley Judd to disco dance. My favourite two moves from it were the 'go in the phone box' and the 'pick up the receiver' . . . I always found myself joining in with those bits.

The disco outfit I'd got ready for her was some spangly hot-pants, some American tan tights, and then this beautiful bright yellow blouse with angel wing sleeves and a massive penny round tartan collar with matching tartan cuffs.

'Where the fuck did you get that?' She sounded so impressed.

'The market. They give it me free.'

'Free? You jammy bitch, how comes?'

'Coz I said you might get in the papers with it. What with you entering Holiday Princess.'

'And they bought that?'

'Well, not at first. But when I showed them your photo. They practically threw it at us.'

'Eeh, you weren't behind t'mangle when they handed out brain cells, our Shirley.'

She could be dead nice, could our Josie. Honestly, I thought the world of her.

'Right,' our Josie said, as she checked her watch. 'I better get a wiggle on. Contestants have to be in the green room by seven. Will you give us an 'and carting this lot over? And if you see Jed Jeffers and he tries owt? Knee him in t'goolies.'

Jed Jeffers was a DJ who sometimes did that *Top of the Pops*. Everyone said he was a dirty old man, and he was going to be here tonight to judge the Holiday Princess competition.

'He wouldn't look twice at me,' I said, convinced that was true.

'Don't bet your life on it. Blokes like him aren't choosy, trust me. As long as there's a hole and gob they'll stick it in. Come on.'

I didn't mind having to carry all of Josie's stuff over to the theatre. Like she said, she had to protect her nails; she'd only put the varnish on half an hour ago and it wouldn't do to chip them so close to the event.

'Hitch 'em high, our Shirl! Don't wanna scrape 'em on t'ground!'

I tried holding the coat hangers as high as I could but I was just nowhere near as tall as she was.

'Oh, give 'em here, shortarse,' she moaned, as she snatched them from me just as we got to the stage door. She then turned and barked at me. 'I'll be all right on me own from here.'

And then she barged inside and let the door swing shut before I could even shout out 'Good luck!'

As I turned to head back to the chalet I saw a swanky red MG pull up outside the stage door, and whoever was driving beeped the horn. Some sort of security man came hurrying out of the building. He went and opened the driver's door, which is when I saw the man himself, Jed Jeffers, get out and head to the stage door without so much as a word to the guy in the uniform. Jed disappeared inside, keeping his sunglasses on, while the security guy got into the car and drove it off. How funny. Oh well. Time for me to get back to the chalet and get ready for the big night.

Me and our Josie were staying in one chalet in the red camp, while our mam and dad were staying in the one next door. I gave them a knock to see if they were almost ready and Mam called out that she was just backcombing her wig. I could feel it in my waters. This was going to be a great, great night.

The Gaiety Theatre here in the holiday camp was my favourite thing about the whole blinking place. The other thing I really really liked was the heated indoor swimming pool, with its leafy branches hanging down from the roof making you think you were going for a swim in the jungle or something. And then under the water all those windows that looked into the bar, so folk who were having a quiet pint or chicken in a basket could watch your bum and legs and stuff underwater while you were swimming.

'Perverts' Paradise', our Josie called it. And Mam would blush and say she didn't know what she was on about. When it was quite obvious she did.

Not that I ever really went in and got too wet there. Not because I was anxious that some dirty beggar would be under the water, sat eating scampi and chips and trying to get a glimpse of my noo-noo. I just couldn't take to that swimming malarkey. I often bandied about in the shallow end, walking round with my feet on the bottom of the pool, and pushing my arms in a breast stroke motion to give the effect that I was a top-drawer swimmer. But really, I'd never actually learned to do it. If I went and put me head under the water I'd look even worse. I looked shocking after I'd had a bath. Why on earth would I choose to do that in public?

No chance. Swimming was naff. Stuff that.

The Gaiety Theatre reeked of glamour. It was so big. 'Bigger than anything you'll find in that London!' Dad would boast. And he knew. He was a lorry driver so he'd seen some sights. And nothing, he claimed, compared to this place. My favourite bit was either side of the stage where they had these huge boards on the wall. Above them it said BABY CRYING IN CHALET and then under it was a criss-cross board of all different numbers and if your number and colour flashed it meant there was a baby crying in your chalet so you had to get up and go back. I loved it when that happened. Except the time it happened and they said it was our chalet and our Josie shouted, 'Cheeky bastards! Like I've had a frigging baby! Right. That's it. Get your coat Shirl, we're going.'

As me, Mam and Dad took our seats, Mam forever touching her wig, which made it obvious she had one on as people with real hair didn't make such a song and dance about it, the resident band struck up with my favourite tune of the day – 'Under the Moon of Love' by Showaddywaddy. I couldn't help clicking my fingers along to it and humming as well, which made Mam do this massive sigh before going, 'Honestly Shirley, it's Josie's night, not yours. Have a little decorum.' And then she turned to my dad and went, 'I think to our youngest decorum's a foreign word.'

'It is a foreign word.' I couldn't help myself.

'You what?'

'Decorum. I think it's like . . . Latin.'

'Oh, stop showing off, Shirley. Not everything's about you, you know.'

'I know!'

'Well then!'

'I'm going for a wee.'

'Oh, make your mind up, Shirley. We've only just sat down.'

And then I saw her lean in to the woman sat next to her and said in a showy-offy low drawl, 'Our eldest's in the contest. Very highly thought of in beauty queen circles.' And I squeezed past and ran out to the loos.

I liked to think that everyone could look at me and tell I must be related to one of the contestants. I'd tried to flick my hair like our Josie, but my hair was more flyaway than hers. Flyaway Peter I called it, so it just ended up looking a bit over-singed, like I'd sat too close to the three-bar fire getting ready. And the catsuit I had on was a bit saggy round the gusset as it was one of our Josie's cast-offs and she was so much taller than me. But still. I looked better than I usually did at school, and nobody seemed to be sniggering too much.

When I pushed into the ladies' loos, that's when I saw her. Pretty as a picture. Stood there in a party dress, hair in ringlets and a big silvery bow on top of her head. Can only have been about three. Like one of the Victoriana dolls I'd see on the market all the time and badger Mam to get me when I was a nipper. There'd been one called Tringalonga Trixie. Heavyset doll with ringlets and a bow who had a big red telephone clasped to her ear. She was the one I coveted most. But Mam always said the addition of the phone made her common. 'And clearly into tittle tattle, which must be avoided at all costs.'

'Mother, it's a DOLL.'

'I know. And you're not having her.'

I couldn't help myself. I smiled at the little lass and said, 'Look at you! Tringalonga Trixie!'

At which she right there and then burst out crying. Would you credit it? I meant it as a compliment. Of course, I tried telling her that, which was when I realized she wasn't crying about that. She'd obviously been on the verge as I came in and now that someone had talked to her it had all erupted, so to speak. Hot tears bubbled up like the geysers in my geography textbooks, and between breathy sobs she told me she can't find her mam or dad. Except she called them Mummy and Daddy, of course, what with her speaking the Queen's English, proper and that. Her voice was exotic, like summat off the telly. In ordinary circumstances I could've stood there and listened to it all day but . . . well, a few things really:

One. I needed a wee. So I told her to wait there while I had one. I even left the door slightly ajar for some reason, probably to show her I hadn't legged it.

Two. I wanted to see my sister in the Holiday Princess competition. Well, who in their right mind wouldn't? Eh?

And three. Well, there wasn't a three. But things sound better when they come in threes, don't they? They used to say that about me, our Josie and our Kymberly. Till Kymberly drowned in the sea and air-sea rescue never got to her in time. Neighbours still didn't know what to say and it was over ten years ago now. Some days I wished Kymberly was alive. It'd be good to have another sister who wasn't such a bobby-dazzler and could be more like me. But then other days I was glad she'd gone. Well, not glad, but I didn't mind so much, coz I think if she'd still been around, me and our Josie wouldn't be so close, if you follow my drift. And that's one thing in life that I did like, being great pals with her.

Anyroad up I come out the loo and take the little girl's hand.

'Let's go and find your mam and dad, lass,' I said.

'My name's not lass, it's Abigail.'

'Well, come on then, Abigail.'

But by the time we came out of the loos into the foyer it was nearly showtime, so the place was swarming with people. And none of them looked like they'd lost a little girl. I took her up to a Redcoat and told him we couldn't find her mummy. But he just wanted to know what chalet she was staying in and Abigail was too little to remember – three, she told me – and then the redcoat got waylaid by a woman telling him his bum looked great in those tight white slacks so I dragged Abigail off through the crowd, knowing full well that even though her parents must by now be beside themselves with worry about their missing little girl, my folks would be becoming really annoyed that I'd gone AWOL for so long. And I was only doing a good deed! If only there was some way of killing two birds with one stone.

We went outside and it was getting quiet out there now; everyone was taking their seats. Was it possible that her mam and dad weren't that bothered she'd gone walkabout?

'Were you coming to see the Holiday Princess competition, poppet?' I asked her.

'My name's not poppet, it's Abigail,' was all she said.

They must've been bringing her here. Why else would she be in the girls' lavs all dressed up like a dog's dinner?

Inside I heard a drum roll and an announcement being made.

Ladies and gentlemen. Please take your seats and put your hands together for the Redcoat dancers!

And right there, right then, I had the most brilliant idea imaginable. A way in which we'd find Abigail's family, but also let my mum and dad know what an amazing person I was.

I tugged her back inside. The foyer was quiet now and I ran at high speed, dragging the poor thing behind me like a light suitcase and as if I were running for a train that was just pulling out of the station. I pushed open the theatre doors and the heat from the auditorium hit me like a Bunsen burner. I looked to the stage. YES! There was a small ramp leading from the front of the stalls up onto the stage. I walked Abigail down the side aisle and stood at the bottom of the ramp.

'Luck Be a Lady' was being played by the band and the Redcoats were doing a funny dance to it, zipping across the stage even faster than I'd zipped through the foyer with this little one. At the end of the piece the lights went low and the dancers stood in an upturned V shape, arms pointing out to the back of the stage, and there was another announcement . . .

Ladies and gentlemen. Please welcome your host for the evening. The one and only . . . Mr . . . Jed Jeffers!

Circles of light spun round the stage as the spotlights went to find the star, and that's when I did it. That's when I held Abigail's hand real tight and started to walk up the ramp.

Jed Jeffers was talking into his microphone and the audience were laughing. He was saying something about having been in the changing room and seeing more knockers than in a front-door shop. But then he faltered as he saw me taking to the stage, holding hands with Abigail.

'Oh, look. My favourite pastime. Babes in the wood. Only joking, mums and dads, only joking. You all right, love?'

And I just said it: 'I can't find this girl's mam or dad.'

You'd've thought I'd set a bomb off, the way Mam went on about it later.

'You held up the beginning of that pageant by a good twelve minutes, I counted. And all coz some daft brush had taken her eyes off her kids, daft apeth.'

'The little girl was upset.'

'I'm upset, Shirley. That lost twelve minutes put our Josie off her stroke.'

Turned out that because the show had 'gone up' late, thanks to the general pandemonium caused by me 'storming the stage' – Mam's words, not mine – half the girls in the changing rooms had helped themselves to a free bar and were half cut by the time they came on to do their turns. By the time they did the talent round, well, let's just say our Josie Harlem Shuffled so far to the left that she fell off the stage into the orchestra pit.

Mam was not best pleased.

Our Josie was dead to the world, fast asleep fully clothed in our chalet.

And I was in the doghouse.

'It's not my fault they all helped themselves to the free booze,' I'd complained.

But Mam had an answer for everything. 'Well, not all of them did, did they? Busty Bernice from Poulton-le-Fylde never. And she waltzed away with the flamin' crown. Of course you're responsible. Go to your chalet and we'll speak in the morning.'

So I lay in mine and our Josie's chalet, listening to the croak of her snoring and the rumble of the funfair in the distance, the occasional squeal of laughter from people passing, and I tried to remind myself that I'd done a good thing. I'd found a lost little girl and now, thanks to me, she was probably sleeping safely in her chalet, and was definitely back in her parents' company. Well, she could hardly stay in those toilets forever, could she?

Her family weren't even in the theatre. They'd lost her in the bar. The woman from the chalet next to theirs recognized Abigail and went to fetch them. The mother came running in five minutes later, tears streaming down her face, and grabbed Abigail so tight you'd have thought she was going to choke her.

It was no good. I wasn't going to sleep. I decided to take myself off for a late-night walk. Mam and Dad would never know, would they? They'd be spark out by now.

The holiday camp looked so different at night. A world of fences, shadows and bright lights. Ghoulish waves of noises from corrugated-iron boxes that passed themselves off as centres of fun and games. I decided to take a walk down to the outdoor swimming pools as I reckoned nobody'd be round there this time of night. I wasn't sure what time it was but it felt late.

There was a little hill that blocked the chalets from the pools. As I got to the top of it I saw so much of the funfair reflected in the rippling waters of the pools. I wasn't sure what was making the ripple; it wasn't that windy. Maybe it was the reverberations from the late-night funfair rides. At each end of the pool area were the tiered fountains that looked like wedding cakes. Even though it was probably nearly midnight, they were still bubbling with water.

I heard a sniff to my right. I looked. Some fella was sat on the hill. He had his head in his hands and it looked like he was crying.

I wasn't used to seeing fellas cry. My dad certainly never did, and none of the lads at school, except maybe the jessies. But not a proper full-on bloke like this one. He looked old, but in the moonlight I could see a wash of freckles on his muscly arms. And he had sandy hair. I wanted to reach out, stroke it, like he was a dog or something.

I couldn't help myself. I wanted to make him feel better.

'Are you all right, mister?' I said.

He looked up. And he seemed dead embarrassed to have been caught crying.

'Oh, take no notice of me. Domestic.'

'No woman should make you feel that rubbish, though,' I said. And I don't even know why I said it. It made me sound worldly wise, and I can tell you for nothing, I most certainly wasn't.

He rolled his eyes. 'You haven't met my missus.'

He had a nice voice. The accent was familiar. Not quite posh but definitely from Down South somewhere.

'Is she a right cow?' I said. And that made him snigger.

'You're a tonic, aren't you?' he said, impressed.

'Better than being a gin,' I said, sounding like a minx. It's the sort of thing our Josie would have said. The sort of thing pretty girls said, the sort of girls who knew they could get away with being saucy or cheeky. It was like the cloak of darkness; the cape of night time had allowed me to pretend to be someone else, as if nobody could properly see the real me.

It made him chuckle again. The way folk would chuckle at the pretty girls.

It made me feel all warm and gooey inside. Like a marshmallow on the fire.

'My little girl went missing. It was only for about ten minutes. We got her back. But there's been hell to pay. And of course, it's all my fault.'

I felt a rush of excitement. This man was going to think I was really ace.

'Is her name Abigail?'

He looked right shocked, he did. 'How did you know?'

I sat down next to him. 'I'm the one what found her.'

And his eyes lit up.

'You really are a tonic. What's your name?'

'Shirley.'

'That's a pretty name. I'm Doug.'

'Hello, Doug.'

'Hello, Shirley. Shirley? Can I buy you a drink? Say thank you?'

'I'd love one,' I said. And he took me up the Continental Bar.

I didn't even need to think it wasn't like he was ashamed to be seen with me; it was just a fact. He wasn't. And for the first time in my life I felt powerful. Like I called all the shots. This man owed me a debt of gratitude and it's like he was the first person on this planet, except maybe our Josie, to see that I was okay, that I was a decent person, that I was capable of doing good things.

I ordered a Bacardi and Coke coz that's what I knew sophisticated girls ordered and even though each sip made me wince, soon I was relaxing and we were chatting away like old buddies. Which was weird as I was only sixteen and he had to be dead old, like, thirty or something. I still had my make-up on from going to the contest, and my catsuit, so I knew I looked older, but he didn't even ask if I was old enough to drink. He thought I was the bee's knees, I could tell. But that was okay. Coz I thought he was too.

The bar was busy but he didn't seem to care who might clock us. At one end of the huge room there was a stage and a white woman was singing 'Brown Girl in the Ring'.

'We've got a brown girl lives next door to us,' Doug said.

'Have you?'

'We have.'

'That's novel,' I said, ever the sophisticate.

'Really nice tits on her,' he said.

'You mucky pup,' I said.

'What?!' He sounded all offended. 'I'm a red-blooded male, we notice these sorts of things.'

'And what have you noticed about me?'

'You?'

'Yeah, me.'

He shook his head.

'Well, I couldn't possibly say, could I? Because you strike me as a lady.'

'Someone once told me I had very nice ears,' I offered. Which was true. And I saw him having a good look at them.

'And they were right,' he agreed. 'They can be very sensuous things, ears.'

'Can they now?!' I chuckled.

The singer started to sing 'By the Rivers of Babylon'.

'Must be a Boney M. medley,' I said.

'You know your music, then.' He winked.

'Aye. I love me top-twenty countdown.'

'I bet you do.' And he gave me this dirty wink that I didn't quite know what to make of.

After the one drink though he looked at his watch and then winked again. Less dirty now.

'Won't your boyfriend be wondering where you've got to?'

'I haven't got one.'

'Thought they'd've been queuing round the block for you, Princess.'

'I've not looked.' Nonchalant, that's what I was being. That's what they told you to be in *Jackie*.

He nodded. 'Well. My missus'll be sending out the dogs.'

'Best you walk me home, then.'

'Well I'm a gentleman, so I'll have to.'

When we got to my row of chalets we started to walk dead slow. Conversation became intermittent. And then we got to my door.

'Gonna invite me in for coffee?' he said, quietly, jokily.

'Our Josie'll be in bed. And we haven't got any coffee,' I said.

'I'll just have to settle for a kiss, then,' he said.

I shrugged as if to say 'if you like'. And he leaned in and cupped one cool hand behind my neck and then drew me in for this kiss. He slipped his warm tongue into my mouth and as he did he made this kind of whimpering sound, bit like the dog used to do when he had all the cysts and you patted him on the back. It was a weird feeling, someone else's tongue inside your mouth, but I quite liked it actually. He pushed me up against the chalet door and I could feel something warm and hard press between my legs. Well. I knew immediately what that monstrosity was, and there'd be no funny business. Not tonight, thank you. Not all over our Josie's catsuit, thank you. Oh yes, and not with a married man.

He moved his hand round and started caressing my left ear lobe. It really tickled, but in a nice way. And I felt a funny feeling between my legs.

Oh no, this would not do.

This catsuit was dry-clean only.

Eventually I pushed him away with a quiet, 'That's your lot, Doug.'

'Spoilsport,' he said, but all teasing, like.

'I need my beauty sleep.' I didn't. But that's what the girls said on the telly.

'Can I see you again?' he whispered. 'You've got to let me see you again. I have to say a proper thank you for finding our Abigail.'

'I'll see you tomorrow.'

'Where?'

'Same time same place.'

'Shall I bring some johnnies?'

'If you want.'

'Not that I'm assuming anything.'

'No, neither am I.'

'And you won't tell my missus?'

'I think she's a bit of a cow.'

'She is.'

'Okay then. See you tomorrow.'

'By the pool. Half eleven.'

'Okay then.'

'Bye, Princess.'

'Bye then, Doug.'

I let myself into the chalet. It was dark and I went and sat on my bed. I was shaking. I was scared. I was excited. I was all sorts of things rolled into one.

Oh Christ, Shirley. What have you gone and done?

RACHEL

2017

Chapter Six

'Jane Veronica Taylor was a kind woman. A solitary woman, but a kind one, who led a very quiet existence in this wonderful forest that we all in some way or other call home.'

Jamie's here. He doesn't call it home. He used to call it The Land That Time Forgot. Mostly on account of the fact that everywhere, bar the pubs, winds down and closes at about 4 p.m.

I can't blame him. He's absolutely right.

'Jane . . . was a happy woman.'

As happy as you can be when you're clinically depressed.

Ah yes, you see I've diagnosed her, incidentally. Here I am, all these years a high-end travel agent, when clearly all along I should have been a mental health practitioner. Oh well. You win some, you lose some.

I have an overwhelming desire to eat an apple. I could quite easily do this; I have one in my coat pocket. The problem at the moment is that I have a craving for them most of the day long. It would be so easy to pull it out of my pocket and bite into its crisp green goodness, but I can't. I can't sit and eat an apple during my mother's funeral. It would give the impression that I wasn't interested.

But all I can keep thinking about is that bloody apple. It's a

Granny Smith. God, how I wish I could look at its rich green loveliness. I love the crunch, the texture, the sharp taste, the way the core seems to spit at me when I put it into my mouth. It fills so many cravings all in one.

I used to think women saying they had craved coal in pregnancy was just an old wives' tale. But I seriously think if I lived in a world where I had coal delivered, I would have sampled at least a mouthful of it by now.

Oh well. At least apples are healthy. It could be a lot worse.

I try to imagine the smell of coal. It comforts me.

I put my hand in my pocket and rub my apple slowly. That too comforts me.

I need to focus on something else.

I distract myself with the view.

Father Tom O'Neill is looking more handsome than ever in his cassock and dog collar and freshly gelled hair as he stands at the front of the quaint chocolate-box parish church, a few villages away from Beaulieu. Tom – and I have to say that as he is prone to exclaiming, 'Don't call me Father, call me Tom!' – felt this more intimate venue was better suited to my mother's service than any of the other churches in his team ministry, probably because he could tell there wouldn't be many people coming. I'd joked that catering-wise all I'd need would be a flask of coffee and three Penguin biscuits, which had really made him laugh. As he threw his head back and guffawed I'd spotted a gold tooth.

What sort of vicar was this?

Hardly the sackcloth and ashes type.

Anyway, I'm glad the service is here. I feel like I'm in an episode of *The Vicar of Dibley*, and the fact that there are only a dozen people in attendance doesn't feel so desperate in these cosier surroundings.

My mind wanders and my eyes drift, from Father Tom to the altar where three candles burn proudly. But all I can think is, has Tom recently been to the loo and these are his holy version of air freshener?

'. . . Close to her daughter Rachel. Of whom of course she was immensely proud.'

And what, I wonder, of her other daughter?

For I have cracked the code.

The secret that Mother was taking to her grave. The reason she seemed to spend my childhood floating around in a cloud of denial. Denial of her feelings, of happiness, everything. She was depressed. She was depressed because she had lost a child. My older sister, Diana. I had it all worked out. I didn't even have to check the details with Pam, I was so sure. It was like everything had slipped into place.

And today at her funeral I don't just mourn my mother, I mourn Diana too, poor little mite.

Diana. My sister. The one I never met.

'And she loved *Hetty Wainthropp Investigates*, of course. And owned every single episode on DVD. In fact we will pause now to listen to the theme music from that particular show, Jane's favourite, and take stock. And meditate on . . . our memories of Jane.'

Heaven help us. I really hope I don't get a fit of the giggles. Every time I've thought about this moment in the past week I've done a roll of eyes heavenwards and bitten my bottom lip, as if trying to stop myself from crying. I suppose you could look at it as Mum's little gift to me that when she was gone I wouldn't always be wallowing and bleary-eyed.

Tom nods to the back of the church and the music starts to play. Quivering strings and then a genteel trumpet trip along the ceiling of the church and bounce off the kind of stone walls that folk in Shoreditch would pay a small fortune to emulate. It conjures up a feeling of warm familiarity and I want to cloak myself in its dulcet tones. It also conjures up an image of Mum, in front of the telly as ever, eyes misty in the semi-light, watching her favourite northern detective crack those domestic crimes in Clitheroe. Did she always look so sad because she was thinking about Diana?

Of course she did.

She must have given birth to Diana and then she had a cot death or something and so she had me as some sort of Band-Aid baby to help herself get over the pain, only I never ever did. I never made her happy. She always missed Diana.

As the trumpet continues to trill in its increasingly annoying happy-go-lucky, heart-warming Sunday night TV way that smacks of yesteryear, I find myself crying. Not just for the mother I have lost, but for all the life she lost along the way because her daughter was gone. For all the things she might have been, for all the things she might have done, for all the things we might have been and done together, for God's sake. Diana's death. The ripples were still reverberating today.

I've had to make my peace with Pam. Not just so I could get her to do the sandwiches afterwards, but I felt it's what mum would've wanted and I don't really feel any anger towards what she might or might not have done.

And I wanted her to make the sandwiches afterwards.

'And of course Jane was so excited about her forthcoming grandchild, who she will now sadly never meet.'

How does he know? How does he know if she was excited or not? I never said she was.

And I wonder now, was Diana ever born? Was she a baby that Mum lost? Was it hard for her to see me pregnant, reminding her of some awful memories? A curtailed trip to a hospital. A tiny coffin. I just don't know.

I decide that over the sandwiches later I will ask Pam what she knows. And she does know. I can tell.

I feel an arm creep round me and give my shoulder a tender squeeze. Cliona is sitting with me. She looks to die for (handily for a funeral) in a killer combo of grey pencil skirt and ruched black blouse. Heels, of course, like stilts. Little pillbox hat. She makes me feel dowdy in my sensible camel coat and plain black frock. Margaret decided she didn't want to come. She doesn't really do funerals, she said, as she feels her own is nigh on imminent. She may pop along later, she'll see. But Jamie has ventured down from London, bless him, and is crying even louder than me.

'Drama queen,' Cliona whispers in my ear, which makes me smile.

I've opted for a burial. It's funny, I would never have dreamed of this a few days ago, but since finding that baby jacket, I've felt it's the right thing to do. I want solemnity today, protocol, tradition. This is no longer just for my mum; it's for that lost little baby too. Hence the church. Hence no crematorium. It's all that bit more expensive, but I can afford it at the moment. So why not?

Finally, to the strains of 'Moon River' by Audrey Hepburn, we follow the coffin out to the graveyard. It's then that I notice the undertaker stood outside the church gates. She has indeed got her hair up in a bun, with a cutesy little top hat perched on top of the bun. Sort of thing that wouldn't look out of place on a Christmas tree. I wonder if she's only just put it on as I don't remember seeing it before the service. She gives me a conspiratorial wink as I pass her and she whispers, 'It's going really well, hon. Think she'd love it.'

Which I just ignore. Because I am a sane, sound human being. I hope.

What will she do next? Set off some party poppers? Or blow a vuvuzela during the 'ashes to ashes' section?

Fortunately she does neither.

Pam breaks down at the graveside and I have to hold her in my arms. She sobs uncontrollably for a while and then it's like she's caught sight of herself in a mirror and she is embarrassed by how she looks, as she suddenly flips upright and says she has to get to the church hall to get the cling film off the sandwiches. I link her arm to walk her there but she attempts to shrug me off. In the end I let her.

Before anyone else can get to the church hall I hurry over and watch Pam as she busies herself in the kitchen.

'I know,' I say.

She looks up, furtive, like she's been caught out doing something naughty at school.

'Know what?' she says, shrugging it off.

'I know what happened.'

'When?'

'The secret she's taken to the grave.'

She rolls her eyes, disinterested, and pulls a foil tray of vol-au-vents from the fridge. There's far too much food here for our measly number.

'I have absolutely no idea what you're talking about.'

'About baby Diana.'

And the blood drains from her face. She freezes. It's like she's a statue. But then she takes a huge sniff of air through her nose and looks me square in the face.

'Who's baby Diana?'

And I know she's lying. I know she knows full well who baby Diana is.

Well, was.

'Mum had a baby who died. Didn't she?'

She offers no response.

'I wasn't her first child. She'd had another, before I was born. I've worked it all out.'

And now I can see she is relaxing.

'And how on earth would you work all that out?'

So I tell her. I tell her about the baby jacket. And the name knitted into it. And how I've put two and two together and I sound pathetically showy-offy as I say it.

Her eyes well with tears. And finally she smiles.

'Well done, Rachel. I always said you were a clever girl.'

I smile, but she's not looking at me.

'Much cleverer than working in a fuddy duddy old travel agent's.'

'Pam, it's very high end.'

But that's not really the point right now.

'Pam . . . what can you tell me about Diana?'

'I didn't know Diana,' she says gently. 'It was before I met your mum. And she rarely talked about it. I don't even know how she passed on. In those days . . . you didn't really discuss things like that.'

I nod. This makes sense.

'Now. How about getting some hundreds and thousands for the trifle?'

I feel someone poking me in my ribs. I turn to see the undertaker. She's winking again.

'So. What did we reckon to that send-off? Here. Pretend it's *Strictly*. Marks out of ten?'

She sees me hesitate. So shouts an answer herself. 'TEN!'

And then the room falls silent.

Why did I have to hire a madwoman to be my mother's undertaker?

She looks to Pam.

'Pam, I was pretending to be Darcey Bussell or Bruno Tonioli.'

Pam nods, disinterested.

'Good score, though,' the undertaker reiterates, and then hurries out.

Jamie fusses round me, as per, as the small huddle of us tuck into Pam's bland spread. He wants to fetch me a chair. He wants everyone to agree that my ankles look a bit puffy. Nice. He wants to make sure there's no soft cheese in any of the sandwiches.

Pam's face is a picture there. As if she's ever touched a tub of soft cheese in her life.

General post-funeral chit-chat ensues for about ten minutes. Then dries up. So I tell Cliona and Jamie what I've learned about baby Diana, and they're suitably intrigued. Actually, Jamie gets a tad over-emotional, and it seems to send him into a tailspin of tears and 'what if?'s and I have to placate him with everything even remotely positive that a doctor has said recently about the health of my unborn baby. Okay, so it's his too. But I have to say mine every now and again when he's around or else it feels I'm being ram-raided into having it and he's taken over and I've no say in anything. Fortunately, before he's whittled an ultrasound machine out of the bamboo sticks lying oddly to one side of the hall so he can 'just be on the safe side', his cab is here to take him back to Brockenhurst Station because, as he explains proudly, he's got a second date off Grindr and he needs to stop off en route and get poppers.

Everyone looks suitably horrified.

And then he does, realizing it really is a case of TMI.

'I'm so sorry, Rachel. It must be the grief.'

I just push him towards the exit.

When I look back the vicar is blushing like a beetroot.

'Take you back, eh Tom?' says Margaret. And that's when I realize Margaret has slipped in unannounced.

The vicar's eyes nearly pop out of his head.

And I hear the undertaker emit an enormously filthy cackle, then shout, 'TEN!'

There is so much to sort out in Mum's house. I have scheduled a week to do everything and four days in I don't think it's enough. Well, I know it's not enough. Because thus far I was meant to have got the house on the market, filled a skip full of rubbish, put a load of things on eBay, given a load of stuff to charity shops . . . oh, the list is endless. But the skip only arrived this morning as so few companies round here were prepared to drive up the dirt track. And no, that's not a euphemism, I only wish it was! You'd think I'd asked them to crawl over razor blades, but finally I found a company in Holbury who were reasonable, both in price and in attitude. So I only started filling it up this morning. I have to get it all done soon as it's Thursday today and I've promised Ben I'll be back at work next week.

Margaret comes over to help each day and Cliona comes in the evenings after the cafe's shut. But even between the three of us I don't see it being sorted any time soon. There is just too much decayed old life here. Too much stuff.

'Too much SHIT,' adds Margaret. 'I mean, Christ, I'm as bad a hoarder as the next person, but at least my stuff's nice.'

Pam drops by intermittently, asking if I've come across Mum's paperwork yet. When asked what she means by paperwork she flusters a bit and says she means things like policies.

I tell her I found her life insurance stuff and her will just after she died, and ask if there are any more policies I should know about. Again she flusters and beats a retreat when she sees that Margaret is drinking wine before teatime.

The will was pretty dull, really. She had one life insurance policy which covered most of the funeral, and the proceeds from the sale of the house will be split between me and Pam and, ah yes, a cat sanctuary in Greece, of all places. I get the lion's share at 50 per cent of the income but I am not holding my breath. This house is so dilapidated, it might be easier to just pay someone to knock it down rather than expecting someone to buy it in the state it's in. But then Margaret is convinced it might be worth half a million – she does say this after the better part of a bottle of wine – which gives me fantasies beyond my reach and ideas above my station.

Cliona is filling one room with stuff that she thinks a mate of hers who runs a bric-a-brac place in Brockenhurst might like, and she's scheduled her to come tomorrow. Personally I think it looks like a load of old seventies tat, but Cliona's assured me she'll take most of it off my hands. 'She deals in kitsch,' she explains.

Is that what Mum's life is reduced to? Kitsch.

What was your mum's life like?

Oh, it was really kitsch. She filled a bric-a-brac shop. Now that's what I call an achievement!

I am ruthless in my own bedroom. If I've thrown one H from Steps poster away I've thrown twenty. Anything I've ever really wanted to hang onto over the years I have taken to my basement pad in London. How different from this place it is. All state of the art. And yes, I did pay a small fortune to have the lights and electrics in the flat remote controlled via an app on my iPad. Compared to Mum's cottage, that place only exists in the future.

I sit on my sad single bed and pull out the baby jacket I've hidden under the eiderdown. I lift it to my face and try to imagine little baby Diana. I try to conjure up and feel her in my arms to tell her that someone is thinking of her, that she did make a mark on the world, that her existence was significant. But just then I hear Margaret calling through from another room.

'Rachel?'

'Aha?'

'I think I might've found some paperwork stuff?'

'Okay, just leave it on the side.'

'No, come and have a look. I don't know what to make of it.'

I squeeze the jacket back under the eiderdown and follow Margaret's voice to Mum's bedroom.

'Actually, Margaret, I'm just going to get some air.'

Margaret is shoving some papers back into a faded pink cardboard folder. She plonks it on the bed and looks at me.

Margaret has a very odd look on her face. But she just says, 'Okay.'

The sun's fading as I step out into the back garden, and a route I've taken a thousand times before. I head to the bottom of the garden and the narrow gate in the picket fence that leads out into the woods. I know these woods like the back of my hand, and I know where I am going. I trudge deeper through the trees, not caring that my footwear isn't suitable for the increasingly muddy ground I tread on. These woods were my playground as a child, these trees my friends. I've neglected them in my adult years and they've changed somewhat, as friends do. But they're basically the same and they lead me on to the tiny stream that trickles into the river further down the slope. I want to feel water at my feet. It will make me closer to my mother. That was what she wanted as she was dying. She wanted to feel the sea on her toes.

And I took her. I took her to the seaside and although she was happy then to sit back and watch, the desire had been there and now that desire is mine. She would understand. It is something that bonds us.

When I reach the stream I bend down and splash my hand through it like a kid soaking their chums in the swimming pool. I then stand back up again and hurry down to the river. I kick off my court shoes and clamber down into the petulant waters. I'm six again. I'm eight again. I'm any age I want to be again. But I am definitely me, touching the earth that raised me, the riverbed that nourished me.

God, I sound pretentious.

And of course I have to be careful. Although I have no proof, rumour has it that there are quicksands that will drag you in, just as the river turns the corner. And if the sands don't get you, the current will, as it crashes from river to ocean. Mum and Pam always warned me not to go far into the water for fear of getting sucked under. I never knew if this was a reality, or if it was just them putting me off venturing too far from home.

I can hear Pam calling me when I was a little girl. The voice so vivid in my head.

'Don't go too far, Rachel, it's not safe! You'll get sucked under! River to ocean, Rachel! River to ocean!'

Why was it so often Pam's voice I would hear and not Mum's? At times, it was like they co-parented me. Well, I suppose that's what friends do, help each other out. Single mum, best friend. Of course they do.

In the distance I hear a scream. When I first heard that scream as a child I was petrified. It's the sound of a baby crying. Well, not just crying, but crying for its life. And then my mother explained it wasn't a baby. It was a fox calling out to its mates. The scream reassures me.

I hear crunching twigs, footsteps, and they startle me. I go to cry out when I see Margaret appearing at the riverside. She is clutching the fading folder.

'There's something you should see,' she says.

She sounds serious. And it must be serious if she's followed me all the way down here.

'Has she got some other policies?' I suggest.

Margaret opens the folder and pulls out some papers.

I clamber out of the water and stand barefoot in the mud as she passes them to me.

The top one is the front page of a newspaper. Which is as faded as the folder it's been in.

The headline says 'SHE'S ALIVE'. Underneath is a smiling woman holding a baby.

I look more closely. The light might be fading but I can still see what it is. Who it is.

That smiling woman is Mum. There, in black and white, that's my mum when she was younger. The bigger hair. Wow, that smile. I've never seen her smile like that. She looks so happy, so full of life, so excitable. I've never seen her look so positive.

Margaret has brought a torch. She flicks the switch on it and the page is illuminated.

It is. It's definitely my mum.

And yet . . . and yet . . . underneath it says, 'Linda Wilson is all smiles as she leaves hospital with baby Diana, who had been snatched from her back garden about a month earlier.'

It says Mum's name is Linda Wilson.

That has to be Mum.

Wait. Wait.

I check the date of the paper.

1981.

Diana can't have been born in '81; I was born in '81.

That doesn't make sense.

I look again at the baby in the picture. Mum's really showing her off to the camera.

Oh my God.

That baby must be me.

Baby Diana.

Linda Wilson?!

'I remember that story, darling,' Margaret says. 'Is that your mum?'

Chapter Seven

I wish I could drink wine. Wine would numb the pain, the confusion. What is going on? What happened all those years ago? And the even bigger question . . . who the hell am I?

I hunger and thirst for wifi. It's a craving. Like apples. Like Granny Smiths. I want wifi! There's no internet in the house and it's too late now to go knocking anywhere other than Cliona's and she's out for the night.

I've tried a fruitless search on my phone as there isn't any signal here. I toy with borrowing Margaret's car but she came here by cab and that means I'd have to get a cab with her, then borrow her car, then drive about three miles to somewhere that DOES have 3G or 4G and sit by a pond with my tiny phone trying to learn about my life.

Was it my life? It must be. I must be baby Diana. The dates tally with my date of birth. But then . . . was that my date of birth? How many secrets has my mother kept from me? Am I older than I think I am? Younger than I think I am? None of it makes sense.

'Tell me all you remember about the case,' I say to Margaret, once we're back in Mum's kitchen, and I sound for all the world to hear as if I'm in an American cop show and I'm opening an old investigation.

Margaret looks stupefied.

'I just have to think. It wasn't that important to me.'

Which is clearly, obviously the case. Why would it be important to her? Though it takes all my strength not to bellow at her . . . WELL, IT IS IMPORTANT TO ME!!

I feel the baby kick. I instinctively touch my tummy. Maybe she is sensing my stress. I don't want her to be stressed. I take a deep breath. I have to remember her in all of this. I have to make sure she is safe.

Did Mum not make sure I was safe? Did she leave me in a pram outside the house? They used to do that in the olden days. Is that what she did? Did she leave me outside and some lunatic passed by and stole me?

It all sounds so implausible. I don't know why.

I take another deep breath.

'Of course it's not important to you. Wasn't . . . important to you. Why would it be? And it was a long time ago. But please. Just try and think.'

'Well, I'll tell you what I remember.'

I'm literally hanging on her every word. Like every word is another rung on a stepladder and by clinging on and hauling myself up onto the next one I am getting myself nearer and nearer to the truth.

'It was on the news. Every single night. She seemed to be missing for ages.'

'The baby?'

'Yes.'

'Baby Diana?'

'That rings a bell. I can't remember. But seeing that picture . . .'

'What?'

'Well, I remember the mother's face. I don't remember names of . . . or when it was or . . .'

'Do you remember how the baby was taken?'

'Well. It says in the paper. Back garden. Was it really back garden?'

'I don't know, Margaret. You know more than me.'

'I've no memory of any of it being linked to the New Forest. I'd have remembered much more if it was.'

'Well . . . I don't know. Maybe it was in Southampton?'

'I don't think so. I could be wrong but . . . it had nothing to do with this area. You remember things better when it happens in the area you live in or . . . if the area you live in had a big story going on in it once upon a time. I just remember it being on the news a lot. Never thought it would end really.'

'So I was . . . perhaps . . . taken from a hospital. And then . . .'

'Yes, I just remember it being on the news a lot. Never thought it would end really.'

'How long? How long was it on the news?'

'Well, I've absolutely no idea but it felt like months. But you know how time stretches. Maybe it was weeks. You think this baby was you?'

'I don't know for sure but . . . I think so.'

'I don't know how they found the baby, but I know they did because I remember everyone thinking, "Well there's a surprise; I thought they'd never find her".'

'Right.'

'And then of course that photograph. That's so familiar.' And she looks at the picture of Linda Wilson holding baby Diana. Overjoyed. 'It must have been on all the front pages.'

'Well, I've . . . always said I was . . . kind of a . . . front-cover gal,' I joke.

'That's honestly all I remember, darling. I'm so sorry. I don't remember where it was or when it was or how it happened. I'm useless.'

It would be unfair to agree. No matter how much I want to.

'Everyone used to leave their babies outside in prams in those days. This was such a wake-up call.'

And I then see she has a new thought.

'Didn't you say your neighbour here knew about the dead baby?'

'Pam?!'

'When you thought Diana was your dead sister.'

'Oh my God, Margaret! You genius!'

I hug her. And she has absolutely no idea why.

She probably also has no idea why I suddenly run to the front door and flee the house.

I stop as I do. My baby has hiccupped. It's the most bizarre feeling. Most of the time I feel like she's my constant companion. She is my constant companion. She stops me feeling lonely. But at times like this it's such an alien feeling that another human is definitely inside me. And the hiccup makes me think she is an alien. But I can't think like that for too long. She is my friend. I try to hurry on.

I stand in the lane and look up at Pam's house. The light's off in her bedroom but I see an encouraging flicker through her thin living room curtains. Ah. She is watching television. Or snoozing in front of the television. Either way, a flicker was never more inviting.

Fast forward two minutes and I'm sitting in Pam's kitchen and she's making me something milky on the stove.

'She didn't die, did she?' I say. 'Baby Diana.'

I sense the milky drink-making is a displacement activity. God forbid she'd usually want to do anything for me.

'Pam? I'm baby Diana, aren't I?'

The pan in her hand rattles on the stove and I realize she is shaking. She replaces the pan on the hob, switches off the gas, then comes and sits at the table, whereupon she does something I've never seen her do in my life before. EVER. She huddles over the table, her head in her hands, and starts sobbing her heart out. It's a completely OTT display. The sort of thing that if you saw on the telly or in a film you wouldn't believe. You'd say to the director, 'Have a word, love.' But this is real, and for once I really don't know what to do.

'What's the matter, Pam?'

She doesn't answer. Just continues to convulse and sob.

'Pam?'

I reach across the table and touch her hand and she grabs it desperately, but still doesn't look up.

I feel like I'm in some surreal comedy. A pregnant Amy Schumer pulling a succession of hilarious faces as her non-speaking neighbour continues to have a breakdown and she feels increasingly out of her depth.

'Come on, Pam,' I say in an odd, high-pitched, overtly kindly voice. I sound like Minnie Mouse taking holy orders. 'You can tell me.'

She looks up. She takes a death rattly breath in, and pulls her hand away from me, still gasping for air.

'Pam?'

'What do you know? Tell me everything you know. And I'll tell you what I know.'

And so I tell her. I tell her about the newspaper clipping. And the two names. Linda Wilson. And baby Diana. And how I thought baby Diana had died and how she'd corroborated it, but I now think baby Diana was me. But I don't know. And I won't be able to look anything up on a decent computer for a wee while. As I speak she gathers herself in and becomes more like her normal self.

'Let me make you some nice hot chocolate and I'll tell you everything I know.'

She gets up and busies herself at the hob again. This is more like the Pam I know. Practical. Stoical. Bit rude.

As she talks I notice her dressing gown is stained, despite having the motif 'PRACTICALLY PERFECT IN EVERY WAY' embossed on the back in studs. I remember my mother telling me about her buying it on the market and not realizing it had lettering on the back and how they'd laughed.

'The thing you need to remember is. Your mum's and my generation. We weren't all chitty chatty cosy tell-all-over-a-bottle-of-wine sort of women. Some of us burnt our bras and discovered the orgasm. But some of us just shut up and got on with it.'

I have no idea what she's talking about.

'And so therefore you have to remember that your mother and I never really spoke about what happened in any detailed way. Even if I was her best friend.'

I nod, wishing she'd get on with it.

'I wasn't exactly the *Sex and the City* generation.'

'Actually, Kim Cattrall's sixty now, so she's only a few years younger than you.'

She bristles. I've mentioned her age. She hates me mentioning her age.

'But she's American,' she points out, albeit incorrectly.

'From Liverpool.'

'Britain always takes a while to catch on.'

LOOK, JUST GET ON WITH IT, WOMAN!

She's actually made the hot chocolate and still hasn't told me a single thing. I decide a few prompt-style questions might get her talking.

122

'So. Am I Diana?'

She turns and looks at me. Almost reluctantly, it seems, she nods her head. 'Yes, yes you are.'

'But why wouldn't my mum tell me that?'

'She was trying to protect you.'

'From what?'

'I don't really know. But I suppose if you've had your baby stolen from you, you just want to hide away and not let anyone near you. I don't know.'

'Was she living here when I was taken?'

'No. God, no. This is where she ran away to after it all happened.'

She hands me a mug of cocoa.

'I recognized her immediately. Well, she'd been headline news for a fortnight. But she said her name was Jane. And you were baby Rachel. And I guess I just thought . . . fair enough. She seemed so shell-shocked. And . . . well, that's about it really.'

'So you never said, "Aren't you Linda Wilson?"'

'No. Never. I think because I just sort of got why she was here. Why she'd want to hide away. It wasn't nice what she went through.'

'And what had actually happened to me?'

'She'd just given birth to you. And this . . . mad woman came along and took you. Right from under her nose. And then . . . the rest is history.'

'Yes. My history, and this is the first time I've ever heard it. Where was this?'

'I forget now, it was so long ago. The Midlands somewhere?'

'The Midlands? Mum was from . . . the Midlands? I thought she was New Forest born and bred?'

'I'm sorry, Rachel. I tried to get her to talk to you about it before she . . . before she went.'

I remember the conversation I overheard.

'But you know how stubborn she was.'

I do indeed.

'Where did they find me? What did the mad woman do?'

I suddenly feel sick. What did that mad woman do to me? Did she hurt me? Did she interfere with me?

'You were found perfectly safe. She'd cared for you like you were her own.'

'Who was she? Where was she?'

'I can't remember. I'm sure if you . . . get hold of some old newspapers you can find out.'

'And what happened to her?'

'She was sent to the loony bin. That much I do remember. She was only a young thing, I think.'

'My God, this is incredible. And you never even discussed it with Mum?'

'As I said, Rachel. You and I both know how stubborn she was. Drink your cocoa.'

I take a sip and it burns my mouth.

'You know when you said I was found perfectly safe?'

'Aha?'

'Are you just saying that? Like . . . to make me feel better?'

'No!'

'Coz I can take it, you know. I'd rather know all the bad things from someone like you than . . . learn the truth, further down the line from . . . I don't know. Google.'

'You were safe,' she says. And I believe her. After all, when did Pam ever feel the need to sugar-coat things?

'Thanks, Pam.'

She wrinkles her nose and shakes her head like it's nothing.

'So I am baby Diana.'

'I can only think you are.'

'And Mum's real name was Linda Wilson?'

'I can only think it was.'

'I wonder who she was hiding from. Coming here.'

'Who do you bloody think?! Bonkers Beryl who took you in the first place!'

'But . . . she was locked away.'

'I know but . . . oh, I dunno, I've never had kids, but when you were little if anything had happened to you I'd have strung the buggers up.'

'Something did happen to me.'

'I mean after you moved here. She was safe here. You were. You both were. Away from prying eyes. She was well known. Oh, everyone had an opinion on her. The woman who left her baby unattended for five minutes. Half the country felt sorry for her, half saw her as a bona fide pariah. But here . . . everyone left her alone. She could go days without seeing anyone. And then by the time she was ready to go back to work, she'd changed her hair, changed that bloody name. No-one was any the wiser. Clever girl, really.'

'She lied to everyone.'

She lied to me, is what I really mean.

'Survival mechanism,' Pam says.

So I say it. 'She lied to me, Pam.'

And she says it again. 'Survival mechanism.'

I go home to bed with too many questions in my head.

Christ, I sound like Morrissey.

I lie in the dark. And hark . . .

Oh God, I've got to stop trying to make everything rhyme.

I'm clearly going mad.

They say grief sends you mad.

That's it. That's what's happened. The grief of losing my mum has kicked in and I have hallucinated ALL of this. This hasn't happened. Margaret didn't come to the river with a piece of paper. I didn't go to Pam next door and demand answers and – sort of – get them. In a moment I will wake up from my reverie to someone slapping me round the face and saying, 'Rachel? Are you all right? It seems like you were having a bad dream? You kept shouting, "Diana!"'

If I can just go to sleep. If I can just nod off it will all be all right. I will wake afresh and be back to my normal self.

My name is Rachel Taylor.

My name is not Diana Wilson.

Rachel.

Rachel.

When I wake up, of course, nothing has changed. It's not the grief that made it happen. It did actually happen. This is actually happening. It is the oddest of feelings. To find out you're not who you thought you were. To find out your mother wasn't who she said she was and lied repeatedly throughout your childhood. To you and to everybody else. And the effort that must have involved. The worry that someone might tell me, or realize; that I might realize.

I know one thing. I need to know more. I need to know the full story. I need to know who the hell I am. Was there a dad? Was she a single mum when I was taken? Why was I taken? Who was this fruitloop? Whatever happened to her? Where did she take me? Why did she take me? How long was I with her for?

The newspaper article said about a month. If I had a month alone with someone, that's a significant amount of time. Is she still incarcerated? Has she been released? Is she still alive?

So many questions. So many bloody questions.

I haul my body out of bed and try to reason with myself as I walk around the piles of clutter that now make up Mum's house.

Look. It doesn't matter. None of this matters. It was thirty-six years ago.

She was still your mum.

You've only known yourself as Rachel, so sod it. It's not like you've found out you were adopted. Your mum still brought you up. All that you have really found out is that you had a different name when you were born and that . . . well, I try to look on it as if I had a short break with someone else for a while when I was tiny.

But I still want to know more.

And I know where I want to be when I find this information out.

I don't want to be here. Well, I can't be here; there's no signal. But I don't want to be in the flat above Cliona's cafe either. I want to be comfortable and in my own surroundings, surrounded by my things. My proper things. My nice things.

I want to be home in London.

The landline rings. I answer it.

'Hello? Fiddler's Cottage?'

'Darling, it's Margaret. How are you?'

'In shock, I think. I just want to go to London.'

'Is there anything I can do to help?'

'Well . . . not really.'

'Go on. There must be something.'

'I suppose you could come and stay here for a few days and stick everything in the skip and meet the people who want to buy stuff.'

'I'd love to.'

'You are joking? Coz I was. Sort of.'

'I'm a nosy old crow. I love looking through your mum's stuff. And who knows what I'll find next. Maybe she was an alien.'

'I wouldn't put it past her.'

By mid-afternoon I'm walking into my flat in Bloomsbury and my fingers are itching to get onto my computer.

I've been so good. All the way home on the train I resisted the urge to tap the name Diana Wilson into the search engine on my phone. I wanted to do this properly.

I switch the computer on at the wall. Press the button at the back. I hear it spring into action.

Finally.

Here goes.

I type four words into the search engine: *Diana Wilson Baby Snatch.*

SHIRLEY

1980

Chapter Eight

There'd been a right old giddy-up and a hoo-ha and it were all kicking off. Why?

Our Josie were pregnant.

She swore me to secrecy when she told me up Handbags, this new nightspot on the Chadderton Road.

'I can't believe it,' I said, swishing my Malibu with a straw.

'Neither can I,' she sighed, sucking on a ciggie. 'I were convinced we'd only done anal. Promise you won't tell Mam?'

'Cross me heart and hope to die,' I said. And I meant it. If there was one thing I was good at, it was keeping secrets.

So. Josie. She'd been seeing this lad called Jimmy, who had a look of Bob Carolgees, which I thought wasn't something you'd be shouting from the rooftops but Josie seemed to think was okay. She wasn't that mad keen on him, but apparently he'd done the right thing and offered to pay for an abortion. She just didn't want Mam knowing because she was actually thinking of keeping it.

Needless to say, Mam found out quick smart. Before you could say 'bun in the oven' she'd overheard some tittle tattle in the cafe where she worked about some poor lass falling in the family way. She was shaking her head in a disgusted manner, apparently, seething at the slack morals of our disaffected youth, when she heard that this lass was called Josie Burke.

Well, of course Mam saw red, kicked everyone out of the cafe, locked up for the night and went straight round to Barnes Wallis, the new trampoline park that had just opened off the Manchester Road, where our Josie were working. Mostly her job there involved walking up and down between the trampolines, yelling at kids to take their shoes off. Other times she helped out in the Snacketeria, which had a healthy menu to go with the keep-fit theme of the trampolines. The healthy menu was mostly jacket potatoes with various fillings. But as one of the fillings was 'chips', I didn't think *Boomph with Becker* would be dropping in any time soon for a filming.

Becker was some tired old exercise instructor. The only reason I'd heard of her was that my mam had one of her books on a coffee table. She was a racy redhead who always wore a bathing costume and apparently she yelled at anyone fat.

I always dreaded meeting the woman, to be honest.

Now. Before I go any further, I have to say I was there that day at Barnes Wallis. Things were going really well for me. I'd been seeing my lovely Doug ever since we'd met that fateful night at Butlin's when I'd found him crying by the outdoor swimming pools. And we'd been pretty much inseparable ever since. Thank God we lived in the same town. (I always met people from my hometown at Butlin's. Once even the next-door neighbours!) And even though I'd thought he was a Southerner, turned out he were a Northerner just like me!

Oh. Did I say inseparable? That's how it felt to me. There was of course the small matter of his wife and three kids. His wife were called Vera. I'd never actually met her, but Christ on a bike, she sounded like the biggest piece of work to ever walk this planet. Apparently she was the size of, not just a house, but the whole terrace. And she had really bad hair and spent half her housekeeping on perm-fixing products. She was also a bit of a feminist, and the sort who refused to shave her armpits because it's what God gave her. Even though, Doug would often point out to me as he nuzzled my bare pits, she didn't actually believe in God. What a walking contradiction in terms. And what a walking nightmare with perms! So of course, despite what the ladies' mags would have you warned, I really believed him when he told me he had every intention of leaving Vera. Who wouldn't? She sounded like a pigging nightmare.

I saw my lovely Doug every day, weekdays, but not that much at weekends as obviously it was hard for him to get away when The Dragon, as I unaffectionately called Vile Vera – soon to be Jilted Vera – was really needy and wanted him to do Family Stuff with the three girls. It was all an act, as far as I was concerned. She couldn't have been that good a mam if she'd lost sight of her youngest and let her wander free round the lavatories of Butlin's Pwllheli that time. What sort of a mam was she?

Useless, that's what.

And the kids didn't sound much better. But I bit my tongue about that as Doug seemed to have a soft spot for them. Even though the more I thought about it, the more I thought that Abigail was a bit of a spoilt brat on account of the fact that Doug said Vera let her get away with murder. And she did seem very ungrateful when I found her that night in the bogs and she kept correcting me about her name. It was as if you'd say, 'Hey, honey bunch. Here's a million pounds' worth of Barbie dolls,' and she'd turn her nose up and go, 'My name's not Honey Bunch. My name's Abigail.'

Ungrateful cow.

Anyway. How did I know that Doug was serious about our

relationship and not just stringing me along like some part-time hooker? Because – ta dah! – he had bought me my own little flat. Our love nest, he called it. It was a tiny one-bedroom ex-council place that he'd bought for a song on one of the rougher estates in Oldham, and every morning he'd arrive to see me (weekdays only) bang on the dot of six o'clock. We'd make mad passionate love for hours, or minutes, depending on his level of friskiness, and then he'd head off to work to be there in time for eight. They were special times, precious times, and I didn't half cherish them.

'It wouldn't do for me,' our Josie said when I confided in her what was going on. 'Aren't you jealous of his wife?'

'You haven't seen her,' I said, as if that explained everything.

Josie pulled a face. '*You* haven't seen her.'

'No, but she's like a cross between a rhinoceros and a duck-billed platypus.'

Josie didn't look so sure. 'Why did he marry her, then?'

'Coz she trapped him. With a baby. What a heartless and cunning thing to do.'

'And then another? And then another?'

'What d'you mean?'

'You want your head felt. That's what I mean.'

I think our Josie were jealous. Coz I'd got a man. A decent man. And she were bonking some Bob Carolgees lookalike from Poulton-le-Fylde.

So. Anyway. There I was at Barnes Wallis, waiting my turn to have a go on one of the trampolines as our Josie'd got us in for nothing as her boss had gone to have a rogue wisdom tooth taken out – 'They won't find much wisdom up there,' Mam had said. 'She makes Sam Fox look like Albert J. Einstein.'

'Are you not thinking of Michael J. Fox?' our Josie had asked.

'No,' Mam had replied, firmly.

Anyway, so there I was, waiting for my turn on trampoline

four, swaying my hips a bit to 'The Tide Is High' by Blondie, which was blasting out of the sound system. Trampolining was a bit kiddish for my liking; I mean, look at me. Eighteen years of age and already at secretarial college. I was becoming a whizz at shorthand and touch-typing and because of my good-to-excellent spelling there was talk I might end up working for a consultant up the hospital. See, I had a brain in my head. I lived on my own and managed my own affairs. Okay, with some help from my beloved. But beggars can't be choosers when your sister offers you a chance to hang out at Barnes Wallis and use all the amenities for free, let's be honest. Who'd dare turn their nose up at that, no matter what age? Nobody, that's who.

I also had my little sideline. A woman in the area had set up her own company to rival Avon, so as well as hordes of Avon ladies travelling round door to door selling all kinds of skin and beauty products, she'd created the Pretty Company, and I had become a Pretty Lady. I often got shady looks when I rang someone's bell and told them I was a Pretty Lady, but my natural gift of the gab and command of the English language, and my ability to flatter, soon won them over and I was making a nice bunch of money on the side. Enough for a few new tops each week, or to put aside for if I ever fancied a mini-break.

I was watching the plumpish kid with the bucked teeth and freckles bouncing up and down in her purple jumpsuit, thinking *I looked like you once upon a time* and marvelling at how great my life had become. Folk were saying I was growing into an almost handsome young woman. I knew that didn't mean much. I knew that didn't mean I was gonna be a great beauty like Farrah Fawcett-Majors or Barbara from *The Good Life*, but it meant that I wasn't gonna end up too doggy either. Which was a bonus. And, I guessed, a turn-up for the books. Doug reckoned it was all down to him.

'You're blossoming, Shirley, because you've got the love of a good man. Always happens. Woman spends years in the shadows. But shine some good light on her, she flourishes. Like a yucca.'

I was a plant. And he was my sunshine.

'I'm not making it up!' he'd protest. 'It was all there in that song.'

'Which song?'

'"Sorry I'm a Lady".'

'Baccara?'

'That's it. The Spanish twins.'

'I don't think they're twins.'

'They are.'

He was often like that. Defiant even though he might be wrong. I let it go, though. At the end of the day what did it matter? I knew full well they weren't twins because when they were big our Josie was into them and we'd read up about them in *Smash Hits*. But it didn't really matter that Doug thought they were. And like he said sometimes, it wasn't very womanly to argue with a man.

The fat lass was doing the splits each time she bounced up. Mid-air splits. And her a fat lass. Amazing. And she was really good at them. I nearly gave her a round of applause. Well done, that girl!

But something stopped me.

I lifted my hands to clap and they froze in front of me.

Between the fat lass's legs, every time she went up and split them, I saw a face at the other end of the trampoline hall.

A face I was used to seeing at six in the morning.

I saw my Doug.

She did the splits again.

I saw my Doug again.

Oh no. Oh God. What was he doing here?

And my next thought was . . . who's he here with?

But before I had a second to look I heard a familiar voice across the din of the cavernous room, echoing round.

'Josie Burke? I want a word with you!'

Mam was here. I spun round and saw her in the corner by the Snacketeria. She practically had our Josie pinned up against the wall. This was most unmotherlike.

And that's when I knew she knew.

Mam knew our Josie were pregnant.

'Just you wait till I get you home!'

Which was when she frogmarched Josie towards the exit and I had no choice but to miss my turn on trampoline four and scurry after them, just in case there were fisticuffs. It wasn't like Mam to wash her dirty laundry in public, so I wasn't sure what she was going to do, but I knew it didn't look good.

At the door I stopped and turned round. Doug was at the payment kiosk with a girl of about five or six who, even from the back, I could tell was Abigail. Jealousy hit me like an arrow in the chest. He was bending down saying something to her. They were about thirty feet away from me and I was jealous at their intimacy but what's more I was jealous that I thought there was some sort of intrinsic bond between us. That he'd be able to tell instinctively if I was in the same room as him. And he hadn't. Just then a woman approached them who was carrying a few polystyrene containers of salad. A skinny blonde woman. Those pale blue jeans that were really tight around the crotch and had the fly all covered up with like a stitched-up piece of blue string. And bell bottoms. God, she was a few years out of date but . . . God, she was pretty. And God, she looked like Barbara out of *The Good Life*.

This woman was a stunner, no mistake.

And as she passed him a container of salad, I realized. This woman was Vera.

Maybe he hadn't lied to me. Maybe . . . maybe once upon a time she was a real heifer and he . . . well . . . like he said himself. Shine a light on a plant and eventually it flourishes. And let's be honest, he'd shone a lot of light her way over the years and maybe that's what had made her so pretty. Yes, that must've been it.

Or had I been imagining it all along? Had I invented this fat old ugly woman with hairs on her chinny chin chin and warts on her nose, just because it suited me? Or had he told me that's what she was like? I was starting to doubt myself now, as I hurried to keep up with Mam and our Josie as they almost skimmed across the pavements towards home. They said not a word as they soldiered on, which gave me time to think about Doug and not-so-vile Vera.

Maybe it wasn't her.

But if it wasn't her, who was it?

He couldn't be having an affair, could he? I'd kill him! How dare he! How dare he two-time . . . no . . . three-time me with . . .

Oh, it didn't bear thinking about, honest to God.

MEN.

But why? Why would he lie to me? Why would things be so horrible between him and her and he'd be thinking of leaving her because she was so awful and just looking at her made him feel wretched. Why would he feel like that if she looked like Barbara from *The Good Life*?

Or was I a bad woman for thinking that men were only interested in looks?

But he'd told me. I was convinced he had. He'd told me she were a right rhino.

Maybe this was someone else. Maybe this was his new secretary or summat.

Except he'd never mentioned a secretary.

And why would a flaming secretary be going with him and his youngest to a trampoline park on his day off?

It was. It was Vera. That vision of loveliness in crotch-tight denim. It was his wife.

But I'd have to find out for sure. Pointless worrying over nowt, just in case this lady wasn't her.

But how would I find out? I didn't even know what street he lived in. I never liked to ask. But I'd find out one way or another. By hook, as they say, or by crook.

Crook, probably. No harm in breaking the rules if you were taking care of your own future. If you know what I mean.

We were indoors. And Mam wasn't happy. She pointed at the table in the kitchen, and Josie dolefully sat down.

'Is it true?' Mam practically spat at her.

'Is what true?' Josie said in a really arsey way, and folded her arms across her very ample chest.

'Are you in t'family way?'

'What's it gotta do wi'you any road?'

'What's it gotta do with me, young lady? Huh? Well I'll tell you what it's gotta do with me, it's gotta do with the fact that your father and I have scrimped and saved and give you every last penny what we've got to try and make you a success on the beauty pageant circuit.'

Blimey. I thought her angle was gonna be, 'I'm its grandmother, you big wazzock.' I was wrong.

'Josephine Burke.'

Oh, I knew she was in trouble now. The full name. Don't

think we'd heard that since Josie came home steaming from Girl Guides with a love bite and a pram full of potatoes. And no idea why she had any of them. But then that's what happens when you drink absinthe punch, apparently.

'How do you expect to carry on on the beauty pageant circuit when you're eight months gone?'

'Well, I'll have to give it up, won't I?'

'Finally! She's seeing sense!'

And Mam sat at the table and put her head in her hands. 'I thought for a second you were gonna say you wanted to keep it.'

'Keep what?'

'The baby.'

'I do.'

'But you just said you'd get rid of it.'

'No I never. I said I'd give it up. And I mean the beauty queen circuit.'

Mam looked repulsed.

'How dare you! HOW dare you! After everything your father and I have done for you, you throw it back in our faces like this! Get out! Get out before I throw you out! You ungrateful little witch!'

Josie looked gobsmacked. It was like she'd just frozen to her seat.

'Well? What are you waiting for?'

'Are you for real?'

'Don't swing the lead, Josie. Get out of my house.'

And with that Josie got up and walked out.

I couldn't make any sense of it, truth be told. I just sat there staring at Mam.

'Do you really mean all that?' I found myself saying after a while.

'Oh shut up, Shirley. You're neither use nor ornament.'

'But do you really think a career as a beauty queen is more important than having a baby?'

'When that baby's born out of wedlock, yes. When your career as a beauty queen is over, yes.'

'Mam. Josie's pretty. There's no denying that. But don't you think if she were gonna win a contest she'd've won one by now?'

Mam looked at me, horrified. Probably just as much by me raising my voice at her than by the actual content of what I was saying.

'Why are you so obsessed with bloody beauty pageants?'

'Don't you dare swear at me!'

'Why bloody not?! That child in her tummy. It's your grandson or granddaughter. And you don't give that!'

At this I snapped my fingers and was very pleased they made such a loud snap. It seemed to reverberate around the kitchen.

Mam just looked away. She'd often do this when she'd had enough of me. Josie she could indulge till the cows came home. With me, it's like she got bored. And couldn't be arsed.

I stood up. She still didn't look at me. Though she did ask, 'Where d'you think you're going?'

'Out on the street. See how your daughter is.'

But then Mam did look at me. 'She keeps that baby? She's no daughter of mine.'

'And as of now,' I said, 'neither am I.'

And I meant it. And I walked slowly to the door. I didn't care that I knew she'd never call me back, beg me to stay, apologize. But it was the final straw, and I'd had enough. That she'd put bloody beauty queens above babies really screwed with my head.

I went out onto the street to look for our Josie.

In the end I found her sat on the steps that ran up from the middle of our terrace to the old coat factory that now had trees growing out of the windows. Her mascara had run, but she wasn't crying any more. It might still have been light but the moon was up above the roof of the factory. The light was dead eerie. I wanted to tell her what I'd seen at the trampoline park. But I knew what she was going through was more important. So I kept it buttoned. Why change the habits of a lifetime? Why try to make yourself be centre stage when our Josie was about?

'I don't think she meant it,' I said, hopefully. Though both of us knew it was a lie.

'I don't know what to do.' She sounded genuine. 'He wants me to get rid of it. She wants me to get rid of it. But it's nineteen eighty. Not nineteen fifty. Shouldn't I get to choose?'

'And what do you want?'

'I don't know, Shirl. I know I'm pig-headed. I know that much. And maybe I just want to keep it to spite them. To go against the grain. But that's not enough, is it?'

I shook my head. Though I didn't really know. I went and sat next to her on the cold steps. That couldn't be good for the baby, surely.

'You could have it, then give it to me?'

She looked at me side-on like I was mad.

'Since when did you want a baby?'

I just shrugged. I wasn't sure why I'd said it, but let's be fair, it wasn't the worst suggestion in the world.

'You could have nine months off the circuit. Pop it out. Bob it over to me. Get back in your bikinis.'

'Shirley Burke, did anyone ever tell you you're mental?'

I cackled a laugh. 'They didn't have to. I already knew it.'

She gave me the broadest smile at that, did Josie.

'What you gonna do, lass?'

'Don't call me lass.'

'What you gonna do, Lassie?'

And that really made her laugh. And when the laugh died down she sighed.

'Fuck it, Shirl. I haven't got a piggin' clue. But I tell you what.'

'What?'

'I could kill a portion of chips. D'you wanna come Codrophenia with me?'

I nodded. And we headed off to the chippy.

On the way she linked me and because we felt close I dared to say, 'You'll never guess what.'

'What?'

'Guess who I saw in Barnes Wallis earlier?'

'I dunno, who?'

'Doug and his wife.'

'You are joking me!'

'I'm not.'

'Well . . . come on!'

'What?'

'Spit it out! What did she look like?'

I toyed with telling her. But I couldn't be bothered. I was so confused about everything I just decided to say . . .

'Oh, just as I thought. Right old cow she was. Ten Ton Tessie. I've nowt to be worried about there.'

'Oh well,' she said as we entered Codrophenia, 'at least you know he's not a liar.'

'No.'

'Right. These are on me. What you having?'

'Er, curry sauce and half rice half chips, please.'

'Coming right up.'

And she leaned on the counter to order.

Something happened to me the day that Mam found out about the baby. Something happened the second I clapped eyes on

Vera. I wouldn't go so far as to say my whole world fell apart; I still had stuff to be grateful for. But I knew deep down, suddenly, from nowhere, that the magazines were right. I knew our Josie was right. It was pretty much doubtful that Doug was ever going to leave his wife for me.

Everywhere I seemed to look, she was there. Every pretty lady on the street, it was her. Every blonde newsreader, her, laughing at me. Even the beauty products I was selling all contained aloe vera. Her name was everywhere; I couldn't escape it.

What I should have done was confront him. The next time he came around. Tell him I'd seen them and ask why he'd lied to me about what she was like, ask if they were still having sex, ask if he still loved her. But it was easier to play along, to play the game, it was easier to try to block it all out. Instead of asking him I just tried to be better than her in the bedroom, better than her in the laughs department, better than her in the carefree, who-gives-a-toss attitude. But I didn't know if it was working. Because I didn't really know what she was like.

And so I decided to find out.

It was easy enough to discover where he lived. When he went to the bathroom to freshen up after sex one morning I slipped his wallet out of his trouser pocket and quickly found his driving licence. And there it was in black and white – well, black and green.

8 Cloverdale Walk
Royton
Oldham

I pushed the paper back into his wallet and the wallet back into his pocket and wrote the address neatly in pencil in the back of my diary. I then tucked the diary under the bed and felt a rush of excitement. I didn't know how. I didn't know what I would do. But I knew. I would soon be meeting his wife. But what would I do when I got there?

My eyes came to rest on a bottle of aloe vera body lotion, sat on my bedroom dressing table. And right then, right there, I knew.

Chapter Nine

Cloverdale Walk was on a hill. About twenty new-build houses stood next to each other going down said hill, tall brick dominoes ready to fall. Number eight had a neatly kept lawn and a hanging basket either side of the front door. Someone liked their gardens here, all right. There was a small poster in the front room window next to the front door that read BEWARE OF THE CHIHUAHUA.

Chihuahua?

I didn't even know Doug had a dog.

I hated Chihuahuas. I hated any dog where there was a danger you might tread on it by mistake.

Yelp!

And it got me to thinking. How many more things was he keeping from me?

The front room window boasted those net curtains that went up in the middle. I'd never understood them. Either you wanted a good net to stop folk looking in and to afford you some bleeding privacy or you didn't.

She obviously didn't.

She may as well have flashed her knickers for all the road to see.

As my mam would've said. One word. 'Common'. God, Vera. Talk about lousy taste!

I knew Doug wouldn't be in as it was the middle of the working day and I'd phoned his office and asked to be put through to him. And just as I was I'd hung up and headed out. But even so my heart was in my mouth as I reached out and pressed the doorbell.

It played a tune.

I hated doorbells that played tunes.

It played 'Greensleeves'. I knew that from school as our music teacher Mrs Jones had told us that Henry the Eighth composed it. She'd told us this to impress, like we should've thought it was cool. Like Henry the Eighth was practically him off the Bay City Rollers.

I hated 'Greensleeves' as well. Who the heck was Doug married to?!

I saw the net curtain ruffle a bit. Clearly Vera was checking to see who was calling. I picked a bit of fluff off my Fair Isle sweater and got my name badge ready to show, smartly covering my right nipple, but I made sure I had it the wrong way round so I wouldn't actually have to tell my love rival my real name, and as she opened the door I smiled sweetly.

'Hello. I'm a Pretty Lady.'

And I have to be honest. She did look slightly alarmed.

'It's the name of the company,' I added, apologetically. 'Can I ask if you've got five minutes to talk through your beauty regime?'

'Sorry?'

'Have you got five minutes? For a quick chat about beauty. And how I might be able to help you.'

As if. As if I'd ever be able to help this ravishing beauty.

147

'I'm sorry,' she said, closing the door. 'This is a really bad time.'

The door shut in my face. She had sounded like she was about to cry. I instinctively crouched down and opened the letter box.

'Is everything all right?' I called through. No response. 'Anything I can help with, dear?'

Again no reply. I called again, 'Everything okay in your marriage?!'

Still she didn't reply. Then I saw her walking towards the front door.

'What did you say?'

'I was just saying. I hope I've not offended you, madam.'

'No. Not at all. Family bereavement.'

And she walked away.

Family bereavement? Who the bloody hell had died? Doug hadn't told me anyone had died, and he told me everything. Well, he said he did. It would appear my journey here had been pointless. I picked up my Pretty Lady briefcase and walked back down her path and tried to memorize everything I had seen when she'd opened the door.

She was wearing a black pencil skirt and a clingy dark grey V-neck sweater that I would have bet a dollar to a dime that she wasn't wearing a bra under. She had pale tights on and no shoes. Around her neck there was a gold chain with a locket hanging off it. I dreaded to think what was in there. Around one wrist, the wrist that held the hand that held open the door, was a silver charm bracelet that contained many charms. The two I could remember were a dog and a bottle. Like a wine bottle. She had no make-up on. Or if she did it was very subtle. She had no earrings in, but did have piercings. She had amazingly soft blue eyes. And her blonde wispy hair was tied back into a ponytail, but was still short enough at the front to fall into a fringe. A thick fringe. This lady was never going to go bald.

I had a sudden image of her bald. Bald as a coot with one wisp of question-mark-shaped hair bouncing in the breeze. It did make me smile, I have to be honest. Okay, so I was cruel. So what!

Her hall carpet was cream coloured and looked reasonably new. Either that or it had recently been cleaned. The wallpaper in the bit of hall that I could see was shiny, like it had an effect to make it look like mother of pearl. There was an oval-shaped mirror behind Vera's head that I could see myself reflected in.

None of these things really gave me any more clues to what I could learn about the state of Vera, her personality and her marriage. This was most annoying. My cunning plan was that she'd be so interested in talking all things make-up and beauty and hair and the like that she'd practically drag me inside, throw a Mellow Bird's down my neck, and then start inappropriately confiding in me about how bad her marriage was so she was embarking on an extra-marital affair, and then I'd be able to grass her up, somehow, to Doug, who'd then leave her and come and live with me full time.

But nothing ever went according to plan, did it? Oh God.

This was not good. Not good at all. I'd have to find some other way to accidentally bump into her.

And who the hell was she bereaving when they were at home? I needed to know! I couldn't just say to Doug, 'Who's died in your family recently?' as it'd make me look as if I had inside information. And I couldn't go giving the game away.

At the top of the cul-de-sac I turned to look back to the house. No sign of movement. It was then, though, that I saw her neighbour's front door open, and a portly woman with a headscarf tucked back behind her ears like a gypsy from a picture book bent down and put her empty milk bottles out. She then hurried back in.

Now that was what I called a Pretty Lady magnet. I hurried back. And knocked on her door.

'Hiya! I'm a Pretty Lady?'

She too looked alarmed, but not for long.

To say Gwen Jenkins was a pushover would be over-exaggerating, but stuff me with a bag of sausage meat, once I got her going she sang like she'd OD'd on frigging canary food. She practically dragged me into her house because she 'took her beauty regimens very seriously'.

As she was trying out all the samples, neatly laid on her oval dining table in what she described as her 'through-lounge ambience', I complimented her on her serving hatch.

'It's extra large,' she boasted. 'My Malcolm's very good with his carpentry.'

'Just like Joseph!' I quipped, feeling a little bit biblical. But it was a waste of time. Because she answered, 'Oh, is your fella into carpentry too?'

First rule of beauty product selling. Never make your customer feel thick or ugly. So I just nodded and squirted some hand cream into her open palm.

'Thank you!' she said, all overcome, and rubbed her hands together, like this was the very elixir of life.

'I was just next door,' I said casually, taking a sip from the rather bland cup of tea she'd made me. 'You know, with Vera. Isn't she lovely?'

I could tell she was impressed.

'Oh yes. We're very lucky, neighbour-wise.'

Then I sighed dramatically. 'Poor Vera.'

I could see Gwen was immediately up for a gossip.

'Oh I know, it's shocking,' she said, lowering her voice as if the walls might be wafer thin. 'She must be in bits. Well, we're all in shock really. We'd met Muriel several times, truth be told. I mean, I knew she liked a drink but . . .'

'Did she?'

'Strictly between us this is, yeah?'

'Of course.'

Who was Muriel??

'So, anyway.' She leaned in even closer to me. She was about to explain who Muriel was. EXCITING! 'Does Vera take these products, then?'

Oh.

I had to keep her on side.

'Well. I'm not meant to say owt but . . .'

Her eyes widened with anticipation. Vera was definitely the most beautiful woman for miles around. If I made out she used my products I could make a killing.

'She likes to pretend she gets the posh stuff from the department stores.'

Gwen nodded; she knew what was coming.

'And I could never confirm or deny who uses what. I'm not a tell-tale tit.'

'Me neither!' she beamed.

'But let's just say. I'm very familiar with her through-lounge.'

I didn't know where that came from. And neither did Gwen. 'She hasn't got a through-lounge. We're the only ones with a through-lounge in the cul-de-sac.'

'No, I know. It's just . . . a turn of phrase. I get a bit carried away sometimes.'

'Oh, I see!' And now Gwen looked most relieved. 'So . . . which ones does lovely lovely Vera . . . perhaps . . . or perhaps . . . hide away in her cupboards, then?' She eyed the various tubs and bottles eagerly.

I picked a few at random, sliding them across the Formica towards her. She swivelled some of them round to inspect them.

'I've just had a brain freeze,' I said, trying a different tack.

'Is that a new treatment? Is it like a facial? My friend had a facial. Said it made her look like Selina Scott.'

'No. No. My mind's gone blank. Who was Muriel again?'

'Muriel? Vera's mum.'

'What am I like?!'

'It's so sad. So tragic,' she said, her expression suddenly sombre as she squeezed some face cream onto her hand and then started dabbing it on her cheeks.

'Yes. The way she went.'

'And it wasn't a nice car crash, if you know what I mean.'

'No. No.'

'What with them kiddies in the back.'

'This is it.'

'And her three times over the limit.'

'Three, yes.'

Bloody hell. This sounded so gruesome! Muriel, Vera's mam, had died in a car crash? While she was over the limit? And she had Doug's kids in the back? This was like something out of a horror story! No wonder Vera had been all over the place when I'd rung her Greensleeves bell! I almost felt sorry for the cow.

'I said to my one. I said, she sat right by that serving hatch Boxing Day. Polished off a whole box of liqueurs.'

'Blimey.'

'The warning signs were there, love.'

'Weren't they just?'

'And I don't meant to be rude but . . . can I be frank?'

'Of course.'

She took her time. Then eventually said, as quiet as quiet could be: 'She once did a poo in my walk-in wardrobe.'

That did actually make me feel sick. But as I needed to keep plugging her for information I couldn't let on.

'Muriel?'

'Yes. Muriel. And it wasn't a nice poo, if you know what I mean.'

Oh. My. Giddy. Aunt.

'Dirty bitch,' I said, unable to help myself. But Gwen concurred.

'That's what I called her. Vera was the colour of that.'

She pointed to her puce curtains.

'We've not really spoken since. Embarrassed, see.'

'Well, when your mam poos in your neighbour's walk-in wardrobe . . .' I said, letting the potential end of the sentence hang silently in the air. She could finish it any which way she wanted. And she did. Whatever she imagined me saying, she agreed with.

'This is it. I bobbed over with a condolence card when I saw the piece in the *Evening News*. She seemed grateful. Especially when I said she could now ignore the bill I'd popped through her letter box for the carpet cleaning and . . . well, let's just call it the dry-cleaning on my palazzo pants.'

'Very big of you, Gwen.'

'This is it, love. I'm a very big woman.'

You could say that again.

'Funeral's tomorrow.'

'Is it?'

'Yes. At the crem.'

'Will you go?'

'No. And of course . . . he's been banned.'

'Who?'

'Her Douglas.'

WHAT A BITCH! Banning her own husband from her mother's funeral! No wonder he was knocking me off!

'Has he?'

'Well, they never got on. And coz she was always half cut she was always claiming all sorts about him.'

'Like what? I've always found Douglas lovely.'

'Oh, she said he had a roving eye. Bit too easy with his hands when he's hugging you, kind of thing. I mean, we know it's all nonsense. Bit fond of the younger ladies, but then which fella isn't?'

'Not Douglas, surely!' I said in mock horror.

'She said he once got drunk and told her . . . he told her . . . I shouldn't be repeating this . . .'

'Gwen. When we join up to be a Pretty Lady, we have to sign a form.'

'Do you?'

'Yes, saying that whatever we hear in a consultation . . . stays there. I'm practically a priest. You can tell me anything.'

'He said he wished he'd never married anyone as pretty as Vera.'

I was overjoyed, naturally.

'Why would he say that?'

'Because he said ugly women were more grateful in bed.'

And that was like a dagger to the heart. My instinct was to defend him, though.

'Oh, she'd've been making that up.'

'Muriel?'

'Big fat piss-head, course she were making it up. Doug's lovely. D'you want these products or not?'

I was getting snappy. I'd lost patience with her. And that was bad. That was not the way to complete a sale, and I knew it.

First rule of the Pretty Company? Never lose your temper. Hold onto it at all times. So I took a deep breath, and I leaned in to her.

'Forgive my short fuse, Gwen, temper-wise. It's just I have Vera banging on about this stuff morning, noon and night. If she thinks Doug wouldn't stray, I say he wouldn't neither.'

She looked like she knew something but wasn't telling. 'If you say so.'

'Why? What do you know?'

'Nothing.' She was being all nonchalant, and pretending to inspect my products.

'Tell me,' I said.

'I'm sure it was all a misunderstanding.'

'What was?'

'What he was caught doing in Denise McAdam's lean-to after their Cheryl's eighteenth.'

My blood ran cold.

'What was he caught doing?'

'There was probably just an innocent explanation for it all.'

'For what?'

'It's just none of us could think of one.'

'For what?'

'Having his hand up Cheryl's skirt. She said he'd got her tipsy on rum punch and wasn't sure what was going on. He said he walked into the lean-to and she practically threw herself at him.'

'Well, he is pigging handsome. And from what I hear, that Cheryl's got a reputation.'

Gwen looked most interested. 'Has she?'

Of course I was making it up now, but I embroidered a few fancy tales about my sister and made out they were about this Cheryl, whoever she was. And as far as I was concerned she was a bit of a slut. Well, what do you expect when you hurl yourself at my Doug at your eighteenth birthday party?

I did not like the sound of Cheryl.

In my eyes, Cheryl was the ultimate suburban slut.

I didn't dare think the obvious, though. I didn't dare for one second allow myself to think that any of these rumours could be true. I'd gone in search of stories about Vera. Last thing I wanted was mud chucked at Doug.

Jealousy. That's what this was about. Out and out jealousy. Doug were a handsome chappy and they all wanted a slice of the man and so, short of chucking their car keys in the fruit bowl every time they went round each other's houses, what could they do to snare him?

Pounce on him, that's what.

This whole street was a hive of pouncers. And I didn't like it one bit. I'd a good mind to go round to this Cheryl's house and slap her round her lying little face. She'd certainly been asking for it.

I knew her sort. They might've had nicer houses than me and our Josie but they defo had slacker morals and even looser knicker elastic. They were ferried everywhere in fast cars to places like Guides and church hall discos. They got a whole matching outfit for Christmas and Easter. They had pop stars on their walls and a record player that matched the carpet. And they were bored. Bloody bloody bastard bored, and so they mooned over the man across the road and had a cheeky extra drink whenever he came round. And eventually they got tired of waiting, waiting for him to stick his hand up their skirt, and so what did they go and do? They went and did it themselves.

Here you go, Dougie. Don't be shy. I won't tell a soul.

Oh, sorry. Someone's just walked in and caught us.

It was him – it was all his doing!

Oh yes. I'd wipe that smirk off her lying little face all right.

Gwen was looking a bit worried.

I couldn't really remember what I'd just said.

I knew I'd been slagging Cheryl off. But I think Gwen was shocked by how angry I'd got.

'Are you okay?' she asked, then swallowed, like she was scared.

'Fine, Gwen. Sorry. You can probably tell me and this Cheryl have history.'

'Right.'

'She did the same to my fella a while back.'

'Your Joseph? The carpenter?'

I nodded. 'And now it's the talk of the wash house. That he's a dirty old man.'

'I had no idea. I'm so sorry. I'll make sure the neighbours know. She's not to be trusted.'

'She's not.'

Well, I'd certainly put that one to bed, eh?

'If you don't mind me asking, how old are you?'

'I'm thirty-six.'

'My God, you look about twenty.'

Cheeky bitch, I was only eighteen.

'Exactly. And it's all down to the Pretty Company.'

Within five minutes she'd given me the best part of thirty quid. And I'd left there knowing that the neighbours would stop thinking my Doug was a knicker-twitching randy old toad.

Job done, Shirley. Job done.

I felt like I should've got a promotion for what I'd done there. If that'd been part of my job I'd be management level by now. But it wasn't. There was no-one I could tell about what I'd done as it was very much not allowed.

Oh yeah, Doug? I went snooping at your neighbour's. Heard some horrendous gossip but it's okay, darling. I nipped it in the bud.

No. I'd sound like a pigging psycho.

I went straight into town. I went to the library. I asked for a copy of every local paper for the past week and sifted through till I found what I wanted. The death announcement for someone called Muriel and the details of her funeral. I just had to get there. I didn't know how; I didn't really know why. I just wanted to be in the same space as Vera for half an hour to see what I could glean about her. Gwen had said Doug wouldn't be going to the service, and I hoped she was right. Because my cover would defo be blown if he walked in and saw me. But also, I didn't want Vera to clock me and think, *There's that Pretty Lady who came to my door yesterday.*

What I needed . . . was a disguise.

And then . . . on to Narnia!

The woman in Narnia, the fancy dress shop, was either very flattering, very impressed, or trying to make a quick sale. Either way it worked. She told me I had a blank canvas face. Whereas up until now I thought I was a bit of a Plain Jane, she told me otherwise. What I had was the canvas on which any picture could be painted. 'And that, lady,' she said between puffs on a ciggie, 'is a godsend to fancy dress.' She said with the right outfit, the right wig and the right sort of make-up I could pass myself off as anything from a scullery maid to a woman of high office. I quite liked the sound of that, and for once I appreciated the face that God gave me.

At first I'd thought, rather over-dramatically I now realized, that maybe I'd dress up as an old lady and make out I'd been a pal of the deceased. I fancied myself in a white curly wig, lumpy tights, a nylon frock and some sensible shoes, doddering down the aisle with a walking stick and a best handbag. But with some simple advice from the smoking lady of fancy dress, I realized that with a simple pair of specs, a cap and a pretend ponytail, I was unrecognizable. And that would do for me.

Next, I had to find out exactly when the funeral was taking place. That was easy enough to do. Once I got home and leafed through the phone book for the number of the crem I phoned them up and did my doddery old lady voice and asked what time Muriel's funeral was 'on the morrow'. God knows why I said 'on the morrow'; it sounded so wrong as the words left my lips, but the fella at the crem didn't seem to mind, and informed me it was ten in the morning. 'Better than ten at night!' I quipped, over-egging it a bit, I must say. 'I'm tucked up in my three-quarter by then at the resting home!'

Yes, I knew it should have been 'care home', but I was so pigging chuffed he believed I was an actual old woman, I got a bit carried away.

Ten on the morrow it was.

I planned that my name would be Janine, if anyone was to ask. But let's be honest. When you go to a funeral and you see someone you don't know, you don't exactly bound up to them and go, 'Hiya, how did you know the corpsified one, kid?' Well, I knew I wouldn't anyway. Janine, I reckoned, worked in Muriel's local shop and loved serving her coz she was a laugh, and always came in for those little bottles of vodka. Or maybe she was a barmaid in a local pub? Hmm, I wasn't sure what best suited her as I didn't know how secret her drinking was.

The more worrying concern was, I had no idea where Muriel had lived. So if anyone did say, 'Oh, which pub?' or 'Oh, which shop?' I wouldn't have the foggiest where I had worked, or rather, where Janine had worked.

This wouldn't do.

Just in case.

Someone might ask.

And the last thing I wanted to do was arouse suspicion.

I kicked the bin over in the kitchen. I sometimes did that if I was in a foul mood.

I could wait till the morning. Ask Doug when he came round.

But that too might arouse suspicion. Why would I all of a sudden be interested in his mother-in-law and where she lived, etc.?

Maybe I could ask roundabout questions.

'What's going on in your life, cock?'

But Doug didn't offer stuff up about his family. He knew it upset me. And he didn't like to see me upset.

No. I knew what was coming. I got my cap on, my glasses and ponytail, and headed back off to the high street and towards the library. Again!

Janine asked if she could find any more local news articles about the recent car crash and the woman behind the counter was most helpful. Within fifteen minutes, Janine was sat at a desk reading all about Muriel Gatsby's high jinks again, but this time looking for proof of where she lived. God, no wonder she was Vera's mother; this woman sounded like a complete piece of work.

Janine made some notes in a notepad, taking it all in. Muriel lived not too far from me, truth be told. I wondered if Doug ever popped in to see her after deflowering me of my so-called innocence each morning. But then I remembered what Gwen had said about them both practically hating each other's guts, so I decided that was unlikely. She was in her early seventies and had taken to the bottle after her husband had died from cancer five years ago.

God, you could learn a lot from a local rag!

She had been arrested several times for drunk and disorderly behaviour and wasn't meant to have her grandkids in the car that day, but she had picked them up from school as a surprise and taken them for a ride, which is when she'd hit an empty bus which was returning to the depot. The kids had come out pretty much unscathed, but she'd not been wearing a seat belt and had hit the windscreen and hey presto. Bye bye Muriel.

I didn't like Muriel.

Well, she didn't like my Doug.

And what she'd put them kiddies through. I mean, face facts, I was no fan of Abigail, but them kiddies could have been brown bread as well.

Oh, I had to get to this funeral quick smart. And see what a train wreck this Vera must really be, having had a mother like that.

I was beginning to feel very confident about me and Doug's future.

Very confident indeed!

That night I dreamt I was at the funeral. But when they brought the coffin in it all went a bit loopy. I looked to the back of the crem and saw some pallbearers carrying a huge silver platter. And on top of the platter was Vera, in a swimsuit, microphone in hand, singing, 'Have you met Miss Jones?'

I woke up in an oddly confusing sweat, then couldn't get back to sleep again.

Obviously I was very excited about what lay ahead.

Chapter Ten

Oh lordy.

Lordy lordy lordy!

What were you thinking, Shirley?

Shame on you.

SHAAAAAAAAME on you!!

And I really did feel ashamed.

Okay. It was a mistake. And nobody's fault but my own. I'll hold my hands up. Both of them. I should never have gone to that stupid funeral. What was I thinking? I should never have put on that stupid disguise and gone to the funeral of someone I'd never even met just because I wanted to find out more about the orphaned daughter. My love rival. My nemesis. It was one of the worst decisions I'd ever made, if I was honest.

And let's face it. Honesty had nowt to do with my appearance at that crematorium, I'll admit it. I even went in bloody disguise.

Disguise!

Though even if I said so myself, that disguise was pretty bloody good, actually.

And my gut instinct had been right. No-one asked why I was there. No-one was interested, full stop.

Which was pretty annoying because . . .

Oh, I could barely bring myself to even think about it . . .

Which was pretty annoying because against all the odds, and in complete contrast to what Gwen had told me . . .

Doug had gone to the service.

Yup, siree sirah, Doug was there as he lived and breathed, in full-blown Technicolor, as they said at the flicks.

Which is more than could be said for Muriel, of course.

Dead as a doornail, dead as a dodo, dead as you like Muriel. Muriel who pooed in Gwen's walk-in wardrobe and would poo no more.

My heart had done the rumba in my ribcage when I saw that Doug had walked in behind the coffin, cradling a sobbing Vera in his arms. That's how it felt, anyway. It rattled around like those dancers on *Come Dancing*, shaking all over the dance floor in their sequins, all hand-stitched. For my part, all I wanted to do in that moment was run. But I couldn't. That way I'd definitely draw attention to myself. I couldn't exactly gasp, 'Sorry! Wrong funeral!' I was stuck there. For the duration. I was trapped. Caged. No way out.

It was like someone had superglued my backside to the pew.

I had to gasp for air a bit. Hopefully the folk either side of me just thought I was overcome with emotion. But it was too much for me to handle. How long was I going to be trapped there for? This was the worst mistake in my life!

The sweat was peeling the skin off me, I felt tingly and prickly all over and I couldn't for the life of me get my breath. I actually envisaged dying right there and then at the funeral, but the only thing that stopped me was the fear that when I did, they'd rip off the disguise to give me mouth to mouth and Doug would find himself flummoxed. And, even in death, I didn't want to make a holy show of myself. So I stayed alive.

Eventually I calmed down. My breathing returned to normal.

And I began to wonder if what I had experienced was more of a panic attack than impending doom. Eventually I felt almost relaxed. Especially when I realized Doug wasn't going to spend the whole service turning round to see who was there.

Fortunately it wasn't a very long funeral. Muriel's life hadn't been that interesting. And there was only so much positive spin you could put on a woman who was pissed behind the wheel and drove into a bus. The vicar said something about the bus driver being full of humility and forgiveness, which had really made Vera wail, but other than that Muriel's life really hadn't amounted to too much. There was talk of her finally being reunited with her husband. There was the twenty-third psalm. Some old crumbly did a poem about not having really died, and just having gone to the room next door actually.

Er. I don't think that was strictly true. Pretty sure she had died, love. It were in the papers.

And yes, she was about to go through to the next room. Coz that's where the burning furnace was.

Then the crumbly sat down.

And that, really, was that.

As the curtains were drawn and some nondescript music played over the tannoy I held my order of service to my face, all coy like a woman in a crinoline in olden days Paris, hiding behind her fan. I couldn't risk Doug clocking me.

But of course the awful thing, the horrible thing, the thing I really could have done without, was that yet again – just like at Barnes Wallis – I was under the same roof as my beloved and – order of service or no order of service – he just hadn't twigged.

I wanted to scream, I'M HERE, DOUG! YOUR BIT ON THE SIDE! YOUR COURTESAN! YOUR FANCY PIECE! YOUR TOYGIRL! I'M HERE BROAD AS DAYLIGHT!

But he just hadn't realized. And that hurt. Really hurt.

Okay, so I looked completely different from usual. Okay, so he had no reason to expect me to be there – and probably just as well. But that intrinsic pull that I always thought would spring up whenever we were in the same space was completely absent. Yet a-bloody-gain! His focus was solely on her, his wife. Rightly so, you might have said; it was her mother's funeral after all. But this was not the picture of sad family life he painted to me on his daily visits. This was the ultimate show of strength. I could hear folk in the congregation passing comment.

Isn't he great?

They're so well matched.

And after everything Muriel said about him.

Bless him.

Look at him.

Yeah all right, I was looking. And it was knocking me sick.

Vera. Always the bride. Never the bridesmaid.

I'd not been surprised when he'd phoned the night before and told me he'd have to cancel his visit next day as he was feeling under the weather. I'd almost said, *It's okay, Doug. I know you're burning the alkie tomorrow.* But I kept schtum and told him I understood. Even if I knew he was lying. Even though I wanted to say, *I'm onto you, Sonny Jim.* Even though he was old enough to be my dad. I kept my counsel, because that was what good girls did. For I had decided I'd be a good girl. Because good girls always won. Didn't they? They had to.

I would make sure they did.

I kept hearing that voice in my head. Audrey Hepburn in *My Fair Lady*.

I'm a good girl, I am!

I used to love that film. Sat in of a Saturday or a Sunday

afternoon, me, Mam and our Josie, loving the frocks, loving the songs. Mam knew all the words.

I'm a good girl, I am!

Once the service was over I made a sharp exit before Doug could turn round from his front-row seat and realize I might have been there. I hurried away from the crematorium in as sober a walk as I could. It was almost a trot. I didn't want to run to draw attention to myself. I took the first bus that came to the stop outside and, even though it was going in completely the wrong direction for me, I stayed with it to the end of the journey. Just in case.

Just in case what? Just in case he saw me and twigged? Twigged that I was obsessed with his wife, the competition?

Just in case my cover was blown?

Just in case he saw me and said, *What the hell are you in that rig-up for?*

But there was a bigger fear. Just in case he saw me and said, *Do you know what, Shirl? It's over.*

Something was making me feel like he was slipping from my grasp. Something was making me feel like I was always going to play second fiddle to her headline act. It was a feeling I was used to, let's be honest. I had always lived in the shadows while our Josie shone in the limelight. But Doug had led me to believe that one day I'd be the star of his show. And now I was appreciating this might prove unlikely. Did I really want to be the other woman, the kept woman till the end of my days? Vera had already won on so many levels. She had his ring on her finger. She had the kids. Maybe one day he'd get bored of me and turn his attention to somebody else he met by the outdoor pools at Butlin's. It might only be a matter of time. Was I heading for the knacker's yard when I was only eighteen years of age?

I knew there were other men out there. I knew there were better men out there. But for some reason, he was the one I wanted. He was the one who'd first shown an interest, first shone the light on me. He was the first ever man to see me naked and make love to me and tell me I was beautiful and make me feel good about myself, and that had to count for something. It had to. And if it didn't then I would make sure that it did.

But how?

How could I do that?

Looked like it was time to up my game.

Doug had his own business. It was something to do with providing the parts for catseyes in the middle of the road. He had told me, but I'd forgotten what it was. Blimey, I could be useless sometimes. Like when I couldn't remember if he'd told me Vera was a big fat lump or not. You'd have thought I'd remember that kind of thing. Oh Shirl, you daft apeth.

Catseyes. He ran a company that made a bit of them. For the roads. The bit that lit up perhaps, that showed you which way to drive when it was dark. Maybe he made those bits.

I did know he had a couple of Portakabins in an industrial estate between Oldham and Rochdale. And his surname was on the side of those Portakabins.

That, he'd say, was his empire.

He had men working under him and lots of business contacts.

Sometimes I dreamed that that empire would one day be mine.

I could do his touch-typing. His filing. Answer the phone. *Just putting you through . . .*

And yet.

And yet.

I had this sense of foreboding. Call it woman's intuition, call it what you like, but I sensed all would not be well in the future. I remember when our Josie's pet rabbit Gnasher died and she started having nightmares and then was found sleepwalking on Tiberton Street singing 'Hi Ho Silver Lining' and had no idea why she was doing it. Mam said the woman from the Chinese laundry's hair went white overnight when her twin sister died. You see, grief did funny things to people. And people did funny things with grief. No doubt Vera was going to be no exception.

I kept seeing this image of her in a cowshed, milking a cow. Coz oh boy, was she gonna be milking this one! She'd be more demanding of Doug's time, I just knew it, and he'd have to do whatever she said coz let's face it, when your missus had just lost her mam, you had to show willing. I totally understood that, I just didn't think it was fair. I'd waited in the wings long enough. He'd sworn to me that he'd leave her one day. Was the date of that day going to be: the twelfth of never?

I felt like I was going mad. I couldn't think about anything else. My work was suffering, even I could see that. I stopped getting As at secretarial college, I was slipping to Bs. Everybody knew summat was up. I felt there was so much rubbish and information and thoughts and fears bubbling about in my head, I had to speak to someone.

I spoke to our Josie.

I felt bad, like she didn't have enough on her plate already.

She'd come round to mine for a meal and a bottle of pop. She was trying not to drink now she were pregnant with the baby. I was cooking my old favourite: a tin of condensed tomato soup with a tin of tuna and a tin of peas in it, served with this new-fangled invention they'd just brought out – oven chips. She still hadn't gone back to Mam and Dad's and was stopping with the Bob Carolgees lookalike, so she was glad to get out from under his feet, truth be told.

I told her everything I knew. I mean, there wasn't much. I told her I'd seen his wife at Barnes Wallis and she was pretty. I didn't tell her I'd been round with my Pretty Lady products and interrogated the neighbour, then dressed up and gone to a funeral to keep tabs on her. I only told our Josie I'd found out that Vera's mam had died and it had been in the papers and I felt like she had the upper hand. Josie just sat there shaking her head.

'You're not gonna like what I'm going to say, Shirl.'

'Say it anyway, I can be the judge of that.'

'Well, it's not good, is it? Him with another woman. And he lied and said she were horrible. And now you know she's not. Is he really gonna chuck it all away to risk everything with you?'

I shrugged, even though I knew the answer was a resounding no.

'What d'you reckon I should do, Josie?'

'I hate to have to say it but . . .'

'What?'

'Get out. Get out now. Show him who's boss.'

'But he bought me this flat.'

'You'll find another. And you'll meet another bloke. One who'll treat you right.'

'But what if I don't? What if he's the one?'

'He's not the one. There's no such thing as the one. Oh, there's *someone* but . . .'

'There won't be . . .'

'Shirley, there's someone out there for everyone. Even you. They just might not be the John Travolta in shining armour we all had planned for us selves.'

'Well, we both know that for a fact. No-one'll ever live up to John Travolta.'

'This much is true, cock. This much is true.'

I sighed. I'd known exactly what she was going to say, and that's why I'd asked her. But still, hearing it aloud rather than in my head was a tough weight to carry.

'Have you tried talking to him?'

'What about?'

'About all this!'

'No.'

'Well, don't you think you should? You're not gonna get anywhere unless you talk to each other.'

'But what if he just says, "Yeah, you're right. It's Vera over you."?'

'Then it's best you know now, rather than further down the line. The sooner you know what's going on the better.'

I knew what she said made sense. And I knew she had my best interests at heart. But I just didn't know whether I could go through with it.

Why was it that I had no qualms dressing up and putting glasses on and following his wife to her own mother's funeral? But face to face, being honest, that was somehow much more difficult.

'I will. I promise. I'll talk to him.'

And then I changed the subject and we talked about prams. My heart wasn't in it though. And I could tell hers wasn't either.

'How've you been keeping?' I asked Doug the next time I saw him and I'd sorted him out, sex-wise. You know, down there.

'Oh, you know. So so.'

'Hardly seen you lately.'

'I've been having a nightmare, Shirl.'

'Oh aye? What's occurring, Göring?'

He liked it when I said that. He thought it was cute. And I'd have bet you a dime to a dollar that Vera never said anything like that.

Other things I said along these lines were: *You're a stickler, Hitler.* And: *Don't make me yawn, Eva Braun.*

He reached over and pinched my nose.

'Nothing for you to worry your head about, ditsy Dora.'

'I'm anything but ditsy, Doug.'

He chuckled. 'True.'

'Is it trouble at home?'

He sighed. 'I can't lie to you. It's Vera. Her mam died.'

'Oh, I'm sorry to hear that. Was it a long drawn-out death or . . .'

'No, it was quite quick really. Car crash. She was under the influence.'

'Of what?'

'Diamond White mostly. And a bit of Baileys. It's been horrible, if you must know. Coz the kids were in the car with her.'

I did a massive mock gasp. 'Are they okay!?'

'Minor cuts and grazes but, yeah. They're okay now.'

'Oh Doug, that's awful.'

And I reached out and hugged him to me and I could feel how tense he was just talking about it. But you know. This was good. Because I knew he was being honest with me. All this time I'd worried he was stringing me along like . . . I dunno . . . like a massive string of sausages. But look. He was lain in my arms being honest with me.

Some folk would've said that that was a result.

Some folk like me.

'Shit's hit the fan a bit, really,' He said. 'I was gonna tell you but . . . I know you don't really want to hear about Vera.'

'Oh, I don't mind, Doug. Not really.'

Good girls always won, you see.

'What does she look like, Doug? Describe her.'

'She's all right.'

'Is she fat? I can't remember what you've told me.'

'She's not fat.'

'She's thin?'

'Skinny as a rake. Blonde hair. Looks a bit like thingy.'

'Who?'

'Barbara from *The Good Life*.'

'Hmm. She's a pretty little thing, that Barbara.'

'Vera might be pretty, Shirl. But all that glitters is not golden.'

I took that in for a while.

'Can't all have brains like me, I suppose.'

'You might be right there.'

Right. So he as good as said she was thick.

Result.

'Okey dokey, pig in a pokey,' he added. 'I'm going for a slash.'

As I lay in my bed, luxuriating in the comfort of the mattress and my quilt, I could hear him urinating in the bathroom. A loud thudding downpour; put me in mind of Niagara Falls. But I didn't care. It sounded wonderful. Like an orchestra. Doug wasn't leading me on. Doug wasn't lying. One day he'd be leaving that skinny bitch for little ole me.

It was just a matter of time.

Oh, this felt good. This felt amazing, in fact.

This feeling could last forever.

But when he came in from the bathroom, the cacophonous flush rattling around the flat, he looked very red in the face.

'Are you all right, Doug?'

'High blood pressure, doctor says.'

'Oh.' I'd heard of that, though I wasn't that sure what it was. He sat on the bed and took some deep breaths.

'I'll be all right in a minute,' he said.

'Okay.' I still didn't know what to do, really.

But the longer he sat there, the longer he did his heavy breathing thing, and the more ratty he got.

'Fuck me,' he said, under his breath.

'Isn't that my line?' I joked, sounding for all the world like our Josie on one of her bawdy nights out. Not very me at all, really.

He stood, suddenly. 'I can't do this. I need some space.' He started pacing the room, all panicky. 'What if I had a heart attack now?'

'Well, I'd call an ambulance.'

'And how would we explain that to Vera?'

'We'd think of something.'

I really wished he would have a heart attack. Right there, right then; then she'd have to have found out. Straight away.

Why was my husband found in your house in nowt but his undies and a Supertramp T-shirt?

Why d'you think, Bell-bottoms?

But he was pacing again.

'You're not going to have a heart attack,' I insisted.

'But what if I did?'

'You're just having a panic on. You've been through a lot of stress. This is how it's coming out. I do understand. I had one the other day at the . . . at . . . somewhere.'

'I've got to go.'

Talk about nought to sixty in thirty seconds. One minute he'd been lying in my bed being all nice and lovey dovey. The next he was saying he needed to get out and I didn't know where I stood. MEN.

Suddenly I was all on my ownsome in the flat.

Gone. In a puff of smoke. Well, gone in a puff of high blood pressure. He'd run that fast I expected to see skid marks on the hall carpet.

The next week he didn't come and see me once.

The week after that, the same.

I got the odd phone call. Snatched conversations. Lame excuses. *Doctor's orders. Poorly kids. Vera feeling sad.*

I was back at square one yet again.

Well. If he had no intention of leaving Blondie, maybe it was time to make Blondie want to leave him.

But how to do it?

Time to get my thinking cap on.

Chapter Eleven

Dear Vera

I'm sorry to be the bearer of bad news but your husband is having an affair. Yep. You think he goes off to work every morning but I know FOR A FACT he goes off and rogers some flirty young bint on the other side of town. Also, while we're dishing the dirt I can confirm it, it's true that he shoved his hand up that Cheryl's skirt at her eighteenth. Remember? In the lean-to? Yeah, thought you might.

Basically he's a dirty bastard and you'd be better off without him. Read that sentence a few times. It needs to sink in.

It's me, by the way. Gwen. Your next-door neighbour. I know every time you look at me you probably turn your nose up because you're a full-on skinnymalinx and I'm almost breaking the scales, but I write you this letter as a concerned and caring friend.

PLEASE NEVER SPEAK TO ME ABOUT IT. We shall say no more on the matter. It's too embarrassing and will only lead to us falling out, like we did when your late alkie mam dropped anchor in Poo Bay round our gaff. Yes, I think non-discussion is the way forward, to be a tad on the frank side.

She seems like a nice enough girl, this bit on the side. Think she'll grow into a handsome enough young woman. I

175

mean, she's no patch on you, looks-wise, but you know your problem, Vera? You're too vain. You really fancy yourself. Everyone in the cul-de-sac says it. This, as a for instance, is what I heard someone say recently in Scoop 'n' Save: Vera? She calls her own name out when she's coming. I bet when Carly Simon sang that song about Warren Beatty you blushed. I bet you went the colour of my curtains. I bet you shrieked like you was on them roller coasters up Blackpool and thought 'You're so Vain' was about you. Ha. Oh, I do make myself laugh!

I can just picture you now, reading this and shaking your head. I can just picture you in your hallway with the shiny wallpaper going, 'This is all ridiculous! What a carry-on!' It's such a carry-on, I'm surprised Sid James isn't hiding in your rockery.

Well. D'you know what to do if you don't believe me?

Follow him. Follow him one day when he leaves yours so early in the morning. You really think he goes to work at the crack of dawn? He doesn't. He goes off to his love nest and you should follow and confront him. She's a quirky little thing. On other terms you'd like her. But the time for action is now.

I do believe we shall be hearing the ringing of divorce bells in the cul-de-sac very shortly. I will not be laughing at you (well, not strictly true, we do ALL laugh at your 'going up in the middle' nets – SO common! TAKE THEM DOWN, THEY'RE EMBARRASSING, YOU ARE REALLY MAKING A SPECTACLE OF THEM HAVING THEM UP. I KNOW! I'M 'WITH IT'!).

Not a very good year for you this, is it, Vera? First your mam drops the kids off at the pool in my walk-in wardrobe. Then she nearly kills your kids in a car crash, killing herself in the process. And now this!

Keep it under your hat.

And remember. You dare talk to me about it and you'll see

what a good little actress I am when I deny knowing what the
frig you are on about.

All best wishes

Gwen from next door.

Hi Vera

It's Cheryl here.

Hasn't your Doug got big hands?

They look quite normal-sized when you just see them every
day.

But when they're up your chuff, Jesus. It were like sitting on
a really wide lamp post or something.

DON'T MENTION THIS IF I SEE YOU.

Lots of love

Cheryl xx

I was really enjoying this whole DON'T MENTION THIS IF
I SEE YOU thing. It was really tickling me. And the whole
letters from concerned neighbours thing was really tickling me
too.

Except I'd run out of neighbours I knew about.

Oh well. Time to make one up.

Dear Vera

I don't think you know me. Let's just say I live on the street
next to yours and I get to hear a lot of stories, let me tell you.
What's it like being the talk of the town? Flavour of the month?
Le mot du jour? (Look it up, it's French.)

Gosh, this new neighbour was a bit of a bitch. Snooty, full of
herself, holier than Wow!

I quite liked her!

I first clapped eyes on your husband six months ago when I'd just moved in. I'm a recently divorced, taut twenty-eight, you see. I wear them tight T-shirts that I really have to pull down over my pointy tits. And don't get me started on my nipples – they've got a mind of their own! No wonder I was Miss Wet T-Shirt at Pontins last year. And the year before that. You should see my two gold cups. What a sight for sore eyes my pair are!

And now it was getting a bit like a saucy postcard from the seaside. Or a Carry On film. Better rein it back in.

I'd just popped to the corner shop when I met your one for the first time. And honest to God Vera, he mentally undressed me with his eyes. Soiled. That's what I felt after I'd met him. Like he'd made me do dirty things. And I'd only nipped out for a Viennetta. It wasn't a nice feeling, so soon after a divorce. And I have admit, it made my Catholicism flare up again.

I can't actually bring myself to say what happened next time I popped to that shop. It was hot. I needed an ice pop to cool me down as me bay window's jammed tight and nothing seems to loosen it. Plus I'd not got round to putting my summer drapes up yet.

I don't want to say what your husband did to me with that ice pop. But let's just say, it took a boil wash to get those vivid orange stains out of the gusset of my pants.

Your husband is a cad, Vera. And I'm going to have to move house.

Beware and best wishes

Laura-Lyn Lyons

I liked that name. Laura-Lyn Lyons. I kind of wanted to meet her. I kind of wanted to be her.

I reckoned Laura-Lyn might write a second letter.

Hi there
    In case you're wondering. I'm kind of like you. But with an actual personality. Imagine THAT, V!
    Beware and best wishes
    Laura-Lyn Lyons
    P. S. V stands for many things. Including VAGINA.

I know. I was being so childish. And that could have given the game away. When wondering who might have sent these poison-pen letters they might have got to thinking they were all a bit juvenile and so the finger could have been pointed at me, the youngest card in the pack. But the ace I had hidden up my sleeve was of course that nobody would imagine I knew any of Doug's neighbours. Why would I? As far as he knew, I didn't even know where he lived.

I knew that Vera would come looking for me; it was only a matter of time. The way I saw it she had two options. Maybe three. Actually no, four.

One. Read the letters and think they were the work of a mad woman and ignore them, put them in the bin and forget about them – not even mentioning them to Doug.

That seemed unlikely so . . .

Two. Read them to Doug and he would put her mind at rest and advise no further action to be taken.

Three. Read them. Row with Doug and he comes clean.

Four. Read them. Hide them. Don't tell Doug and then follow him next time he comes to see me.

I felt like the last two options were the most likely. So I had to be prepared. There'd be some forewarning with option three as Doug would phone me and say, *She knows. And she's on her way over.*

But my woman's instinct told me she'd choose the silent but deadly treatment and want to strike when neither of us was expecting it.

And I was right.

It was a Tuesday morning. It was bright. I knew we were in for a decent kind of day because by the time Doug left me, his wetness drying between my legs, the sun was blinding, even through my thin curtains. I lay for a little while listening to Terry Wogan. Some'd say he was a bit old for my tastes, but then I'd an older boyfriend. My tastes were a bit on the anti-quey side. And there weren't nothing wrong with that. Classic taste, that's what I had.

Half an hour later I was showered and ready to face the day. I locked the flat door and took the stairs to the ground floor and, as I turned into the car park, I saw her. She was standing by a car, staring at me, chewing her bottom lip. I pretended I had no idea who she was and carried on my way, trying to act as normally as I could. Needless to say she followed me into the entry round the side of the flats.

Which is when it happened.

She caught up with me.

I'd never been in a fight in my life. I was very lucky to have coasted along through the various stages of the education system without anyone so much as punching me in the face. Oh, I'd been called all the names under the sun, but nobody had actually punched me. So when Vera grabbed my hair and smashed my head against the brick wall behind the flats out of the blue that morning as I was walking to the bus stop to go to work, I had to admit. It didn't half hurt.

Such an odd thing to do on such a beautiful day as this.

TWHACK!

It really did sound like a cartoon noise made by a superhero.

CRUNCH!

It sounded like she was breaking my bloody skull. It sounded like a bone was being crushed. I felt the graze of brick against my cheek and a sticky wetness that told me I was bleeding.

And by the time she'd finished with me it was all really bloody.

Still, by the following day, Doug had moved in with me. Bloody hell!

The plan might have inadvertently given us both black eyes, but at least the plan had worked.

I'd nearly shat myself as I took in what was happening and realized who was attacking me. Clearly those letters had had the desired effect.

'Are you the little scrubber who's fucking my husband?'

'You what?'

'You heard, slut!'

Cheeky bitch!

'We don't fuck, we make love.'

And at that she actually pissed herself. Really patronizing 'throwing her head back' stuff, and snorting like the horse in *Black Beauty*. And even though it was clear she was a bit of a beauty, this made her look ugly. Eventually she settled down. She peered at me like I was an exhibit in the museum when, let's be honest, she was old enough to be the sort of thing dug up by an archaeologist. Thirty-five if she were a day.

'Here, don't I know you?'

'Leave me alone!'

'I have. I've seen you before.'

God, her anger made her uglier by the second.

'I've never seen you before in my life! Who are you?!'

'Who are you?!' she mimicked, before slapping me round the face. 'You know full well who I am, you snivelling little tart!'

I spat in her face. I had no idea why I'd done it but maybe 'snivelling little tart' was a provocation too far. And I knew I'd have a reasonably good aim, no doubt better than any slap I could have offered. But, surprise surprise, she really didn't like that.

She wiped her face with the sleeve of her coat.

'How dare you?!?! HOW DARE YOU!!! Right, come here, you.'

And then she grabbed me by my hair again and dragged me back into the square where my low-rise block sat. And here she felt it appropriate to shout to the empty square: 'Lock up your husbands, ladies!'

'There's no ladies round here.'

'This woman –' she looked at me, all side-eyed, and corrected herself – 'this *girl* is a SLUT!!!'

'Most folk've gone to work.'

Vera looked at me like she'd just smelt some dog turd on her shoe.

'As if people round here WORK.' She almost laughed in my face.

'I work,' I pointed out.

'Oh, I'm sure she works very hard for the money.' Her eyes were narrowing. She still had tight hold of my hair.

She leaned in to me. 'You're the not the first, dearie. And you certainly won't be the last.'

Dearie? Blimey, who was she? My NAN? I squared up to her. She didn't like that. And she didn't like it when I said, 'Kind of begs the question what you're doing wrong, then. Dearie.'

'I'd kind of shut up if I were you or I'll smash your face in. Again.'

'You don't scare me, Vera.'

She flinched. Ah. Her Achilles heel. If I knew her name, then it meant we'd talked about her. And this she didn't seem to like. So I used it again.

'I feel so sorry for you, Vera.'

'Why's that? Go on. I'm all ears.'

'Well. You know. The way your arse gives off that hideous aroma when you're in bed. Not many men'd put up with that, now would they?'

She looked genuinely wrong-footed, as well she might. But then she let out this hysterical hyena-like laugh. God, she was annoying. No wonder Doug had strayed, bless him. She was a full-on freak.

'You what?'

'Trumpy Vera. That's what they call you.'

'You are seriously deluded, you batty bitch.'

I shrugged; she wouldn't get a rise out of me.

'Only what I've been told. Oh, and he says my pits smell fresher. We have a right laugh about your personal hygiene issues.'

She laughed again. 'Someone get some Polyfilla. I'm cracking up.'

'Oh, does he not mention it?'

I could see the cogs whirring in her brain. Then she carried on thinking I was bullshitting.

'You make it up as you go along, you do.'

'Maybe what you need to make up, Vera love, is some anti-perspirant deodorant. Know what I mean, kid?

She held my hair tighter. 'I . . . do not . . . smell.'

I sniffed. Smirked, then nodded.

Oh, she didn't like that. She did not like that one bit.

'If you say so, Vera. I'm sure you always smell just . . . fresh as a daisy.'

She yanked my hair down and shoved me against a nearby car. I yelped in pain as the wing mirror jabbed me in the ribs.

'I've got one question for you!'

The square was eerily silent. Every noise echoed around, ricocheting off the walls.

'D'you love him?'

'You what?'

'Do you love my husband?'

She let go of my hair. I stood up to my full height. I looked her square in the face and said one word.

'Yes.'

She had quite a lot of make-up on. But I still saw the silly moo pale. It was as if someone had cut one of her feet off, and all the blood she had in her body just whooshed out and spilled on the floor.

Pale Patsy.

White Wilma.

Faint Fanny.

God, she was grotesque. An out-and-out bully. How DARE she!

She sniffed. The veins on her neck stuck out like wires off a telly. And then she spun round and clobbered me one again. Then, flicking some imaginary fluff off her bosom, and trying to look like a lady, she walked away.

She didn't really know which way she was going; she was clearly in a daze, as she was heading to the corner of the square and there was no way out there. But a few paces later it was like she came to, and she stopped, spun round again and made a beeline for a nearby white car. I didn't know what sort of car it was but it was a smug kind of car. The sort that said, 'Look at me. I've got a second family car. My fella's got the big one, and I've got the cutesy little run-around. Aren't I ace?' She got in and took a few attempts to start the engine up. I had to stop myself from calling out, *WOMEN DRIVERS, EH?* as I realized I couldn't even drive, and maybe it was sexist and that. And then she reversed really quickly and juddered to a halt in the middle of the square. She looked at me and wound her window down.

'Well, at least we know one thing!' she spat out. 'Blokes think with their dicks and not their eyes. Look at the state of you! Marty Feldman on steroids!'

Then she did a sharp turn to her left and zoomed out of the square.

When I came home from work that night I could hear the telly was on.

Doug sat on my corner settee looking half his normal size.

'What are you doing here? Don't ever see you of a night.'

And of course I was genuinely intrigued. And excited. Like I knew what he was going to say.

Say it. Say it. SAY IT!

He said it.

'She's kicked me out,' he said in a monotone voice. My heart skipped a beat. Then another. Then another. Finally, my plan had worked. My illustrious work had paid off.

But I couldn't let him see that. I reached out and stroked his arm, as I might have done through the bars of a pen at the zoo, coyly touching a disinterested goat, unsure whether it was going to buck against you, nibble you, or nip you.

'I'm so sorry,' I lied. 'You must be feeling rotten.'

He nodded. 'Like a bad egg. Talking of which.'

And he shifted his bum and let a cracker of a fart rip out. He wafted it his way to have a quick smell, pulled a face, then batted it towards me.

I dropped my work bag, nabbed some air freshener from the side and squirted it in his direction. Was this what we'd become?

'What happened to your face?' he said, suddenly noticing the cuts and grazes I'd tried, unsuccessfully, to cover with foundation and a makeshift fringe that kept riding up.

'Don't tell me,' he said before I could answer. 'Vera happened to your face.'

'She were right angry, Doug.'

'She's got a temper on her, Shirl,' he said, pointing to his own shining black eye. 'You didn't say she smelt, did you?'

'No?'

'Oh.'

'Why?'

'Well, the last thing she said as she was chucking some of my clothes out the window was . . . "I DON'T STINK."'

And he really shouted it, which I thought was a bit unnecessary. Still, took all sorts to make a world. And I guess in a way this was his flat more than mine in as much as he'd bought it. So why shouldn't he raise his voice if he fancied? Hmm?

'So. You've moved in with me.' I sat beside him on the settee and put a scatter cushion over my knee and hugged it to me.

He nodded again. Though I have to say, he didn't look that chuffed about the whole thing.

'Well, it's good in a way, init?'

'Is it?'

'Well, yeah. We're together.'

But I could see his mind was elsewhere.

'Are you missing the kiddies?' I asked, full of faux concern.

'She's turned them against me. Keeps screaming things like – "His name's not Dad, it's BASTARD!"'

'She sounds a bit unstable. And I mean. Let's be frank. You certainly didn't get that –' I pointed at his black eye – 'by walking into a kitchen cupboard.'

'She's very angry with me.'

'She was very angry with me.'

'I'm sorry, Shirl.'

'How did she find out about us?'

'I'm so sorry, but . . . she got some anonymous letters.'

'No! Who from?'

'Well, if we knew that they wouldn't be anonymous.'

'Suppose. Eeeh, that's so weird. That's the sort of thing that happens in *Coronation Street*.'

'Is it?'

'Mm.' I nodded. I'd forgotten. He were a bit middle class, so never watched *Corrie*.

'One was from a neighbour who completely denied any knowledge of it when she showed her it.'

'What was the handwriting like?'

'They were all typed. At one point . . . and I'm sorry about this, petal. At one point I thought you might have been behind them.'

I did a massive gasp. Really impressed myself with it actually.

'Me? Whatever would I do that for?'

'Well, this is it. And besides. Whoever did write them knew a lot of what was going on in the street I live in.'

'Doug, I don't even know WHERE you live.'

'This is what I thought.'

'You know I'd never do anything to hurt you.'

'I know.'

'Except when you want me to. You know. When you like me to be a bit . . . firm . . . in the bedroom department.'

'I know it goes against your nature.'

'I'm a naive softy.'

'I know, petal.'

'A Manchester Mother Teresa.'

I was pushing it there.

'I know, baby.'

'So what were the letters saying?'

'Well, they knew about you. That's why she followed me here.'

'And then beat me up once you'd gone to work and that.'

'I'm so sorry, Shirley.'

'I feel I should tell the police,' I pretended.

'No, you can't do that.'

'But she's dangerous, Doug. What if she'd killed me?'

'But she didn't.'

'But she could have.'

'But she didn't.'

'Only coz I fought her off. And she shouted that I was a dirty little trollop to all the neighbours. And said I was going to steal their husbands off them.'

'I'm so sorry.'

'They were all out having a good old look. I didn't know where to put myself.'

'I'm going to call her. Can you leave the room, please?'

'Sorry?'

'Go and get us some chips.'

'Oh. Okay.'

When I came in twenty minutes later he was still sat in the same position. Only this time with the phone in his hands, like he'd just hung up. He glanced at me.

'Her version of events is very different, of course.'

'She had the eyes of a natural-born liar, Doug. I've never seen eyes quite like them.'

'I've always quite liked her eyes.'

'The devil's eyes. That's what I saw. She scared me, Doug. And I don't know what to do.'

'How d'you mean?'

'What if she comes back?'

'She won't.'

'With a gun.'

'She hasn't got a gun.'

'Everyone says that. But folk still get shot, don't they?'

'That's not her style.'

'Look at the evidence. She hit me, she hit you. She's completely livid with us. I . . . I'm not sure we shouldn't split up. Now. D'you want extra vinegar on these chips? I've got some in t'pantry.'

'Go 'ed, kid.'

I was playing a dangerous game. Getting him to commit by pretending to dither. It would have been so easy for him to agree with me. But fortunately he jumped at the chance to put me right. He followed me into the kitchen.

'I have to make this work, Shirley. Then none of this will have been in vain.'

'Eh?'

'I can't chuck away all those years of marriage unless it's with good reason.'

'Am I a good reason?'

He nodded.

'Right, then. We'll say no more about it. Shall I do us some bread and marge to go with these?'

Again, he nodded.

Job done.

Chapter Twelve

So. That was it. Eighteen years of age and shacked up with the man of my dreams. Life did not get much better than that, even if I said so myself. I held my head up high now in public; there was a spring, summer and every season imaginable in my step these days. I'd got what I'd always wanted. Shirley Burke was livin' the dream!

Of course, you couldn't please all of the people all of the time.

Needless to say, Mam wasn't exactly over the moon that a married man had left his wife and moved in with me. She came round to see me, so she could, in her words, 'see it with my own eyes'.

'I didn't know you had it in you, Shirley.'

'She's had it in her for ages, Mam,' said Josie, who was just leaving. Mam ignored her as her tone was smutty, to say the least. Even I had to agree with that, and I wasn't a big fan of smut. Doug was. But not me. Anyway, I just kept schtum.

As the front door banged shut Mam came into my living room and, checking the coast was clear, started unbuttoning her coat and making herself cosy on the settee. I say cosy; she always perched there as if the slightest disagreeable thing could make her scarper for the doorway. And she never actually took her coat off anywhere other than in her own home or her own place of work. It always gave the impression that she wasn't stopping long because you weren't that interesting, and there were far more important things to be getting on with else-where. But she'd sensed Doug wasn't here so could at least perch for five minutes without her younger daughter's sexuality being forced in her face.

'Would you like a cup of tea, Mam?'

She shook her head. 'Me duodenal's playing up. I can't keep anything down.'

'Right.'

The window in the bedroom was open and a gust of wind through it made one of the doors slam shut. Mam suddenly looked alarmed and clutched the arm of the settee as if she was about to be hurtled out of it.

'What was that?!'

'Bedroom door, I think.'

'He's not here, is he?!'

'If you mean Doug . . .'

'Well, I don't know what his name is!'

'Then no, he's not. He's at work. He's got a very good job.'

'And dubious morals. What is the world coming to? What is Oldham coming to?!'

'I don't know, Mam.'

'Nobody knows. And yet there you are. One of the main perpetrators!'

'Perpetrators of what?!'

She sighed. I don't think she knew herself.

'I knew kids were sent to test you, but you and our Josie, you've taken it to the max.'

I let that one settle, saying nowt. Just leaving her to her thoughts and words. It wasn't like she was looking for any explanations or answers. She had just come here to be dramatic, and to make me suffer in some way.

'To the max,' she said again, shaking her head.

I still said nowt. Let her witter. Wittering's what she did best. That's what she'd obviously come here to do as well as all the other things.

'Her having a baby out of wedlock. RUINING her chances on the beauty circuit. Unless they come up with Miss Pregnancy 1980, which I might add is highly unlikely.'

All right, Mam, we do know.

'And now you. You who wouldn't say boo to a goose. Suddenly finds yourself box and cox with a married man! What's his wife had to say about all this?'

I lied, of course. 'She's dead happy for us.'

That threw her. 'Is she a simpleton?'

'Not that I know of.'

'Then I do believe you're telling me porkies, young lady. I bet she's livid. Her fella . . . leaving her . . . for someone who's practically . . . a SCHOOL GIRL!'

'I'm at secretarial college, Mother. I'm doing two days a week placement in a proper workplace. You'd know all this if you ever bothered to ask.'

She couldn't look at me. 'You're a child. And he must be mucky.'

'Well if you don't like it, disown me. Like you disowned our Josie. See if I care.'

After that she didn't have much to say to me.

I got up and made her a cup of tea anyway. Well, it's just what you did at times like this, wasn't it? It was as if somebody had died and it was a shock and nobody knew what to say. So you took to your displacement activities: tea making, bedroom tidying, hoovering. I handed her the cup of tea but she just continued staring at the carpet. I pulled up an occasional table and put it next to her.

'Just in case you change your mind.'

'His poor wife,' she repeated. Then she jolted upright. 'I don't know her, do I?'

I shook my head. She looked relieved.

'Are you gonna disown me or what?'

And she didn't reply. She stood quickly, buttoning her coat up again.

'I only came out to get some scrag-end for your dad's tea.'

'Does he know about this?'

'Does he heck as like! D'you want to drive him into an early grave with a heart attack or a . . . a cardiac arrest or . . . or a coronary? Or something similar? Coz that's what'll happen, lady. You mark my words. And when we're standing at his graveside don't be upset when I say, "I told you so".'

'Okay. I just wondered.'

'Well, you know what wondering did.'

I didn't, but I knew better than to ask.

'Isn't a cardiac arrest the same as a coronary?'

'Don't get clever with me, lady.'

There was a lull in the conversation. Well, to be more honest there was a lull in her moaning on, so I just let the silence hang there.

'I brought this all on meself,' she said, right quiet.

'How d'you mean, Mam?'

'I've been here before.'

She stood up and went over to the window.

'How d'you mean?'

But she didn't answer.

'Mam? How d'you mean, you've been here before? To this flat? Your kids letting you down? What?'

'These flats.'

'Right.'

Well, she'd lived in the area most of her life, so I didn't see what was so interesting about that. She took a swig of her tea, then I saw her rubbing her neck slowly with the hand that weren't holding the cup.

'January the twenty-eighth. Nineteen fifty-four.'

'Were these flats built then? I fancied they were newer than that.'

'Go and find Nelly in flat fourteen, they said. This was before I met your dad.'

The way she was speaking. It was so weird. She was speaking with a tone I'd never heard before. All quiet and on the one level. Like she was in some sort of trance.

'Nelly'll look after you, they said. She'll know someone who can help.'

'What you on about?'

'Nelly said I had to take these pills. She got them for me. She said if I took them and they didn't work, I'd to come back and she knew someone who'd be able to help me. So I went away and I took them. Only nothing happened. So a few days later I came back.'

'Pills for what?'

'Of course she didn't really know anyone else who could help. It was her all the way.'

And somehow I knew. In that second. I knew.

She'd been pregnant.

She'd been having a baby.

And she'd come here to get rid of it.

'Were you pregnant, Mam?'

'She told me to get a household syringe from the iron-monger's. She'd provide the rest.'

'Mam?'

'This wasn't her flat, though, where we went. Number fourteen. She was keeping an eye on it for someone. Don't know who. Didn't care then, don't care now. Coz of course she couldn't take me to her real place. In case I told the police. I was so scared. Scared of my mam finding out. Work. I had nothing.'

'Who was the dad?'

'Well, he wasn't yours, Shirley. Don't go thinking that. She had antiseptic. Hot water. Big bar of soap. And she stuck the needle inside me. And it was like the whole world fell out of me. In the end I had to put bandages in my knickers and go home and call for Doctor Elgin. Who of course had to send me to hospital, so the world and his wife found out. Which is what I didn't want. Thirty-six hours I was vomiting for, on and off. And the blood. Near killed me.'

'But you're glad you did it?'

Mam doesn't say anything. Just takes a sip of her tea and watches something out in the street. I hear a car quietly revving up and driving off.

I was suddenly overwhelmed by a feeling of anger.

I almost felt sorry for her.

She had the brass neck to sit there and tell me something so sad and traumatic.

And yet what did she want our Josie to do?

Have a flaming abortion!

I was going to give her a piece of my mind.

I was going to give her what for.

I was going to berate her for her hypocrisy.

But in the end I couldn't be arsed.

'I'm going for a bath,' I said.

She didn't even look round.

And so I did. I went for a bath.

Few minutes later I heard her leaving.

I ended up drinking the rest of her tea, cold. I didn't really mind cold tea.

Living with Doug was actually quite nice. I'd sometimes thought it was idealistic, unrealistic of me to think that living together would be swell. When the only time you got to see your beloved was a few hours each morning it was easy to think that full-time living together would be ideal, when actually the reality might be that you'd both end up hating each other. So I was quite prepared to grow tired of Doug when he moved in with me.

But actually we dovetailed quite nicely in the scheme of things. We stopped having sex in the mornings and started doing it at night-time instead. That was a novelty. And I enjoyed being a good old-fashioned housewife, making meals and cleaning round, making myself nice. He appreciated it and I appreciated his gratitude. It was win-win, really.

And Vera, amazingly, left him alone. I thought she'd be kicking the grate in every night or ringing in the early hours crying that she had a mouse in her kitchen or something. She struck me as that type. But no. She kept well away. I even grew a grudging respect for her, if I'm honest. I'd won and she'd conceded defeat. Fair play to her. Maybe she wasn't as stupid as she looked.

The only downside for Doug, I could tell, was his separation from the kids. Any fool could see it was playing on his mind. But what could I do to put that right?

Oh, I knew! I knew all right.

'Well, we'll have a kid then,' I said one night, as we were watching *Blankety Blank* together.

'It doesn't work like that.'

'Like what?'

'You can't see your kids so you have another one to make up for it.'

'Don't see why not.'

'Behave, Shirl.'

I sometimes didn't like that. The way he affected superiority and made out he was brainier than me. Even though I was, in his eyes, just a girl, I knew I wasn't stupid. And I knew a little kiddie would be just what the doctor ordered. I knew that he'd take one look at a wee baby and he'd melt. There and then. Into a puddle like the Wicked Witch of the West in *The Wizard of Oz*. He'd told me so many times about how overcome he was when each of his kiddies were born, about how he'd almost fainted with excitement at the maternity hospital. I knew. I just knew a baby would make him happy.

'Don't you be taking your cap out, now,' he said, next time we had sex.

'As if!' I guffawed, the cheeky tyke!

But truth be told I'd not put it in for ages. I knew. I knew if we had a little baby together, everything would be perfect. And then Vera, conspicuous by her absence or not, would have no hold over what we had together now. The problem was I'd not got pregnant. Bar making Doug have his sexy ways with me while I was doing a handstand, I'd tried everything. But like the magazines said. It'd only be a matter of time.

And any road. I had the small matter of getting ready to be an aunty to busy myself with.

It was fair to say that our Josie didn't take to pregnancy like a duck to water. She resented the fact that she couldn't get bladdered any more and . . . well, that was it really: she resented the fact she couldn't get bladdered any more. She missed going out and getting on it. She missed boogying the night away up

Handbags on the Chadderton Road. She missed knocking the ale back and snogging blokes and swapping lipsticks in the ladies', then getting chips on the way home and being sick in the gutter. She missed scrapping with other girls in the queue for the night bus. It was stuff like that that made her tick. Like a pigging clock. She felt, in her words, that she'd got . . . boring.

'But you've got to get boring sooner or later, Josie, or t'baby'll end up a bit . . .'

'Mongified? I know.'

'No. Well . . .'

I didn't like words like that. There was a girl on our course whose sister had disabilities and the way she went on about them, it really made you think.

I looked around my small familiar kitchen and tried to change the subject and brighten the mood.

'Have you thought of any names yet?'

'Oh yeah,' our Josie said, taking a swig of a glass of squash, 'I'm gonna call it Parasite.'

'Don't say that, Josie.'

'Why? That's how it feels. Eating away at me, it is. And d'you know the worst thing?'

'What?'

I wondered what it could be. I'd have said thinking your baby was a parasite that was eating away at you was a pretty lousy thing.

'It's made *him* fancy me even more.'

'Bob Carolgees?'

'Mm.' She didn't sound impressed. 'He does me head in, Shirl. He can't do enough for me. Opening doors, telling me how much he loves me. I can't remember the last brew I made; he's always getting to the kettle before me and going, "What would you like, my precious?" And I'm like, "Fucking hell, man. Tea. What d'you think? It's not like I can neck an absinthe." And he thinks I'm joking and goes, "Mood swings, hormones all over the place. Isn't pregnancy great?" And I'm like, "Do one, Tonto." God, he gets on me tits.'

'Well, at least he's attentive.'

'You'd think, wouldn't you? That blokes'd go off women who had puffy ankles and bad backs and mood swings. But no. You're spreading their genes, aren't you? And I don't mean Gloria Vanderbilts!' She had a right laugh at that.

'You what?'

'Gloria Vanderbilts.'

'I don't know who she is.'

'It's a type of jeans.'

'Oh, right.'

'It's dead funny. By rights you should be pissing yourself.'

'Oh, right.' And then I did a really loud, sarcastic laugh.

Which she was completely unimpressed by.

We carried on eating in silence, but there was one thought I couldn't get out of my head. I'd had it before but it was becoming more tangible now. I could. I could reach out and touch it.

If I couldn't have a baby. Maybe I could have hers. She really didn't seem to want this Parasite. Whereas if I had this Parasite, maybe I could pass it off as mine and Doug's.

I mean, Josie'd be in on the secret. She could tell Mam and Bob Carolgees, and anyone who wanted to listen, for that matter, that she'd lost the baby. And if I'd done enough preparation, I could then say I'd had an early labour and – HEY PRESTO! – look! A little baby boy or girl of my own.

Well, mine and Doug's own.

But would Josie buy it?

There was only one way to find out.

* * *

199

Josie was still working up Barnes Wallis so I decided to head there one night after secretarial college. She'd taken up residency on a hardbacked chair near the Snacketeria and was prone to shouting out like a lazy lifeguard at a municipal pool, 'OI! GET BACK ON YOUR OWN TRAMPOLINE, FATSO! I SAW THAT!' And: 'AN ORDERLY QUEUE AT THE SNACK-ETERIA, PLEASE! JESUS!'And then there was: 'GLASSES OFF, FOUR EYES! CHRIST ON A BIKE!'

I could see she was in a grumpy mood, so thought I'd better butter her up, bit like the jacket potatoes on sale in the Snack-eteria.

I knew the way to this woman's heart was always going to be through her stomach. So I offered to take her to the Wimpy bar when she clocked off. She clocked off immediately, the greedy cow.

We both ordered hamburgers and tucked in with gusto. I could see her visibly relax. So I struck while my iron was hot.

'I've been thinking.'

'Oh aye?'

She knew I was fishing for something. I could tell.

'You don't really want this baby, do you?'

She shrugged.

'And I'd love one.'

'Would you?' She looked and sounded surprised.

'Yeah. So I got to thinking. And I know you'll think I'm daft, so hear me out. But when you have the baby. You could . . . like . . . give it to me.'

'You said this before once, but I thought you were joking.'

'Well, I probably was. But I'm not now.'

'Why the fuck would you want a baby, Shirl?'

'Coz it'd round everything off dead nicely. Now that Doug's with me and . . .'

'You want a baby?'

'Well, we've been trying. Well, I have. And it's not really been working so . . .'

'You want a pigging baby, Shirl?'

'Yeah. I was just thinking of something that might suit us both, really.'

She stared at her hamburger. Then took another bite.

'What d'you reckon?' I said, floundering a bit now.

'I don't know what to think.'

'Do you want this baby, Josie?'

She hesitated.

'You should know.'

'Sometimes I do. And . . . and sometimes I wonder if I'm just having it to spite Mam. Coz she's so dead set against it. But mostly . . . mostly I think I do.'

'Right.'

Well, that was news to me. First I'd heard of it and all that.

'Well then, that's good. That's good that you know. I thought you didn't, you see.'

'You know I didn't plan for it, Shirl. But when I'm lying there of a night, and I can't sleep. And he's . . . snoring away beside me. It's just me and the baby. And it feels good, Shirl. It feels right. And I can't get rid of that.'

'No, of course. Forget I ever said anything.'

I was embarrassed now. Talk about making a show of yourself.

'You'll get pregnant, Shirley. You'll have your own baby. You'll just have to give it time.'

'I guess so.'

'I know so.'

And that, it would appear, was that. We quickly changed the conversation and enjoyed our burgers as if we were two normal sisters out for the evening. Not sisters where one had asked to have the other one's baby. The more I thought about it as we ate and chatted, the more bizarre my request appeared to have been. What had I been thinking? No wonder she'd said no.

It was me going to Muriel's funeral all over again. Bloody madness!

I'd have to find another way to round off our family nicely.

And I was sure I would.

One night I had a dream that I was in the square outside the flats and Vera turned up in her car. She didn't see me as I was hiding behind a motorbike, observing. She went up to the door of the flats and rang the buzzer to mine. Only no-one came to see her. She stepped back and shouted up to the window.

'Doug? Douglas?!'

She wanted him back. And I had to stop her.

She was wearing a gypsy skirt and a denim jacket. She'd dyed her hair bright orange as well, though it didn't strike me as odd, this being a dream. And for some reason, instead of a handbag, she was clutching a bright green plastic watering can that dripped water every time she moved.

How was I going to stop her?

Stupidly, but handily for me, she had left the engine of her car running so I darted forwards and jumped into the driver's seat. Despite in real life not being able to drive, I put my foot down and drove straight at her. I was so quick she didn't even have time to turn round to see me approaching. I flattened her. It was most satisfying. I then reversed the car back and parked it before getting out and looking about. Nobody had seen. Vera lay dead in the path up to my entrance, but nobody had seen. Her gypsy skirt had skid marks all up it, and the watering can had exploded into a thousand tiny pieces, so that she was now lying not in a pool of blood but a pool of water.

Without giving it a second thought, the way you do in dreams, I opened the main door and then dragged her by the armpits up to my flat. She was surprisingly light and left only a few watery stains on the stairs. Once in the flat I decided the best place to hide her was under the bed. I stuck a Glade air freshener under there with her, in case she went off and started to smell. Like fish.

Doug came home and I made a nice smelly tea, to try to smell the flat out. It was a spicy curry, something I wasn't that keen on and Doug was surprised I'd made it, but at least it covered up the smell of the rotting corpse. Next we knew his kids had turned up saying their mam hadn't come back from the hairdresser's. What a to-do and a hoo-ha! Next the police called round saying Vera hadn't been seen for ages and rumour was she'd been murdered. They looked all over the flat. Just as they were about to delve under the bed . . .

I woke up.

The dream stayed with me all of the next day. I felt a flush of revulsion and shame every time I thought about it. But then the next day every time I thought about it, it actually made me chuckle a bit. The shame and revulsion were clearly wearing off, and what I was left with was a sense of intrigue. A string of . . . what ifs?

What if this actually happened?

What if I did actually kill her?

No. This was madness, surely. Utter tosh. Come on, Shirl, get a grip! You weren't bonkers, lass. You just had an overactive imagination.

A lot of geniuses did!

I mean. I wasn't going to. Of course I wasn't going to.

I was no murderer.

This was a kind of game I was playing with myself. A game

of dare, if you like. Dare to imagine the unimaginable. Dare to think the unthinkable.

What if I did actually kill Vera? What would happen then?

Well, you'd go to prison, I'd argue with myself.

Not if you didn't get caught, I'd over-rule.

But you'd never get away with it, I told myself.

You might, if you were clever enough, I'd argue.

I really was in a daze thinking about it.

But d'you wanna know something? I liked this game.

The biggest problem was . . . and I couldn't believe I was even entertaining this. But it was only make-believe, it was only pretend. The biggest problem was that if I murdered Vera, then them kiddies'd have to come and live with Doug. And did I really want that?

No, I flaming well did not.

Or worse. I'd have to go and live with Doug and the kids in the smart little street. And then Gwen next door would recognize me as the Pretty Lady and it'd all come out about how I'd written the poison-pen letters. And then one thing might lead to another and then folk'd be thinking that I'd bumped Vera off. And I had. Oh, it was all too ghastly for words, really.

I got back to my typing.

But then my mind would creep back.

If I was going to kill her, how would I do it? What was the foolproof way of bumping someone off and not being caught? How did you actually get away with murder?

These fantasies made me feel all warm inside.

But that's all they were. Fantasies.

Running her over was good. But I'd be seen or heard by someone, surely.

Mind you, I could steal someone else's car and wear some sort of disguise. All it would take would be for me to follow her for a week or two, work out her regular movements. Take it from there. See if there was anywhere she went regularly that was particularly remote, somewhere where the harsh squeal of brakes as I accelerated towards her wouldn't be heard.

And then I remembered that I couldn't drive.

Maybe I could take lessons. Pass my test.

I'd only need a few lessons. Under a false name. I just had to master the basics; I didn't need to know how to do reverse parking or a three-point turn if all I had to do was plough into a Barbara from *The Good Life* lookalike.

Having these fantasies stopped me feeling scared about losing Doug. So there was no harm in them, eh?

Maybe I could go to her house, again in disguise, and present myself as a Pretty Lady.

But that wasn't going to work. No way. She'd recognize me instantly and never let me over the threshold. Also, she might've got gobby on the doorstep, shouting the odds again, and the last thing I needed if I was going to bump her off was for people to know I'd been to her house, been seen with her. That wouldn't do at all.

Well, at least I knew I had to – publicly, at least – keep my distance.

See? Thinking like this stopped me fretting about him.

But it was hard to be distant when you were trying to kill someone, I told myself. I would have to get up close and personal with her if I was to end her life. And thereby lay the conundrum. I had to make sure I was never ever linked to her, so that no-one would say, 'Oh I bet she did it. That Shirley. I saw her with her not so long ago.' Et cetera.

Was it possible to commit murder remotely?

Maybe, if I could work out how to make a letter bomb.

But then she might not pick up the post. She might've got

one of the kids to do it and I didn't want to off any of them, I just wanted to get Vera.

Blimey. Did I really hate her that much?

I realized I was getting a bit carried away with this.

I didn't really want to kill her.

Did I?

And yet the fantasies were more and more comforting. I found them compelling and challenging in a good way, whereas you'd think I'd be unnerved by them, shocked at myself.

No way, José.

I needed some inspiration. I needed advice from someone who'd never ever blab. I needed to feel less alone with my madness.

I took myself to the library. Not my library. I wore my disguise and told them I was a budding crime writer and did they have anything that could tell me how to commit the perfect murder and get away with it. Ooh those librarians, they loved a challenge. After a bit of heave ho-ing and fingering through various shelves, one of them returned and smiled.

'Miss Dubois! You're in luck. I've found just the thing.'

She guided me to a little table in the corner of the library where she'd found a book called *So! You Wanna Be a Crime Writer?!* by Jessamy Brookes.

What a glamorous name that was. Jessamy Brookes.

And within its pages were untold treasures about what to think about when penning a novel that would hit the shelves and the bestsellers lists and make you into the next . . . well . . . whoever the big crime writers were.

Chapter five was called 'How to Get Away with Murder'.

I took a notepad from my bag and got scribbling. Scribbling would continue the game, stop me angsting over Douglas.

Gosh, there was so much advice. The library building was

like a sixties glass cube and I kept expecting passers-by on the street outside to stop and peer in and just KNOW what I was up to.

I made notes such as *Clear up after yourself. Oxygenated bleach is best.*

As if a murderer would leave the place filthy.

Another bit of advice was *Pick someone at random.*

Well, I didn't write that down. I already had my victim, thank you very much. Though I liked the word random. I needed, I felt, to make the killing look random.

There was a section called 'Proximity'. It told me: *Don't be on the road for hours as you might get tired and unfocused.*

I wrote that down. Not sure why.

Commit the crime in another town.

I liked this idea. If Vera was somewhere else for a while I could have killed her there and then not be linked to her. If she was murdered in Blackpool, what links had I there?

But then I read the next piece of advice.

Get yourself an alibi.

Now there was a problem. I would need Doug to be my alibi. But if I was out murdering his wife, he'd know I wasn't there.

Unless I decided to do it late at night and he was sleeping.

But sometimes he was such a light sleeper.

Oh yes.

Oh yes.

I would drug him.

But what with?

I had no drugs.

I might get some.

I'd have to get some.

I could go and visit my doctor and say I was having trouble sleeping and could I have some sleeping pills. I'd never take them and then crush them into his late-night snack so that he was out like a light and wouldn't hear me leaving the flat.

Now that was a genius idea. Even if I said so myself.

So there was my alibi. Excellent.

Don't be in the area when the police investigations begin.

Hmm. Difficult one. Because if I killed her at home I would sort of be in the area as she only lived three miles away.

Maybe Jessamy meant just not to be in the immediate area. Like, hanging round Vera's front garden watching the police get to work. That would look suspicious.

Then there was a list of 'Types of Murder'.

All the obvious ones were there: shooting, strangulation, stabbing, poison.

But then she'd put another on the list.

Crucifixion.

CRUCIFIXION!

I couldn't quite get my head round this. I pictured myself constructing a crucifix in Vera's back garden, then trying to coax her onto it. I couldn't see that happening for some reason.

But still. Blimey. Crucifixion. You certainly couldn't accuse this Jessamy of not trying to cover all bases.

Under the header 'Don't Get Caught' was a list of really obvious things like – yet again – *Clean up after yourself* and *Don't leave any evidence.*

Actually, this Jessamy was starting to get on my nerves. I could have written this bloody book, so much of it was so obvious.

But then maybe not every reader had murdering tendencies like me.

I looked at the photo of her on the back cover flap. All soft focus, not unlike a hazier version of the wife in *Some Mothers Do 'Ave 'Em.*

Jessamy Brookes is the internationally renowned best-selling author of eighteen crime novels as part of her Lucy Lovering Investigates series, famously adapted for TV, starring Joan Van Ark. A graduate of Harvard, Jessamy now lives in Minnesota with her five cats and twins Jesteban and Jester, on a farm where, she says, 'You could bury one helluva lot of bodies!'

What an annoying cow. I flicked back to the inside of the book and a section called 'Timing Is All', which told me to commit the murder in the early hours and not to look out of place wherever I was doing it. This was accompanied by a cartoon of a clown walking through an empty street. I was beginning to feel ever so slightly patronized now. Jessamy added: *Most people are asleep in the early hours of the morning.*

You don't say, Jess!

Maybe I'd picked the wrong victim. Maybe I needed to be boarding a Freddie Laker and getting over to Minnesota with my strangling mitts on.

No. That wasn't part of the game.

Then, in a section called 'Top Tips', there was some better advice. To pay for any tools for the job with cash so you couldn't be traced, to destroy any receipts or plastic bags used in the purchase of said tools. To always wear rubber gloves, and to plan and purchase everything a good month in advance of the killing.

Getting better, Jessamy love. Think you just saved yourself from the noose, honey!

The final piece of advice, after several pages of flicking, was to avoid watching TV or reading the papers for a good month after the killing. Jessamy reckoned the police used this time and the media to psych the killer out. This too made complete sense. One should go about one's daily business as if nothing had happened, act normally, not be wound up by inaccuracies or stuff put out there to wind you up.

Fair enough, Jess. You can rest easy in your bed now.

As I scribbled the last of my notes down I heard some wheels passing me and looked up to see a young mam pushing a baby round in a big old pram. The mam was about my age and quite shabbily dressed. She had a love bite on her neck and as well as clutching the handlebar of the pram she was also clutching twenty Lambert & Butlers. Her hair was lank, though she'd clearly put a brush through it. All signs, possibly, that the baby would be malnourished, or a second thought. But when I looked in the pram the little thing was overdressed to within an inch of its life. Big frilly woollen hat, big frilly woollen coat, and she looked as if she was laughing. Gurgling away as if having a conversation with herself. And in that second I got an actual stab in the chest of jealousy. That's what I wanted. I wanted to be pushing that pram and having that gurgling child, and I didn't.

I smiled at the child but she was too young to clock me really, and her mam swung the pram round and they disappeared down the children's aisle. Well, whatever people might have said about a young mam, she was definitely taking care of that healthy looking baby, even going so far as to be getting books out of the library for her.

And what was I doing?

Sitting on my ownsome, reading a book about how to get away with murder, taking notes. Which one of us had their life more on track, me or her?

Her. Definitely her.

The librarian was walking towards me. Even she probably had her life more on track than me.

'Is that the sort of thing you were after?'

'Sorry?'

Was she asking me about the baby?

'The book. For your crime writing.'

'Oh. Yes. Perfect. Thank you so much.'

'We aim to please. Would you like to take out membership?'

'No, thanks. I'm only visiting. I've made some notes.'

I stood, looked about, like I was leaving a date that hadn't gone that well.

'It's a . . . lovely place you have here,' I said, motioning towards the room with my hand. I sounded posher now. I was good at voices.

'Thank you. We like it.'

I made my excuses and left.

I'd maybe had enough of this game.

Time to pack it in, Shirley.

On one of the buses home I wondered why I suddenly felt so desolate. On paper I had everything I'd ever hoped for. Shacked up with a bloke who loved me, who'd chosen me over his beautiful wife. I was mostly enjoying my time at secretarial college. The few day placements I had each week were going well, and all was on track for me to pass with flying colours. A good job beckoned, hopefully up the hospital, where my spelling and typing skills would come into their own. But something was leaving me feeling incomplete. Was it the lack of a baby? I'd never really craved one before. I didn't really have myself down as the maternal type. I wanted a career first, family later.

Maybe it was that constant niggle that somewhere else Doug had a better offer. Or if not a better offer, then at least an alternative. The wife and the kids and the semi and the garden. Maybe I'd be better suited to a bloke who just had eyes and thoughts for me. Where there was no competition, even if this time I was the winner. Something about the situation didn't sit right with me.

When I got in the flat was empty. I called out for Doug but he wasn't there. I looked at the clock in the kitchen. Funny. He'd usually be home from work by now. I pottered for a bit and had a look in the freezer. I pulled out two chicken Kievs and bobbed them in the oven. Maybe he'd be back by the time they were done. I took a packet of Smash out of one of the cupboards and went about turning the lumpy powder into mashed potato. I was just stirring it into a thick paste when the phone rang.

We had a nice phone. Wall-mounted. When I was on it I liked to pretend I was in some American sitcom on the telly. They had wall-mounted phones with huge cables that meant you could walk the length and breadth of your flat with the receiver.

'Hello?'

'Shirley?'

It was Doug.

'Shirley, I won't be coming back tonight.'

'Oh, right. Why?'

'Well . . . thing is . . . I've got back with Vera.'

The receiver shook in my hand. I didn't say owt.

'Oh. And I think it might be time to move on.'

'Move on?'

'Find another flat. Your own flat. I can't keep bankrolling you no more.'

'I've got to go, Doug. My chicken Kiev's burning.'

I hung up before he could say anything else.

The chicken Kiev was burning. But I ignored it.

I just sat at the kitchen table and remembered one of the words I'd scribbled down.

Crucifixion.

Oh, this would not do. I had to have a word with myself.

I was a normal teenage girl with dreams. I did not want to kill anyone or spend any time behind bars. I had to box cleverer than that. I had to come up with a better plan to keep my man.

I had to be more ambitious for myself. Keep him. Make things on this side of the street the sunnier side. Keep her in the shadows.

I just had to work out how to flaming well do it.

Shirley Burke? Get your thinking cap on. And get it on quick.

RACHEL

2017

Chapter Thirteen

I have spent so much time at my laptop these past twenty-four hours I feel like I'm having an affair with it. It is my life force, my soul mate; I deify it. It's part of me; it's my right arm. I think the world revolves around it. When my phone rang earlier I searched the keyboard of my laptop wondering how to pick up. Thank heavens for the internet. In days of yore I wouldn't have been able to sit in the relative comfort of my own pad in Bloomsbury searching the world's archives, I'd have had to visit a library or a private detective to learn more about my history. But here, thanks to one Sir Timothy Berners-Lee, I have the world at my fingertips.

I feel guilty. I've always felt my baby was my constant companion, my best friend. To be usurped by a piece of technology doesn't seem right.

Stuff that. I have a job to do.

Private detective. Private detective.

Oh my God. I know one. Who's now a vicar. Maybe I should give him a call.

I check my phone and see I still have the vicar's number in my contacts list so, grabbing the bull by the horns, I call him. I'm not even sure what I'm going to say to him. It rings for what feels like an eternity before an answerphone kicks in.

It's his landline so it's an official vicarage message – fancy not being there for your parishioners – and eventually there's a beep and I stumble over my words but finally come out with . . .

'Oh, hi. Father. It's me. Rachel. Rachel Taylor. You like . . . buried my mum the other day. I have a favour. I think. It's just. Well. Certain things have come to light since Mum died and . . . well, I need to pick your brains about something. I need to speak to a private detective, I think. To try and trace someone, well, some people possibly, from when I was little. And I wondered if you had any contacts who might be able to help. In London, preferably. That's just where I am. I think you have my number. But if you haven't it's . . .'

And then I give the number and hang up. I don't even say thank you. Rude!

I then remember it's Sunday morning. He's probably taking a service. So, maybe he is there for his parishioners after all.

Anyway. Back to the internet. What have I learned?

Right. So. If I am baby Diana Wilson, this is what I know about myself.

I was born in a maternity hospital in Birmingham a few days before the royal wedding in 1981. My parents Linda and Les took me home the next day. On the day of the wedding, my Mum was washing-up in the kitchen and she'd left me in a pram on the patio bit of their back garden. She left me there for only a few minutes. When she went out to check on me, the pram was empty. A nationwide hunt began to find me and get me back. Nearly a month later I was found in a cottage in a village in North Wales with the woman who had stolen me. I was well cared for. The woman who stole me was called Shirley Burke. She was nineteen and had been seeing a married man for a while. When he had threatened to end the relationship she had pretended to be pregnant to lure him away from his wife. A neighbour at the North Wales cottage raised the alarm as she felt Shirley Burke resembled the facial composite of the baby-snatcher that had been shown on the news. Shirley Burke claimed to be mentally ill, but was still sent to prison for years. The country was elated that Diana had been reunited with her relieved and jubilant mother Linda.

Right. So.

The most shocking thing about this is that my parents seemed to be married. Well, they were at least an item when the abduction took place. I had always been brought up to believe that my dad was some dim and distant one-night stand that my mum never bothered with and who'd not had the slightest interest in me or bringing me up. He was so dim and distant, in fact, that he wasn't even mentioned on my birth certificate. But then my birth certificate had my new name on it. Rachel Taylor. And it said my mum's name was Jane Taylor. Had Mum forged this? Had she paid someone to make it up? Or could you change names on birth certificates when you changed names by deed poll? That didn't seem right. My mind is swirling at how duplicitous my mum has been.

Where is my dad now? Is he still alive? Did he have any idea where I was living all these years? Or was Mum being honest all that time? Did he have no desire to see me? All those times at school when I was sick with jealousy that all the other girls had dads, no matter how distant they were, and I had a big fat zero. Had that been a misinformed waste of time? A complete waste of energy?

It certainly is starting to look that way.

I was apparently discovered in a house called Lovers' Leap Cottage in a village in Wales called Loggerheads. I have searched and searched on YouTube to see if there are any documentaries or news clips, but there is nothing. I certainly don't register there. If I enter 'Diana Wilson Baby Snatch' it just comes up with similar cases in America from very recent years.

All this searching has certainly made me interested in Loggerheads. In that cottage. In that street. Having read that it was a neighbour who had tipped the police off, I want to go there. I want to find that person and say thank you. Thank you for twitching your net curtain and being nosy enough to know that something was awry.

The last article I managed to find – and I couldn't find many because of course my abduction predated the invention of the internet – was an interview with Linda a few years after we had been reunited. It explained a lot, and left a load of new questions too. I found it in a collection of interviews by some old tabloid hack. Ursula Sanders was a middle-aged woman, long since dead, who did emotional pieces with high-profile women. My mother being one of them. Some student in Durham had typed out all the recordings of her interviews and put them online as part of their dissertation.

God knows what they were studying, but I was very grateful they'd done this odd thing.

Oh, and she interviewed Barbara Taylor Bradford, but that's for another day.

I've printed it out and will carry it everywhere from now on. Proof of who I am and what I went through. Proof I'm not who I always thought I was. They feel like magic papers that hold the keys to a weird and wonderful kingdom. A kingdom I was once part of but now have no idea whether it really existed or not. But here is the proof. For what it's worth.

This is what it says.

US: Linda, if I may . . .

LW: Of course.

US: I'd like you to cast your mind back, if you could, to those dark, dark days when Diana was taken. Can you talk us through what actually happened when . . .

LW: Shirley Burke?

US: When Shirley Burke broke into your back garden and took tiny little Diana.

LW: We'd had her home from hospital a few days. It was the beginning of the summer holidays and the weather was lovely, so I'd taken to putting her in her pram and parking her out on the back patio for a bit each morning, before it got too hot at midday. Les was off work as it was the Royal Wedding and he was pottering and I was washing up. The radio was on. 'Stand and Deliver' was playing by Adam and the Ants. I quite liked them so I turned it up. How I wish I'd never turned it up. And then I popped out to check on Diana and that's when I saw . . .

US: What did you see?

LW: The pram was empty.

US: What did you think?

LW: I thought Les must've come round the side of the house and taken her so I called to him. Asked if she was all right. When he came into the kitchen empty handed I knew immediately something was wrong.

US: A lot of people let their babies sit outside in their prams, don't they?

LW: They do. I did. And I regret that.

US: It wasn't an open invitation.

LW: Looking back it feels like it was. On one level I know it's normal. But on another, I know I kind of hated myself more than I hated Shirley Burke back then.

US: Which must be hard.

221

LW: It really is.

US: Going back to that day.

LW: Okay.

US: I believe the next thing that happened was that the area went into lockdown.

LW: Yes. But it was too late. By the time the police arrived we'd lost twenty minutes. Shirley Burke was already driving off in a car with Diana in the back. From then on in it was bedlam. I can't remember too much about it if I'm honest, but it was when I saw policemen searching the bins outside the house that I realized they thought that I might have had something to do with it. They'd cordoned off all the local streets, thinking if might have been a neighbour or a kiddie but . . .

US: Take your time Linda.

LS: I don't remember much about any of the time Diana was away. I just catch images of myself sometimes. Hoovering the nursery. Scrubbing everything with bleach to within an inch of its life. Watching stuff on telly. Inoffensive, daft stuff. Happy families in adverts. I'd be sat there thinking, oh it's all right for you. With your home-cooked meals and your ten million kids. Where's mine? My baby had just vanished into thin air. I was worried no-one believed me. I thought I was going mad. Thankfully some-one had seen Shirley Burke at the bus stop over the way and they were able to help the police with a facial composite, otherwise who knows if we'd've got Diana back?

US: The police were pretty convinced she was alive all along, weren't they?

LW: They were. They said they were sure whoever had taken her had lost a baby and would be looking on Diana as their own and so wouldn't harm her. Whatever the circumstances were, this woman would be treating her well. I just hoped this was true, of course.

US: It seemed that the whole nation was holding its breath.

LW: Well, I certainly was. I had a few fainting fits actually. Never had them before or since. I think it was because I just kept forgetting to breathe.

US: And then almost a month later . . .

LW: We got the phone call. Les and I were in the middle of . . . well, let's just say a very heated argument. He was trying to get me to face facts.

US: Which were?

LW: The facts as he saw them were that Diana was dead and I needed to get used to the idea.

US: You're no longer with your husband, are you?

LW: We were put under a lot of strain.

US: Do you think if Diana hadn't been taken you'd still be together?

LW: Who knows? I don't like to think about it. At the end of the day she was taken and we did split up. I can't change either of those things, even if I wanted to.

US: And getting her back wasn't exactly a bed of roses, was it?

LW: No. I found it really hard to bond with her. I'd not seen her for about three or four weeks. I couldn't settle and as a result neither could she.

US: You couldn't settle?

LW: I kept thinking someone was going to take her. I still haven't let her out of my sight really. But no. I found it very difficult to bond with her at first.

US: And now?

LW: It's a lot better.

US: I'm pleased to hear that, Linda.

LW: Thank you.

US: How do you feel about Shirley Burke now?

LW: I hated her for a long time but now I feel sympathy for her.

US: I think some people will be surprised by that.

LW: I'm only being honest. She was a kid. She was desperate. I think it's pretty evil what she did, but I do, I feel sorry that she felt she had to do that. It was never going to end well for her. But she was too young to see that.

US: It might not have ended well for you.

LW: But it did. So . . .

US: You're quite the tabloid star now aren't you Linda?

LW: I'm not receiving a penny for this interview. I never set out to be a tabloid star, to have my face in the papers, and I don't enjoy it one bit. But I understand that people are interested as it's such an unusual story. But I am doing this one interview, and then that's it. No more. I will disappear and no-one will ever hear about me or Diana ever again.

US: Bold words, Linda, if you don't mind me saying!

LW: Well, I mean it. I will not have let Shirley Burke destroy my life, and I swear to God I'd never let her destroy Diana's.

US: So you will disappear?

LW: I'm toying with going to Australia. Maybe New Zealand.

US: But your infamy may follow you.

LW: I won't let it. No offence, Ursula, but this interview will be tomorrow's chip paper.

US: I'll try not to take offence at that.

LW: I will. I'll disappear. And you watch. Shirley Burke might have messed with my family. But Diana will be the one to have the last laugh when she's a happy, content child, and a well-adjusted grown up. We will have the last laugh.

I have read and re-read that interview what feels like a million different times. It is so illuminating. And it means that Linda and my mum were definitely the same person. It's so interesting to me because here she is, having gone through one of the most gruelling ordeals imaginable, and on the one hand she is being all sweetness and light and forgiving and, *Oh the poor wee thing, Shirley Burke* – but then her passive-aggressive side comes out and she can't help but be vile and hideous and all, *You won't be hearing from me again even if you're fascinated by me, as well you might be.*

It made sense why she had changed our names. She was clearly a household name. Or maybe I was. And by moving to a brand-new place, somewhere she had no ties, presumably she felt she could have her well-earned anonymity.

And how clever of her to make out she was heading down under. It meant no-one would be looking for her in this country. It meant she could retreat to the New Forest and get on with that anonymous life.

But what about my dad?

Les.

Les Wilson.

How did he feel about all this? Did he believe I was living in New Zealand?

And did I want to find him? And if I did, how would I?

Surely there couldn't be that many Les Wilsons knocking about. It isn't exactly a common name. But how old would he be now? Mid-sixties? Surely he'd still be alive. I couldn't be the one who has all the bad luck and loses both their parents before they hit seventy, could I? The sort of person who tracks down a parent and finds they only died the week before.

I don't want that happening, so it's probably best to get cracking with any sort of search immediately. I fire up Facebook and enter the name Les Wilson in the search bar. Several profiles come up and they are all women. Maybe he's transitioned? If he has he is looking pretty good on it. Or she is. Or they. No, she.

Anyway.

I re-enter Leslie Wilson and scores of them come up.

Okay, so it isn't as uncommon a name as I originally thought.

I scroll through them and click on their profile pictures and on the whole they look too young to be my dad. There are a couple of Leslies who have non-committal photos of tigers or place settings at a dining table; one even has a picture of his pick-up truck. I feel I should contact them all and explain who I am, but as I go to do it my fingers freeze above the keyboard. I just can't.

What do I say?

Hello, Les. Remember that baby who was nicked?

IT'S ME!

LOL.

Actually, LOL would be hugely inappropriate. But as I think that, I realize the whole thing is completely inappropriate. Contacting someone out of the blue and telling them you're their child? It's a Jeremy Kyle wet dream, isn't it?

But then I remember someone saying it was quite the done thing these days and that Facebook is littered with kids getting in touch with parents who never knew they existed, and within seconds of a friendship request you could be checking out your long-lost mother's taste in soft furnishings by nosing at her photo album, headily titled 'Through-lounge since decorating', etc.

Do I really want to see what Les Wilson's taste in home decoration is like?

No. But I want to reach out to him. Let him know I've not really been ignoring him all these years. Let him know that Jane/Linda kept him very much a secret from me. See if there is anywhere we could go with this. Whatever this is. Whatever this might be.

I have to say I haven't hankered for the presence of a father figure in a very long time. I pretty much got accustomed to that before I hit puberty. But now I know that Jane/Linda was lying all those years . . . well, it feels impolite not to reach out the hand of friendship.

This is a man who must have been as traumatized by what Shirley Burke did as my mum was. For God's sake, he'd tried to sit her down and get her to contemplate a scenario where not only had I been abducted, but I had also been killed. He had had to think about, and no doubt believe, that his baby daughter, his first-born, had been snatched from beneath their very noses and was probably dead. He then had to convince his wife of this. The poor man, to have to go through all that – his heart must have been breaking. It really didn't bear thinking about.

And then what did his missus do? After they split up she disappeared into the night with a change of name, not only for the baby but also for her, never to be seen or heard of again. What must that have been like for a young man? A young man who had been through so much?

Had he met someone else? Remarried? Had he gone on to have other children?

Oh gosh. That is something I've not considered.

Has he got other kids?

Do I have a brother or sister out there? Brothers or sisters, maybe?

Or maybe he was so traumatized by what happened to me he couldn't face having any more.

I have to find out.

I look at my phone to see if the vicar has returned my call, but I know he hasn't. Maybe he, with his hotline to God, can find out through the power of prayer and by tonight I'll be Skyping Les and reminiscing about the good old days.

But of course there were no good old days.

Everything about this story of mine is bad. Sad. Maybe he won't want to hear from me.

I check the phone again. No missed calls. Oh well.

Instead I Google 'Hire Cars: Central London'. I need to take another bull by the horns.

I also need to get more Granny Smiths.

It's easy enough to work out where the police found me with Shirley Burke. The address is there in black and white in each internet article I have found. And renting a car is a lot easier than I thought it would be, though admittedly the drive from Bloomsbury to North Wales takes a lot longer than I anticipated. Nearly six hours, but that's mostly down to roadworks on the M6, and the fact that I enter the wrong postcode in the satnav to begin with. After several wrong turns, and another that sees me going halfway up a mountain called Moel Famau, I eventually wend my way to the bizarrely named Loggerheads. For some reason the name alone makes me think that Liz Taylor and Richard Burton should have had a house there. And then another in the next village, Divorce. 'We were at Loggerheads, then moved to Divorce.'

But of course there is no village called Divorce.

I am wittering in my head.

I am nervous.

Time to face the music.

Eventually I find the street and park up.

I stand in this, the very street where I was once held captive, and hope against hope that I will feel something. That there'll be some flash of recognition. But of course . . . the last time I was here I was about four weeks old, no more than that certainly. I feel nothing but disappointment.

I soothe myself with a crisp apple. It improves the mood.

I can't even work out which house was once upon a time Lovers' Leap Cottage. None of these houses look like they could ever have warranted the moniker 'cottage'. I was expecting a pretty street, a backwater of holiday homes, luxury gaffs where rich footballers might not look out of place. I expected to see a van parked up with POOL CLEANING SERVICES written on the side. I wanted this to be more of a cul-de-sac than a street, the sort of place where you'd expect to see Renée Zellweger popping to the shops on a dirty weekend with Hugh Grant.

Instead I am greeted by a row of non-descript three-storey council maisonettes. How bloody grim! Cottage, my foot! Is this all Shirley Burke could afford? Poor cow, literally. What do I do now I'm here? I can't just stand here, take a few pictures on my phone, then go home. I have to do something or today will have been a complete waste of time.

I look up beyond the maisonettes and see the mountain disappearing into the clouds. The weather is bright on the ground but I can't see the top of the mountain. It's eluding me. Like this street is eluding me right now, the truth is eluding me. Which house was my hiding place? I have to find out.

I walk up the path nearest to me and ring on the doorbell. I know there is someone in as I can hear a telly blaring in the living room. Through the glass of the door I see a silhouette approach. The door swings open and a woman about my age is there. She gives me a *Yes, how can I help you?* look, though says nothing. She is fashionably dressed and immaculately manicured. She's too cool for words. In the split second before either of us speaks I wonder if this is her second home. That she has another in London and this is her Welsh getaway. Bizarre choice but hey ho.

I realize neither of us is speaking and the ball is in my court. Here goes.

'Yes, I wonder if you could help me? I was wondering if you knew anything about the history of this street?'

She sort of shakes her head and looks a bit confused.

'Do you know, for instance, which house used to be called Lovers' Leap Cottage?'

She shakes her head. 'We've only been here six months. Try Norma in the post office. Her family have been here forever.'

I look around, but can see no post office.

'Sorry, the old post office. It's that house there.'

She points to the dilapidated prefab opposite. I thank her and trudge across. Before she shuts her door I hear her calling to someone inside, 'Lettice? Turn that down, please! Mummy needs to express.'

So. These houses may look incredibly ordinary, but it seems they're inhabited by posh people.

I ring my second bell.

And this time I have a bit more luck. Luck in the shape of Norma.

It turns out Norma's family have lived here forever, though Norma – a sprightly sixty-year-old – was working away when the drama unfolded on this street so has little first-hand recollection of it. But she knows a woman who will remember. Her old pal Sandra's mum Myrus was the woman who tipped the police off.

Myrus. That's not a name you hear every day. It's a wonder that didn't make it into any of the articles I've read. But maybe she too wanted her own anonymity.

'Myrus?'

'Yes. Myrus.'

Sounds like a mash-up of Miley Cyrus. But I keep this to myself.

'Is she still alive?' I ask.

'Why do you want to know?' Maybe she thinks I am a journalist or something.

'I'm baby Diana.'

And at that Norma pales and invites me in and says she'll find Sandra's phone number. It's odd seeing her reaction. It's almost as if at the sound of my name she has become a quivering wreck. Her hands are shaking as she checks through pieces of paper on her messy kitchen table, and she keeps brushing her hair back nervously. Eventually she finds a number scrawled on a notepad and picks up the phone to call. But then she drops the phone and screeches a loud 'SORRY!' It's like she's about to burst out crying.

Gosh. What an effect I have on people, suddenly.

'Are you all right?' I ask quietly. And she turns to me.

'You have to realize. You were the biggest thing that ever happened in this village.'

I feel myself blushing. I feel a piercing of shame. I put this village on the front pages of the newspapers. Through no fault of my own, but I did. It was so long ago, but look, it may as well have been yesterday as far as this woman is concerned.

She makes her call.

Long story short, an hour later I'm in an old people's home about ten miles away, chatting to Myrus. Her daughter has come to sit in on the conversation, probably for ghoulish nosiness more than anything. She warned me on the way in that Myrus has a dreadful short-term memory now, but remembers things from the past with crystal-clear precision. Thank God.

She's a very ordinary looking woman. This wrong-foots me. She could be any old lady you see walking down the street with a drag-along shopping trolley. Any old lady at a bus stop. Any old lady fumbling in her purse at the checkout. And yet she is quite extraordinary in my personal history. Without this woman I might still be in thrall to my abductor. Without this woman I would not be the person I am today. I want her to look incredible. I want her to turn heads with her eccentricity or importance. I want every step she takes to create seismic shocks. But she's not that sort of person. She's me, she's you, she's everyone. She's ordinary. She just, once upon a time, did something out of the ordinary. And I am extremely grateful.

She looks to be in her eighties. But she is perkily dressed in a grey leopard-skin puffa jacket that's quite slim-fitting and trendy looking, and she is wearing smart black slacks and has definitely put a brush through her white hair. She seems to spend forever when I first arrive holding my hands and looking at me up and down, turning her face this way and that, like she's eyeing up a cow at auction. Will I pass muster?

I eventually sit down and her daughter serves us tea and biscuits and – no idea why – explains that she bought Myrus the jacket last Christmas. With vouchers. Maybe she's trying to explain why her mother is wearing a coat indoors.

I ask her if she remembers much about when I was a baby and ended up staying on her street.

She smiles at my polite use of the word 'staying', and I instantly know this woman is good news.

'Oh yes. Like it was yesterday. You were quite the story.'

It's now I realize that although we are in Wales, Myrus has a cockney accent.

I ask her what Shirley Burke was like.

She has a think.

'She was a funny looking thing. You wouldn't look twice at her. Small. But not petite, if you know what I mean. I was always interested in newcomers, being a bit of an outsider myself. I mean, look at me. Eighty-four this March, been here since nineteen sixty-three, and they still don't see me as a local.'

She drops a sugar cube into her tea with some dainty silver tongs. I marvel at how I've not seen such an action in a very long time. I wonder if she had the tongs in 1981. Whether she used them to sweeten her tea when I was crying in a cot a few doors away.

'She had the sort of face you'd want to slap, actually. Sorry. That's an old saying of my mother's. She certainly weren't no oil painting, dear.'

Dear. No-one has called me 'dear' in forever.

'She was pregnant of course. Or so we thought. Well, we know now she was only pretending . . .'

'Sorry?'

'She was here a week or so before the baby appeared.' She corrects herself. 'Before you appeared. Forever walking up and down the lane, all fat with the baby due. Then she disappeared for a few days. Then she come back.'

'She was pregnant?'

'Well, it turns out now she was having us all on, leading us on a right old merry dance. But I remember vividly her ankles were all puffy.'

'I don't understand.'

'She was wearing some sort of padding, to make out she was pregnant. And she had the walk down to a tee. Always stopping on the corner and rubbing her back and sighing. I felt sorry for her. That's why I noticed her. Plus she was on her own. Back then it was very unusual for a woman with child to be on her own. Specially round here. Ain't exactly Hackney Marshes, is it?'

'No. No, I suppose not. But what made you suspicious of her?'

'It sounds daft now, but . . .'

'I'm sure it doesn't.'

'I got talking to her one day. The way you do. And something just didn't add up.'

'In what way?'

'It was the way she talked about her husband. Yet she didn't have no ring on her finger. And I know the couple what owned that house was a married couple. I just got the feeling she weren't telling me the truth. I felt sorry for her, truth be told. Thought she was the mistress. A kept woman. I turned out to be right.'

'But that's not necessarily, in itself, that odd. Or was it, back then?'

'Oh, it weren't that, dear. It was just that she told me she was having a boy. Quite adamant about it, she was. Nice little boy, and she was going to name him after his daddy. Douglas. And of course Douglas was the name of the man what owned the house.'

'You've got such a good memory.'

'For back then I have. I can remember stuff from the war like it was yesterday. But ask me what did actually happen yesterday and we'd both be buggered.'

We share a smile.

'And then of course she came back from the hospital and . . . well, you weren't a little boy. She was all flustered about it.'

'So you met me?'

'Only on the path. Taking you from her car.'

'How did I look?'

'You were sleeping. But you were ever so bonny. But of course this was the same day it was reported the baby had been taken from the lady's back garden. And that baby was a little girl. Something in my gut said it was you. Only I didn't dare say. Then Douglas turns up and they seemed perfectly happy so . . . what business was it of mine?'

'So what made you contact the police?'

'Douglas seemed to have disappeared. God knows where he'd gone . . .'

'Back to his wife, probably.'

'Well, this is it. And I popped round with a little cardy I'd knitted for the baby. And she seemed ever so put out about it. And I asked if I could see you. And she was adamant I couldn't coz you were sleeping and . . . well, something didn't add up.'

'How d'you mean?'

'She didn't seem to have any friends popping round. Or family. And most new mums love nothing more than showing their baby off to all and sundry, and she really didn't.'

'Of course. Yes, that would be odd.'

'And I went home and I found the artist's impression thing in the newspaper. And the more I looked at it, the more I thought, oh God. It's her. So I called the police. Next day I had a few of 'em camped out in the house, binoculars at the window, the works.'

'Watching her?'

'Well, they weren't waiting to pay the milkman.'

I'll give her that. God, she's sharp.

'Two days later the whole street was cordoned off. Coppers everywhere. I watched it all from the attic window. Heart thumping in my chest. The main one knocked on the door. I saw her open it. Bit of chat, then I remember, clear as day, she stood to one side and they went in. She looked . . . she looked resigned to her fate. She looked relieved. A minute or so later he comes out with you in his hands. And that was it. 'Course, the whole village was glued to their TV sets for days after.

Biggest thing that'd ever happened round here, as you can imagine. Still is, really.'

'We still get people talking about it in the pub,' her daughter pipes up. Gosh. I was paying such attention to Myrus I'd forgotten she was here. 'Mum was quite the celebrity, weren't you, Mum?'

'They asked me to open the village fete.'

'She said no, like.'

'Oh, I said no. Didn't want a fuss. Just wanted, I don't know, order restored.'

'Were you called to be a witness? At the trial?'

'I'd have been happy to, of course. But no. Silly little girl pleaded guilty to everything so they didn't kick up much of a fuss, trial-wise. Which was probably just as well, for your mum. How is she?'

'Oh. Well. Sadly she died a little while ago.'

'Oh, I'm sorry to hear that.'

'Actually I knew nothing about any of this till . . . till after she died and . . . and I found some old newspaper clippings and put two and two together. She changed my name and . . . well, it's all been a bit of a shock.'

'Blimey, really?'

'Yes.'

'Might be for the best,' the daughter chipped in.

'Sure she knew what she was doing,' Myrus agreed.

'I'm sure. But it's left me with a lot of questions, obviously.'

'Of course. Gosh, that must've been a shock, dear.'

I nod. No flies on Myrus.

'Can you tell me which house on that street was Lovers' Leap?'

She looks at me like I am mad. 'Of course I can, dear. It's

236

changed hands a lot over the years but it's Christine's place now. She does Hair B&B now.'

She's looking at her daughter.

'Airbnb,' her daughter corrects her.

Myrus shrugs. 'People'll stay anywhere these days. Still, the views are nice.'

I look at my watch. It's past five in the afternoon. A quick estimate of driving times mixed with a rising sense of excitement urges my next question.

'I wonder if anyone's staying there at the moment.'

It's the daughter's turn to shrug. 'One way to find out.'

Lovers' Leap is now named Moel Famau View. As we stand outside I hear Sandra on the phone speaking rapidly in Welsh. I gaze at the house, hoping it will spark some memory. It sparks nothing. It's possibly the worst-kept house in the street. When Sandra hangs up I'm not surprised when she says, 'You're in luck. No-one's staying here this week. It's yours for the night.'

I imagine the reviews on Airbnb to be pretty harsh.

But then I am not staying here for five-star luxury. I am staying here as a trip down Memory Lane.

'D'you think I'm weird?' I hear myself asking. I can't help it. She shakes her head.

'What happened to you was weird. I'd want to do exactly the same.'

And this makes me feel better.

She says the owner will be here within the hour.

I'm about to make small talk when my phone goes and I see it's the vicarage calling. I answer quickly.

'Tom. Hi. Father. Sorry.'

Sandra looks at me like I'm mad, as well she might.

I point to the phone and mouth the word VICAR. Which I

don't think she gets. And as I do I hear Tom saying, 'Rachel. Hi. I've got the details of a private detective for you. Still need them?'

'Yes.' And then I almost shout, 'YES!'

Chapter Fourteen

An owl hoots. I hear the ticking of the clock. Somewhere someone screams. It sounds like a baby. But then I remember that's
what foxes sound like in the dead of night, but it sure reminds
me why I am here.

It's something Myrus said, just before I was leaving her. She
remembered something. I knew she had by the look on her
face. And I knew that what she'd remembered had taken her by
surprise.

'What is it, Myrus?'

'I've remembered another reason why I was so suspicious of
her.'

'Oh, right. And what's that?'

'I saw her out digging one night. In the garden.'

'Lovers' Leap garden?'

Myrus nodded. 'I could see their back garden from my bedroom window. She was there in the wee small hours. At first I
thought she was gardening. But she didn't have the look of a
gardener. And why would you do gardening so late?'

'Digging?'

'The light was on in the back kitchen so it was lighting the
garden and I could see her in her nightie with a big spade.'

'Maybe she couldn't sleep.'

'She was meant to be nine months' pregnant, dearie.'

She pointed to my stomach.

'Would you get out there in the dead of night and spend the better part of an hour digging into the earth?'

I shook my head.

'Did you say anything to her?'

She shook her head.

'None of my business.'

'Did it make you think she wasn't really pregnant?'

'Not at all. It just made me think how odd she was.'

'I'm sure.'

'Did you tell the police?'

'I can't remember. I don't think that I did, as it was before she brought the baby back.' She corrected herself. 'Before she brought you back. Didn't seem relevant.' She faltered. 'Actually, maybe it was after. I'm sorry.'

But why was she gardening so late at night?

Maybe it's a clue. Maybe Shirley Burke is a gardener. Was a gardener.

Why did I think staying in Lovers' Leap was going to lead me to her?

All reports about her online say she went to prison for abducting me. But then the trail runs cold. There is a theatre in Australia named after someone called Shirley Burke. At first I wondered whether she had done what my mum had wanted to do, which was to run away as far as possible and start a new life. But when I did further searches for the woman who inspired this theatre in Melbourne, I found that she was already a Melbourne resident by 1962. And a photo of her in that year showed she was certainly in middle age, so this wasn't the ingénue who stole me, that's for sure. And then, to top it all, I saw that she had died in 1975. Even I know it's difficult to die and then steal a baby six years later.

Shirley Burke is elusive.

I suppose part of me thought that by gaining access to this so-called cottage I'd – miraculously – find a clue that would lead me to her.

But what?

I must be the only person who has rented this Airbnb who has practically done a fingertip search from top to bottom looking for something from their past.

You can imagine the sort of thing. A dusty snakeskin handbag that I find under a settee. I blow the cobwebs off it, snap open the clasp and pull out a piece of paper. It has some fading handwriting on it: *Property of Shirley Burke. 1981. In the event of loss, please return to . . .*

And then an address. And I get in my car. And head to the address. And knock on the door. And wonder of wonders, she hasn't moved house in over thirty years and is still there . . .

And then what do I do?

Well, it doesn't matter. Because she breaks down in tears and throws herself in my arms, begging forgiveness. I don't even have to explain who I am. She just knows. She has never forgotten me. She has never stopped loving me. And then I go into labour. And she helps deliver it. And she saves the baby's life. And all is forgiven.

Or there's another scenario. I find some graffiti. It's behind a curtain in an upstairs bedroom. My old bedroom, probably. It says: 'SHIRLEY BURKE WOZ HERE. 1981.'

Below it she has drawn an arrow, pointing to the floor. I bend and find a bit of carpet missing. A floorboard is exposed. And Shirley has written 'OPEN ME' on it in nail varnish. And so I do.

Inside is a set of house keys with a cardboard tag attached to them. An address is written on the tag in pencil.

This time, in my fantasy, I take an Uber to her address and this time I am unable to get any answer at her front door. Losing patience, I eventually break in. It's then that I find Shirley Burke lying dead in the bath. Scrawled across her breasts in lipstick she has written 'SORRY, RACHEL.'

Because of course there must be a distinct possibility that Shirley is dead. She might have left prison and become a heroin addict, or a prostitute. She couldn't have come out of a place like that and ended up with a joyous life, could she? Life just doesn't work like that.

I lie in my strange bed, ruminating on all of this.

What on earth am I doing here? I don't feel safe. I don't feel happy. And I want to feel both of those things. I need to, especially here. But was I ever going to feel safe in a house with so many bad associations for me?

Talk about revisiting the scene of the crime!

This was a mistake. I don't know what I thought I'd gain from staying in this draughty Airbnb. And even though it's cold enough to feel like an old house, it can only have been built in the sixties. Low ceilings, a pine kitchen that's been painted white, those vertical choppy blinds that old people have. There is a flat-screen telly on the wall, some rooms smell of paint, and the carpets have plastic sheeting over them here and there. Nothing about this house says 1981. Of course it wouldn't. In order to be rented out it will need to feel a little bit contemporary. This was such a bad move.

The curtains are too thin. There must be a full moon because it feels like I've left the main light on, even though it's the dead of night and I've not a switch on in the house. I feel sad, I feel lonely, and I feel stupid.

242

Why did you come here, Shirley Burke? Why did you bring me here? Well I now know the answer to that. Your married boyfriend owned this place. How depressing. Were you that much under his thumb? You must have been more than that to take me.

I feel like I've had enough. The only thing keeping me going is the knowledge that tomorrow I will get in my car and drive back to London and go and meet this detective. She sounded so warm and friendly on the phone. And she sounded delighted to hear from me.

But maybe that's a bad thing. Maybe she's so unsuccessful she's thrilled to get any job going.

I have to stop thinking like that. I must try to get some sleep. Might have an apple first, mind you.

I look at what I've written in my phone. Kelly Hopper, Enquiry Agent.

I wonder if I've written it down wrong and he actually said Kelly Hoppen. I know the name Kelly Hoppen. She's off the telly. What does she do again? I quickly Google her. Okay, so she's an internationally renowned interior designer. It's doubtful she does detective work on the side so maybe I heard it right and wrote it right. And, also, if Ms Hoppen was a private dick I doubt she'd have an office above a 'mixed sauna' on Kentish Town Road.

What is a mixed sauna?

It has paintings of palm trees on its white-brick walls, and a photo of some happy couples looking overtly jovial in a sauna hanging by the door, which, I have to say, has seen better days.

I toy with nipping into the mixed sauna, just to see what's going on, but I realize I'd have to walk round in a towel tucked over my boobs with the bottom of my bum showing, and I decide I'm really not ready to inflict my huge pregnant fatness on the world of swinging. Because it must be full of swingers.

Who else goes to a sauna that claims to be mixed, and shows photos of couples looking thrilled to be semi-naked?

No. Kelly Hopper's offices are above the sauna, so I ring the bell of the door to the side of the main entrance. No-one replies. I ring again; then a frustrated voice squawks at me through an intercom.

'Yes?'

'Hi, it's Rachel Taylor? I've got a two o'clock appointment with Kelly Hopper?'

'Who?'

'Kelly Hopper.'

'No, who are you?'

'Rachel Taylor?'

'Who?'

I find myself shouting. 'RACHEL TAYLOR.'

Then silence.

Then, 'Oh, you may as well come up.'

I hear a buzz and the door disengages from the lock and I push my way in.

The carpet on the stairs is filthy. All I can smell is cats. It's gloomy. The staircase twists and turns. Up ahead I hear a door open and an aerosol being sprayed. The smell that hits my nostrils says it's very cheap air freshener.

'Sorry!' the voice calls. 'Wasn't expecting you till tomorrow! Come up!'

At the top of the stairs I'm greeted by a mixed-race woman in a tweed two-piece and a string of pearls wearing mismatching shoes. They're both court shoes, but one is shiny, one is not. Maybe she's just the secretary. Which detective worth their salt wouldn't detect that they weren't wearing matching shoes? But she stretches out her hand and beams, saying, 'Kelly Hopper. Lovely to meet you, Rashelle.'

'It's Rachel.'

'Oh. You pronounce it like that, do you?'

And she ushers me in. Is this woman mad? Why would she think 'Rachel' was pronounced 'Rashelle'?

I can't tell if this woman is in her forties or sixties. If she's forties she's looking a bit jaded. But if she's sixties, she looks amazing. And I usually hate the word amazing. But it's true. She does.

If she's eighty she's incredible.

If she's thirty, she had a very long paper round.

My mind's jumping. I must be nervous.

The smell of cats gets stronger as I enter her offices. She points to an empty desk in the first room she leads me into. It feels like an outer office, and it's thick with dust and litter trays. She kicks one tray under the desk and some of the small white stones fly off it onto the thick, dark carpet.

I don't see a cat. Maybe it's in the other room.

'I did have a secretary. But between me, you and the gatepost she was an utter bitch, luvvy.'

She sounds a bit like Kim Woodburn from that cleaning programme.

'Can I get you a drink?'

'Oh, yes please.'

'Scotch?'

'Erm . . .'

'I'd say tea or coffee but I've run out. Or I've a tiny bit of Baileys left.'

'Erm. I'm actually pregnant.'

It's clear even to a blind person that I'm pregnant. But she looks surprised and her eyes dart to my stomach. She still looks unsure.

'One won't harm the baby, will it?'

'I'd rather not. And I don't need a drink, I'm fine. I had a coffee earlier.'

Politeness will be my downfall.

'My kind of gal!' she says, and she really jabs me hard in the upper arm. 'All the more for yours truly!'

And she opens a cupboard and pulls out a half-drunk bottle of Scotch and pours two glasses out. She's a bit haphazard with her pouring and some of it ends up on the abandoned desk, but it doesn't seem to bother her. She passes me one.

Can she really be that scatty?

'I'm pregnant.'

'Congratulations.'

'Thank you.'

Oh God. She's pissed.

'Who sent you, again?'

'Oh, Tom. The vicar? Tom O'Neill.'

'Bloody hell. Tom, eh?'

'Yes. My mum died recently and . . . he took the funeral.'

'Violent?'

'Sorry?'

'Was it a violent death?' she asks, suspiciously.

'No. Well, it was cancer.'

Her eyes narrow even more.

'Assisted suicide? Or . . .'

'No. Cancer.'

She nods to herself and looks out of the window as if she is in a scene in a TV crime series and she is weighing up the evidence. I wonder if she is showing off to me, whether she feels this is some sort of audition, to prove she can cut the mustard as a private dick.

'Cancer, eh?'

'Yes.'

She takes another hit of her drink.

'And why did he send you to me?'

'Well, he said you were good.'

She nods to herself again, not averting her eyes from the window.

'Well, you know vicars, Tracy. They don't fucking lie.'

'It's Rachel.'

'What is?'

'My name.'

'I know that. We spoke on the phone.'

'We did.'

'Cancer, eh?'

'Yes. And I need your help.'

She turns to me quickly. 'Did he really say I was good?'

I nod. And think she is going to cry. But instead she moves to another room.

'I need to make notes!' she calls back to me. 'Come through!'

I have a feeling this is a disastrous waste of my time. But I follow her through anyway, into her main office. I know this because in the glass on the door linking the two rooms it says in gold lettering: 'MAIN OFFICE'.

A cat is sat on her desk, looking for all the world like a brown Bagpuss. It sees me and jumps, rather nimbly for a fat cat, onto the floor and hides under said desk.

'Ignore Prudence.'

'Okay.'

'She's a little shy.'

'Okay.'

'She's a Norwegian Forest cat, don't you know.'

'No, I didn't.'

'They love the rain.'

'Gosh. That's . . .'

'But she doesn't go out.'

'Oh. She's a house cat.'

'She sits on the windowsill. Staring at the rain. It's almost moving.'

'Right.'

Why is she telling me this?

I look about. Her office could do with a good dust and a good vacuum; no surprises there. It's a larger room than I expected and the window looks out onto the busy high street. The lack of double-glazing on the sash window means I can hear very clearly every rev of an engine, every squawk of a pigeon. I can even hear the chatter of passers-by, despite the fact we're on the first floor.

'Cats are like detectives.'

'Are they?'

'Verrrrrry intuitive.'

'I see. Well yes, I suppose they are. Though I imagine detectives get out more.'

I laugh, but she doesn't join in. I realize she either hasn't heard me or she just doesn't think my jokes are very funny.

And who could blame her?

'What's your name again?'

'Rachel.'

'Friend of Tom's.'

'Kind of.'

Kelly plonks herself on a swivel chair and almost misses and the chair skids a bit and I think she's about to hit the wall behind her, but she stops herself by braking with her feet.

'Nearly,' she says, with muted emotion. Then offers a smile. 'Now. Notes.'

And she whips out a notebook from a drawer of the desk and clicks the top of a biro.

'Take a seat.'

I sit the opposite side to her and pretend to take a sip of my drink. I don't know why I'm doing this. I just feel like I've entered some mad alternative universe and am going along for the ride.

'So,' she says, scribbling something down. 'You want to know why your mum died.'

'No. I know why my mum died. I . . . I want to trace two people from my childhood.'

'Who?'

'Well. I don't know how old you are.'

'That's no business of yours. I ask the questions.'

'Sorry. Well it's just I was at the centre of a big news story in nineteen eighty-one.'

'You don't look old enough. And I thought black didn't crack.'

'I was a baby. A newborn. And I was snatched from my mum's back garden. Went missing for nearly a month before I was found.'

'Are you shitting me?'

'No.'

I've brought some papers with me. Everything I've found on the internet, printed off. I take them out of my bag and hand them to her. She takes them but doesn't look at them.

'What are these?' she says, as if I'm trying to wrong-foot her.

'Newspaper reports. Stuff like that. About the incident.'

'Who do you want to trace?'

'My dad.'

She writes something in her book. I look. She has written 'DAD'. And then drawn a massive question mark.

'You said two people,' she says, like she's trying to catch me out.

'And the woman who abducted me.'

Now she writes 'WOMAN'. And an even bigger question mark. And then for good measure she adds a massive exclamation mark. Blimey. She'll be doing emojis next.

I'm getting cold feet. Any sensible person would have run a mile when they smelt the cats and the alcohol. This woman probably can't even find her handbag, never mind Shirley Burke or my dad.

'Look. Maybe this wasn't such a good idea.'

'What wasn't?'

'Me coming to see you.'

'I'm cheap.'

'I'm sure, but . . .'

'I'm good.'

'I'm sure you are, but . . .'

'Tom recommended me. A man of the cloth.'

'I've just got a funny feeling about it.'

Then she leans across the desk, and suddenly she seems to sober up and mean business.

'I'll find them. I give you my word.'

'But . . .'

'I know what you think when you look at me.'

'I'm not forming any judgement.'

'Washed up. Washed out. Has been. Oh, I'm all of those things.'

'Well . . .'

'But I'll prove to you I can do this. Give me two weeks.'

'It's okay.'

'It's not okay, you stupid bitch. You were kidnapped. I'll find her. I'll find the woman who did this.'

And now she looks at the printouts for the first time. She studies them and I don't know what to do. She looks up.

'I remember this.'

I nod.

'Baby Diana. Named after Princess Di. Stolen the day she got married. I remember this.'

She flicks through the papers. Then takes a sharp hit of her whisky.

'So,' I say, 'I need to find my dad. And I need to find the woman who took me.'

'Why do you need to find her?'

And now I falter.

The real answer is I don't actually know. I have no idea why, really, I have this overwhelming desire to find Shirley Burke. What will I say to her when I find her? If she's even still alive.

'I was with her for weeks. I want to know what I was like.'

'You were probably some mewling puking little brat. Box ticked. Why do you really want to meet her?'

'I'm not sure.'

'Do you want to kill her?'

God, that hadn't even crossed my mind.

'No. NO!'

'Wreak some sort of revenge?'

'No. I don't know.'

'She was one of the most hated women in Britain. I'd want to hurt her. Like she hurt your mum.'

'I don't think I want to hurt her.'

'Even if you do. I'll still find her for you.'

'How? How will you find her? This is the bit I don't understand.'

'I could tell you. But then I'd have to kill you.'

And now she's scaring me. But then she emits a throaty chuckle.

'God, it's just a joke, luvvie. Get over it.'

She stands and starts walking round the room, a bit like I'd imagine Columbo would have done.

'This job,' she says, 'is an unusual beast. It's ninety-five per cent boredom, five per cent fear.'

'Fear?'

'Big dogs, mostly. But they don't scare me. I was brought up with dogs. I get them. They get me. If I'm going to recover a debt they always set the dogs onto me. And they always. ALWAYS end up licking me.'

I smile awkwardly. It feels like she's showing off.

'I wanna track someone down? I go to ex-employers. They love to spill the beans. "Oh, she's a hairdresser now"; "Oh, is she?" Then I speak to all the bloody hairdressers in the world till I find who I'm looking for.'

'But Shirley went to prison.'

'I'm an attractive woman, Philippa.'

'I'm Rachel.'

'And I've got a copper so bent he's practically convex.'

I roll my eyes. She sees. I didn't mean her to see.

'He'll give me any info I want about people who've been in trouble with the law.'

'Even if it was thirty-odd years ago?'

'He wants me.'

'She might have changed her name.'

'The police know everything. They are big brother. And they are watching you. He came round to check me out.'

'Who?'

'My source. Let's call him Billy.'

'But . . .'

'I was operating from a bedsit. Put up a website. He came sniffing.'

'Right. Well . . .' I think it's probably time to go now.

'Probably because "enquiry agents", as I called myself back then. Enquiry agents were mostly ex-cons. Like Tom.'

I feel my eyes widen.

'Tom's an ex-con?'

252

'He wants to check me out.'

'Tom's an . . .'

'You heard. Other enquiry agents tended to be ex-cops. So he wanted to know which I was.'

'And what were you?'

'Neither. Just naive. Few too many Miss Marples in the school library. That kind of thing.' She smiles. 'So he wanted to check I was kosher. Which I was. Which I am. Now he's putty in my hands. Philippa? I will speak to him.'

'Rachel.'

'And he will unlock the secrets. And we will find whoever you want.'

'Okay.' It feels best just to go along with this. 'And how much will it cost?'

'You don't trust me.'

'I do. Well, I don't know you, but . . .'

'How about this. No win, no fee.'

'And if you win?'

'Five hundred.'

Blimey. That's a lot.

'Each.'

'Each?'

'A grand if I find your dad and your abductor.'

I can just about afford that, I guess. And if this is just pissing in the wind, which it certainly feels like, then I've lost the grand sum of precisely nothing.

I stand, wanting this over.

'Deal.'

I hold out my hand. She shakes it.

'Deal. Now sit back down. I need to know EVERYTHING.'

Oh God. I'm beginning to feel like I'm not going to get out of here alive.

Chapter Fifteen

When I first moved to London, this particular area, it has to be said, was a bit of a shithole. All the locals called the area Kings Cross, but these days it's reverentially referred to as Bloomsbury. My flat is in a red-brick apartment block overlooking the Brunswick Centre. These days the Brunswick Centre is a dazzling white slab of architectural quirkiness, staggered flats going up in steps, each one retreating away from you, all around a courtyard of destination shops and wannabe swanky restaurants. When I first came here it was the sort of grey colour I imagined you could only find in the liver of an alcoholic, and it always reeked of urine. In those days you took your life in your hands if you dared brave it inside to visit the large Iceland for some frozen foods, and when you did so you had to brave the elements, and a one-legged crack whore called Lisa, who spun round in circles in a tiny wheelchair with 'PROPERTY OF GREAT ORMOND STREET HOSPITAL – DO NOT REMOVE' written on the back.

These days the Iceland has been replaced by a Waitrose and Lisa and her ilk have long gone, more's the pity. Bloomsbury has been gentrified. And most agree that, unlike other areas of London, it has come out the other side smiling.

The area is populated, it appears, by students from local

universities, doctors and nurses from the local hospitals, arty farty types who love a good second-hand bookshop, posh people who escape to the country every weekend, and then the dyed-in-the-wool locals who've had their council flats on the many nearby estates since the year dot.

And me.

As I am back in London and my mother is well and truly deceased and dealt with – although there is still the small matter of putting her house on the market and kissing goodbye to the New Forest – it appears I have no other option but to go back to work.

Great.

I take the route I always do, walking up Marchmont Street, past the launderette where I kind of have a girl crush on the woman who works there – 'Oh, I can always do a service wash for you, Rach' – and the off licence where the girls are uber friendly, though I can never quite place their accents, and then I cut across the street and into Cartwright Gardens.

When I first moved to London, my boss Ben and I were really good friends. We hung out together all the time. In fact I moved round here because it was his stomping ground. Anyway, he told me that Cartwright Gardens was where they'd filmed that big song and dance number in *Oliver!* the movie. At first I'd believed him; it's a beautiful semi-circular sweep of houses overlooking a park which is shaped like a slice of melon. But he'd soon owned up to making it up to tease me. These days all the houses are hotels. I love walking through the gardens at this time in the morning because you can see all the guests of the hotels sitting in the large picture windows tucking into their breakfasts. This sight always lifts my spirits. These people seem so full of hope. Most of them aren't heading off to a job they can't stand; most of them are checking out tourist maps and planning their day, which will be filled with the stuff that memories and Instagram posts are made of. Seeing the sights, getting lost on the tube system, hoping that they'll see, but inevitably failing to see, a Pearly King and Queen.

I cross the gardens, where two Chinese blokes are on one of the tennis courts having a knockabout, and head for Burton Place, where our offices are.

But as I near the gate at the exit from the gardens I see a pram. It's a big blue old-fashioned mother trucker of a pram. The sort 1950s nannies used to push across Hampstead Heath. It's sitting there unwatched. I look inside and see a baby sleeping in it.

I look around.

Whose baby is it? Who has left the pram out here in the sunshine?

Is it someone walking their dog who has left the little mite here to snooze? But apart from the tennis players I realize that I am the only person in the gardens.

Which is when I start to panic.

Someone has left their baby there and I now realize how easy it would be to take it. I could just start wheeling the pram away and nobody would notice. I could be home, with my stolen baby, within four or five minutes. Less, if I ran. The whole fragility of life and the courses and directions it can take suddenly hit me slap bang in the face like a monumental smack.

This is what happened to me. This could be me. It's as if when I lean into the pram I am looking into a mirror. This baby has been left alone just as I was left alone. And for the first time I feel angry with my mum for leaving me so exposed and vulnerable. I don't care that 'everybody did it'. Not everybody got abducted.

Why has this baby been abandoned?

It can't be some newborn abandoned by a teenage mum who couldn't afford to look after him – I'm going with 'him' as the baby is dressed in blue and who am I to say this abandoner has gender-bias-challenging issues – the pram is too posh. This baby reeks not of baby sick, but of privilege.

'Excuse me?!' I shout out to the tennis players. They ignore me for a bit, so I march up to their mesh fence. 'Excuse me, do you know whose baby this is? Just by the gate here?'

A ball hits the fence and one of the blokes looks round.

'Sorry?'

'Is this your baby?'

I point to the pram. He shakes his head and returns to his game.

Does nobody else in the whole wide world care that there is an abandoned baby in a park?

And through my panic I feel that, God, this is so apt. The whole *Oliver!* connection. Wasn't he an abandoned baby? Didn't his mother give birth on the steps to the workhouse? But there just *aren't* workhouses in Bloomsbury.

There aren't workhouses anywhere, mind you.

Well. Not unless you count a zero-hours contract at Sports Direct.

I peer into the pram. This golden child is sleeping, rosy cheeked, not a care in the world.

Just as I'm taking out my phone to call the police I hear footsteps approaching.

'Er, can I help you?'

I look round. A woman in her twenties, officious, chicly dressed, is stepping out of some of the bushes, her hand attached to that of a toddler.

'Is this yours?' I say, motioning to the pram.

She nods curtly. Then hisses, 'Keep away from me.'

'I thought he'd been abandoned.'

'I know your game.'

And with that she grabs the handle of the pram, and starts pushing it away down the path, her toddler struggling to keep up.

My legs buckle from under me. I stagger to a nearby bench and sit. I slide the water bottle I have in my bag out and unscrew it and glug from it greedily.

She thought I was like Shirley Burke.

She thought I was going to steal her child.

And the look that she gave me.

These days, when people take kids it's to do terrible, nasty things to them. I can't even bring myself to think the words or see the imagined pictures in my head, too too ghastly for words.

And it makes me wonder if something bad like that happened when Shirley Burke took me away. If maybe all this talk of her being in love and pretending I was hers to win over some bloke was a falsity. That she and he were reckless paedophiles, who took a baby so that they could escape to the middle of nowhere and do whatever took their fancy with it.

With me.

The thought makes me vomit. I lurch forwards in my panic, but still some sick splatters on my shoes.

But wait.

This can't be right.

It just can't.

All the news reports said I was returned unharmed.

Unless that was just a cover-up, because the truth was too unsanitized for the mainstream public.

Is that why Mum never bonded with me once I was back?

Because I was soiled goods? Because it was obvious terrible things had befallen me?

I try to get my breath back. I try to find a way through my paranoia.

Well. If I was abused then there don't appear to be any long-lasting side effects. I have always had a perfectly decent sex drive and sex life. I have managed to conceive okay. And the thought of this calms me.

But what if she did? What if they did?

But then why would those news reports lie? They had nothing to gain from pretending.

No. She stole me. And the awful thing, the crushing thing, the dreadful thing is . . . she didn't just steal those weeks when she had me from my mum; she stole most of the years afterwards too. The years when Mum couldn't bond with me. The years when Mum found me hard to deal with. The years when Mum thought the best thing to do for all of us was to shut down and ignore me. It would be overly dramatic to say she had stolen the best part of my life, but she'd certainly screwed quite a bit of it up.

Thank you, Shirley Burke.

I feel my phone pulse in my coat pocket and pull it out to inspect it.

It's Ben, asking if he'd got it wrong but he thought I was coming in today.

Much as I'd really like to throw the phone into the bushes where the narky woman was lurking, I reply telling him I'm on my way but had to sit down as I've been sick.

He replies with a shocked face and two kisses.

Actually. What was Narky Woman doing lurking in the bushes?

How do I actually know that was even her baby in the pram?

How do I even know that that child she pulled out of said bushes was even hers as well?

I am now convinced that sooner or later I am going to switch on the TV news and learn that a child in a pram and a walking toddler have been abducted in the Bloomsbury area. And I did absolutely nothing to stop it.

I can picture the tennis-playing Chinese bloke being interviewed as an eye witness.

This fat bird wanted to take the pram. She asked me if I minded.

I did no such bloody thing!

And she was just about to when Narky Knickers pulled a small child from the bushes and legged it with the lot.

It's good that I've imagined this. It's so ridiculous that it means it will not happen, it cannot happen.

I guess I'd better get myself to work.

With a heavy heart, I take a paper hankie from my bag and wipe my shoes. Then stand to face the day. God help me.

Here we go. Back to the mad house.

Why am I dreading going in? Well . . .

Ben has had the travel company for what feels like forever.

Ben used to like me working at his wonderful travel company.

That was, until muggins here went and did the worst thing imaginable that a woman could do.

That's to say, I went and got pregnant.

It's not like I'm just waddling in looking as if I am carrying another life inside me. To him I may as well be walking around carrying a severed head in my hand.

And making a big song and dance of it, too.

'Hi, gang!' I may as well say each time I arrive in the morning. 'Anyone got somewhere I can stick this skull? Thanks, hon!'

Ridiculous.

Like my PA Didi once said, 'How was he born? Out of a fucking egg?'

Actually, I wouldn't put it past Ben.

As I traipse this small part of Bloomsbury – when you're this heavily pregnant, that's all you can do, traipse – I imagine the area in the Second World War. I imagine it all in black and white, a headscarfed woman leaning over the front gate, a Woodbine hanging loose from her lips, saying to a neighbour in screechy sing-song cockney: 'Well, you know that Rachel Taylor got herself in the family way, duntcha? And her not so much as in wedlock, strike a light. I said to my Cyril, I said, "You know what happened to her fancy piece, duntcha? He ran off with a load of homowhatsits, he did." Bold as brass, so he did. More front than Woolworths, dear. You wouldn't catch me bringing a little bastard into the world. Well, it's the shame, you see. Never leaves you. Anyway, best get in. Left some brawn on a low light. I'd hate it to foam over.'

And the black-and-white lady disappears inside. And suddenly I'm back in the here and now. And outside my place of work.

It's only when I walk into the office and see the posy of flowers on my desk with a small card next to it with my name and a sad face drawn onto the envelope that I realize no-one from work sent any sort of condolence card or flowers for Mum's passing.

Fuck them, I say to myself.

And who on earth draws a sad face on the card you're giving to a bereaved person?

Fuck them again. This time up the arse, I say to myself. And rip open the envelope.

The card shows a picture of a drink. Around it, it says:

WHEN LIFE GIVES YOU LEMONS
MAKE A MEAN WHISKY SOUR.

It is the most inappropriate card, I think, to give a grieving pregnant woman. I flip it open and see everyone in the office has signed it. Tracy has even written after her name: '(I'm now on Twitter. Follow me! @transtracydiamond xx)'.

What I want to do now is swipe the flowers off my desk and put them and the card straight in the bin. That's what a ball-busting woman would do in an American movie. But I'm not. I'm a sweaty pregnant person who today has puffy ankles. So instead I sit and look round the office and smile.

Three sympathetically smiling faces stare back at me. All of them are frozen. It's like they're doing the mannequin challenge. I should run up to each of them and wave my hand in front of their faces to see if they flinch.

They don't know what to say.

They don't know what to say to a grieving person.

Best not to tell them about my newfound identity and the whole abduction scenario of my early days. They'd probably all keel over and die.

Or failing that just tut and go, 'Golly.' Really quietly.

I can see they're too nervous to say anything for fear of upsetting me. Or they might just be being lazy and enjoying being seemingly frozen in time. So I break the ice with a perky, 'Hello!' and again I do some weird Scottish accent. Maybe that's my default accent for when I'm irritated.

And with that they all relax.

'Are you okay?' Didi asks, all faux concern, before rapidly checking her phone – probably to see how many likes she has got on Instagram for the photo of the bog roll she eats to stop herself gaining weight.

'Yep. All good, thanks. Hi, Ben.'

I look to Ben in the corner. He seems to be on the verge of tears, nodding sagely, a bizarre expression that appears to say, *I'm too choked up to speak. I know pain in its many forms and your recent loss has brought them all back.*

Idiot.

And then Tracy at the other desk gives me a wink and says, 'My hips are really coming on.'

I wink back. And tell her that's excellent.

'Do you like the flowers? Aren't they adorbsy?' Ben asks.

I go to say yes, but he's already interrupting.

'Moyses Stevens. What the Queen uses. And Joan Collins.'

'He got this discount from—'

'Shut UP, Didi!'

And then they all return to their computers. So I sit and switch mine on.

This is going to be fun.

'Any news on JuJu Whatserface?' I ask, to get it out of the way.

Tracy and Didi look to Ben, whose typing slows, and he turns to me with a fixed grin.

'Well, as you know, your mum took ill halfway through your JuJu trip to Marrakech—'

Didi interrupts with, 'Ben says every street looks like it's been designed by . . . you know . . . a designer.'

I stop myself from rolling my eyes and return my gaze to Ben.

'And of course she is too good a client to lose. So I took over the rest of your stay.'

'I thought the riad was good,' I say, businesslike, before he can start trying to make me feel guilty for making him go. Which I don't. If Mum hadn't died I might do, but she did, so I don't.

'Yeah, but what were those tortoises all about?'

'Oh my God!' gasps Didi. 'Those tortoises sound IMMENSE!'

'They were quite small, actually,' I say, puncturing her bubble of ridiculousness.

'Anyway, all is good in the hood, as the yoot of today say. And JuJu flies out there . . .'

He looks at his watch.

'In about an hour.'

'Back of the net!' Tracy caterwauls, then rolls up a Post-it note and chucks it through the air into the nearest wastepaper basket, trying for all the world to look like she's a basketball player.

She then blushes and returns to her work.

An orange light at the top of each phone flashes, and they all ring in unison. I feel duty bound, as I've been absent for so long, to answer this so I snatch up the receiver, glad to not have to talk to my colleagues.

'Venus Travel, Rachel speaking?'

I recognize the person on the other end of the line immediately.

'Do you know what time my flide is?'

This person is English, believe it or not, but pronounces flight as flide. Like she's American.

'Oh, hi JuJu. Let me just check for you. Gonna pop you on hold.'

And I do. Before adding quickly, 'You talentless sack of shit.'

And three colleagues' eyes zoom up, looking at me in panic.

'She can't hear. I've put the music on.'

And then I hear what is playing on the holding music. It's her latest single, 'The Ballad of Peckham Sly'. I can't bear it. She thinks she's Lily Allen, but she's more like Alan Partridge before his voice broke.

> *I wanna go, go, go, go to Peckham, Peckham, Peckham*
> *If I see any frenemies you know what I'll do?*
> *I'll deck 'em, deck 'em, deck 'em*
> *Coz that's street life in Peckham, Peckham, Peckham*

See? Hardly Philip Larkin with a beat, is it?

'I can't believe you're playing that to customers,' I say to Ben, with a built-in eye roll for good measure, like a surly teenage brat.

'What does she want?' hisses Ben. Everyone's hissing today.

'She can't hear you. She's on hold.'

'Oh, put her through to me.'

'Yes, Sir.'

I click JuJu off hold. So the singing stops.

'That music is so cool.'

'How clever of you. JuJu? I'm going to pop you over to Ben, my darling, and he can fill you in. Ciao!'

And I tap in Ben's extension number and now his phone is ringing.

He answers it with the very corny, 'Oh my God, is that the best singer-songwriter since sliced bread?' and then roars with laughter. I look to Didi and Tracy to do that 'what a complete bell end' shared look we usually do, but I see Tracy's ignoring him, and Didi is guffawing herself, like she's trying to get in with JuJu, even though she isn't even on the phone to her. The sort of 'look at me' laughter you might do at parties to get noticed by a potential mate, which means very little apart from 'I am here and I am cool. Or at least I think I am. Or try to be.'

Ben has clearly brainwashed Didi in my absence to think that he completely rocks. I don't mind this so much, as long as one of the by-products of this isn't that he's also brainwashed her into thinking I totally suck. Which is the sort of thing he'd do.

'Mark my words,' I say aloud, punctuating that thought. And Tracy looks over, wondering what I'm on about.

But there's no time for me to explain, or make something up to cover my moment of madness, as A CRISIS has broken out at Ben's desk. I can see he's trying not to hyperventilate as he types stuff into his computer and goes the colour of a beet-root, as it becomes clear JuJu has chucked some kind of hand grenade into the itinerary for today, and Ben had to fix it or else he fears she will go to a rival travel agency.

Let her go, I say.

But no. She pays top dollar. Which is why I hear him say, 'JuJu? I'm going to call you back. Give me fifteen.'

And he slams the phone down.

'She's changed her mind. She's gone off BA because they lost her cousin's luggage or something.'

'Who does she want to fly with now?' I ask.

'Private jet. She wants to leave in two hours.'

'Oh, that'll be a piece of piss.' I clearly use sarcasm in my tone when I say that. But it's not enough to placate Didi, who looks alarmed and says, 'I don't know if it will actually, Rachel.'

'ALL HANDS ON DECK!' Ben suddenly screams. 'Private jet! We need to find a private jet!'

'Where does she want to fly from?' Tracy asks what I think is a somewhat obvious, but nonetheless valid question.

'Don't be so fucking stupid, Tracy! Everyone get on the case!'

We must be pretty good at what we do. Two hours later, JuJu is heading to London City Airport, from where she is going to take a private jet to Marrakech.

I high-five Ben and Didi, just like we used to. But when I hold up my open palm to Tracy she claims it's 'triggering' and returns to her rice cake.

All day long I'm aware of my phone in my bag. I really want it to ring. I really want Kelly Hopper to have found some miraculous answers and tell me everything I want to know. I want her to say, 'Guess who I've got sitting here with me?! Shirley Burke! Oh Rachel, she's a SCREAM!'

I obsessively check my phone to see that I've not missed a call, so much so that Didi comments, 'Expecting a call?'

To which I shake my head. No. No way!

And then her eyes widen and she's all, 'Oh my God, Rachel's been on a date! Oh my God, is he really into preggers women and stuff?'

'I've not been on a date, Didi. I've been burying my mother. Not that conducive to romance, believe it or not.'

'Rachel,' Ben says, in an admonishing, patronizing way.

'What?'

'Don't be cruel. Didi's not to know.'

'To know what?'

'The shape grief takes.'

Did he actually just say that?

'When my Uncle Norman passed over. And it wasn't a nice pass over—'

'Was he Jewish?' Didi asks.

'No.'

'Oh, you said—'

'He didn't mean Passover like—' I interject, but Ben snaps so loudly he overrules the two of us.

'When my Uncle Norman died I went fucking mental. Shagged anything that moved. I'd've probably even have shagged you, Rachel. That's how horned up I was.'

Even Tracy looks up at that one and wonders where it came from.

He says the most pathetically, unthinkingly unkind things sometimes.

'I'm not saying you're ugly,' he adds.

'Well, I'm glad we've cleared that up.'

'It's just. You know. With me being –' he hates saying the word 'gay' – 'musical.'

'Musical?' I nearly spit out my chai latte.

'Yes. That's what they said in the olden days.'

'And what instrument do you play, Ben?' I ask. 'The pink oboe?'

Fortunately the phone rings then and he is distracted by someone he wishes was an A-lister.

Ben says he wants to take me to lunch. That's sweet – he says he needs some Rachey Time, and we need to reconnect. Fair dos.

'You choose where we go. Your choice.'

I'm about to mention that tapas place round the corner when he gasps, 'What about YO! Sushi in the Brunswick?! I love the conveyor belt approach.'

The path of least resistance is always best, so I say I'd love to.

YO! Sushi is too busy to sort us a table immediately so we decide to go to the tapas place I was originally going to suggest. But not before Ben snaps at the waitress, 'I hope your conveyor belt breaks!' as we retreat from the restaurant.

The Spanish-style tapas restaurant is located in a very British-looking pub and staffed mostly by Filipinos.

'Brexit?' Ben muses – well, I'm assuming he's musing; he's pulling that *I'm hilarious* face – 'What Brexit!'

And then a fit fella walks past, heading to the toilets.

'Ooh. Steady,' Ben gasps, watching the bloke's arse as it passes. 'Wouldn't mind giving that a hard Brexit.'

I return to my miniature chorizo toad-in-the-hole accompanied with minimal greengage relish.

'Okay, so Racheybaby, you know I tend to shoot from the hip, so I gotta talk to you about something.'

'Oh right, okay?'

I didn't realize there was an ulterior motive to us two doing lunch.

'So. You've been missing in action for a couple of weeks now.'

Sorry, missing in action?

He sees the look on my face.

'And it's of course unavoidable. What with your close family bereavement and all that shiz.'

'My mum dying, yes?'

'And of course, that's some really heavy shit right there. But also. You have . . . quite a bit of time off coming up, am I right?'

'No, I thought I'd give birth in the office, fielding calls and booking flights for Z-listers all the way through.'

He looks at me as if I'm being serious, then says with tension and judgement in his voice, 'Very funny, Rachey. Don't give up the day job.'

'So what are you going to say next? Actually DO give up the day job? You're firing me?!' I chuckle, finding myself hilarious.

Well, someone's got to. But then I see his face. 'Oh my God. You are. You're firing me.'

'Oh fuck off, Rachel. I'm NOT firing anyone.'

And . . . relax!

'But I do think we need to look at your circumstances. God, this Manchego is to DIE for.'

'What d'you mean, my circumstances?'

'Well, I'm paying you an awful lot of money.'

'Are you?'

'Well, yes. Considering you're so rarely in. Also . . .'

'What?' I do. I want to punch him in the face. That's so not a good look for a pregnant woman.

He leans in conspiratorially.

'I think your pregnancy is triggering Tracy.'

'In what way, triggering?'

'Well, reminding her of her . . . background. And how she can't have kids.'

'What, so now I'm running round rubbing my womb in everyone's face?'

'Well, kind of.'

'Are you for real?'

'Sorry?'

'Has Tracy actually said this?'

'Said what?'

'That I'm oppressing her, by being pregnant in her company.'

'Well . . .'

'Has she?'

'No. But you can see it in her eyes, Rach. You can really see the trans-y pain, hon.'

'Oh fuck off, Ben.' And yes, I did actually say that out loud. 'You make a bigger deal of Tracy's transition than she does.'

'I do not. I just want to make Venus a safe space for my trans employees.'

'And what about people who aren't trans?'

'They're always safe.'

'Oh, really?'

'Yes. I've read up a lot about all these issues lately.'

'Where are you getting your information from?'

'Twitter. I follow some very angry disenfranchised people. And I don't want Tracy going the same way.'

'Are you firing me or not?'

'No. I said I'm not.'

'Then what are we talking about?'

'I'm promoting Tracy.'

'Why?'

'Because you're not going to be around.'

'Right.'

He smiles at me. I'm so confused.

'And what about me? Am I being demoted?'

'God, no. No!'

'Oh, good.'

'But I am going to drop your wages.'

'By how much?'

'A third.'

I have to stop myself from stabbing him with the bread knife.

Chapter Sixteen

'What were you digging for, Shirley Burke? What were you hiding? What were you trying to find?'

When I find myself saying these words out loud to myself in the bathroom mirror I know I am going mad.

I'm now at that stage where I'm taking lots of naps. The slightest exertion, be it opening a book, rolling my eyes at something Katie Hopkins has come out with – you name it, it's knackering me. Plus my stomach is so Mount Everest-esque it's rare to find a position, be it sitting, standing or lying, that's actually comfortable, so it's easier to block everything out with forty winks here and there. It must look like sleepy bye bye time in the elephant house down my end of Bloomsbury, the size of me. But it's all in a good cause, I tell myself.

One day my mobile rings. A withheld number. I really hope it's Kelly Hopper as I take the call, but instead it's Pam.

'Pam. I wasn't expecting to hear from you. Is there a problem?'

And that seems to faze her.

'Problem? Well, yes, I'd say there was a problem. Your mum's died.'

'Right. Well—'

'Your mum's died; I'm not allowed in there; instead you've

got strangers traipsing through like Larry-oh, chucking out her knick-knacks.'

I've never heard the phrase 'Larry-oh' before.

'Pam, is there a problem apart from the fact I've asked my friend to sort Mum's stuff out?'

'Well, yes.'

And then silence.

'Well, what is it?'

'Well . . . I don't know.'

And I sigh quite loudly.

'This is very hard for me, you know, Rachel. Very hard indeed. I was friends with your mum for an extremely long time.'

'Oh yes, of course you were. Such good friends you never even asked her if she was baby Diana's mum? What sort of friend doesn't ask that kind of question? I'll tell you what sort, Pam. A fair-weather friend.'

'You always were an ungrateful little bitch,' she says.

'Well, look at who I was surrounded by growing up.'

'I hope you don't mean me, there.'

'And forgive me if I'm a little bit ungrateful now that my mum went to her grave without the balls to tell me about my real identity.'

'Oh well, I shouldn't worry about any of that. Least said, soonest mended.'

'How d'you mean? I'm allowed to be angry if I want to be.'

'Yes, but . . . no point raking over all that . . . history stuff, is there?'

She is now sounding much friendlier and gigglier, like the fact I'd been abducted as a baby and made front-page news was akin to me getting a new pair of slippers. No point making a fuss about it.

'Well, I have been raking over it actually.'

'Oh, have you?'

'Yes.'

'In what way?'

'I've been to the place I was abducted to.'

'How did you find that out?'

'The internet.'

'Bloody hell, is it all on there?'

'Yeah, you should get it, Pam. You can look up recipes for jam.'

'Where did you go?'

'North Wales.'

'Where?'

'Loggerheads.'

'Loggerheads?'

'That's the name of the village. I know. Weird. I stayed over-night in the shithole where Shirley Burke took me.'

There's silence on the end of the line.

'She's the woman who took me,' I explain.

'Shirley Burke.'

'Does it ring a bell?'

'Just racking my brains. No. Don't think it does. What was it like?'

'When she kidnapped me? I can't remember.'

'What was it like now?'

'Oh. I don't know. Bit dull, really.'

'Well, I suppose you'd . . . go somewhere like that hoping to get answers. But what you just get is more and more questions.'

Suddenly it feels okay. Suddenly it feels like I am talking to family. And now that Mum is dead I guess Pam is the nearest thing I have to my own flesh and blood. And part of her understands me. I've nobody else really I could be having this same conversation with right now.

'I met the woman who tipped the police off that I was there.'

'Sorry?'

'When Shirley Burke took me there. One of the neighbours got suspicious and called the police.'

'She's still living there?'

'Well. I got in contact with her through one of the neighbours. Long story short, I went to meet her.'

'How was that?'

'She was sweet, really. Remembered it all like it was yesterday.'

'What was there to remember?'

'Oh, just how Shirley kept herself to herself.'

'And that's suspicious, is it? I suppose to some people it is. I like to keep myself to myself. Careful, Pam, you might get arrested.'

'She saw her digging in the night.'

'Digging?'

'She's got no idea why.'

'Maybe she was planting carrots.'

'Or evidence.'

'Evidence of what? Wasn't very successful, was she? She still got caught. Silly cow.'

I can't help but laugh.

'What?'

'Well, I'd argue she was a bit more than a silly cow.'

'Point taken.'

'She did something really shocking and tried to get away with it. She ruined my mum's life. Our relationship. Loads of things. She stole years from us.'

'Was it years? I thought it was weeks.'

'But the repercussions went on for years.'

'I'm sure, I'm sure. I just meant if she was burying . . . what d'you call it?'

'Evidence?'

'Yes, then she was a silly cow.'

I really don't understand Pam sometimes.

I really don't understand Pam most of the time.

As much as I want to get into an argument about her suddenly having an opinion on a woman she's never met, and who she couldn't remember much about at my mum's funeral, I decide to let it drop. She is the nearest I have to family. Now is not the time to rock the boat.

'Pam, I'm sorry if you feel I've excluded you since Mum died. But I had to get the locks changed because I locked myself out.'

'Oh forget it, it's fine. What's done is done.'

'And maybe it's good that my friend is going through her stuff. It would only upset both of us.'

'Yes, and let's face facts. You've already found out the biggie.'

'This is true.'

Is it possible? Is it possible that Pam was nervous about me finding out? That she was honouring Mum's wishes and so didn't want me going through her stuff? That that's why she was angry that I'd changed the locks and she no longer had access to the house? Did she promise Mum on her deathbed that she'd get rid of the evidence for her?

I don't like to think that's a possibility.

I believe now might be the correct time to bury the hatchet. And I don't mean in Pam's head.

'Pam? I'm really sorry.'

'For what?'

'That I made out you . . . that you might have put a pillow over Mum's head. Or a cushion.'

'What a thing to say.'

'I was in shock. I was grieving. And I'm sorry.'

I haven't said I've changed my mind. I haven't said that's not what I think any longer. I've just apologized for using those words.

I still think she did it.

But maybe she did her a favour.

'Thank you. Will we be seeing you in the New Forest soon?'

'I'll be sure to let you know next time I'm coming.'

I keep dreaming I'm back there. I keep dreaming I'm in that street and the mountain is towering above me. It's always black and white in my dreams; it all takes place in a time that knew no colour. In the dream I'm always Myrus. I'm not unlike the gossiping housewife from the Bloomsbury doorstep, with my arms crossed across my cracking bosom, and a ciggie dangling from the corner of my mouth. I'm standing in my bedroom at the back of my maisonette, looking down onto the garden at Lovers' Leap. I can see a girl, not unlike Dorothy in *The Wizard of Oz*, same black-and-white gingham dress, same hair in pig-tails, only in my dream she's attacking the ground with a pickaxe.

I wake. And I always think the same thing.

There's no place like home.

Dorothy. Dorothy in *The Wizard of Oz*. She went missing. Okay, so she went on the most incredible journey and saw the most fantastical things, but all the time she hated it and wanted to get home.

Is that how I felt? Did I know? Was I as scared of Shirley as Dorothy was of the Wicked Witch of the West? Or did I love her like Glinda the Good Witch?

What were you, Shirley? A good witch or a bad witch?

I remember Ben telling me the story of the woman who'd

played Auntie Em in the film. About how she killed herself draped in a gold cape, surrounded by all her publicity shots and press clippings from her successful career. Ben had always found this image so camp; who wouldn't? The ageing star daring us in death to tell her she was no good.

No kid, I was a star!

But when I investigated further I found that the poor lady had been crippled with arthritis and was going blind, and she hated every minute of the pain she found herself in. So. Not so camp after all. Though the added flourish of the press cuttings and head shots was definitely a coup de théâtre.

Is that how you felt, Shirley? When it was all over? Did you end up killing yourself? Could you, too, no longer live with the pain? You'd done something quite extraordinary and it had gone and what were you left with? Nothing. And that's a lot to deal with.

Christ. What am I sounding like? Enough with all the *Wizard of Oz* analogies. That way madness lies!

Although I do think that film, now, is very skewed in favour of the journey that Dorothy goes on. I mean. What about her poor family? Left behind in Kansas, having to deal with the aftermath of a twister and thinking that their child has been killed in the tornado. You don't see any of that in the movie. That's where the real story is.

Or is it?

Isn't my whole driving force at the moment to work out what happened in Oz, rather than what happened back in Kansas?

I know. I really do need to drop it.

Even if the analogy is a really good one.

Oh no. Am I too camp? Is that why my last boyfriend turned out to be gay? Did I drive him to it with my camp analogies?

Stop. This. Now.

I'm at work, bored, when finally Kelly phones me.

'Is now a good time?'

'Hang on,' I say, getting up. I address the room: 'I'm just going out for a breather. Won't be long.'

And I head out onto the pavement.

'Okay. Shoot,' I say.

'I've found something interesting,' she says, deadpan, as if she's concentrating on something else.

'Right,' I say, all giddy and excited.

And then there is silence.

'Okay, I'm all ears,' I prompt, my giddiness levels still remaining high.

Yet again. Silence.

'Kelly? Hello?'

Then suddenly she says, 'I've got to go. I'm so sorry.'

'Kelly?'

There is an urgency in her tone I don't like. In the background I can hear a hammering sound. Like someone striking a wall with a heavy object. Is she being attacked?

'I'll have to show you in person. Meet me outside Kentish Town tube station.'

'When?'

'Half an hour.'

'I'm at work.'

'Six?'

'I don't finish till half past.'

'Seven.'

And then she hangs up.

All afternoon I'm frantically wondering what it is she's found, what she's going to show me at the station. I worry that I've acted too ungratefully towards her. She's had some sort of breakthrough. It's the first time she's made contact since we met. What's more, she sounded sober. And I just acted all, *Oh God, it's really inconvenient right now, soz hon,* to her.

What a rude bitch I am.

I realize the error of my ways and so spend the afternoon phoning her mobile, but every time it goes straight to answerphone. I leave a variety of 'Actually I'm free now if you want me to come straight away' type messages, but she doesn't call back so by four I decide to leave it till our seven o'clock meet.

Ben, Didi and Tracy keep looking at me, wondering why I keep nipping out to make umpteen phone calls. As the obsession is eating away at me, I can't help myself. I'm going to tell them. I'll put some spin on it so they don't think it's me, but you never know . . . one of them might have some good advice about the situation.

'So anyway –' I try to sound as chirpy as possible – 'I've got this friend, right, in the New Forest and she just found out that when she was little she was abducted.'

Didi gasps. 'By Isis?'

'From her back garden. People used to leave their babies outside all the time back then. 'Anyway, she was missing for weeks on end before they caught her abductor.'

'Who was it?'

'Some random woman who'd told her boyfriend she was pregnant when she wasn't and so she needed a baby to keep the lie going.'

'Blimey,' says Tracy, and I'm inclined to agree. It is indeed a blimey situation.

'Wasn't baby Diana, was it?' Ben asks. And I nearly fall off my chair.

'Yes! How do you know?'

And then of course I remember that Ben is quite a bit older than me and presumably saw the news items as a child.

'Oh, I just remember her dad was really fit.'

'Oh, right.'

'I had my first wank over him, actually.'

Okay, this is now the seventh circle of hell that I'm finding myself in.

'He was really fit. I loved seeing him cry.'

Now I want to change the subject. But Ben might have some welcome information.

'I was quite disappointed when they got the baby back. He just disappeared like that.'

And with that Ben snaps his fingers dramatically.

'What's he like now?' he asks. 'Have you got a photo?'

'Why would I have a photo?'

'Well, he's your mate's dad.'

'Oh, yeah. Oh, she doesn't really see him any more.'

Ben looks most put out.

'What was her mum like, then?'

He shrugs. 'Like I'm gonna remember her.'

Typical.

'She had big hair, though. I remember that. Well, it was the eighties.'

'How old were you?'

'Thirteen. Fourteen? When did it happen?'

'Nineteen eighty-one.'

He nearly coughs up his windpipe with embarrassment.

'Oh scrap that, I must have been about six.'

As I've always thought. This bugger lies about his age.

'How is she? This Diana?' he asks, in a rare moment of kindness and interest in others.

'Yeah, she's good.'

'You'd think something like that might scar you for life.' He sighs.

'Do you remember anything about the woman who took her?'

Ben thinks. Chews the end of his vape. Then shakes his head.

'Nothing whatsoever.' Then his eyes widen as if he's remembering something. He adds, 'I always wondered if Lisa Stansfield's song was based on all that.'

'Which song?'

And he bursts into a heavily vibrato'd rendition of 'Been Around the World'. And when he sings the bit about not being able to find his baby, Didi gasps and looks at me.

'Someone wrote a song about your friend. That's so awesome.'

'Right?' echoes Tracy.

'Awesome sauce!' adds Ben. Just then the phone rings. He snaps it up. 'Hello, Venus?'

I feel like hitting my head against a brick wall.

It's dark by seven and Kentish Town feels mobbed. The pavement outside the tube station is too narrow for the volume of people walking past. Alongside the entrance an awning is down, sheltering a greengrocer's who's put tables out on the pavement crammed with plastic bowls full of the most vibrant-coloured fruit and veg. It all looks like someone has painted them, or they're a pre-filtered Instagram moment waiting to happen. It starts to drizzle and the colours all around me seem to smudge. The headlights of passing cars, the neon shop signs, the white cubes of iPhone screens, make me feel like I'm in a work of art, a drawing smudged by the artist's thumb.

At twenty past seven I'm getting a bit tired of waiting, and starting to feel the cold. I try calling Kelly on my mobile but it goes straight to answerphone. At half seven the rain eases off a little so I decide to walk down the high street and see if she's in her office. But when I get to the sauna I see that there is an ambulance outside, its back doors open, lights off. Maybe someone has collapsed in the heat of the sauna. But then I see that the door next to it is open, the door up to Kelly's office. A few seconds later I see a flash of lime green and a paramedic is backing out through the door, carrying a stretcher. Another paramedic is carrying the other end. Lying on the stretcher is none other than Kelly. I freeze, suddenly feeling the blood drain down through me. Her eyes are closed and she looks dead. Selfishly, the first thing I think is, *She can't die. She's made a breakthrough in my case. Please. Don't let her die.*

'What's happened to her?' I call out to the paramedics. Then realize I must look like an incredibly nosy passer-by, so I add by way of explanation, 'I do know her.'

'Not sure. Taking her to the hospital,' one of them replies, cautiously. 'We found her collapsed.'

'She'll live, though, right?'

'We just need to take her in, love.'

'Of course.'

'What's her name?' one of them asks me.

'Kelly. Kelly Hopper.' I then add, 'Not Hoppen, like the interior designer.'

And they both look at me like I am mad. I am obviously speaking a foreign language to them.

'Jeez!' I joke. 'What are you doing at eight o'clock in the evening when her reality design competition programme's on?'

'Saving lives,' one of them replies.

'Yeah, that was . . . part of the joke.'

I watch as they hoick Kelly up into the back of the ambulance, then strap in the stretcher so that it doesn't roll about on its wheels.

'Which hospital is she going to?'

'Royal Free, love.'

283

As the ambulance pulls off I realize I am standing in the entrance to Kelly's office. The ambulance men haven't closed the door, thinking I was going in, judging by how I have positioned myself. Would it be rude to go up and see if I can make sense of any of Kelly's notes?

I would only be quick.

I am going to pay her if she gets any results.

Therefore I sort of have a right to go up.

Sod it. I will.

It's a shock when I get to the office at the top of the stairs. The door is unlocked and open; light is streaming into what feels like a white cube. Every single stick of furniture bar none has been removed, and every soft furnishing. The windows stand naked, stripped of any curtains, oblong marks across the floor showing where rugs once lay. Every shred of evidence that Kelly Hopper was once here has been eradicated. Gone. In a puff of paramedic. All the built-in shelves are bare, and in some places the actual light switches have been unscrewed from the walls. This is no longer a detective agency.

Was that what she was trying to tell me? Was that what she had discovered; that she'd have to move on, try something new?

Perhaps I will never know.

SHIRLEY

1981

Chapter Seventeen

Which film was it where they said 'when the Good Lord closes a door, somewhere he opens a window'?

Well that's what had happened here and no mistake. Because no sooner had Doug put the Oldham place on the market and I'd dropped my clanger.

'I've got a bun in the oven, Doug . . . And I've nowhere to live, like . . .'

Well he only went and revealed that he was a man of property. I'd always known he was a man of means, show me a man who deals in catseyes who wasn't, but turned out he had a few hidey holes dotted about the place and he suggested I moved to Wales.

Wales! I know!

He said it had been a holiday home for him and 'Vee'.

I didn't like him calling her Vee. It was far too over familiar for someone he was practically on the verge of leaving.

But when I'd got here, well, you couldn't have imagined anything less like a holiday home.

Don't get me wrong. On many levels this was ideal. It was hidden away from the eyes of the world. Doug couldn't get here all the time so it allowed me space to put my plan into action. And nobody seemed to pay me much heed.

Apart from her. Nosey Neighbour Extraordinaire. It felt like she was always out there, watching me, so I was having to keep my head down and stop in most of the time. Which was kind of all right as there was naff all to do round here except wait for Doug's next visit.

'Hello, sweetheart,' she'd say, every time I'd pop out for a breath of fresh air. 'How's the little monkey doing?'

I hated her calling her the little monkey.

'Yeah, she's fine thanks, Myra.'

'It's Myrus, actually.'

'Sorry.'

'Apology accepted.'

It was a bright sunny day and I couldn't take being cooped up in the cottage a second longer. I'd come and sat on the back doorstep. And there she was, poking her head over the garden fence.

'Having a little lie down, is she?'

'Yeah, she's asleep.'

'Aww, they dunn'alf sleep a lot at that age. I remember it well.'

I didn't say owt. Hoping that'd shut her up, like.

'Course, it never.

'You wanna get her outside, dumpling.'

I nearly said, *How many times? I'm not dumpling, I'm Shirley.*

But I didn't want a row with her. Pointless making a show of yourself, getting a reputation.

The phone started to ring inside. I jumped up.

'Gotta go. That'll be my fella.'

She smiled – God, even her smile looked nosy – and I dashed back inside.

I'd have to tell him it was time to move on. I could say I was bored or something. I did not want Myrus flaming Withy snooping on me any more, the nosy old trout.

I snapped up the receiver, only it wasn't Doug; it was a wrong number.

I was so bored.

I was so lonely.

I had done the most ridiculous thing in the world.

I was completely and utterly in the shit.

Baby started to cry. I went up and took her out of her carry-cot and jiggled her about a bit in my arms and stuck that cute little dummy in her mouth and wondered if it was time for another feed. It's all I did these days. Feed her. Change her. Talk baby talk to her. Try and get her to be quiet. Try and get her to be sweet. But she was grouchy. She knew damn well I wasn't her mammy. She hated me.

Please, I prayed to God, *please let it start going my way. Please let her start liking me.*

Maybe I was scaring her, every time I looked down at her. Maybe she got a shock seeing my ugly mug and not her own mum's. But I'd now had her longer than her mum had her. She should've been buddying up to me now. What on earth was the matter with her?

You could go off people, you know.

Sometimes I wanted to run away from her. Sometimes I wanted to tell Doug she'd died. Just leave her there, or on Myrus's doorstep, and run.

Sometimes I thought the easiest thing to do would be to kill her. I knew how horrible that sounded, but it really did feel like it would suddenly make everything all right.

I could dig a hole. In the garden. Nobody would know. The only person who really knew what I looked like round here was that Myrus, and why would she be any the wiser? Folk already knew Diana was missing. Nobody thought Diana was the baby I had; I'd told them her name was Rachel.

'It's a pretty name, is Rachel,' Myrus said. And she was right. It was a pretty name.

Loads prettier than Shirley, any road.

I couldn't kill her, though. I just knew I wouldn't be able to go through with it. It was one thing having mad fantasies about knocking off Doug's missus. But a newborn baby. No way.

Though I bet a load of people wouldn't put it past me, if they knew what I had done. If they realized what a terrible, shocking thing I'd planned and gone through with. But it was meant to be a decent thing. I would look after her.

And the good news was Doug'd never doubted me once.

Never.

The bad news was . . . he didn't seem to be any closer to leaving that needy bitch Vera.

Oh, he'd stepped up to the plate. Passing us money left, right and centre, splashing the cash like Larry-oh. Like nobody's business. He'd given us a roof over our heads, away from prying eyes.

But it didn't alter the fact that I was still here in the middle of nowhere with a bloody kid, on me tod. And that wasn't easy, not in anybody's book.

He was coming up at the weekend, though. Said he was looking forward to seeing Rachel. Happen he'd fall in love with her when he saw her.

Wish I could've. But she was so grouchy and grizzly. She was like a bear with a sore head.

Two days I'd had her, now. And it felt like an eternity. It was as if I couldn't even remember what it was like before she came. And I was so ill prepared. It's not like I knew a midwife or a health visitor who came and visited me through the pregnancy

– they'd've got a shock if they had've – and warned me what it was all going to be like.

I hadn't got a pigging clue, had I?

I'd read somewhere that gin was good for babies. Not loads of it, mind. Just a bit, now and again, to make them shut up and nod off. I was really careful I never gave her too much. Just the odd bit when she was screeching enough to drive any poor bugger mad. And last thing I needed was her annoying the neighbours. And then them calling social workers and the like and them asking too many questions.

And then them calling social workers and the like and them asking too many questions, and I certainly wouldn't put that past nosy parker Myrus Withy. Eyes and ears of the village, by the looks of it. I was surprised she didn't bomb round with binoculars all the time. And an ear trumpet.

She had a nose like an ear trumpet, too. Like she could grab hold of it and knock out 'The Last Post'.

She was obsessed with Doug. Probably had the hots for him.

'Oh, he was often here with his lady wife,' she'd say, inferring of course that I was anything but. And then she corrected herself, 'His former lady wife, obviously.'

'Obviously.' I agreed, as if it was obvious.

Though she said something really weird as well.

'And, of course, with looks like that she was the talk of the village. Never quite seen the likes of it before, they hadn't.'

What? They'd never seen a beautiful woman before?

It had to be said. Myrus Withy was weird.

'I mean I'm more in touch with these things, dear. What with me being from London an' all.'

She beggared belief. And I had to get away from her.

I supposed one thing I could do, one way to get out of this

mess, would be to take the baby and leave it somewhere and put a note in with her saying who she was and how sorry I was. No harm done.

But then I'd have to tell Doug a tale or two to cover it. I mean, she was live and kicking now. Even if I pretended I'd found her dead in her cot he'd want proof, wouldn't he? Not saying he'd want to see a corpse, but he'd want to know what I'd done with her.

I could say I'd had a little funeral for her. There'd been a cancellation at the crem and I'd done it on the spot, got it over with.

But I just knew somehow he'd twig.

I'd have to go through with this now, now I had a real live baby on my hands.

I looked out the bedroom window while Rachel finally got off to sleep as I rocked her in my arms.

'There's a good girl. There's a good Rachel. I'm so sorry, kid,' I said softly as the tears fell.

This was not the way it was meant to happen at all.

The poor little thing didn't deserve all this. She certainly didn't deserve me. She'd put me off having kids for life.

But then . . . but then I did have a kid. I had one now.

What a frigging mess, Shirley.

I could tell Doug she'd died and I'd buried her in the garden coz I was scared folk might think I'd killed her. But then wouldn't he just assume I'd killed her anyway?

But then I could blackmail him and say if he dared tell anyone what I'd done I'd tell his Vera about the baby.

He'd not told her about Rachel. He said he was mulling it over. Whatever that was meant to mean.

Every turn in my head, every thought I had, I just felt more and more sick.

'This afternoon,' I said to the baby as I rested her down in her carrycot, 'I'll take you up the mountain. See the sights. Peace and quiet and nobody looking. Just the two of us.'

I went and sat in the garden again, and up popped Nosy Hole.

'I'm thinking of going up the mountain later. Take the little 'un.'

Myrus pulled a face. 'Have you got walking boots?'

'No.'

'You're gonna need walking boots.'

'Why? It's a nice sunny day. I'll push the pram up to the top. Be lovely.'

Myrus pulled another face. 'It might be sunny down here, sweetheart, but up the top it's snowy. You won't be able to push a pram up there and you certainly can't be going up in them heels. What size shoe are you?'

'Three.'

'Hang on. I might have some. Let me look.' And with that she went inside.

Right, well, if I couldn't push the pram up I'd have to carry her up. She wasn't a fat baby. And happen the fresh air'd tire her out.

The phone rang. I went inside. Finally, it was him.

'How you doing?'

'I'm all right. I miss you, though.'

'I miss you, baby.'

'Have you told her yet?'

'No. You know I haven't. I'm still trying to find a way to make this work.'

'How d'you mean?'

'Well, for me to keep seeing you on the QT and give you money and that, and still keep her sweet.'

'Your place . . . is with me and Rachel now.'

'So you keep saying, but I've got responsibilities here. And what if Vera fancies a weekend break in her holiday home?'

'She won't. Look. I'll be with you at the weekend.'

'We're going mountain climbing.'

'You what?'

'This afternoon. Up the mountain.'

'Are you off your head?'

'No.'

'Have you lost the flaming plot, Shirl?'

'I've always liked mountain climbing.'

'You only gave birth two days ago. Haven't you got stitches in your fanny?'

'Nurse came round today and took them out.'

'You are in no fit state to go mountain climbing.'

'It's only a little hill.'

'You need to rest up and take it easy.'

'Yeah well, that's a bit difficult when you're a single parent.'

'I will make this up to you, Shirley. I will make sure Rachel never goes without.'

'Without what, though, a dad? She already has, Doug.'

'I'm gonna hang up if you carry on being like this.'

'I just find it hard, Douglas. Being a single parent, all on my own.'

I just wanted him here, with me, with the baby. But as Mam had always said – I want, doesn't get.

He littered the airwaves with a warming stream of apologies and my heart was lifted temporarily.

Then I became aware that I wasn't in the house on my own. Well, I became aware someone had stepped inside and might be able to hear me.

'I'm going to have to go now. I've got company.'

'Who?'

'One of the neighbours.'

'Okay. Hey. Have you seen the news?'

Why was he doing this? He knew I had to go. Well. He thought I did, any road.

'What news?'

'That poor family. Where the baby's been taken.'

'Oh I know, it's shocking.'

Was this some sort of test? My heart started racing. Was he saying this for a reason? Had he worked it all out and felt the need to confront me? Time to nip it in the bud.

'That poor woman. I can't stop thinking about her. What she must be going through.'

'Dunt bear thinking about, does it?'

'I keep looking at Rachel in her cot. And thinking. It could so easily have been her. You know they were born on the same day, Doug? So she'd be exactly the same age.'

The line goes quiet.

'Aye, it makes you think.'

'Ah, don't get too sad, Douglas. That's the difference between us and them, int it? We've got our baby. We know exactly where she is.'

'Aye.'

'And that's here. In this beautiful village. Waiting for you.'

'Lovers' Leap,' he said tenderly.

'Yes, Douglas,' I said, equally tenderly, trying not to let him hear the big bass drum beat of my heart. 'Let's hope they do.'

'Just don't leave her outside on her own, eh?'

I turned and saw Myrus hovering behind me with a pair of muddy walking boots.

'I feel like Prince Charming in *Cinderella*. Whosoever

weareth these shoes shall marry the fine prince! Was that Douglas on the blower?'

I nodded. How much had she heard?

'I can't wait to catch up.'

I took a deep breath, to quell the overbeating heart.

'He'll be here soon enough,' I said, and had to catch myself because I knew I had just snapped at her, and that was not a good move when I'd just arrived in a street in the arse end of nowhere with a baby that was born on the same day that one was nicked. One that was making front-page news. I saw her staring at my hand. I knew what she was thinking so I just came out with it.

'If you're wondering where my wedding ring is, I lost it.'

'Ooh dear, that's a bit rum init?'

'Me hands swelled up something rotten in my last stage of pregnancy and I took it off, only I can't for the life of me remember where I put it.'

'Oh dear. Sure it'll turn up soon enough.'

'I hope so, Myrus. But you know the good thing? Douglas was so understanding about it.'

'Was he?'

'If they handed out prizes for nicest bloke on the oil rigs, they'd have to give it to my hubby.'

'That's a lovely thing to say, Shirley.'

'I know. But what's even lovelier is . . . it's the truth.'

And with that we shared a smile. She held my gaze a little bit too long.

'Was he disappointed, though?'

'When?'

'When you realized you'd had a girl and not a boy. See, I wouldn't mind. I like little girls, always have. I used to dress mine in ribbons and all kinds of finery. But blokes, see, they can be a bit funny, dear. If you know what I'm saying.'

I sighed. This woman could so easily have become the bane of my life.

'Honest answer, Myrus? I don't know. He said he was fine about it. But like you say. He's a bit of a man's man.'

'Oh I like a manly man, dear. Don't get me wrong.'

'Which is why you probably won't see much of us when he's down at the weekend.'

She winked at me. 'I get your drift, dear; pretty unshockable here. Lived through the Blitz, didn't I? And after all, dear. A man has needs.'

'Now, I must – thank you for these boots – get on with getting ready.'

'That hill won't climb itself, dear.'

'No it won't, Myrus, and thank you again.'

She gave me a cautious smile and headed back out. In the doorway she turned, looked at me again, then walked off. I followed her and shut the front door. I did what I'd been avoiding all day; I put on the television.

And there she was. The other woman weighing heavy on my life and my mind right now. Linda Wilson in all her Technicolor glory. Another news bulletin. Another shot of her silently roaring with pain. Turning her head away from the camera to nestle it on her husband's shoulder.

I'd only seen them the day before yesterday, but they looked like they'd aged ten years.

I'd thought he was pretty dishy, actually. But he'd looked like he could have been a bit of a handful.

And what about her?

How did I feel about her?

She was quite pretty, really.

Actually, she was very pretty.

I mean, grief didn't make you pretty. And that's what she was doing. She was grieving and I was the cause of it. That little crotchety bundle of screams and snot and shit and piss. She was grieving that. There was probably milk leaking from her breasts, whereas I had none.

I wanted to hate this woman. If only I could try, really try to dislike her. If I could seethe every time I saw her. Like, if she reminded me of someone I hated from school, say, then I could feel better about what I was doing. But she didn't. She just seemed straight up and decent. And the whole bloody country had fallen in love with her. When you were a plain Jane you knew a pretty girl when you saw one. And she was pretty. So the tabloids loved running pictures of her on their front pages, looking more and more bereft.

I turned the sound down when the next news item came on. I'd heard enough. Basically the police were screwed. They'd had no leads. Nothing to go on. No-one had seen me.

I suddenly thought of that woman who came to the bus stop. She'd been crying. I really hoped that would have blinkered her view of me. Surely she'd've come forward by now, forty-eight hours after the baby was taken, and given a description of me if she'd remembered me? Never mind the folk who actually saw me walking along the street, bold as brass. Or seen me in my hire car. Or seen me at the service station playing my music too loud to drown the noise of the baby crying in the boot. I couldn't have risked being seen driving around with a baby in the back, not that day. And me getting changed in the loos, out of my costume and wig into my normal clothes.

Actually, she'd not been bad at all. She'd only cried for ten minutes or so.

But folk notice things. I knew that.

God, I couldn't think about this. It was doing my head in. That familiar panic was rushing through me like red stuff in a thermometer. Any second now I'd get too hot and blow.

I had to get out. Into the air. Breathe deeply and feel better.

Myrus was right. It was snowing and I was glad of the boots. I'd wrapped up and had the baby tucked in my coat so that she wasn't obviously visible at first glance. It would have been quite an odd sight to see a girl as young as me carrying a newborn like this up to the top of a mountain. Though now I'd done it, it was definitely just a really big hill. I held her close to me, constantly aware that she was too young, too fragile, and the slightest thing could harm her. Suddenly my feelings of guilt towards her mum and dad were overtaken by a strange mixture of vulnerability and a desire to protect.

At the top of Moel Famau I looked down and saw the city of Liverpool, across two rivers, spread out for me to see. It was clear at the top. I could see for miles around. I could pick out blocks of flats, power stations, bridges.

Being so high up lent me a feeling of invincibility.

I could do this. I could. I could get away with it, because feeling this little girl lying close to my chest right now . . . it meant something.

It meant she was mine.

And as long as I banished all thoughts of that poor sodding crying woman on the telly box. As long as I could, like . . . totally forget all about her, this child would be mine.

She was mine.

Maybe. Maybe, just maybe I could keep going through with this after all.

When I got back to the house I picked up the phone and

called our Josie and told her I'd had Doug's baby and was recuperating in North Wales. She said she'd come and visit.

As soon as I hung up I started to panic.

Chapter Eighteen

The night before Josie was due to visit I hardly slept a wink. I lay there in the dark and the shadows through the curtains scared me. There weren't any lights on in this street, so how come it felt like there was a concentration camp spotlight pointing right into this room? I got up and ripped the curtain back. To the left of the mountain I saw a full moon shining. A saucer of pulsating blue-white light. I had to screw my eyes up, it was so bright.

I went and looked in on Rachel's cot. She was sleeping soundly. Maybe I should have had some gin too. But I didn't like the taste of it. It might've knocked me out, but I couldn't afford to be grouchy and hungover tomorrow. Tomorrow my sister would be here.

And my sister was canny.

She didn't miss a trick.

And since she'd lost her baby so late on in her pregnancy she didn't suffer fools. In fact, she suffered them even less gladly.

Hard-faced, that's what she'd become.

She'd sounded so excited on the phone at my good news, and she'd bought the lie so quickly. She'd believed me when I'd said I'd not told her about baby Rachel because I hadn't wanted to upset her in the wake of her bad experiences lately. She sounded like it had almost made her cry, that bit.

'I knew you were pregnant, I just didn't think you'd have it and not tell me! I've been ringing the flat but someone else is living there. Thought you'd done a runner on us!'

'Douglas wanted to do a bit of travelling and that.'

'Has he left his wife?'

'No comment.'

'Oh, Shirl. What are you like?!'

But there was no malice in her voice.

So far she hadn't smelt a fish.

But she was going to in the morning, I could feel it in me waters.

I was to meet her up near Conwy Castle, because her Bob Carolgees lookalike liked old relics and he could take in the castle while me and her could take Rachel to the tea shop.

Even if our Josie didn't clock who Rachel was . . . someone was going to. Weren't they? Some bright spark in the tea rooms was gonna nudge their mate and head for a payphone and before we'd had our toasted teacakes it was gonna be like an episode from *The Sweeney*. And gullible Josie would watch on from the sidelines gasping, 'No! Not my sister. Not our Shirley.'

But that was the problem. Our Josie wasn't a bit gullible. I was going to fall at the first fence.

I must've eventually nodded off because I woke with a start and it was bright daylight. The phone was ringing downstairs and I panicked that Rachel had died in the night as she wasn't making a sound. But I quickly saw that she was just lying staring at the ceiling quietly. She was fine. I legged it down the stairs.

It was our Josie.

'Oh, Shirl. You're never gonna believe this.'

'What?!'

'I've only gone and woke up with conjunctivitis in both eyes.

I think I caught it off the pillow coz Him Indoors had it last week. I told him to wash the pillowcase, bastard.'

'Oh, you poor thing.'

I tried to sound disappointed.

'Upshot is, I don't think I can come.'

'Oh no!'

'I can't see my hand in front of my face. When I meet my niece I wanna see her good and proper, d'you know what I'm saying, Shirl?'

'And I want you to see her too.'

'Plus if I've got an infection, last thing I want's to be passing it onto the babby.'

'Well, I was thinking along them lines, Josie, if I'm honest.'

'Honesty's the best policy, kid. I'll give you a bell when me eyes've cleared up.'

'And make sure you see a doctor.'

'I can't see me own frigging tits at the minute, kid. But I'll phone 'em anyway. See you, love.'

'See you, Jose.'

'And give that little belter a kiss from me.'

I hung up. And nearly danced my way back to bed.

Josie down. Only Dougie to go now.

Oh heck.

Rachel was stirring when I next looked in on her. She seemed grouchy, so I sung her her favourite little nursery rhyme thingy. It had been mine as a nipper, and now it was hers. I tickled her legs and arms, moving up and down as I went:

> *'Itsy bitsy spider climbed up the waterspout,*
> *Down came the rain and washed the spider out,*
> *Out came the sun and dried up all the rain,*
> *Itsy bitsy spider climbed up the spout again.'*

* * *

I was getting some fresh air before Doug's arrival when I saw Nosey Neighbour pegging out. I could feel her staring at me, but I didn't let on.

'Did he not have any babies with his former lady wife?' she called across.

I looked at her. 'You what?'

'I suppose he didn't or he'd have said.'

'You've lost me.'

'I was wondering if Doug had any babies with his former lady wife.'

Was she trying to catch me out?

'Mind you. Probably just as well.'

'How d'you mean?'

'It ain't always easy for half-castes is it?'

'For what?'

'Half-castes.'

'I don't know what you mean.'

And then she approached the fence, arms full of wet clothes.

'You do know his last wife was a thingamabob. Coloured.'

What was she on about?

And then it dawned on me.

Myrus had never met Vera.

Vera had never been here.

Douglas had set some other girl up in this house. A girl who was a black girl.

'She was black?' I asked, my voice faltering.

'Oh yes.' She smiled. 'Funke came from Nigeria, darlin'. She was as black as the ace of spades.'

Vera had been right. Vera had been right that day she's accosted me in the street. She'd said something like, 'you aren't the first and you won't be the last'.

Douglas was a serial philanderer.

Why did I think I was so special?

No wonder he was so confident that Vera would never come here. Vera probably didn't even know this house existed.

This wasn't his holiday home for him and Vera. This was his love nest for him and Funke.

Oh Shirl. When will you live and learn?

'Int she lovely, Shirl?'

'Aww, glad you think so.'

I linked Doug as we leaned over the carrycot.

'Int she funny looking?' he said, after a while.

Cheeky bastard. Though of course, I don't say it out loud.

'Well, some folk say I'm funny looking, so happen she got that from me.'

'She dunt look like any of my other kids.'

'Yeah, coz Vera hasn't had an 'and in this one. What are you like, Doug? She's ours. Nobody else's. Aww, I love her so much, you know.'

'It shows. You've kept her ever so nice. Clean and tidy, and . . .'

I cut him off. 'I keep everything nice. It's what I excel at.'

What I didn't tell him was I'd given Rachel an extra dab of gin before he got here. I didn't want her waking up all the time and bawling and showing me up so he'd see that sometimes I couldn't cope with her. Coz most of the time I could.

I needed to prove I was better than Vera. I needed to prove I was a better investment than Funke.

He went to the window and opened it, then struck up a cigarette.

'What, you've started smoking?'

'It's the stress.'

'But what about your heart?'

'Don't you start an' all.'

'Oh, does she have a go, does she?'

'Shurrup.'

'Well, good. It's bad for you, smoking. It's a killer.'

He rolled his eyes. 'I didn't come down with the last shower, you know.'

'Have you told her yet? About Rachel?'

He shook his head and looked up at the mountain.

'But you will do. Eventually. Yeah?'

And he nodded his head, took a drag on his ciggie and said, really quietly, 'Yeah.'

And that was the thing with him. I couldn't tell if he was being quiet because he was dreading telling her. Or he was going all soft because he was lying, and he had no intention of telling her. Either scenario didn't bode that well for me.

'I can't be a kept woman forever,' I added, trying to sound all virginal.

He flicked half his ciggie away, out of the window and into the garden.

'Litterbug. That's how forest fires start,' I gently cajoled him, and he turned and shut the window.

'They're a bugger a lot, the Taffies, you know,' he said, all cocky.

'You what?'

'They find out you're English? They'll set fire to this place and kill the pair of you.'

'Don't be soft.'

'They do that! The Welsh nationalists. They set fire to English people's country cottages. That's why me and Vera hardly ever come.'

Liar!

'Well, her next door, she's from London. She's never had her house set fire to. Plus she's a nosy beggar. She'd spot anyone coming down this street with a petrol can and call the police.'

He nodded and looked down into the carrycot. And said again, 'Funny looking fucker.'

This was beginning to upset me, as if she was my own. I really wished he wouldn't say stuff like that.

'So, go on. What was the labour like again?'

'Oh, you know. I cried a lot. Screamed a lot. Nurses were nice. Bit put out you weren't there.'

'You or them?'

'Both!' I said with a wink, and my best Alma Cogan chuckle.

'I thought you were having a boy.'

'Yeah, but that was just a gypsy I met. She was meant to be a good gypsy. Maybe she'll grow up to be a tomboy.'

'It's weird, int it? Usually such a foolproof thingy.'

'It's an old wives' tale and well you know it, Dougie.'

'Thought you said the gypsy had never put a foot wrong.'

'I'm happy having a little girl, Dougie. Whether you are or not.'

'Oh no, I am happy, Shirley. Dunt make any difference to me.'

Huh, sounded like it. He were sounding right common today. I could tell from this he was stressed. I were so glad I weren't common.

'Weird though, int it?'

'What is?'

'How you were so sure.'

'She were meant to be a good gypsy.'

And now he turned to me and looked at me and grabbed me by both arms. I could see fear, terror in his eyes. They seemed to well up from nowhere.

'Be honest with me, Shirley.'

'Eh? I am being honest with you.'

'Be honest with me and I'll cope with it. I promise I will.'

'About what?'

And now he let go of me so I sort of skidded across the carpet, while he went in his bag, his little one he'd packed for his overnight jaunt. It was then that he pulled out a *Sun* newspaper.

There on the front page was a pencil drawing of a woman, carrying a baby.

I felt sick.

It could've been a drawing of me.

Sod that. It *was* a drawing of me.

'They've done an artist's impression of you, Shirley. So please . . . stop lying to me.'

'I don't know what you're on about!'

'This!'

And now he jabbed his finger on the picture, then hurled the paper at me.

The headline just said 'BUS STOP LADY'.

'What? Who's that?'

'Never mind who that is, Shirl. Who's this?' And he pointed to the baby. 'Is it baby Diana?'

I started to cry. 'How can you even say that, Doug?'

'Because none of this adds up!'

'How d'you mean, though?!'

'Your baby's three weeks early. That does not look like a baby who's premature!'

'Maybe I got my dates wrong!'

'PLUS. She's the double of baby Diana.'

'Is she heck as like. Oh what, so I drove down to Birmingham and took a baby from under the noses of a new mam and dad? Do you really think I'm capable of doing all that? Well, thanks a flaming lot, Dougie. Thanks a flaming lot!'

I went careering down the stairs and ran out into the back garden.

How dare he?

How DARE he!

How dare he think me capable of doing such a horrible thing? And he was meant to be in love with me. How could he love someone who could be capable of that? It's the worst thing to imagine about someone you like, never mind are meant to love. Fancy thinking I'd stolen a baby! It didn't bear thinking about.

It didn't bear thinking about because he was onto me. He'd worked it out. What did I do now? Run?

And why was I being so incensed when all he was thinking was the truth?

I had done that horrid, horrid thing. I was worthy of his condemnation.

That bitch at the bus stop had dropped me in it. That bitch at the bus stop had been staring at me after all. Well enough to be able to describe me in intimate detail.

How was that even possible? If someone said to me, *What does Dougie look like?* I'd be hard pressed to ring up an artist and describe him so well that they could jot down something worthy of the Tate gallery.

I realized I was getting angry, and I realized I was getting angry because I had been rumbled. And I'd not spent too much time working out what the implications of this would be. The worst-case scenario for me was going to be Doug not wanting to know me or the baby, and so it all having not been worth the while. I didn't seriously think I was going to get rumbled. And certainly not by HIM.

My sphincter was doing a real ten-pee/two-pee contracting motion. My insides were dancing a rumba. And all this was not due to excitement. Jesus, I was stood here in the garden and for all I knew he was inside on the phone to the cops already.

But how would I stop him?

He'd want to stop me, wouldn't he? He seemed so angry about it all.

Typical. Probably fancied Diana's mother. Probably saw this as his way of getting to meet her. I was probably as throwaway as his last piece of fluff.

What did I do now? What COULD I do now? I couldn't lie to him forever. And if he called the cops that'd be the end of me. They'd lock me up and throw away the key. And everyone would know. Everyone would know it was me.

I'd thought if it all went tits up with him I could just get the baby back to her mum, the proper one.

But I'd thought he'd take one look at her and melt.

What I needed to do now was get him onside.

Get him onside for what, though?

Right. This would look bad on him, too, I fancied.

If I said he'd told me to do it, would they believe me? Probably not.

But if I was honest, and said I'd only done it to win him back . . . his name'd be in all the papers, and folk'd know I was his mistress. He'd hate that.

Yes. I had to get him onside.

I'd tell him he was right, I'd tell him I'd made a big mistake. But now I needed his help to put it right. Then we could get the baby back to its mother together. Then we'd be in on it together. And that way nobody would know we'd ever had a thing.

And if losing him was the price I had to pay to get out of what I now saw was an incredible mess, then so be it.

That was better than going to prison.

I did not want to go to prison.

Going to prison was one of the worst things I could imagine. Ever.

But would he go along with it?

We could drive together to the nearest hospital. I could leave her in a bin. Or pull my hood up and just leave the carrycot by the entrance to the casualty department. He'd probably have a better idea.

Right. The game was up. But there was a way of coming out of this unscathed.

I'd appeal to his better nature, and then I'd be free. Free of him, free of this, and free of this pea-souper of anxiety that overwhelmed me every waking hour.

I'd appeal to his vanity. Say how poorly this was going to reflect on him. Say how angry Vera was going to be. I'd be contrite. I was good at being contrite. And I'd say I only did it for him.

Well, which was, let's be honest, God's honest truth.

I turned to head back in. I could see him through the door off the kitchen, in the sitting room, putting the television on.

As if things weren't already bad enough I could hear the opening music of the telly news. Like we didn't need reminding I was already in the shit. No doubt that picture of me would be the leading story.

Here she is!

I wavered. There was the small matter of Myrus next door.

But then I reminded myself that she had no idea who I was. And by now, no doubt she'd have clocked that my 'husband' was back. All we had to do was get out of here, drop the baby somewhere, and return to our normal lives, and it'd never cross her mind what had gone on. Baby Diana would've been found, and she'd never put two and two together and think *I bet it was them lovebirds next door*.

Thank God I was a thinker. I could think things through rationally, and see all possibilities.

Now I just had to convince Doug about the next step.

311

And at least I hadn't walked in to find him on the phone to the boys in blue.

As I stepped cautiously into the living room he mustn't have heard me coz he shouted out, 'Shirl! Quick! Come and listen to this!'

'What is it?'

'Shh!'

And he knelt in front of the telly and turned the sound up.

Selina Scott was reading the news. And what she said shocked me so much I nearly fainted.

'Police are following a tip-off that baby Diana's abductor is living in the Paisley area of Glasgow. A woman today called a helpline anonymously to say that she had Diana and that all was well. She asked to be left in peace and to tell the baby's mother . . . not to worry. Some people might find the following report upsetting.'

And then there was some Scottish woman walking down a high street, through the shoppers, saying someone had come to 'this phone box', and she pointed to an actual phone box where the anonymous call was made and said that we were going to hear it, as the police thought the caller was genuine and that 'someone must know who she is'.

Then they cut to a close-up of a tape recorder playing.

And then we heard this voice.

And I felt the room was spinning.

The voice sounded young. Scottish. A young girl. Sounded like she was still at school.

'Hello, yes, I've got her. I've got little Diana. See, I lost my baby and now I've got one. I'm sorry. Tell her mammy I'm sorry and not to worry. But she's in good hands and she's well cared for. And tell everyone to stop looking for her, coz she's safe.'

312

And then for good measure there was a baby crying in the background, and then the caller hung up.

I couldn't listen to any more of the programme. It was going on in front of my eyes and the noises were heading into my ears, but the room was spinning too much. I felt like I was on a carousel and I couldn't jump off. I had to push myself into the settee so I wouldn't drop to the floor, fighting that gravitational pull that was gonna drag me down.

I felt something on my hand. It made me jump and shriek. But I looked and it was Doug sitting beside me.

'Oh, Shirl,' he said, tears pricking his eyes. 'I'm so, so sorry. How will you ever forgive me?'

I looked back to the TV screen. Selina Scott's lips were moving but no sound was coming out.

Where the fuck did I go from here?

It appeared that where I went from there was that I was completely exonerated in Doug's eyes, and he clearly felt so guilty about what he'd thought me capable of that he felt he had to roger me all weekend long in every single room in the cottage.

'Not surprised this place is called Lovers' Leap,' he'd say, 'coz I wanna leap your bones every time I look at you!'

And then he'd take my titties out and ask me to give him some milk.

'I can't do that yet,' I'd say. 'Nurses said what with me age it might take a while.'

And guess what? He bought it.

Though, cheeky bastard, guess what he said when he saw me with no clothes on?

'Hey, you're not looking TOO bad, considering you've just give birth.'

What could I say to that apart from go along with it?

'Oh. Ta.'

'I mean, few months from now and you'll be normal-sized.'

'Yeah. Thanks Doug. Means a lot.'

I supposed I'd better be grateful for small mercies. Thought this was God's way of telling me it was time to go on a diet.

When we weren't bonking each other's brains out we were going for runs out in his car. He had a lovely saloon on him, with quite the impressive gearbox, and once we'd tucked baby on the back seat in a special strap for her carrycot he liked to get out there and 'open her up'.

'I'm a chancer,' he'd say, 'a risk taker. I grab life by the pubes, Shirley. By the down-and-dirty, good-for-nothing pubes.'

And with the general public thinking the police were look-ing in Paisley for the missing baby, nobody suspected a thing as we ate in pubs, and drank tea in cafes. North Wales was our plate of oysters. And we got high on them. He lavished me with love. He lavished me with sex. He lavished me with nappies for the baby and food for the larder. And best of all, he lavished me with cheques that I could cash once he was gone. He was only meant to be staying till the Sunday night but he ended up leav-ing Monday lunchtime. So you could say he lavished me with time as well.

On the Monday morning we'd just been to Kwik Save and piled the boot high with provisions for my week ahead and we were unpacking in the driveway. I wanted to be quick because I could see the nets at Myrus's place twitching away like Larry-oh.

'Let's get this lot in,' I said to Doug, 'quickly! I don't want Nose Almighty sticking her oar in.' We ran between the Lada and the front door, dropping off bags and running back for more. Ever the gent, Doug offered to take the carrycot and get the baby changed upstairs. I stayed behind to check the car.

Which was when I found a plastic bag under the driver's seat.

A plain boring white plastic bag.

But I checked inside in case it was something for Lovers' Leap.

Inside was another plastic bag, a Mothercare bag.

Oh God. Was this a little present for me? Was he going to give me this as he left? Oh, God love the BONES of him.

I couldn't help myself. I had a little peek inside.

I was right! I must've been. Inside was a little yellow Baby-gro. And a card in an envelope.

But. Hey up. The card had been ripped open. I pulled the envelope out for closer inspection.

Scrawled on the red paper in biro were three words.

Douglas and Vera.

I pulled the card out. It showed a dull picture of some balloons. Inside it said:

Congratulations on your fantastic news, Mummy and Daddy! Love Gwen, Charlie and the twins xxx

I felt sick.

I left the car door open and took the Babygro and the card inside. Doug was in the kitchen, aggressively opening a baby's mobile from an overly wrapped cardboard box using a pair of scissors.

'Is Vera pregnant?'

I almost didn't recognize my own voice. It was so listless and one level. It took him a while to realize I'd said anything. He slowly put down the scissors and looked over at me. He saw what I had in my hand.

'Is she?'

He said nothing.

'Well, come on, Doug. Either she is or she isn't.'

He nodded.

I snatched the scissors from his hand, held the Babygro in front of his eyes and tore away at it with them, ribboning it to frig.

He didn't make any effort to intervene. Just stood there watching me hack the Babygro to death.

I was so angry. I was raging. The blood in my veins seemed to bubble up like hot soup in a tiny pan, no room to breathe, nowhere to go but upwards and out, to spill over and hurt, boil, sting. I hurled the offending item of clothing across the room, then the scissors too.

'Well, that was grown-up.'

'Oh, fuck off.'

'You don't have the monopoly on having kids, you know.'

'Oh, do I not? I thought I did.'

'No need to be sarcastic.'

'No need to be a pathological liar.'

I'm not sure he was that, but nevertheless.

'What the fuck have I lied about?'

'Not telling me Miss Prissy Goody Bloody Two Shoes was up the duff!'

'And what difference does that make?'

'Do you not know?'

'No!'

'Really? Are you that bloody thick?'

'I'm not psychic, Shirley!'

'No! I'll tell you what you bloody are! A waste of space!'

Upstairs I heard the baby cry. I really wanted to grab the gin and go and calm her down, but I knew that'd only be giving Doug ammunition to slag me off.

'I was going to tell you,' he said, more calmly. 'But I didn't wanna rain on your parade.'

It was useless. This had all been for nothing. I was meant to be giving him something Vera wouldn't be giving him. A treat, a surprise, the next in line to the throne. And there she was, joining the bloody queue.

'I didn't want to say, "Oh, guess what! Vera's having one too!"'

I turned and looked at him. 'You're never gonna leave her, are you?'

He dropped his eyes to the floor.

'Look at me!'

He looked up. 'I don't think I am, no.'

'Is that why Funke left? Is that why this place was empty?'

He looked completely gobsmacked. But quietly said, 'Yes.'

And finally, finally . . . I realized what a completely silly cow I had been.

As if I was ever going to compete with the likes of Vera.

As if my thorny branches were ever going to magnetize him away from the heady scent of her rosewater petals.

She was honey. I was castor oil.

And castor oil made you sick.

I saw it now. And once it'd been seen and I knew I'd be a mug to see it any other way, I saw what I had to do.

'Get out, Doug.'

'Eh?'

'Go back to your wife.'

'But . . .'

'Me and Rachel don't need you. We'll be fine on our own.'

'But . . .'

'Just go, Doug.'

I didn't even look to see if he did. I knew he would. I was giving him the get-out clause he'd probably been looking for ever since that night we'd met in Butlin's all those years ago. I wearily took myself upstairs. I couldn't even be bothered to bring the gin.

Outside I heard Doug revving the car up and slowly driving

away. I didn't even remember him packing his bag. Maybe he'd done that earlier.

I went and lay on the bed.

Here lies Shirley Burke. Stupidest woman in Christendom. Does the stupidest things, for the stupidest reasons. And worst bit of it all? It's all about her. Not content with finding her own boyfriend, she had to go with someone else's husband. And then not content with having a brief fling she had to drag it on. And on. And on. And she was soooo full of herself she didn't stop there. Instead of going out and not being lazy and finding a nice new bloke all for herself, someone not old enough to be her dad, she decided she wanted him all to herself, and screw his wife and kiddies. And when she couldn't think of any other way to trap him, she lied. She told him she were pregnant when she wasn't. She even offered to bring up her sister's baby, thinking that might win him over. No such luck. So what did she do then? Told him she was still pregnant and came up with the weirdest, most horriblest plan you could think of. She decided she was going to go and steal a baby right from under the nose of its mother. A boy baby, coz she thought he could do with one of those. She taught herself to drive so she could go anywhere in the country. She bought herself elocution lessons, coz someone had once said her voice sounded dog rough, and then she stole a baby. Only what she assumed was a boy was a girl, but that didn't matter. She had her own little baby. And sooner or later he'd come running. And stay.

How wrong Shirley Burke was.

And the worst thing was . . . through it all, she didn't really stop to think what effect this would have on the baby itself. Through it all she only ever cared about herself. Because Shirley Burke was the ultimate selfish cow. She was the lowest of the low.

I thought about killing myself, as I lay on that bed. But that felt like the coward's way out. And that way I'd've had no guarantee that the baby would be okay. What if she lay in her cot unattended and died of negligence before anyone found her? I may as well have killed the baby now.

Time to stop calling her Rachel, it seemed. Time to own up to who I really was.

Time to say enough's enough; I couldn't handle this. I'd done the worst thing, an evil thing, but the good thing was there was a way of making this right for the real mother, by getting the baby back to her.

The eyes of the press were on Paisley. Nobody would be expecting a baby to be left at a casualty department with a note. It'd be like that kids' show I watched years back, *Paddington*. He'd been left in some railway station, with a sign attached to him saying, 'Please look after this bear'.

I'd have one more night with the baby, and get her back tomorrow.

In the meantime I'd have to cover my tracks.

I went downstairs and looked around at all the baby paraphernalia.

I couldn't leave it behind when I left. That would arouse suspicion.

Myrus was bound to remember me, and if a baby had been abandoned not far from here and I'd left toys in Lovers' Leap . . .

No, I'd have to get rid of them somehow.

I'd have to get rid of the bloody Babygro, too.

I looked out at the garden, and had an idea.

That night, after digging in the garden, I wrote a letter.

Dear Linda

I am so sorry to have caused you pain. I return her to you intact. Your need is greater than mine.

She really is a lovely baby.

A friend.

X

I folded it up, ready for the morning.

The next morning the radio seemed to be screaming at me. I put the telly on too. Same story everywhere. The girl in Paisley had turned out to be a hoax. A national search was back on. Myrus knocked at the door about something, but to be honest, I didn't really listen to her; my heart was racing as I stood on that step.

I went back in and thought. Did I still go through with my plan?

There was another option.

Kill the baby and bury her in the garden, too. If Douglas ever got in touch there'd be no reason for him to see her, I'd just say I wanted some space. And eventually I could say she'd died. No questions asked. It'd be easier for him that way.

The baby started crying.

Looked like it was time to give her some gin again. Just until I made my mind up.

I tore the letter up and put it in the bin. No rush.

I could always write another.

I took the bottle and looked to the stairs.

'Hush, Rachel. Mummy's coming!'

As I climbed the stairs I sang to myself.

> '*Itsy bitsy spider climbed up the waterspout,*
> *Down came the rain and washed the spider out,*
> *Out came the sun and dried up all the rain,*
> *Itsy bitsy spider climbed up the spout again.*'

RACHEL

2017

Chapter Nineteen

I am so excited at the prospect that one day soon I am going to meet this baby who's inside me. I wonder what she'll look like. I wonder what her soul will be like. At the same time the thought fills me with dread. Once she is out I will be without my constant companion. My life will change and I'll have to share her with the rest of the world. Just like normal people.

I can't stop cleaning the flat. I thought nesting was just something from the olden days. A bit like rickets and penny farthings. But I get these surges of energy and my flat has never looked more like a new pin.

I can feel her growing and growing. I can feel her wriggling inside. I can always tell what position she is lying in. I pushed her little feet before and she pushed back.

On the downside, I could do without this water retention. As she grows so does the girth of my legs. They look like they're made of Play-Doh. Press your fingers into my knees and the indentations stay awhile, like they would in freshly kneaded dough.

I have even started cleaning the office instead of taking proper breaks. I must stop this. The others will get used to it and the next thing we know, Ben will have fired the cleaner and added it to my job description.

It's lunchtime. I can go to the shops, get some air.

One of my favourite things to do when I go to the local shops is to look down. No, I don't mean that I am glued to my iPhone like everyone else on this planet; I would much rather my unborn child spent her life looking up, at the sky, avoiding bumping into people, anywhere but down at a phone. But this particular 'down' is an unusual one. Daily, scores of workers stop at the Brunswick Centre to buy their lunchtime quinoa or grab something for supper from Waitrose. Even the pigeons read the *Guardian*, that's how middle class it is. But on this site in the 1700s there stood the Foundling Hospital, set up by one Captain Thomas Coram. Coram was a philanthropist – not a philatelist, as I'd mistakenly thought when I first heard about him and wondered why a stamp collector had been so ruddy generous – who grew so shocked by the sight of children dying in the streets with no-one to care for them that he fought and strove to set up a place of safety for them. Mothers could then abandon their children at the hospital knowing they would be cared for, rather than dying in the street.

The reason I care to look down as I walk to the Brunswick Centre is that an artist called John Aldus has cemented replicas of tokens left by mothers for their children into the paving stones underfoot. The originals of these tokens can be found in the museum round the corner. They were items that the mothers would leave behind with their children as a keepsake, in the hope that one day they and the item, and no doubt the child, would be reunited. To the untrained eye they just look like pieces of silver set into concrete to make the area look more 'jazzy'. But one day I happened upon a sign, half hidden behind a nearby hedge, explaining what the silver shapes represented. I find them heart-breaking. For me they show the poignancy of women born into poverty, who had no other option than to give up their children. One is in the shape of a heart with a name etched on it: *Maria Duchene, born August 8th, 1759.*

Another is a floral brooch. Another looks a bit like a knuckle-duster, but I can only imagine it's meant to be something like a child's rattle. The hopes and dreams of these women from so long ago. Would they one day return to reclaim their child? I can only think it doubtful.

Of course, today as I tiptoe over the hopes and dreams of various eighteenth-century women, I can't help but think how lucky I have been, compared to those children. Whatever my fate, whatever happened in those first few weeks after I was born, I was raised with my mother, I was returned to her. These children were not so lucky.

Or maybe they were the lucky ones.

I am fed up of thinking like this. Thinking like this is going to drive me mad.

But I can't help it. Would I have been better off in a found-ling hospital, had they still existed? Away from my distant mother, who was clearly traumatized by what had happened to her and thus unable to bond with me.

I think of the playing fields on the other side of the shopping centre, Coram's Fields, the sign that stands outside saying no adults can enter unless accompanied by a child. A wonderful tribute to the man who gave the area its name, and a sign I so frequently dismissed in the past. I had no reason to go in, not knowing that many children. But once I got pregnant I realized that sooner or later I'd have a good excuse to venture in.

Is this why Shirley Burke stole me?

Did she want a reason to go into Coram's Fields?

Was she in fact a resident of Bloomsbury?

No. No. I'd have known if this was the case, wouldn't I? All the press reports described her as being from the North-West. Why on earth would she be familiar with my local children's playground?

But then I wonder . . . why can't adults go in unaccompanied? Is it really because it's so child-centric that they are more important than adults? Or is it that a garden designed for children to play in might become a target for paedophiles, so best warn them off? No unaccompanied adults welcome here! I hope it is the former.

I wonder if I'd dare to enter, then if I was stopped, point out that I was with child.

As I'm thinking this and being very self-indulgent all round – plus ça change, Rachel! – I become aware of someone crying. A woman is crying somewhere nearby.

I turn and see a woman on a nearby bench with her head bowed. I recognize her immediately.

'Tracy?' I instinctively hurry towards her and sit alongside her. She looks up, immediately mortified to have been found, and found by someone she knows.

'Oh, take no notice of me,' she says, batting me away, even though I'm making no attempt to touch her.

'What's the matter, Tracy?'

'Please. I'm fine,' she insists.

'You're not.'

'Honestly.' But there's a catch in her voice that almost breaks my heart. I've never seen her like this before. I've not seen her for ages outside the confines of the office. She is always so plucky, so strong, laughing in the face of the many adversities she has to face along the way. It's upsetting to see her so distressed.

'What's happened?'

She's not able to speak. Maybe she's not ready to speak.

'Shall we go for a walk? Go and see the goats by Coram's Fields?'

I don't expect her to nod quite so readily but she does, and soon we're walking arm in arm round the corner towards the goats.

Milkable animals. Who knew they could be a cure-all?

Along one side of Coram's Fields there are a few pens where goats are kept, kind of a children's petting zoo I suppose, though I've never seen children pet them, possibly because as an unaccompanied grown-up I'm not actually allowed through the gates. But one side of it can be seen through railings from the street without having to venture in. Tracy and I stand and watch three fat goats snoozing in the lunchtime sun.

'They look happy, don't they?' I venture.

Tracy nods. 'Blissful.'

And we watch them in silence for a while.

'Sometimes,' Tracy says, 'I wish I was a goat.'

I let the words hang in the air a bit, then look to Tracy, just as she looks at me, and we both immediately burst out laughing.

'Are things that bad?'

'Oh yes, so bad I wish I was a goat.'

'We've all done it.'

The goats aren't doing much – even children passing with their parents en route to the fields are getting bored – so we move on.

'What's so bad? Is it transitioning?' I ask.

She looks at me, shocked.

'Oh shit. I got that hugely wrong, then. Great.'

She can't help but giggle; looks like I did.

'Blame Ben. It's all he ever talks about.'

She rolls her eyes. 'Well, this time it's nothing to do with that.'

'Is it a man?'

'No.'

'A woman?'

'NO!' She sounds horrified.

'Then what?'

And she sighs.

'Look, you don't have to tell me if you don't want to. I'm just a nosy cow and it's none of my business. We can go for a walk. Do some window-shopping. Spend a thousand plus pounds on a smoothie with added cactus. Then head back to the office.'

I catch her smiling at me.

'You look so pretty when you smile,' I say, involuntarily. And she pulls a face.

'Okay. I'm patronizing you. I'll treat you to an apologetic smoothie. I've got a spare second mortgage.'

'Promise you won't tell Ben?'

'About the smoothie?'

'About what I'm going to tell you.'

'Guide's honour.'

'Were you in the Guides?'

'No.'

She looks almost disappointed. 'I was in the Scouts. Was desperate to be a Guide.'

I don't really know what to say to that apart from, 'Dib dib dib.'

'I'm adopted.'

'Okay.'

I try to work out what that's got to do with the Scouts. Is it some sort of Scouty phrase, where they swear an allegiance to

328

the Queen by pretending to be adopted by her? Then I realize she is actually telling me she's adopted. Like, in actual real life.

'Oh, I see! Okay!'

Now that wasn't what I was expecting. 'Why wouldn't you want Ben to know that?'

'He sees the oddest of things as a sign of weakness. It's like he sees your pregnancy that way. Or you losing your mum. I don't want to give him any ammunition.'

Well, she's got that spot on.

'Yeah, but you shouldn't be ashamed about the fact that you're adopted, Tracy.'

We go and sit by the over-designed pond thing at the end of the Brunswick Centre.

'Oh, I'm not. I'm not at all. I just traced my birth family recently and that's what I don't want him to know about.'

'Was it horrible?'

'Kind of.'

'Do you wish you'd never done it?'

She seems taken aback by my line of questioning. Talk about 'to the point'.

'Er, I don't know. Sort of. But . . . but I know I've always wanted to answer a few questions, so . . .'

'The reason I'm asking is . . . you know I said at work that my friend was that baby who was abducted?'

She nods.

'It wasn't. It was me.'

Her eyes widen. I nod.

'I only found out when my mum died. I had no idea. Bit of a headfuck really.'

'Massive,' she agrees.

'I've not told Ben, obvs.'

'Obvs. Oh my God, he said he had a wank over your dad, then.'

I nod.

'I thought that was pretty gross even before I knew it was your dad, if I'm honest.'

I nod again. 'He is a bit of a wanker,' I say with a wink, and she giggles. 'And he's clearly had a lot of practice at it. Hence being so accomplished. But the reason I'm asking you about meeting, you know, your birth family . . . is because I wonder whether I should try to find my dad. Or the woman who abducted me.'

'Why would you want to find her?'

'I don't know.'

'I get your dad. Everyone wants to know where they come from. But her?'

She raises a good and valid point.

'I suppose I'm keen to know what happened to her. That's all. I don't think I do want to meet her. Oh, I don't know.'

'Did she go to prison? Was she caught?'

I nod on both counts.

'I suppose she must've been if they got you back.'

'But I don't know what happened to her after that. I'd like to ask her why she took me.'

'I wanted to ask my birth mother why she'd given me away.'

'And what did she say?'

'It was awful . . .'

I wait for her to tell me. And tell me she does.

Tracy's ten years younger than me. She found out she was adopted around her seventh birthday and from then on her middle-class mother always used it as a bargaining tool. She'd say things like, 'If you don't tidy your room I'll take you back to the children's home.' She'd often make out that she'd chosen the wrong baby, if ever Tracy misbehaved as a kid. Life was comfortable in Twickenham, where Tracy was raised, but two things played on her mind. One, she knew she was a little girl and not the little boy her body presented her as, and two . . . she would one day trace her 'real' mum. She knew very little about her, just what her adoptive mum had told her. Then on her eighteenth birthday she was allowed access to her adoption files.

'I'd read a lot of Armistead Maupin. I had this romantic notion that I was like Anna Madrigal and I'd been born somewhere exotic like the Blue Moon Lodge.'

'Wasn't that a knocking shop?'

'A brothel, yes.'

Hardly romantic, but I don't say.

'Out in the desert somewhere. A mum who wanted me but was too caught up with some cowboy.'

A cowboy punter, no less. Heavens.

'Tracy, there is no desert in Britain. And the only cowboys you're gonna get are . . . probably in some camp sort of Village People tribute act.'

'So you can see I was destined for a fall.'

I nod. She certainly was.

'My birth certificate said I was born in Solihull. I had no idea where it was.'

'Well, at least you were saved from having a Brummie accent.'

'Right?' she says with a twinkle.

Jesus, I'm on fire today!

'Long story short. I only met up with my birth mother for the first time a few months ago. Of course, I knew it wasn't going to be easy. As far as she was concerned she'd given birth to a boy. How was she going to feel meeting Tracy and not Tommy?'

I nod, trying to get my head round what it must have been like for her. For both of them.

'A social worker spoke to her and she didn't seem to mind.'

'Why did she give you up?'

'She didn't. It was only really in the sixties that babies were relinquished so freely. I was taken off her. She was a heroin addict.'

'And is she clean now?'

She nods. 'Clean of drugs. But she's found God.'

And then she starts to cry again. I pull her to me and hug her, stroking her hair. I don't care that we're in the middle of a busy shopping area. Nobody knows anyone else's pain. I want to cry too and she's not even told me what happened. But something did. Something to cause her distress.

'So how was it awful?'

'It was okay at first. Very polite.'

'How old is she?'

'Nearly fifty. I thought she had a kind face.'

'Okay.'

'But appearances can be deceptive. I thought it had gone so well. But at the end of our meeting . . .'

'Where did you meet?'

'Fucking Solihull.'

'You poor thing.'

This is unfair of me. I've never been to Solihull.

'At the end of the meeting she just said, "Well, it's been nice to meet you, Tracy, but I don't think I want to see you again. What you've become is not something Jesus would approve of."'

'So much for an all-loving God.'

'I should have bitten my tongue, shown her I was the bigger person. Bit difficult when she's about twenty stone.'

'Really?'

'And I said, "Well, that's good. Because I don't think Jesus would approve of you." When my adoptive mother asked me how it went I told her the truth. And she gave me this look. It just screamed at me, "I told you so."'

She pulls herself away from me, clearly embarrassed to have shared so much.

'But you had to go there.'

She nods. And looks me square in the face. 'And if I could give you one piece of advice?'

'Aha?'

'Just be prepared for disappointment.' She takes her phone from her pocket. 'We better be getting back.'

'I suppose we better had.'

Though it is the last thing in the world I want to do.

Is she right? Is the universe trying to tell me to give up? Even if part of me wants to find my dad and my abductor, will it really change anything for me? And thus far it seems that the things I have tried to do in order to seek them out have gone, well, tits up to say the least.

Not that I've tried that much.

I've tried the internet.

I've tried Facebook.

I've tried a private detective, who for all I know is now dead.

Do I just quit now while I'm behind?

I can't help but keep thinking of that interview Mum did with the gossipy journalist. If I was to do something similar, that might flush a few things out. I'm sure, for instance, that a tabloid newspaper would be able to find out the whereabouts of both these people.

But the more I think of Tracy's story, the more I wonder, is it really worth it? Won't it just lead to further heartache? Maybe the reason I've never known my dad is that he never wanted to know me. Mum's story to me was that my father was a one-night stand called Ambrose. AMBROSE. Where the hell did she get that name from?

But maybe there really was an Ambrose.

Maybe Dad had just found out I wasn't his kid when I was taken. But he couldn't say publicly as I fancy the eighties were a bit more judgemental about extra-marital affairs and so on. And as the pressure mounted and I continued to be missing it all got too much. And then, hey presto, I was returned and he was probably saying stuff like, 'But she's not mine, she's Ambrose's. And by the way, what a ridiculous name for the father of this baby who isn't mine!' type thing. And it all became too much and he walked out on her, telling her he never wanted to see her or me ever again.

Actually, the more I think about it, the more and more plausible it becomes. It would certainly explain why he's not been in touch all these years.

Or maybe he'd just had enough of my mum. I mean, it's not like she and I saw eye to eye all the time. Maybe he found her distant, too.

Plus, if he thought I was living on the other side of the world, why would he bother to keep in touch? Especially if Mum had said she wanted a new life for us both.

Or maybe, you know, he was just a bit useless. Like we're all a bit useless sometimes. The confrontational shows of daytime TV are littered with feckless men who've not kept in touch with their offspring. Maybe he was just one of them. Maybe life has a way of making you think that there are Machiavellian secrets behind everything. Whereas in fact the main reason I didn't know my dad was just laziness on his part.

And, the more I think about it, why haven't I been bothered enough to trace my dad over the years? I am no spring chicken. And yet at no point have I gone in search of the man who helped give me life. Even if I really believed all those years that he was a one-night stand called Ambrose, why haven't I sought him out? It's not like Mum stood in my way. Admittedly, she never seemed that interested to talk about him, so I probably thought it was best to leave well alone, but she never forbade me from finding out who he was and trying to make contact.

Though to be fair the cover story was a good one in as much as . . . how easy is it to track down a one-night stand from over thirty years ago? Not very, would be my humble opinion.

By the time Tracy and I get back to the office I have resolved that I've had enough drama for the time being. I have no desire to seek out my errant father or that weirdo who nicked me. The more I contemplate it the more ridiculous it sounds. Why on earth would I want to find out what had happened to some mad woman who kidnapped me thirty-odd years ago? It was almost laughable.

Apart from the fact that she stole me and denied my mother and me precious bonding time.

Oh yes, there was the little matter of that.

But it was so long ago now; does it really matter?

I breathe anger in, I breathe anger out.

No. It doesn't matter. And deciding it doesn't matter makes me feel like a weight is being lifted. I saw an episode of *East-Enders* recently where a runaway bus came hurtling into the square. You know, the way they do. Nobody was killed, you know the way they sometimes never are in soaps, but someone got stuck under the wheels of the bus. I can't for the life of me think who it was. But the residents of the square lifted the bus up and the bloke was pulled free.

That's how I feel, having made my decision.

There really is no going back now, I will only look forward. No more dwelling on the past.

Dads? Who needs 'em? Abductors? Even more so!

I return to my desk and log into Facebook. Jamie comes up in my feed. I wonder how his date went after Mum's funeral?

And then I see. A change of status that proudly heralds: *Jamie Stafford is in a relationship with Paolo Batti.*

'Paolo Batti?!' I hear myself saying. Everyone looks over. And I just can't help myself. I say, 'Jamie Stafford is in a relationship with someone called Paolo Batti? It's not even been two weeks since their first date.'

'Batti?' says Didi, perturbed. 'Sounds Brazilian or something. Is there a picture?'

There bloody well is as well.

Why does it make my blood course with anger?

I click on the picture. A sweet-looking twenty-something is staring back at me. He's done too much plucking on his eyebrows. I hate that look on guys.

Batti, eh?

It takes me all my strength not to message Jamie and say, *I see you've bagged yourself a Batti-boy.*

But I wouldn't be that childish.

Would I?

I tell Ben to do it instead.

Just as we're all chortling at my all-round hilarious sense of humour, and how genius it is that the joke is slightly homophobic so sounds fine coming from the fingers of Ben, my mobile goes. It's a number I don't recognize. I answer.

'Hello?'

'Hello, can I speak to Rachel please?'

'Speaking?'

'Oh, hiya Rachel.'

The man on the other end has a Brummie accent.

'I was given your number by someone called Kelly Hopper.'

'Oh, right?'

'My name's Les Wilson. I think I might be your dad.'

Chapter Twenty

I've looked so many times at the face of Leslie Wilson. Grainy black-and-white images of him clutching his wife's hand. A hollow, faraway look in his eyes. He has a moustache, stubble, jet-black hair, a square jaw. His eyes are black, too, and his cheeks sunken. He looks like a lad, a poor lost young lad. The sort of lad you'd pass every day. Ordinary, average, nondescript. And yet there he was, at the centre of a controversial news story. He had in the early eighties what so many young people now seek, crave. He had instant celebrity.

He also had a natty line in sports casual sweaters. Well. I've only seen two of them. Both Le Coq Sportif. I guess I'm generalizing.

In those pictures, in those newspapers, the very few online, I feel so sorry for Leslie Wilson.

He looks like the sort of lad who'd work in your local garage. He looks like he was probably very good to his mother and never strayed far from home. I've read so much into those few photographs over the past week, and now he has been in touch and said he wants to meet, I can definitely only see good in those pictures. I want to only see good.

I want Leslie Wilson to be a good person.

I need Leslie Wilson to be a good person.

If Leslie Wilson is a good person it means I can have inherited that from him.

If Leslie Wilson is a good person it means that these recent shocks won't have been in vain.

Look Rachel, it was all worthwhile. The shock, the weirdedoutness. All absolutely fine. Because some good came out of it; you learned that your dad was okay.

Well. A girl could hope, couldn't she?

He sounded half decent on the phone. Attentive, interested, could hold a sentence together. He said Kelly Hopper got in touch with him last week and explained she had got his details from a police contact and that she was working on my behalf and I wanted to meet. She said she'd give him a day to think about it and then call him back. She had then called him back and he'd jumped at the chance. But then she said something that he found a bit odd. She'd said, 'I'll set up the meeting. It has to run smoothly. I'll take care of everything as I don't want Rachel to be upset. She's with child.'

She did, apparently – she used the biblical phrase. Oh well, she is a friend of Tom the vicar.

'However.'

And this is the weirder bit.

'In case anything happens to me, I'll text you her number in a minute.'

Then she'd hung up.

He received the text with my number on, but then never heard from Kelly again. He waited, and waited, and tried calling her back on the number she'd called on. He'd looked her up online and found an office number. Both seemed to be cut off.

Which is when he bit the bullet and called me.

And I am very glad he did. I think. No, I am.

Oh God, what am I doing?

This is obviously going to go hideously wrong. I just know it is.

The afternoon before I decide to meet him I half tell Ben the truth at work. Well, I tell him I'm meeting my dad. I miss out the bit about him being the first man he ever masturbated over. I might save that for another time. Doesn't feel right somehow.

No shit, Sherlock.

I just pretend he's come out of the woodwork since Mum died.

'Oh, out of bad comes good,' he says.

I see Tracy looking over from behind her computer screen.

'Yeah, he contacted me.'

She looks away.

God. What is her problem? Just because she warned me not to go digging, the deed was already done by then, the die already cast. This just . . . well . . . happened. It's not like I've tracked down Shirley Burke, is it?

Gimme a break, Tracy.

'Where are you meeting him?'

'Euston station. His train gets in there and . . . well, we can walk somewhere from there.'

'You shouldn't be walking!' shrieks Didi. 'Not in your condition!'

'Take an Uber,' insists Ben.

'On the company?'

The only Uber account I have is a work one. Is he seriously offering to pay for my father and me to go and find a restaurant?

I see him blush.

'Oh, do you not have your own account?'

I shake my head.

'Well, stick it through the business,' he says, acting distracted, checking his computer screen, 'and then we can sort it out with next month's wages.'

And then I say something awful. It's involuntary. As soon as the words come out I wish I'd not said them. I say, 'God, you're such a cunt, Ben.'

And it's so shocking that Didi and Tracy don't speak. I just notice Didi's eyes widen and hear all their fingers tapping faster and faster on their keyboards.

Ben looks up slowly from his screen and gazes my way.

'I'm sorry,' I say. Then realize that actually I'm not. Not in the slightest. Yes, I wish I'd not said it as it gives him ammunition to dislike me. But I do think it, so why not admit to it? And then it all comes tumbling out. 'I didn't ask for a taxi. I was quite happy to walk. You told me to get an Uber when you should know full well none of us earns the money you earn, so none of us has our own Uber account, we just have the Venus one. So, no. I won't take one so you can dock it out of my wages. I'll walk. Like I walk everywhere else.'

Not sure I do walk absolutely everywhere, but hey ho, he's not to know.

'Look, I know you've had a hard time of it lately—' he goes to say, but I cut in.

'Hard time? Hard time? You don't know the half of it, Ben, you great big knob.'

Didi and Tracy appear to be sinking further down into their desks, as if there is some sort of magnetic force pulling both women into them.

And then it all spills out. How I haven't just lost my mother, I've lost my complete identity – okay, so I'm laying it on a bit thick, forgive me, but it's Ben and he's – you know – an absolute prick – and how I was abducted as a newborn baby and kept away from my parents in a place called Loggerheads. LOGGERHEADS. And how I was all over the news. Et cetera, et cetera. And how he is punishing me for being a woman and being pregnant by docking my wages, how he has no concept of human suffering or emotion. In fact, I tell him, he's an emotional retard.

'We shouldn't really use that word,' Didi says, grimacing.

'Oh, do one, retard,' I snap at her. And she looks even more surprised than ever.

And of course, then, to really ladle it on I end with . . .

'And now, Ben. I am going to meet my father for the first time. And what is going to be running through my head?'

'I don't know.' He's so sheepish. GOOD.

'I'm going to be sitting there, thinking. My boss had his first wank over you. So thanks for that, Ben, you know. Nice one, babe.'

He is now the colour of a beetroot. I actually feel a bit sorry for him. Yes, he said something ridiculously 'him', but there was no need for me to call him on it and then give it to him with both barrels, whilst calling my assistant a retard. I am clearly taking out all my recent frustrations on him, and a little bit on Didi.

'If I'd known he was your dad,' Ben is saying, 'I would never have said that about . . . you know what.'

I nod. I get that.

But then he adds . . . 'Have you got a photo of what he looks like now?'

I want to punch him.

Leslie Wilson is still good-looking. I spot him immediately as he emerges from the platform with all the other arrivals from Birmingham New Street. He is carrying a small bouquet of flowers. His eyes are still dark; he looks almost Italian. And although he must be in his late fifties he has only recently started greying at the temples. Ben'd have a field day. He once came into work wearing a T-shirt that read 'DADDY ISSUES'.

Well, he'd have them now, that's for sure.

He's not wearing sports casual any more. But he is wearing quite a trendy North Face anorak, jeans and – wow – Kickers. His hair is a bit Paul Weller. If I didn't know already I'd say he was an old rocker, or someone who used to be in a Britpop band. The drummer. The roadie.

But then I realize I have no idea what he does for a living. He could well have been in the charts and I never knew. But it feels impolite to ask him just yet.

He could be Liam Gallagher's older brother.

Okay, so that would make him Noel Gallagher. I'll rephrase.

He could be Noel Gallagher's older brother.

But I know that he's not, as I know he's not from Manchester.

It's like I know him instantly. Well, it's not like I'd have spotted Leslie anywhere. But there is something familiar about him, if that doesn't sound trite. He still looks like that lost lad, except there's a paunch at the waist, and wrinkles on his face, which only make him look more rugged.

'Leslie?' I say, because he is eagerly looking around to see which waiting woman might be me.

Then his eyes light up and he does a *God, how stupid am I?* look, because of course I am the only woman waiting by the platform entrance who looks in any way heavily pregnant. And I have told him on the phone that I am heavily pregnant. Anyway, the flowers are practically a goner because he drags me in to him for a massive bear hug and they get squashed between us. The realization that this is happening then sends us both into fits of nervous, embarrassed, *I don't know you but this is kind of hilarious even though it's not* kind of laughing, that only strangers who don't want to be strangers can do.

'Look at you!' he says, all Brummie, which makes me laugh in itself. It sounds at once so alien, yet at the same time it feels like coming home.

Blimey, there was me taking the mick out of Tracy's birth family being from Solihull. And look at me now!

He rubs my cheek, taking in my face, as if searching every inch of it for some sort of recognition. I don't know if he finds it but he grabs me in for another hug, only this time he makes sure he puts the flowers behind my back so they remain unsquashed. And this time as he's hugging me I feel his body jerk and I realize he's starting to cry. I hold him there and, quite quickly really, the tears subside. He pulls away from me and hands me the flowers.

'Sorry, sorry. Promised myself I wouldn't do that,' he says, taking a hankie from his coat pocket and wiping his eyes.

'Thank you,' I say, sniffing the flowers like people do in movies.

'You don't have to thank me for anything, sweetheart.'

'How old are you?' I ask, incredulous. He looks so young.

'Fifty-five, babs. I was a nipper when we had you.'

Gosh. He's as old as I feel!

He indicates the flowers and says, 'I'm a bit crap with flowers so I have to be honest. The missus chose them.'

'You're married?'

'For my sins.'

'Have you got any other kids?'

He shakes his head. 'She's got a problem with her tubes.'

I nod. I'm his only child. No wonder he's bloody crying.

We walk across the concourse of the station hand in hand.

Oh my God, I am walking across Euston station hand in hand with a complete stranger.

I never hold hands with people.

I hated holding hands with Jamie.

Later he would go on to say, 'Was it because you had an inkling?'

'An inkling of what?'

'That I was gay.'

'No, I just hate holding hands in public. Sorry.'

He'd seemed most put out.

We walk to Pizza Sophia, which is just across the road from my flat, and a ten-minute walk from the station. It does the best pizzas in the area and everyone seems authentically Italian (and if they're not, then they're very well cast). And I think, well, working-class bloke in London for what might be his first ever time . . . He can't be intimidated by some homely pizza.

'You live round here? Very posh, bab.'

'I've done all right for myself.'

'So! When's the baby due?'

'Week before Christmas.'

'And d'you know if it's a boy or a girl?'

'No.'

'Oh well, maybe you could call it Noel or Noelle.'

And we laugh. We laugh so casually. Anyone else in the restaurant would just think we were casual friends. Or a normal father and daughter meeting for a catch-up.

And let's be honest, this is way different from that.

There is a chasm between us that we must cross.

'I'm so sorry I never tried to find you before. Mum told me she got pregnant by a one-night stand.'

He rolls his eyes again, and the smile instantly drains from his face. 'That'd figure. She was a fantasist, your mum. If I'd not been with her when you were taken, I'd have said she'd made the whole thing up.'

I never had Mum down as a fantasist. Okay, so she hoodwinked me my whole life, but – oh God, I guess he's right. It's just usually I'd assume a fantasist would make up slightly more glamorous stuff.

I'm Joan Collins' cousin but we don't speak.

Tina Turner stole her act from me.

One of my ancestors was Peggy Lee.

'Where did you think I was?'

'New Zealand.'

Oh good. I was right. I was right!

'She told me she was going over there for a fresh start. And I believed her. Well, of course I believed her. Why wouldn't I? We were both of us recognized wherever we went, but more so with her. I just wanted to get back to normality and the rot had set in with both of us. Then I . . . well, I went and made a fool of myself . . .'

'How?'

'Oh, I had an affair with a woman who took a shine to me. I had my head turned. I played the field a bit. So Linda was angry with me. We split up. She said she was shipping you both abroad. And she felt it was best to make a clean break.'

'How did that make you feel?'

'Oh, I was glad to see the back of her, don't get me wrong. I mean, I know she was your mam and that, but fuck me, she was hard work.'

'Well, I have first-hand experience of that.'

He then reaches out and takes my hand.

'But saying goodbye to you was one of the hardest things I'd ever had to do. I'd lost you once. Didn't seem fair to have to lose you again.'

'Did you ever try and keep in touch?'

He shakes his head.

'You just vanished . . . off the face of the earth. She promised she'd write with an address and send pictures. But she never did. It was horrible. I lost you twice. Once was bad enough, but . . .'

'Well, you've got me back now.' And with that I'm much more soppy than I ever thought I could be. He takes my hand again and gives it a little squeeze.

'I hope so, bab.'

'What do you do for a living?'

I know. So weird. Asking your own dad what he does for a living. This whole thing is too surreal.

I just know he's going to say he's a scaffolder, or a bricklayer, something reassuringly manual and working class. So I am quite taken aback when he says, 'I'm a drug and alcohol counsellor in a private rehab clinic in the Lickeys.'

'The what?'

'The Lickeys.'

'Oh.'

He smirks and explains it's a nice bit of countryside near Birmingham.

'After your mam left and took you with her, I had nothing. I sold the house and moved into a flat and spent the profits on wine, women and song. Oh, and cocaine. Well, anything I could get my hands on. I went to a very dark place.'

'But you came out the other side?'

'Eventually. Took a while, mind.'

'And now you help other people in similar situations?'

'I try to. Although of course, up till now I thought I'd never meet anyone who'd been through something quite so similar as me.'

I nod.

'But then of course I met you. And even though you won't remember a thing about it. You're one more person involved in that story, in that bit of my life. And I've never had that in my adult life. Well, this part of my adult life. My clean, sober bit.'

'Someone to share it with?'

'I guess so. It's hard to articulate really.'

'I know what you mean.'

Our pizzas arrive, but we're so engrossed in the conversation we don't even thank the waitress, except for a quick nod of the head.

'For so long it's felt like it never actually happened. It was so long ago now, you . . . you don't see things online about it as it was all pre-internet. It's not something most people remember. So it's like I made it up. Made it up as an excuse to drink. Or snort whatever.'

'It did happen,' I tell him. 'It happened to me and it happened to you. It happened to Mum as well. It's just a shame she never bothered to tell me.'

He shakes his head. 'I can't actually believe that, bab.'

'Well, I guess denial was an easier place for her to settle.'

'It must've taken so much effort, though, keeping up the pretence. The new names, all that.'

'I guess so. And it goes some way to explain why I always felt I was looking at her through perspex or something. Hard to get to. There was definitely a division between us and I assumed she just didn't like me.'

He ponders these words. We eat in silence a while.

'Sorry,' he says, 'I'm really comfortable with silence. Because of my work. Time to reflect. But I appreciate it can be disconcerting for some.'

My God, my dad is really brainy.

He uses words like 'disconcerting', 'appreciate' and 'reflect'.
Yikes. Suddenly he puts down his knife and fork.

'D'you wanna know what's freaking me out?'

'What?'

'When Shirley took you. When she tried to pass you off as her own. Obviously she couldn't call you by your real name.'

'Aha?'

'So she called you . . . and this is too weird . . . Rachel.'

'What?'

'It's true.'

'Really? Bloody hell. Did Mum know this?'

He nods.

This is too much.

'So it's not just coincidence?'

He shakes his head.

'I guess it was a name she thought you were used to hearing.'

I think about this. This is too bizarre for words. Mum latching onto something Shirley Burke had done. You'd have thought she'd want to run a mile from anything associated with her.

'Did you go to Shirley Burke's trial?' I ask.

He nods vehemently as he takes a bite of his pizza.

'I wanted to see the guilt in her eyes. I think I had fantasies about trying to kill her. But as always, I was too much of a coward.' Then he adds, and it sounds like he's joking, 'Maybe one day!'

'What was she like?'

'She was a little girl playing dress-up, that's what she felt like. She was completely out of her depth. If I thought Linda was a fantasist, she met her match in Shirley Burke. I mean, what did she think she was trying to achieve?'

349

'Happiness?'

'Her boyfriend saw right through it. He was there as a witness. Bit of a twat, if you ask me. Oh, it all came out, how Shirley had been stalking them. Well, his wife mostly. Hate mail. Talking to her neighbours. She'd even turned up at his mother-in-law's funeral.'

'What, and kicked off? Oh God, she sounds nuts.'

'I don't know. Think she just observed from afar. She came out with all this herself on the stand. Like she was showing off how clever she was. When in fact the jury were just thinking – you complete and utter fruit bat.'

'Blimey.'

'And they called her sister in too. She had more nous about her. I quite warmed to her; she seemed sane in comparison. But Shirley had cut herself off from her family so they'd not seen her in the latter part of her pretend pregnancy, and they'd not visited her with the newborn baby.'

'So her family were normal, then.'

'Dead normal. I remember her mum was there every day, sitting ashen-faced in the public gallery. She did once shout out, "Control yourself, Shirley!"'

'What?'

This sounded like a trial from a soap opera.

'Well, she went to pieces on the stand. Hysterical, she was. Made a right show of herself, didn't warm herself to any of the jury there. Give her her due, though. She did change her plea.'

'What, she was going to plead not guilty?'

'She did plead not guilty. Silly bitch.'

'But everyone knew she took me.'

'On the grounds of diminished responsibility. Tried to make out she was bonkers. But trust me. I've met loads of loonies in my time. What she did was bonkers, no doubt about it. But she was just manipulative. Thought the world revolved around her. A lot of mad people do believe that.'

'A lot of psychopaths, too,' I say, trying to sound like I know what I'm talking about. 'Like a certain President of the United States.'

He chuckles. 'Mentioning no names!'

'Exactly.'

'Sadly, in his case, he might be right. The world does revolve around him.'

He sighs.

'And for a very short while it did.'

'Sorry?'

'Revolve around her.'

We share a sad smile and eat in silence for a bit.

'How long did she get?'

'Ten years, bab.'

And he gives a look that says it should've been longer.

'Do you know what happened to her?'

He shakes his head.

'I was obsessed with her for a while. I did. I wanted her dead. If they'd had the flaming death penalty over here I'd have been first in the queue to give the injection, press the button.'

'She did a very bad thing.'

'Aye, she did. You're right there. But I know myself very well now, bab. Sorry. Feels weird calling you Rachel. It'd feel weird calling you Diana, mind.'

'Bab is fine,' I say.

'But it wasn't that with me. It wasn't that she'd taken you. You were well looked after from the sounds of things.'

Oh good, that wasn't just a press story, then.

'I wanted to kill Shirley Burke because she'd dented my macho pride. She'd come into our garden, onto our premises,

351

and got one over on me. Made me feel less of a man, see. No matter how much people argued with me. No matter how many mates told me they'd have done the same thing. She'd taken the piss. And that offended me more than her hiding away with you for weeks on end.'

I nod. I get it. I really do.

'Sorry. I'm probably being a bit too honest here. But life's too short for bullshit.'

'So you don't know where she is now? Even if she's alive?'

He shrugs, which I find a bit non-committal. Either he does or he doesn't.

'She was released. And I was gutted. And I still wanted to kill her. I'd follow her around.'

'What?!'

'I was obsessed with her. She'd wrecked my life. I wanted to wreck hers.'

'Where was she living? Where was she from?'

'Manchester way, Oldham. But then I had to let go.'

'I don't understand.'

'I don't remember half of it myself. So I don't explain it very well. It was when I was drinking a lot. I went there thinking I'd sort her out. But truth be told I just sat in a boozer round the corner from hers and drank myself into oblivion. Slept on a park bench. Eventually the police were onto me and . . . well, they said it wasn't a good idea to be hanging round there, no matter how much sympathy they had for me.'

This story. This life. It doesn't fit with the sprightly, clean-cut man in front of me. The handsome matinee idol gone slightly to pot. This man with his clean fingernails and his shiny white teeth does not look like the sort of man who has ever slept on a park bench.

'And what would you do if you met her now?'

'What would I do if I met her now?'

'Aha.'

'Oh, that's simple.'

'What?'

'I'd kill her.'

He takes a swig of his Diet Coke, and then continues to eat his Fiorentina with a runny egg. Suddenly he says, 'Rachel, I've got a confession.'

His change in tone alarms me.

'What?'

'Me and your mum weren't getting on during the pregnancy. I'd already started hitting the bottle.'

'That's okay. She'd drive anyone to drink.'

'The day Shirley took you, I was pissed. Well, it was a national holiday. That's why Linda turned her back on you. She wasn't washing up. She was rowing with me about starting drinking so early. She blamed me.'

'It's okay.'

'She said all sorts. Said if I'd not been pissed and we'd not been rowing we'd've known a complete stranger was walking off with you.'

'It didn't cause the abduction though, Les.'

He looks so stunned that I would think this.

'Thank you,' he says. Then says it again, before adding, 'You don't know what it means to me to hear you say that.'

'Shirley Burke did this. Not Mum. Not you. And not your drinking.'

'I hate her, Rachel.'

'The feelings are still that raw?'

'Rachel. Look at you. I've missed out on all this.'

He motions with his hand to show he means my whole body.

'I never saw your first day at school. Exams. Boyfriends. I

never saw you blossom, I just see the end result. And then on top of all that, it sounds like you had a gruesome childhood.'

'Oh, it wasn't that bad.'

'You weren't close to your own mum, and whose fault is that?'

'Shirley Burke's.'

'So forgive me if it sounds a bit harsh. But yeah. I'd push that bitch under a bus tomorrow.'

He calls the waitress over and orders another Diet Coke. I think that is the end of it. I am about to change the subject to something jollier – mass genocide, maybe – when he continues.

'I could kill her, you know. I could kill her tomorrow. And just knowing that, d'you know what that gives me?'

He's leaning in towards me a bit now. Like mafia bosses do in gangster movies.

'It gives me power.'

I am speechless. I have no words. I honestly do not know what to say, so I find myself nodding in slow motion. I may as well be underwater, I am going so slow.

He continues to eat.

'How d'you mean? You could kill her tomorrow?'

'This is good pizza.'

'I don't understand.'

'I have her mother's address.'

I gulp. It's what people do in cartoons, but I am doing it now. Who knew? I am a gulper. At times of stress, receiving surprising information . . . I gulp.

'I made some friends. When I hung around those pubs all those years ago. They might be alkies but they're decent people. Fucking decent people. And they keep me in touch. Plus there's the electoral register. I check that every now and again. And her mother, Mrs Mary Burke, she still lives where she always lived. Seven-three-nine Springfield Avenue, Oldham.'

'That must be a long road.'

'Well, it's a long story, isn't it? My friends tell me Mary doesn't see too much of Shirley. But they must see something of each other, eh?'

'Eh,' I find myself echoing.

'All it'd take would be to break in. Or get one of them to break in . . .'

He's starting to – not quite scare me – but he is alarming me somewhat now. This is all turning rather cloak and dagger, rather Machiavellian. I preferred it when he was being avuncular. But then is he being any different from how I have been since I found out what happened? And this man before me has had to live with the incident, those lost times, for thirty-odd years.

'Break in and go through her stuff. Find an address book. And bingo.'

'Bingo,' I say, unconvinced. And slightly weary.

'Do you want to find her, bab?'

I think. I know he'd do it for me. I know he'd lead me to her, dead or alive.

'Do you think she's alive?'

'They reckon she is. And they'd know.'

I think some more. I'm obviously taking too long as he says it again.

'You don't have to tell me now. But if you do want to see her. I'll get you to her.'

I take a deep breath. Then I say it.

'No. No, I don't want to meet Shirley Burke.'

'Fair dos.'

'Once upon a time I thought I did. But I don't think I need or want to now.'

And then we discuss mass genocide.

Chapter Twenty-One

'It's a shame they don't have apple restaurants.'

'Shut up and answer the question.'

'Don't tell me to shut up.'

'Rachel! What was he like?'

'My name isn't Rachel, it's Diana!'

'RACHEL!!!!'

I like winding him up.

My life seems to be spent in restaurants at the moment. And it's true about the apple thing. Talk about a lost market!

I give in.

'Yeah, he was nice.'

Still, at least I'm really making this 'eating for two' thing work.

'Did you tell him that Ben had his first wank over him?'

'Jamie, what do you think?'

'Well, sometimes we say really inappropriate things through nerves.'

'No, I didn't say that. I wasn't inappropriate at all.'

God knows why I have done this, agreed to come for tapas with Jamie. Though I did put the proviso that Mr Batti didn't come with him. Fortunately for me, Jamie shamefacedly had to admit that he and the Batti-boy were no longer an item, and he really regretted putting that relationship status on Facebook.

'So you should be,' I'd said, like a reproachful mother. Which is how I feel about him now. Is that bad? It doesn't feel bad. It just feels . . . odd.

'And you haven't heard from this private investigator?'

'No. By rights she should be invoicing me for five hundred pounds I don't have.'

'What have you done about finding her?'

'Well, nothing. It's up to her to find me now.'

'She could be dead.'

'Don't be dramatic.'

'Well, you're the one that saw her being cartwheeled into the back of an ambulance, love, not me.'

'Stretchered.'

'Cartwheeled's camper.'

'I know. I'm still getting used to it.'

'Oh, behave. You love a bit of camp. Basing your look on Doris Day?'

'Shut up.'

'Going out with a bloke with a bigger handbag than you? Pur-lease!'

It's been a month since I met Les. We've not seen each other since but we've stayed in touch via the odd text, email and phone call. He wants me to go to the Midlands and meet his wife. I said maybe after the baby is born. Well, definitely after the baby is born.

So much has happened this past month.

I feel like I'm treading water somewhat right now. I'm a month off my due date. It's an exciting time, as it feels like Christmas is coming. Actually scrap that, it feels like ten million Christmases are on their way. It's an exhilarating feeling.

But not one I can do much with or about, except just go along for the ride. The positive side of this is that my feeling of euphoria has returned and is overriding most things. I get teary at adverts on the TV. I cry at videos on Facebook of deaf kids hearing for the first time. But mostly I am going round with a ridiculous smile on my face. I am now one of those irritating people who will post an inspirational meme on Facebook saying things like 'DON'T SWEAT THE SMALL STUFF'. With a picture of a still lake behind it.

And that is probably just as well because, well, it's all kicked off at work. JuJu Quick has dumped Venus and gone to our biggest rival, Earth Travel, because – and I quote – 'I got sick of hearing myself sing every time you put me on hold.' So, it doesn't always pay to be a sycophant. The lack of this income stream has sent Ben into a tailspin. He's running round like a headless chicken, threatening us all with the sack if we don't 'pull in someone big'. I jokily pretended I'd set up meetings with Christopher Biggins and the Chuckle Brothers and he visibly blanched.

Apparently that's 'not funny'.

Whereas I found it highly amusing.

The way I am feeling I would be more than happy for him to lay me off. More than happy. I'd be happy to walk away now, but I won't. If he dares get rid of me, rather than the other way round, he'll have to pay me a month's income for every year I've worked there, and he'll begrudge that. Oh, he will really begrudge that! So I'll leave the ball in his court, thank you very much.

Mind you, I don't have this blasé, gung ho attitude towards the job and my precarious position therein because I am high as a kite on pregnancy and impending motherhood; it's because I now have a buyer for Mum's house in the New Forest, which means that, kerching, in the next few months I will be more or less quids in.

And if you were wondering whatever became of my private investigator Kelly Hopper, well, only yesterday I got the following email:

From: EastBoldreVicarage@cofe.co.uk
To: Rachel@Venus.net
Subject: KELLY HOPPER

Dear Rachel,

I hope this message finds you well, and adjusting to life without your dear mum.

I really hope you don't mind me writing to you like this but I have a visitor staying with me. Kelly Hopper.

Anyway, long story short (I usually hate that phrase but seems so appropriate here LOL) she's not in a good way. Been in and out of psych wards past few weeks after collapsing at work after the bailiffs took everything she had. Poor lamb. But worry not, she is getting better. Think more than anything she just needs some TLC. (And some prayer LOL.)

Now she has become more lucid she has asked me to pass on a message to you, which is that she discovered two things. One, the whereabouts of your father. He is living in the Midlands somewhere but she can't remember where. But she did find and speak to him, she just can't remember what was said. But she will – as soon as she's back on her feet – get in touch with her contact and make inroads again. She's really sorry about that, but the bailiffs took her notebooks.

The other thing to tell you, and hopefully this will make sense to you: Shirley Burke is dead. Not been heard of for years, has literally vanished off the face of the earth. So either dead or living homeless on the streets. Hopefully that will mean something to you.

She has asked me to pass on her bank details as she is going to write an invoice for her services. I will attach it. (But between you and me I won't blame you for not paying it till you have at least a phone number, etc. LOL.)

I really do hope this news is of some comfort. It's the best that I could get out of her as she appears to be somewhat incoherent, to say the least.

Love and light

Tom x

I was less perturbed by the content than by the fact that I'd discovered a LOL'ing priest.

So it turns out Shirley Burke is definitely dead.

Well. Definitely dead or possibly living on the streets. There's decisiveness for you!

A thousand pounds, eh? I read the invoice and thought . . . well . . . there's no hurry, is there? It's not like Kelly's been kicking my door in.

I respond when I get in this evening. Just a day later. No biggie.

From: Rachel@Venus.net
To: EastBoldreVicarage@cofe.co.uk
Subject: Re: KELLY HOPPER

Hi Tom

Great to hear from you. All good here, getting bigger every day LOL.

Oh God, now I'm at it!

361

Thanks for letting me know about Kelly. I went to visit her just as she was being taken off in an ambulance, so I wondered what had happened to her.

If you could please let her know I have met my father. She had got in touch and passed on my phone number. It was a very positive, productive meeting and we have kept in touch. So naturally I am very grateful.

I am of course happy to pay Kelly's invoice, but I need to wait till payday, sorry. I'm sure she will understand – it has been a while since I've seen her.

Thank you for everything you did for my mother's funeral. I'm not sure how much I will be returning to the New Forest as I finally have a buyer for the house, so I will have fewer ties there. I still have two friends in Beaulieu so no doubt I will be down now and again, so who knows? Maybe one day our paths will cross again.

Once again, thanks for everything – all best

Rachel x

I'm just about to shut my laptop down when I hear an email ping into my inbox. I think it might either be an out of office from the vicar, or he has replied incredibly quickly, but instead I see it's an email from my dad.

From: LWilson1962@hotmail.com
To: Rachel@Venus.net
Subject: Just thought you should know

Hi Rachel, Les here.

Hope you've had a good week.

Listen, I've had some info from one of my pals 'oop north' which I thought I better share with you.

Shirley's mum died a few days ago and it's her funeral tomorrow. I know everyone reckons Shirley's not been seen for a long time and they weren't in constant touch. But if she was ever going to return home, it would be for her mum's funeral, right?

I'm going to go. I want to see what she looks like. Don't worry, I'm not going to cause any trouble. But I just want to go and see for myself if she is there, etc.

Do you fancy coming with me? I know you said you had no desire to see her, but thought I would check on the off chance. If you wanted to come, it'd mean you'd have to get a train from Euston to Birmingham New Street by ten tomorrow morning and I'd drive us there. It's a palaver but you never know.

I was thinking about what I told you about what SB said at the trial. About how she'd been stalking the other woman, going to her family funerals and all that. Well, now it's my turn to stalk her. Nobody's going to wonder who I am, are they? People aren't too nosy in a crematorium.

You probably won't want to come, but thought it best to check anyway.

Hope you and brewing baby are okay.

Love ya

Les x

P. S. Her Indoors sends her love.

I reply immediately.

From: Rachel@Venus.net
To: LWilson1962@hotmail.com
Subject: Funeral

Hi there
    You know full well what I said at the restaurant.

But isn't a girl allowed to change her mind?
Fuck it. I'm in. See you at New Street at ten.
R x
P. S. Love to Her Indoors!

I wonder if this was such a good idea. We're not even at the crem and my heart is racing. Is that good for the baby? Surely it can't be. But there's no way I couldn't come today. I know. I know I said all those weeks ago that I had no desire to meet Shirley, but I just can't help myself. She's what bonds Les and me. She's what broke Mum and me. Maybe I could just catch a glimpse and make do.

My mind is telling me she is dead.

Kelly Hopper said she is dead.

But my heart is telling me, you just never know.

My heart is wanting her to be here.

But I know full well that whatever you want from life you rarely get. So I know today any hopes will be dashed.

But at least I have Les for company.

We sit on Springfield Avenue, watching the house. The funeral isn't for another forty minutes but cars are pulling up outside and people are venturing into the house.

We sit there, eating burgers from a Burger King we passed. I feel for all the world like Cagney and Lacey or Scott and Bailey on a stakeout.

None of the women who've gone into the house yet have been old enough to be Shirley.

'How old would she be again?' I ask, as we stare at the blandly painted white council house. The one next door is far more racy. It has wagon wheels attached to the brickwork either side of the door.

'Nineteen in 1981?'

'Aha?'

'Fifty-five.'

'That's nothing. But all of these look too young.'

'Maybe they're her daughters.'

We quickly look at each other.

I have never stopped to think that Shirley Burke might have children of her own. Maybe she has. Maybe she is a good mum. Maybe they have no idea, like I had no idea. Maybe they know and don't care. Maybe they didn't know and found out and all sorts went down. I want to go over the road and knock on the door and ask.

'Where are you, Shirley?' I say quietly, then realize I am feeling slightly repulsed by my burger. It must be the acid reflux. I fear I am going to be sick. I take the Gaviscon from my coat pocket and have a swig. I drink this stuff like it's milkshake these days. I return it to my pocket and pull the collar of my coat up.

'Incognito?' Les asks.

'No. Bloody freezing.'

And with that, as if by magic, it starts to snow.

I see he's smiling.

'What you so happy about?'

He turns and beams at me. 'Just realized.'

'What?'

'I've never seen snow with my daughter before.'

And we both sit there and watch it fall together. Our first snow.

And through the snow we see the hearse arrive and pull up outside the house.

'Let's get to the crem. Ringside seat.'

He turns the key in the ignition and puts the car in gear.

* * *

At the front of the crem is a huge iced bun made of flowers. It makes me quite emotional. As I bring a hankie to my eyes I see people looking round and know that they think I am crying for the loss of – what was her name? – I check the order of service.

Mary Burke.

The flowers tell me that Mary liked cakes, or made cakes. It's such a simple thing, but it tells me so much. It also tells me that she was loved. Someone has gone to the trouble of getting a load of flowers made to look like an iced bun. You don't go to all that bother if the person is a pain in the arse. As the crem starts to fill up, I am reminded of my own mother's funeral, not so long ago. That affair was much more spartan and sparsely attended than this.

Mary Burke obviously did a few things right.

But of course, she also did a few things wrong.

Like – give birth to Shirley Burke.

But then, was that Mary's fault?

I look at the order of service again. There is a picture of Mary on the cover of the booklet. It shows a sweet, white-haired old soul in a hand-knitted cardy, possibly in a nursing home, smiling vacantly at the camera. She looks lovely, inno-cent, incapable of being the mother of someone who did such a dreadful thing.

But then I flip the booklet to the back cover. There is a pic-ture of Mary in what looks like the seventies. She's standing at a counter. It looks like she's in a cafe. She's got tongs in her hand and she's posing with a scone in the tongs. She's wearing a uni-form and a little hat. The smile is frozen on her face. And I have to say, it's not a nice smile. She looks tough in this picture. Hard-faced. You wouldn't want to get on the wrong side of her.

She does look like the sort of woman who could have given birth to Shirley.

She looks like the sort of woman who'd steal a baby herself.

I don't like the look of her in this one.

I open the order of service to see if it says who is doing the readings. It does.

I don't recognize some of the names.

Shirley isn't mentioned anywhere. If she is coming then she isn't taking part.

But one of the readings, a poem I've never heard of, is going to be read, it says, *By Mary's daughter Josie.*

Josie must be the sister that went on the stand at the trial. The one Les thought was sensible. I elbow him – he's busy scouring the room for potential Shirleys, but I've examined them all and I don't reckon any of them are her; none of them are sat on the front two rows, for a start – and I point to the name in the order of service. His eyebrows rise and he checks out his own booklet.

It's impossible, isn't it?

Shirley Burke is not going to be here.

This really has been a pointless day.

We are both being vaguely ridiculous.

Yet at the same time it is reassuring to know that I am not alone. I am not the only person on this planet who has these strange feelings, who wants to know what a woman is like that I've not seen for thirty-odd years. Thirty-six years. A woman I wouldn't know if I passed her in the street, and her me. If I were here alone I'd feel like a freak. But the presence of Leslie proves that I am not losing the plot. I am not stalking my lover's mother-in-law or partner like Shirley Burke was once upon a time.

Or . . . am I? Are we really that different?

Yes. Yes we are. I would never do what she did. I would never . . .

God, I could really eat an apple right now.

Why didn't I bring any with me?

Suddenly some music comes over the loud speaker and a vicar instructs us to stand up. The music is familiar but I can't pinpoint what it is exactly. It's from an advert. Possibly for British Airways. Anyway, who cares? The coffin is being brought it . . . hurry up, coffin, I'm not interested in you . . . and behind it a woman walks, linking a man. I look quickly to Les.

Is it her? Is that her?

He shakes his head.

'Think it's the sister.'

She's very gorgeous, the woman at the front of the procession. Possibly had a bit of work. Big flicky hair. Wouldn't look out of place on *Knots Landing*. Tiny waist, sort of woman you could hate. Looks very good for her age, but is probably sixty, or just under.

There are other women behind her but they are all much younger, more my age. And then some younger than that, and various blokes. But nobody who could fit the right age group for Shirley.

The gorgeous one turns out, of course, to be Josie, the sister. When she reads her poem she has a broad Lancashire accent. Very *Coronation Street*.

I wonder if this is the sort of accent Shirley has or had.

It must be. They were/are sisters.

During the eulogy Shirley gets a mention from the vicar. But only in passing.

This is a family who do not acknowledge her presence. The eulogy is all about how proud Mary was of Josie and her modelling career.

We hear all about Mary's life. So much so that when I'm heading towards Les's car in a foul mood afterwards – how dare

Shirley really be dead! How dare the family be so decent as to not warrant her with anything more than a fleeting mention? – he hurries after me and says, 'We're in.'

'We're what?'

'We're in. We're going back to the house.'

'Which house?'

'Mary's house. Josie invited me. I said I was a regular at the Station Cafe.'

I roll my eyes. The vicar had gone on and on about that blessed cafe in the eulogy.

'We're going to her house, Rachel.'

'What's the point? She's clearly dead.'

'We're going. And that's that.'

He opens the car and climbs in deftly.

I enter like a medium-sized elephant would. And with half the grace.

'Oh. And if anyone asks. You're my wife and that's my baby.'

I give him such a look. 'That is gross. That is . . .'

'That's gonna put them off the scent, bab. Now come on. I'm gonna find out one way or another. You don't even have to say a word.'

'You haven't got any apples, have you?'

'No, bab.'

This really is proving to be an impossible day.

I don't know how he does it. I'm a nervous wreck. He's gabbing away quite merrily to everyone in the house, whereas I am a pathetic mess. I am convinced I have a neon sign above my head that says, 'I AM BABY DIANA. YOUR SHIRLEY STOLE ME.'

Any time one of the family comes towards me I just panic.

It's a shame, as they all seem quite nice. Lovely, in fact.

I might go to the toilet. That'll kill some time. I'm not really in the mood for small talk.

As I pass Les en route to the hall he is in cahoots with a woman who's about twenty.

'Shame what happened with Shirley, isn't it, eh?'

'Oh God, yeah.'

'Do you still see her? I wasn't sure if she'd passed on or not.'

'Haven't a bloody clue, Geoff.'

Right. So he's saying his name's Geoff. Good to know.

'So you haven't heard from her?'

'None of us have. Nana Mary, never. Not for bloody years. Can you imagine that?'

I hear Les whistling through his teeth.

'She came about ten years ago. Flying visit. I think Nana Mary had just had her cancer scare. I think it was then. Think she'd just finished her chemo. But I never saw her. She just saw Mary and Mum. Didn't say much. Apparently she looked dreadful. And she'd gone all la-di-dah.'

I'm about to head up the stairs when I see something I'd not seen before.

Under the stairs there's a little table.

On the table is a bowl of fruit.

Crowning the bowl of fruit is a beautiful Granny Smith apple. It is beckoning me.

I look around. No-one can see. So I lean in to take it.

Which is when I see another thing.

It's a photograph in a frame.

Mary has a headscarf on. Josie is standing next to her in a back garden.

There is a woman on the other side.

My legs buckle and I feel sick.

And I realize that Shirley Burke is not dead at all.

SHIRLEY

Oldham, 1988

Chapter Twenty-Two

I wasn't sure how people still recognized me. What did a girl have to do? I'd altered my hair drastically, completely modulated my voice – some strangers assumed I was from the West Country and I certainly didn't dissuade them – I'd even taken to wearing glasses that I most certainly did not need. And yet people pointed and sniggered.

But I couldn't be Shirley Burke; I didn't look or sound like her. She had puppy fat, she had a coarse northern accent. I had the deportment of a young Audrey Hepburn. You'd never have known I was from 'oop north', as they say.

And yet some unruly kids near the hostel shouted out, 'There she is! Maggie Thatcher! Baby snatcher!'

I just kept my head down and hurried by. They really were the most hideous creatures. The lot of them, they wanted locking up. Locking up and throwing away the bloody key!

Now where had I heard that before?

You know, it was very hard, trying to make your way in the world when you had absolutely nothing. And what's more, you didn't even have your reputation. Even for most people living in poverty, they had at least that. What did I have? Correct. A big fat zero.

It was nigh on impossible to get work. I really fancied

working with kids. Nursery nursing, that kind of thing. Or being a teacher. Yep, really fancied that. But apparently, just because I'd had one misdemeanour involving a small child, working or coming into contact with little nippers was a no-go area. How ridiculous was that?

The prison service had said I was completely rehabilitated. Completely cured, for want of a better word. I was, in their eyes, a success story.

So please, pretty please, can I work in a nursery? I've grown fond of kids now. In fact, I really miss looking after baby Diana. She was a sweetie. And once I'd lost her I mourned her. She really had started to feel like she was mine. I missed the purpose my life had when I had her. The routine, the schedule, knowing what I had to do every hour of the day. I want that back, please.

Can I? Can I? Pretty please?

That'll be a big fat no, thank you.

Life just wasn't fair.

I'd paid my dues. I was meant to be a success story. One of the screws, Marion, she said to me, 'You're one of our best success stories, Shirl.'

It made me feel like a star. Like a brainbox. Like the top of the class.

Like once I was back on the outside, my life was going to mean something. I would finally find my purpose.

How wrong was I?

This life, this shitty little life. D'you know what it was? It was beneath me.

This was not the life I was destined for; existing was all I was doing, existing in a hovel of a hostel where every time it rained, water came through the window and I'd wake to a wet pillow.

It always wrong-footed me and I wondered if I'd been crying in my sleep.

No. I was just living in a shitty hostel.

No wonder I couldn't wait to get out each day. Thank heavens for the buses. I could just about afford to get in and out of Manchester every day, and in Manchester town centre there was a veritable feast of things to do for free.

I used to just bob into town every few days, but recently I'd had to move to daily because he was here.

Her dad.

Leslie Wilson.

How I wished there was someone I could have talked to, but I had no-one. Zulema in the hostel was the nearest thing I had to a pal, but she didn't speak any English. Well, except to say 'Kevin Keegan'. And I wasn't even sure she knew what that meant.

How awful it must have been to be all alone in a foreign country and only to be able to say the name of a has-been foot-baller.

But he was there. Watching me. I was sure of it.

I did hope it was him.

I did hope I was not – and this was my big fear – going mad.

This would have been my punishment, you see. For pretend-ing to be going mad to excuse my actions. Karma would come and defecate on me from a great height to remind me to be careful what I had wished for.

Was I imagining him? Was I? No, I couldn't be. It was defin-itely him. He had the same face, the same build; he looked haunted, as well he might.

But was I just imagining him? Was he in fact a figment of my – let's be frank here – sordid imagination? Was it my para-noia that was making me see him, hanging about on the corner, swigging from a lager can at any given hour of the day – there was vulgar for you – saying nothing, but his silence of course speaking volumes?

I didn't know. And rather than confront him, I did what I always did, and ran for the bus. What was he doing in Manchester? He lived in Birmingham. I was going mad.

One day, they said, it will be like the old days, and you'll be able to take a tram from Oldham into Manchester. How quaint. How odd. When the world was moving forward, what interest had we in looking back?

I for one refused to look back.

I did not recognize the girl I used to be.

I had no time for her as, I'm sure, she'd have had no time for me.

Shirley Burke was as dead to me as she was to my mother.

I'd campaigned vociferously during my final months inside to be granted a change of identity. But that change had never come. I knew what they were up to. I wasn't behind the cowshed when they handed out brain cells. They wanted me to suffer. Every day of my life it would be there, in black and white. Two words: Shirley Burke.

Honestly. Hadn't I suffered enough?

So since my release I'd been visiting the library in Manchester and looking into how I'd go about changing my name all by myself, changing it by deed poll. Then I could be whoever I wanted. I could be someone else. I could feel like me again, the new, improved, better me. Not the old one who made some, let's be frank, pretty catastrophic decisions.

I had to get away. That is what I knew, deep down, I had to do. The reason I kept imagining I was seeing Leslie Wilson was because I was still in my old stomping ground, and that would not do. If I could just get away, find the money to ship out to pastures new, everything would improve. And if I had my new name, no-one would ever associate me with the girl I used to be.

I mean. What was keeping me in this neck of the woods?

Nothing, that's what.

Every day I'd follow the same routine. I'd go to the phone box outside Central Library and dial in the same old number. And every time she'd answer the phone with the same speech.

'Shirley. Stop calling me. You've brought humiliation and shame on me, your father and our Josie. Yes, even Josie. No-one wants to know her on the beauty queen circuit now. She's having to diversify. And whose fault's that?'

And every day I'd say the same thing back. 'I'm so sorry, Mum.'

'Mum? MUM? Please don't call me that. You're dead to me.'

Told you.

And then she'd hang up.

Once a week I'd phone our Josie.

Gosh, I'd have to stop calling her that. That is so northern.

Once a week I'd phone my sister, Josephine. But it was pretty much the same story.

'You lied to me, Shirley.'

'I was desperate.'

'I had to look into that poor woman's eyes in court. And see her thinking I was in on it. I could never be in on something like that. Anyway . . .'

'What?'

'I'm pregnant.'

This time it was my turn to hang up. But still. At least that beat her usual routine of 'Fuck off and leave us alone, Shirl!'

Is it any wonder I strayed, coming from a family who used such filthy language?

I had been on this bus to Manchester for nearly twenty minutes and the woman sat beside me was beginning to get on my nerves. She'd got on at the same stop as me and had plonked herself next to me, forcing me to be squeezed up against the window. I'd not yet deigned to turn and look at her, as I didn't want to give her the time of day, but all journey long she had been fidgeting and moving about and sighing and now . . .

Well, now her body was jerking. Very small jerks. And it became obvious to me that she was crying.

Oh, this was all I needed. First, a woman who had no concept of one's own personal space. And secondly, an emotional mess who was going to be embarrassing enough to cry in public.

I'd had enough.

I turned towards her and tutted. And then pulled this face. It was quite a good face. Audrey fforbes-Hamilton in *To the Manor Born*. I loved the re-runs of that in prison. It was a part withering, part disgusted look that I'd really managed to perfect.

I then turned away and looked out of the window.

Which is when I felt an elbow in the ribs.

And I heard a voice say, 'You don't even remember me, do you?'

WHAT?

I turned quickly and saw she was staring at me, wide-eyed. Those eyes were red with tears and immediately I wanted to be sick.

I knew exactly who she was.

I had felt my blood run cold only once before, and that was when I realized that the police were surrounding Lovers' Leap, and I had this woman's baby in my arms. And I felt it run cold again now. The blood literally drained from me. I could feel it sinking towards my feet. Yet at the same time I felt my forehead go sweaty and my heart start to race.

Linda Wilson was sitting next to me on the bus.

'What do you want from me?' I said, in barely a whisper. I was so scared. Finally it had happened. She had come to kill me. Was this a vision? Was this my paranoia? First the father, now the mother?

'I want your help,' she said.

I then noticed she was gripping tight onto the handrail in front of us, the handrail on the back of the seat. Her knuckles were white, she was gripping so hard. And the knuckles were digging into the back of the woman in front.

That woman now wriggled and turned around as if to say, *Can you move your hands, please?*

And move them Linda did.

She was not a ghost from my imagination. I had not conjured her up.

This really was Linda Wilson.

And she said it again. Linda Wilson said it again, in her tiny tinny voice.

'I need your help.'

She was very pretty, Linda Wilson, the sort of girl I might have developed a crush on if I were that way inclined, which I wasn't.

Oh, don't get me wrong, I'd had the odd experience in prison. Once with a lifer called Babs, who smoked cigars and thought me stealing a baby was 'cute', the other with a prison officer called Connie, who I thought always had a truncheon in her slacks side pocket, only it turned out on several occasions it was her vibrator. She had a name for her vibrator; it was called Sky. Or it was, till it got stolen. Her house was broken into and they took the TV, video player, stereo system and, would you believe, Sky. This led Connie to believe that it was lesbian robbers, probably ex-cons. I had to pretend to be interested because she got me special privileges.

Her hair was bleached blonde and cut in the style of Diana, Princess of Wales. I'd attempted this look myself, but it hadn't been such a success. Some twisted people asked if I was trying to emulate the look of Wendy Craig in *Butterflies*.

Actually. I'll tell you who Linda Wilson reminded me of. She reminded me of Vera.

I can't actually physically handle thinking of that evil witch any more. Focus on Linda. Focus on Linda.

We sat in the Little Chef just by Piccadilly Station and Linda Wilson looked, to all the world, like a frightened little girl. 'I Think We're Alone Now' by Tiffany was playing on a radio behind the counter while Linda wittered on over her hot chocolate, though I was in such a state of shock that I only took in the odd sentence here and there. Why had she sought me out? What would she be interested in me for? I had caused her great pain. This did not make sense. I tried to focus on what she was saying, but it was hard; I just caught snippets.

I've never bonded with her.

I don't know what to do with her.

It's like she doesn't love me.

I don't know her.

What did you do? Did she respond to you?

No-one must ever know.

That woke me up.

'No-one must ever know what?'

'What I've suggested.'

'What have you suggested?'

'I just said it.'

'I'm sorry. I'm not thinking straight.'

'I know you're not a danger, I read your reports. I asked to see them before you were released. You're no longer a danger to society, they reckon.'

'You want me to do something?'

'Just come and see her. Spend the day with her. I can't do it on my own. You know her.'

'I haven't seen her for seven years.'

'I'm struggling. I've got no-one else to turn to. She was fine when she left you. I want her to be fine again.'

'What's the matter with her?'

'Nothing's the matter with her. I just never feel good enough.'

'Linda, this is a terrible idea.'

But I didn't mean that one little bit. It was the most exciting idea I'd heard in ages.

What harm could it do? Me spending a day – no, a few hours, with little baby Diana.

'What if someone found out who I was? It's not fair. I'd have to go back to prison. Part of the deal for me getting out early is that I never see baby Diana ever again.'

'I won't tell.'

'How do I know this isn't just a trap? How do I know the police aren't going to come in now?'

'I don't know.'

And with that she burst out crying again. The crying was so painful. Those silent gulpy sobs. Awful.

'How do I know you won't have the police waiting for me if you take me to her? Your final punishment, your way of telling me I haven't suffered enough, not yet.'

'I don't know.'

All I knew, looking at her, was that this was a broken woman.

And another thing I knew, looking at her, was that I was the one who could fix her.

If she really meant what she was saying, this could be my redemption.

This would make me the good person I always knew I could be.

'I'll need to think about it,' I said.

I'd just say you were my friend. Or a new neighbour. I've never told her what happened. We have new names now.'

And that was the clincher.

I lay in bed that night, my mind racing. It was incredible, what had happened that day. Unheard of. A first. And of course it had happened to me – of course it had, the more I thought about it. I'd been right all along; I wasn't like other criminals. I was the best. It's not that I had got away with murder, far from it, it was just that even the mother of my 'victim', for want of a better word – and boy did I hate that word; that baby was cared for to within an inch of its life, thank you very much, psychiatrists of the world – could see I'd been better than my crime.

She had given me a chance for redemption.

She was vulnerable.

Interesting.

Some might say I'd made her vulnerable.

Even more interesting.

I could work my wonders on her.

I could start to make myself invaluable to her. Her shoulder to cry on, her child psychiatrist, her mentor. I could show her the way.

I could adopt a new name.

Oh yes, this was very good. This was exactly what I'd been looking for.

What did the Bible say again? Seek and ye shall find?

I'd sought. And now I'd found.

I'd have to take it slowly, of course. No doubt about that.

But suddenly there was light at the end of the tunnel.

I'd wasted so much of my life on inconsequential things that I wrongly thought were of consequence at the time. I'd spent year upon year upon year chasing and then trying to pin down a married man, and what a waste of time that had been. He'd lied through his back teeth about his feelings for me. He'd pushed me to extremes to keep his love. And it had all been the lousiest waste of everybody's time. How I wished I'd never crossed paths with Doug. How I wished we'd never gone to Butlin's that year and I'd never found his pig ugly daughter in the toilets. How I wished I punched that impossibly irritating *Good Life* wannabe Vera in the teeth when I'd seen her at Barnes Wallis, knocked her out good and proper.

All of it, every last second of it. A waste of time.

If I'd not met him, not met them, how different my life would have been.

And since my release from prison, again, days drifted by and I was wasting all this life. It was disgusting, it was offensive. It was wrong. Like I was treading water waiting for something to happen, and finally it had.

Finally, I had found my purpose.

RACHEL

2017

Chapter Twenty-Three

The satnav said it would take four hours to drive from Oldham to the New Forest. Clearly that didn't factor in the heavy snow, or the fact that a pregnant lady needs to wee every now and again. It also didn't factor in a stunned Les driving at what felt like twenty miles per hour all the way, taking in what he'd just heard, what had just unravelled before us. We drive most of the way in silence, punctuated sporadically by a comment of his or mine on this bizarre situation. Neither of us can quite believe it. And if he can't get his head around it, I can't even begin to explain how I feel.

It's nearly ten o'clock at night by the time we pull up on Sparks Lane. I see Les looking around, wondering where the hell I've brought him.

'This is where you grew up?'

'My stomping ground.'

'Blimey.'

And I can't tell if, by that, he is impressed or in fact he feels the opposite.

'I want to do this bit on my own,' I say suddenly. 'Is that okay?'

He considers this. There's no rulebook here. He then shrugs and tells me he'll be waiting.

The snow is deep underfoot. I want to say it's crisp but it's not. It's crunchy and the sound my feet make seems to echo round the forest. I push open the gate to the path. Nothing seems familiar any more; it's like I'm seeing it all with new eyes. I've seen clips online of deaf babies having hearing aids put in their ears and becoming aware of sounds for the first time. The unbridled joy on their faces is a sight to behold.

Well, this feels like that in reverse.

Every positive image, every happy memory of my time here as a child feels like it has now been ripped from my brain and tossed in the river that runs behind the cottages. I remember going and standing in that river the night we were going through Mum's stuff. The night that Margaret first found the newspaper front page. How little I knew then. And little did I know that finding that front page would change everything.

There are no footprints in the snow on the path. No-one has walked here recently, and for some reason this makes me think I am going to find her dead. With each step I take, my senses are becoming increasingly heightened. It's as if I can smell the snow, I can taste the oxygen in the air, I can hear every single branch crack in every single tree.

And then I am here.

I bang on the front door.

I thought I would feel angry. I thought I might cry. I just feel uncomfortably numb.

The lights are on. She is still up.

I hear her call from inside. 'Who is it? This time of night!'

'Sorry! It's me! Rachel!'

'Oh!' And she sounds excited.

A few bolts are unlocked and the door creaks open and there she is, standing before me.

Pam.

She goes to open her mouth, probably to say hello, but I cut in with, 'Hello, Shirley. Long time no see.'

And her face completely freezes.

'I think we need to talk. Don't you?' I add.

And then suddenly she moves. And I can't believe what she does. She rushes to shut the door in my face. But even though I am so bloody huge at the moment I am faster than her and kick my foot forward to jam the door and keep it open.

'Oh no you don't!' I snarl, and I push her out of the way to show I mean business. I barge straight into the kitchen and I hear her following. I swing round. She is ashen-faced, pulling at the sleeves of that ridiculous Mary Poppins dressing gown of hers.

Practically perfect in every way? I don't think so.

'Well? Have you got anything to say for yourself?' I certainly am giving good snarl tonight.

'I don't know what you're talking about.'

'Don't you dare. Don't you DARE! You've been lying to me for thirty-six years. Count them! Don't you dare think you can carry on with it now.'

'How do you know? Nobody knows!'

'Mum knew, presumably.'

'Of course she bloody knew. This was all her idea.'

'It's sick.'

'It worked, didn't it?'

'Worked? WORKED? If it hadn't been for you. If . . .' I realize I am trying not to cry now. 'If it hadn't been for you, I'd've had a half-decent relationship with her.'

'Oh, do me a favour!'

'What?!'

'If it hadn't been for me, sweetheart, you'd've had *no* relationship with your mum!'

'Oh, piss off!'

'No, I won't piss off. If I'd not stepped in when I did, your mum would never have bonded with you. She'd've probably . . . I don't know . . . handed you over to social services or something. And that's the truth of the matter.'

'Well, maybe that would've been preferable to growing up with you keeping your beady eye on me all the time.'

'This was all your mother's idea. Not mine.'

'Force you at gunpoint, did she?'

'I knew I should never have gone along with it. I blame myself.'

'Oh, drop the woe-is-me act, Pam. You had thirty-six years to back out of it.'

'You're making up numbers now.'

'What did she do? Greet you at the prison gates?'

'Oh, will you listen to yourself?'

Something suddenly hits me.

'You weren't . . . lovers?! Oh my God!'

'Don't be disgusting. I have never slept with a woman in my life!'

By now I should know when Pam/Shirley is lying. Her lips move. Can I trust anything she says?

'It's just too weird! Two women with false names hidden away in a forest. It's the stuff of fairy tales! No! It's the stuff of nightmares! It's *Grey Gardens* without the glamour!'

'I knew this would happen!'

'You knew what would happen?'

'It'd all go tits up! I can't believe she kept hold of those bloody newspapers. I told her to throw everything away. She told me she had.'

'No, Shirley. What you can't believe—'

'It's Pam!'

390

'What you can't believe is that you've been caught out at your . . . stupid little game.'

'It is not a game. It was never a game!'

God, she's sounding desperate. She's sounding like a stuck pig.

'Are you not even going to apologize for kidnapping me?'

'Oh, don't be so dramatic.'

'But you did!'

'I was a very different person then! We all make mistakes. Have you never done something you've lived to regret?'

'What, like accidentally walk into someone's house and walk out again with a newborn baby? Erm, let me think!'

'I didn't walk into . . .'

'Don't split hairs!'

'I'm sorry, okay?! I had mental health issues!'

'You did not. You were just selfish, and desperate.'

'Oh, and you're suddenly an expert, are you?'

'My dad told me.'

Now she really does look horrified.

'The piss-head?'

'He's not had a drink for years.'

'How about heroin?'

'He's not taken drugs for years.'

'He was a useless waste of space. Ask your mother.'

'I can't, she's dead. And she always insisted she didn't really know my father, let alone was married to him. She always said he was a one-night stand called Ambrose.'

'Sounds like you've been keeping yourself busy these last few months. Proper little Miss Marple, aren't you?'

'Maybe my dad got into a mess because of what you did to him,' I suggest, but she is adamant.

She shakes her head. 'Your mum told me. He was three sheets to the wind when I took you.'

'Oh right, so he deserved it, then?'

'Well, maybe if he hadn't been pissed I wouldn't have got away with it.'

'You've been getting away with it for far too long, Shirley.'

'Nobody. Nobody calls me that, you cheeky little bitch.'

Ah, see, she just can't help herself. She just can't help but let that anger seep through. I decide to kick her where it hurts. I say, 'I went to your mum's funeral today.'

Her eyes flicker. I don't know if this is because she didn't know, or just that she is offended by my presence there.

'And?' she says.

'They all think you're dead, too.'

'Well if I am, they killed me. Weren't prepared to give me a second chance. You gave your dad a second chance. I take it you've met him, then?'

'No. I'm giving him his first chance. Because you took the original one away from him.'

'God, you're obsessed with him. Well, all that glitters is not gold!'

'Because he's decent now!'

'See? SEE? We all change, Rachel.'

'No wonder you look so old, carrying around that terrible secret all these years.'

'Oh, we're getting personal now, are we?'

'It'd age anybody. But you can only be about fifty-five.'

'And carrying that terrible secret's what killed your mother. That's what gave her cancer. It was madness, inviting me into her life. And we both knew it but I was lonely. I was an outcast. And the olive branch was given from the most unexpected source. I think a few years later she regretted it. But by then we were, sort of, bound together. And there was no escape for either of us. I had nowhere else to go, and love me or hate me, I was here.'

'So, what? Struggling with the secret, with not having been honest with me, that gave her cancer?'

'Who knows?'

'Or maybe . . . maybe she died because she was going to tell me the truth. And you wouldn't let her.'

It has only just occurred to me, and I don't know if it is true.

'Well, that would suit you, wouldn't it? Always painting me as the bad guy. But yeah. You go ahead and think what you like.'

Time hasn't softened Shirley Burke of any sharp edges, I think to myself. Forced to face and own up to the truth there is no sense of regret, no feeling of culpability; it's everyone else's fault, not hers. And what's that smell permeating the kitchen? Well, it's the fish cakes she made for tea; it's certainly not the piquant tang of remorse. She really is quite the piece of work, I realize. She's a porcupine, backed into a corner, and the spikes are out. She doesn't care if they hurt you; they are merely there as a protective shield for her.

I am tired all of a sudden, so lean against the sink.

It's as if Shirley/Pam is too. She pulls out a chair and sits at the kitchen table, leaning her elbows on it, staring into the middle distance.

I can just tell what's coming. Confession and forgiveness time. I can now read her like a book. A rather complicated book. A very dark book. But a book all the same.

I cut in first, 'And don't you dare tell me they were asking for it, leaving me outside in a pram.'

'Rachel. I did a very, very bad thing. I was very young. I was very confused. I was very stupid. I never hurt you physically, but I know that by removing you from your mum, well, you missed out on important bonding time. So in a way I hurt you more than if I'd hit you or . . . worse. I hated myself and what I'd done, and if it's any consolation, by the time the police caught up with me my feelings of guilt were insurmountable and I was about to hand you back. Anonymously, mind. I wasn't that bloody honest or noble.'

She looks at me briefly and shoots me the smallest of smiles. I don't shoot one back.

'I was nineteen, Rachel. And a very naive nineteen at that. But I did my time. And I came back into the world, determined to do things right for once. So when your mother came to me, well, I was scared. I thought it was a set up, to get me back inside. But when she asked for my help. It took me a long time to understand it. Now, maybe that was her madness. Thinking I could mend something, put something right. I couldn't, by the way.'

Well, that sounds like honesty.

'But I was so lonely, and grateful for her attention, because it felt like forgiveness. I, well, I jumped at the chance.'

Again, this sounds like honesty.

'It was probably so wrong, for both of us, but it felt so right. We didn't do too badly, did we?'

She's seeking my approval. I really don't want to give it to her. I have no desire to make her feel any better. Right now that doesn't feel like my job.

'We'll see what my dad's got to say about that.'

'How is he?' She sounds concerned. Yeah right, that's faux concern if ever I heard it.

'Cold,' I say.

She doesn't understand. Then thinks she does. 'I see. Distant. Bit frosty. Hard to reach out to. Plus ça change, eh, Rach? Plus ça change.'

She's sounding almost pally. How dare she!

'No, he'll be cold. Seeing as he's sitting outside in the car.'

She takes a deep breath. Well, she wasn't expecting that. She sits there, thinking. I can see panic is rising up inside her. Finally she says, 'Does any of this make sense to you?'

'In what way?'

'When you found out. Was it a surprise?'

'Of course.'

'Not even a part of you thought, well that all feels familiar. Like you knew it had happened subconsciously.'

'No. Not a bit.'

She takes this in.

'Do you remember, Rachel? Do you remember the little song I used to sing to you? It always made you happy.'

'Of course I don't. I'd just been born.'

And then, very quietly, while staring at the table, she starts to sing:

'*Itsy bitsy spider climbed up the waterspout,*
Down came the rain and washed the spider out,
Out came the sun and dried up all the rain,
Itsy bitsy spider climbed up the spout again.'

She then looks me straight in the eye.

'Please don't hate me, Rachel. I named you.'

That pierces my skin. Like she has ownership of me. I don't want her to have ownership of me. And yet, and yet . . .

'I'm not sure what I think of you, if I'm honest. But I doubt my dad'll be as confused.'

'You're not bringing him in here,' she says quickly. I can see she is petrified.

Good. I want her to be. Maybe that's what I wanted all along.

For her to feel the same sort of fear and anxiety that my mother must have felt all that time I was missing.

Well, maybe this is the result I was aiming for.

I see beads of sweat on Pam's forehead. Rather repugnant beads of sweat. No beauty there.

She is, she's scared.

'Maybe you could apologize to him,' I suggest, and I notice her eyes darting round the room, like she's never been here before. Like she's trying to work out where she is and whether she's safe.

'I shouldn't worry, Pam. I don't think he's going to kill you. I don't think he's got it in him. He's actually quite a nice person.' Why am I trying to make her feel better? So I add, trying not to let myself down, 'Unlike some.'

She's speaking again. 'Will you excuse me a moment? I need to use the bathroom. I was on my way when you arrived.'

And she gets up gracefully and almost glides out of the room, quite the performance.

I feel my belly tightening; my whole chest seems to tighten with it. It's as if my body is going into spasm. I lurch forward and grab hold of the table, then lower myself into a chair. A gripping pain clutches me inside. And then I feel it subside. I know why this is happening. This is happening because, despite what I claimed, that song, and the singer, they sounded so familiar. The familiarity, the circumstances, they're so overwhelming. I do, I must have some memory of my time with Shirley. I can, I can remember something. Well, remembering isn't the right word, but something is stored inside me from those days. And it just comes flooding back, as if my DNA is recalling it, and the effect it had on me.

I suddenly feel very calm. I feel so calm I could sit here all night, just savouring the feeling of the song. It has placated me, put me back on an even keel.

It is so distracting a feeling that it takes me ten minutes or so before I realize that Shirley/Pam has been gone a long time.

And then I realize that I am chilly. And it's the sort of chilly that can mean only one thing in a house such as this. The front door is open.

But why would the front door be open?

I get up and move slowly to the hall. I look up the stairs and see that the bathroom door is ajar. Shirley/Pam cannot be in there.

'Pam?' I call. And there is no response. 'Pam?!'

I pull the front door further open to see if she's outside. And that's when I see there are two sets of footprints in the snow. Mine arriving and someone else's leaving. The leaving prints were not there when I arrived.

Pam has run away on me.

'Pam?!' I shout out into the night. And then decide to follow the footprints. I slip, I slide, and I'm fearful of falling and hurting the baby, so I do a sort of sideways walk, which for some bizarre reason I think will keep me upright. The footsteps head into the woods. They're visible, crisp and deep and even, as the old Christmas carol says. And even here amongst the trees I can see them; the moon must be pretty full tonight and reflects off the snow. I know now where she is heading.

'Pam?!' I shout again.

And then they disappear into the stream. Gone. They are no more.

It's too cold for me to walk in the water so I edge my way along the bank of the stream, knowing I am getting closer to her. Somewhere an owl hoots and I hear myself shouting, 'Oh shut up, don't be such a cliché!'

But the owl doesn't answer back. I hear the machine-gunfire flutter of wings as birds in trees nearby make their escape as they sense danger approaching.

But then I feel that gripping pain again and I am rendered useless and have to sink to my knees. I am wet and cold now, and shriek out in pain. What is going on? Is the baby telling me not to follow? When the pain subsides I force myself to my feet and carry on.

It's now that I hear a man's voice calling me; Les must be following. He's clearly had enough of waiting and has gone to the house and found it empty. He too must be following the footprints.

'Rachel?!'

And more flapping of wings. The water beside me is getting noisier now as I know I am nearing the section where it bends into the river. A few trees are blocking my view of the inter-section. I grab hold of one, and pull myself round to see.

And there she is. She is standing in the river. The water is up to her waist. The current laps past her. Her dressing gown floods out all around her, like a pool of black ink under the bright moonlight. Her body is twisting as the quicksands pull her down. Her back is to me. I see the silver thread, the word 'PERFECT'.

'You coward, Shirley! You fucking COWARD!'

I want to get in and pull her back, but I don't know if I have the strength.

Another gripping pain shoots through me and I realize what is happening. I am two weeks early; can my contractions really have started already?

As much as I hate her I want to save her. I step forward to the water's edge.

I hear Les behind me.

'Rachel! What you doing?'

'I don't know!'

The alarm in his voice brings me to my senses.

'Is that her?'

'Yes!'

'Leave her be.'

'But . . .'

'Let her get on with it.'

Her body isn't sinking. She slips and rights herself. Why isn't she sinking? She always said these were sinking sands. Did she make it up? Just to scare me, a little white lie to stop me from being naughty? She slides again and then moves further away.

'Pam! What are you doing?!'

It's a pointless question. She probably can't hear, as the rushing of the water seems to be getting louder now. And also, it is quite clear what she is doing.

The question is . . . what am I doing?

I am scared of more pain. My body is recovering from the last contraction, and I realize I have two options.

I either go in the water and try to save her.

Or I stay here and try to save my baby.

This is a no-brainer.

I feel an arm around me, pulling me back.

'Just leave her, bab. Just leave her.'

I fall into Les's embrace, unable to look any more.

It's over. The past is over. It's the future that's important now.

But then I hear a scream. She is screaming at me. I turn, look.

'What's she saying?' I say to Les.

And she screams again.

'DO YOU FORGIVE ME?'

But before I can answer she slips under the water and is

gone. She has reached the cusp of river to ocean. The currents have carried her away.

And in that moment I am glad that Shirley Burke's parents never insisted she learned to swim.

EPILOGUE

4 Woolf House
Tavistock Place
London WC1H
15 January 2018

Dear Margaret,

Thank you so much for the beautiful knitted sailor suit you sent for Otis. It fits him like a glove. Well, like a sailor suit. THANK YOU YOU'RE A STAR!

I stayed away from Pam's funeral – feel I can call her that now, not sure why – just because I couldn't be arsed, basically. I couldn't be bothered getting involved in the dramas of whether her family went or where it took place or what she was called. Not my circus – not my monkey. Though I did get a much nicer surprise than the others I've had recently when it turned out she'd paid off her mortgage and left the proceeds of any house sale to me. Blood money, I know, but it means I don't need to go back to work once my maternity leave is over – no point telling the boss that yet, though; make him sweat. I can be a lady of leisure. Just like yourself!

I'm toying with buying myself a little flat in the New Forest, so you won't have got rid of me just yet. And Otis will need to see his Aunty Margaret, won't he? Who else is he going to get his drinking skills from when he's 'of age'?

I'm in absolute love with him, of course. He's completely adorable. His smile doesn't just light up the room, it lights up the whole block, the whole postcode. See photos enclosed. Fortunately he looks like his dad and not like me, thank God for that! Jamie was a pain in the arse at the birth, once he finally got there (I know, I didn't want to have the baby so far from home, but then I didn't want to be abducted at just a few hours, etc.). He fainted when he made the mistake of looking down at my lady bits. Plus ça change, eh, Margaret? Plus ça change! He's got a new boyfriend. This one's an architect. I give it six weeks.

I spoke with Cliona on the phone last night and I'm going to plan a weekend staying at hers once I feel more confident about travelling with Otis on the train. So once I know when that is I'll give you a bell.

My dad continues to be a little star. That's the big positive I take from all this. And with his encouragement I've decided to start doing some voluntary work for a (tiny) charity that helps families who have had children go missing. I find it quite daunting, but at the same time my experience is so weird I need to make something positive out of it. If that makes sense. Les stayed at the hospital with me all the time I was in there. Determined to not let anyone take Otis, of course! Bless him, I don't think he slept for a week, and he now bombards me with texts every few hours checking up on the grandson. I think him and his missus are even toying with a move down south to be nearer to him. In that respect I feel very lucky. See? Not all bad.

I can't begin to fathom how Jane/Linda must've felt when I was taken. The thought of Otis not being by my side makes me physically sick. I am starting not to judge her so much. I know it's a cliché and I know it's obvious, but what she went through was so appalling I can't be too harsh on her for how she was as a result.

I'm going to take Otis out for a walk in a minute and post this. He is such a happy baby so I'll try my best to keep it that way. There are so many lovely parks round here, and there's a special one that's aimed at kids, so we go there every day. Adults can only go in there if accompanied by a child, so he's my free pass now!

Thanks again for the sailor suit. You are very generous. One day soon I will get around to sending some photos.

Lots of love, Margaret, hope life is treating you okay and you're not missing me too much. The ten o'clock club just WON'T be the same without me! I might have to start my own: Blooms-bury Division.

Miss you . . .

See you soon . . .

Rachel xxxxx

ALL SHE WANTS

There are some things in life you can always rely on. Living in the shadow of your 'perfect' brother Joey, getting the flu over Christmas, and your mother showing you up in the super-market.

Then there are some things you really don't count on hap-pening: a good dose of fame, getting completely trashed at an awards ceremony, and catching your fella doing something unmentionable on your wedding day.

This is my story, it's dead tragic. You have been warned . . .

Jodie Xx

'Utterly original, sharply written and very funny'
JOJO MOYES

THE CONFUSION OF
KAREN CARPENTER

Hello. There are two things you should know about me:

1. My name is Karen Carpenter.
2. Just before Christmas, my boyfriend left me.

I'm not THE Karen Carpenter. I just have the most embarrassing name in Christendom. Particularly as I'm no skinny minnie and don't play the drums.

I can't even sing. I'm tone deaf. I work in a school in the East End. (Where I came third in a 'Teacher we'd most like to sleep with' competition amongst the Year 11 boys.)

My mum's driving me mad. She's come to stay and is obsessed with Scandi crime shows and Zumba.

Oh yeah. The boyfriend. After eleven 'happy' years, he left me. No explanation, just a letter sellotaped to the kettle when I got in from work. I think I'm handling it really well. I don't think I'm confused at all. What was my name again?

'I enjoyed it HUGELY . . . a total page-turner,
very entertaining, then very moving'
MARIAN KEYES

THE GIRL WHO JUST APPEARED

LONDON – THE PRESENT

Holly Smith has never fitted in. Adopted when just a few months old, she's always felt she was someone with no history. All she has is the address of where she was born – 32B Gambier Terrace, Liverpool. When Holly discovers that the flat is available to rent, she travels north and moves in. And in the very same flat, under the floorboards, she finds a biscuit tin full of yellowing papers. Could these papers be the key to her past?

LIVERPOOL – 1981

Fifteen-year-old Darren is negotiating life with his errant mother and the younger brother he is raising. When the Toxteth riots explode around him, Darren finds himself with a moral dilemma that will have consequences for the rest of his life.

Moving between the past and the present, Darren and Holly's lives become intertwined. Will finding Darren give Holly the answers she craves? Or will she always feel like the girl who just appeared?

'Absolutely delightful. Jonathan Harvey
writes with all his heart and all his soul'
LISA JEWELL

THE SECRETS WE KEEP

It's hard being *that* woman, the one whose husband disappeared. It's made me quite famous. I just wish it was for something else.

He went out five years ago for a pint of milk and never came back. So here I am with a daughter who blames me for all that's wrong in the world, a son trying his best to pick up the pieces and a gaggle of new neighbours who are over-friendly, and incredibly nosy. Then we find a left-luggage ticket in the pocket of one of his old coats and suddenly I'm thinking . . . What if he's not dead? What if he's still out there somewhere?

You think you have the perfect life, the perfect kids, and then it's all turned inside out. What if I don't like what I find? And is it a chance I'm willing to take?

THE HISTORY OF US

What happens in the past doesn't always stay in the past . . .

LIVERPOOL 1985

Kathleen, Adam and Jocelyn are three teenage friends who bond over an unconventional nativity play. They all have ambitions, they all have dreams.

Adam wants to be a writer, Jocelyn wants to sing and Kathleen – well, she wants to be an embalmer.

LONDON 2015

Kathleen is a borderline alcoholic, Adam is holding on to a shocking secret and Jocelyn is dead. Where did it all go wrong? How did having the world at their feet turn into having the weight of it on their shoulders?

Filled with Jonathan Harvey's trademark wit, warmth and outrageous humour, *The History of Us* is a novel about friendship and secrets, the choices we make and the consequences we face.